Ron Berry
Collected Stories

edited by
Simon Baker

First Publication—2000

ISBN 1 85902 639 7

This book is published with the financial support of the Arts Council of Wales.

THE *A*SSOCIATION FOR
*W*ELSH *W*RITING IN *E*NGLISH
*C*YMDEITHAS *L*ÊN *S*AESNEG *C*YMRU

Printed in Wales at
Gomer Press, Llandysul, Ceredigion SA44 4QL

Contents

Foreword

This edition is part of a series of publications sponsored by the Universities of Wales Association for Welsh Writing in English which brings together collected editions of Welsh authors who write in English. The field has received relatively little attention in the past and it is hoped that, by republishing major work from earlier in the twentieth century and before, critical interest will be stimulated in writers who will handsomely repay such attention. The editions are conceived of on scholarly lines and are intended to give a rounded impression of the author's work, with introductions and bibliographical information.

JOHN PIKOULIS
General Editor

Introduction

When Rhys Davies, that prolific Valleys' short story writer and novelist, was asked, 'Do you consider yourself an Anglo-Welsh writer?' he replied, 'Down with passports to art.' The last time I wrote to Ron Berry I asked him what he would have replied. He wrote back, 'No offence meant. I don't give a damn for Anglo-Welsh. Tapeist gurus and shorthand dabs from the University and Arts Council be buggered.' It was a characteristic reply, in typically forthright language, something that could have come straight out of the mouth of one of his characters.

Yet art is defining ourselves, at least in one of its aspects, by our sense of place. What Frost called 'locative values' are fundamental to most works of literary imagination, and the Welsh writer in English is a poor relation in a double bind—first to England, and second to Welsh-speaking Wales. After all, those whom the Gods wish to destroy they first afflict with a language problem. However, marginalised by language and history, apparently rootless and detached, many twentieth-century artists—Joyce, Kundera and Rushdie all spring to mind—have relished this kind of dislocation, especially in that most marginalised and oblique of literary genres, the short story. The English language has expanded its usage by different consciousnesses, different parameters of imaginative (re)construction. In fact, the Welsh short story writer Glenda Beagan has queried the 'Englishness' of writing in the English language:

> I read English, speak it, write it, but as I learned most forcibly at Lancaster, it's not *English* English. Perhaps, paradoxically, I write in the first place because I'm uncomfortable with the language I have to employ, that I'm trying, somehow, to define my personal territory through it, this historically embattled patch of what was the old Flintshire.

Look at the English of James Kelman's stories, or Rushdie's novels. The terminology may be the same, but the meanings have changed. There is a perceptible shift away from the kind of Anglo-centric glorifying and ethnic humility formerly implied by the now defunct term 'Commonwealth Literature'. The commonality was always difficult to perceive—and we all know where the wealth went! It is a shift towards a refashioning of the language, a reappropriation of it by writers of the new literatures in English.

If Welsh writers in English are to produce comparable work, the best place to start is by following Seamus Heaney's advice and re-envisaging the region as the central point, and they must predicate this re-envisaging on some form of cultural style that defines them as Welsh, not provincial English. Heaney goes on to identify the principal difficulty of this imagined homeland:

> I think there are two ways in which place is known and cherished, two ways which may be complementary, but which are just as likely to be antipathetic. One is lived, illiterate and unconscious, the other learned, literate and conscious. In the literary sensibility, both are likely to co-exist in a conscious and unconscious tension.

If we transcribe this notion into the terms of the Welsh writing in English, it means attempting to secure a balance between writing from *within* a community, and positioning the narrative voice *outside* of it. To appreciate a lived, illiterate and unconscious sense of place one must implicitly acknowledge the validity of its codes and values, for instance Lewis Jones in *Cwmardy* and *We Live*. And yet, in order to remain learned, literate and conscious, the writer must transcend the narrow, circumscribed boundaries of the purely parochial by maintaining a distanced scrutiny of those codes and values, as Gwyn Jones does in *Times Like These*. The really difficult thing to achieve is the co-existence of both, to write from *inside* and *outside* simultaneously. Such a talent is conspicuous by its absence from Welsh novels in English this century. Perhaps only Raymond Williams and Emyr Humphreys have come close, though Christopher Meredith and Lewis Davies offer hope.

This is rarely the result of a lack of sympathy or political empathy on the part of the novelist. (Llewellyn's neo-conservative *How Green Was My Valley* is the exception that proves the rule). There is no doubt that Gwyn Jones and Lewis Jones would have agreed with Calvino when he wrote in *The Literature Machine*: 'Literature is necessary to politics when it gives voice to whatever is without a voice . . . especially to what the language of politics excludes or attempts to exclude.' Their problem was not lack of intent, but failure of execution.

To steer a course between the demotic and cultivated, between the reinvention of urban consciousness and the necessity of dramatic plot, requires a kind of realism beyond the scope of most Welsh writers.

The Valleys, as a product of empire not nation, whose population, drawn from a despoiled hinterland, witnessed 'the great dream and swift disaster' of imperial expansion and contraction, provide both a literal and a metaphorical imagined community for successive generations of Welsh writers. The difficulties of producing coherent urban realism are all too apparent. As James A. Davies has argued, the first difficulty is to write about working communities—which are subject to agencies beyond their control—without resorting to the artificial fictional devices of melodrama, sentimentality, propaganda or raucous comedy (Llewellyn, Cordell, Lewis Jones). The second problem is that a narrative voice from *outside* of the community it depicts is invariably compromised by its intellectual, cultural or sociological superiority to the characters still locked in the dialogue, whatever the sympathies of the author (Gwyn Jones, Humphreys, Raymond Williams). The third problem is that too close an identification with the narrow horizons of its urban discourse results in a reiterative symmetry of voice and situation leading to tedium (Gwyn Jones, Jack Jones). As Harri Webb remarked in 'Synopsis of the Great Welsh novel', one is not quite sure whether it is fiction or not. In contrast, an emphasis on overt fictionality has been one of the foremost aspects of the Welsh short story. The stories of Caradoc Evans, Dylan Thomas, Glyn Jones, and Rhys Davies have usually excelled because they have eschewed the limiting confines of social realism. Their partial and oblique narrators indulge in surreal, bizarre and violent stories, often from an adolescent or a child's point of view, or an adult's rural visit or return journey, but always somehow dislocated, detached, observing from the outside, a fractured vision which lends itself perfectly to the story form.

Which brings us back to Ron Berry. The three problematic areas I've outlined: depiction of working-class communities; voices in the narrative/dialogue; coherence of realistic structure/plot, have all, to different degrees, defeated the Welsh novel, and been avoided by the short story. I believe that Ron Berry, more than any other contemporary Welsh writer, has consistently tackled and, especially in his short fiction, overcome these difficulties, so why has his writing been ignored? One of the problems of national or regional patronage is that certain writers are over-praised, presumably because they can claim an easy identification with national or regional group-identity, and others are undervalued, shuffled off into corners, and given an equivocal acceptance at best. The most obvious example of this in Wales is Caradoc Evans, who told us what we did not want to hear. It has always seemed to me that he was so secure in his Welshness that he assumed a similar maturity on the part of his readers. If we cannot be sardonic about ourselves, what weak selves do we live with! Nostalgia is not enough, sentimentality is a cosy trap, and spurious political commitment is even worse. Caradoc Evans kicked against the easy way to national acceptance, and in a similarly caustic manner, so has Ron Berry. Perhaps that is why we have not given him the attention he deserves.

To begin to rectify this omission, some basic facts. He was born in Blaen-y-cwm in 1920, a mining village at the far end of Rhondda Fawr. Although his parents were bilingual, he was never a fluent Welsh speaker, so typical of his generation in an English-medium education system. More interested in sport than lessons, he had little formal education, either at Secondary School or Junior Tech., and left early to descend briefly down the pit. Throughout the rest of his life, he never really settled into a steady job. His vocational career reads like a series of advertisements in an Employment Office: miner, limestone tunneller, Merchant Navy, Ordnance Corps, amateur footballer, carpenter, farm labourer, steelworks plate-layer, student, journalist, assistant manager of swimming baths, and so on *ad infinitum*. But it was a rich vein of experience to be mined in his fiction, which has steadily amassed since the late 1950s. Despite settling back in Blaen-y-cwm with his wife and five children, he was always an ousider, a political agnostic and religious atheist, sceptical of all systems and institutions. His respect for one or two literary peers, chiefly Gwyn Thomas, was always qualified by his suspicion that they had 'never sampled the muck and mire.' His own fiction he believed to be 'entirely original', and it caused him 'damage' to be so consistently and casually overlooked. His aim was to lay down for posterity the life-experience and language of the

Valleys' world he knew, even as it passed out of history into oblivion. As the title-quotation of John Pikoulis's article asserts, 'word-of-mouth cultures cease in cemeteries'.

By way of reference, the closest contemporary analogy for Berry's writing is surely that of James Kelman, the Scottish novelist. One can imagine Berry assenting to Kelman's words, 'I wanted to write as one of my own people . . . to write and remain a member of my own community.' Such a desire has little precedent in either Scottish or Welsh fiction, where the indigenous population is confined to the margins, kept in their place, stuck in the dialogue. Berry's work is that of a proselytizer, bearing witness from *inside* his community, explaining, celebrating and judging its myths, conventions, rituals, languages and constant evolution to a querulous outside world. His writing conveys the intersection of both personal and communal 'his/story' with the larger historical moments and movements, and it does this in what might be called an *'ecriture masculine'*, spare, terse, caustic prose, often sardonic and crabbed, the idiolect of Rhondda Fawr.

This style is unique and enables him to succeed in those three crucial areas mentioned above where so many other Welsh writers have failed. Central to all three is Berry's refusal to accept the definitions of what counts as 'Literature' in contemporary society, his defiant rejection of the categorisations within which modern writing is created and consumed. At one end is his determination to make writing connect directly with the 'lives of ordinary people'. At the other end is his denigration of the modes by which fiction is constructed to avoid the 'real world' in which those ordinary men and women have to survive:

> Our quota of the Good, the True, the Beautiful comes from telly adverts, mail order catalogues and the usual hire purchase facilities. We have no architecture, no statuary, no paintings, a few male voice choirs, no bookshops; we have empty chapels, betting shops, a fifteen-minute bus service, cinemas for bingo, and the crappiest films ever made; we have petty crime, shifting iceberg politics, failing pubs, flashily extended clubs, and cemeteries full of dead miners.

There is little demarcation between his narratives and his characters. Indeed, sometimes inverted commas between narrative and dialogue seem superfluous. Choose any passage from the proceeding stories and the reality and physicality of his world immediately strike you. For Berry, the bulk of fiction—and even of literature—is an evasion of this reality, in content or in form—and literature itself is really a way of preventing writing from being engaged with that reality, since it is the product of an education system with which he had little contact, and for which he had little time. With that central thrust to his conception of writing, perhaps it is not surprising that his work has received so little academic or critical attention.

His novels and stories have been dismissed in the past as 'sexual comedy involving sad and tragic characters'. This is wholly inadequate. In his fiction, love is the desire to give what his characters do not possess, and sex is its poor substitute. The biting humour and jagged wit is a defence mechanism, an epitaph for feelings which are dying or have died. And surely, judged in the sombre light of tragedy, his protagonists are always found wanting, not even the heroes of their own stories. Theirs, to quote Nedeszha Mandelstam, is 'the privilege of ordinary heartbreaks'. Ron Berry was the chronicler of those ordinary heartbreaks, and, thirty-eight years after his first publication, we have still failed to appreciate his talent.

SIMON BAKER

Editor's note and acknowledgements

Editing Ron Berry's stories has not been a straightforward task. The variant spellings, syntax, grammar, indeed the entire tenor of his language is far removed from 'standard English', and is meant to be so. I have, with his help, made over two hundred changes, deletions and additions, but whenever in doubt, the original has been left as it was written. Errors and solecisms which were present in the first published versions have been rectified. My decision to alter as little as possible, as with my decision not to write a more scholarly, analytical introduction, is made in the spirit of his work.

I would like to acknowledge the help and support of Robert Fleming, Joanna Furber, John Pikoulis and Mairwen Prys Jones in the preparation of this manuscript. My chief debt is to Ron Berry for his letters, books, advice and patience. It is a source of huge regret that he is not here to see its completion.

S.B.

End of season

Jeering from his wife. 'You must be desperate. Look, it's teeming down.'

'Heavy showers,' he said. 'Fine this afternoon.'

'Well, mind yourself then, that's all I can say.'

'See you, Bella.'

'You've gone your own way since you retired five years ago, never a thought for anyone except Hopkin Lewis.'

He felt innocent, shameless, nodding to avoid confusion.

'Cheerio, love.'

'You don't understand the meaning of the word.'

'Visit Sylvia,' he said.

'She's having enough trouble with her own husband.'

Still nodding, 'We know why too.'

'Our son-in-law's a weak-minded waster. We've been over this umpteen times.'

'Right, hopeless case. So-long, Bella.'

No response.

'So long, Bella.'

'Selfish,' she grumbled.

He thought, no, just daunted by bickering.

She insisted, 'Selfish,' accusing him eye to eye, his careful grin tormenting her.

'At least I can bear my own company,' he said.

She slammed the door. Next, her sullen face edging the front window curtain while he stowed his fishing tackle in the car.

Storm rain fizzed off the bonnet as he drove up the mountain road to a lay-by. Late October coloured the landscape, great invasions of sodden bracken spreading over rough, fawny pasture. Flood water draped whitely fixed in distant gullies. Whiffs of mist thinning like ectoplasm. Patches of glacial bog treacherously green. Hopkin savoured his isolation. Lifelessness everywhere, all Wales preparing for winter. Winter-time of my life, of Bella's, but she can't accept it. We'll share animosity and indifference for the rest of our days.

No matter.

Forget remorse. Too expensive.

By five o'clock a bleak aftermath of toneless grey sky, Llyn Glas deserted, only one angler casting off the dam wall by the

1

inflow. Hopkin tied a size 14 Iron Blue nymph on the dropper, size 12 Teal and Green on the point. He smeared his twelve foot tapered leader with a paste of Fuller's Earth and liquid soap. Luck, he thought, I need more luck than Robinson Crusoe. Conscience ruled Crusoe. Haemorrhages of fear. Bella's afraid. Fears accumulated over the years. Sylvia's already stuck in her rubbish heap.

First cast aimed lee-side of a boulder hulking above the ripple. Smooth 25 yard throw assisted by wind driving from the north-west. He saw his flies briefly slurring through wrinkling cats'-paws. Wait. Allow the leader to sink. Gusts bellied his dark green flyline. Concentrating now, he retrieved in jerky inches between long and shorter pauses. The tail fly snicked the boulder on his second cast. Hopkin retrieved at a crawl all the way in. A minnow lipped the Iron Blue at the water's edge and instantly dropped off.

Hopkin continued casting.

The angler bawled, 'I've had enough! It's all dead!'

Hand raised, Hopkin merely acknowledged a variation of defeat. He felt blessed, set apart, past and beyond gossip, the jargon of Izaac Walton disciples. Contentment surged. Huge rainbow trout were slugging along in the deeps of Llyn Glas— this pensive indulgence scrubbed by five mallard flurrying up from a spiky mattress of dying sedge. They skidded down in mid-water, planted askew, perfectly still for moments, then they paddled in echelon, sideways-on to the ripple. Hopkin appreciated wild creatures. They signified what they appeared to be in themselves. As for wilderness: leave it alone. Private certainties, vagaries of his own existence, sufficed. Behind him, fifty odd years of hooking trout, rudd, perch, less often mackerel, dabs, whiting, cod, dogfish and skate.

Hopkin considered a truth: The best rod men are merciless. They persist like barbarians. Long ago I was a killer. Forty-two brownies from Cwm Carw squashed in my bag. Seven mile tramp over the mountains. August 1948. Forty-two beauties, lots of them spoiled by the time I got home, shredded fish meat fouled with black faeces. Killer-diller Lewis.

Days gone by.

Crossing the shoreline, he slowed through shin-deep peat sludge to Hawthorn Bay, the gravelly far side layered with stained foam by the north-westerly. He changed the point fly for a Badger Matuka. The weighted artificial plumed a thin bubbly wake as he stripped in line. Hopkin clucked his tongue. Modern fishing. Chuck it and chance it. So he changed the Matuka for a Stick Fly. He retrieved very slowly. Too slowly finally. The caddis artificial snagged on the bottom. Releasing line and backing, he walked around to the outermost corner, hoping the slanted pull would release his fly. Top ring under water, he reeled in line, felt solid hardness, tested it, and the Stick Fly remained snagged. Hopkin hauled by hand until the nylon snapped at the water knot. Two flies lost.

Hopkin tutted. He rested, smoking, beaker of coffee warming his hands. Staring across Llyn Glas, he saw the periscope head of a cormorant rising, gliding, and the big fisheater coiled downward, resurfacing several yards away. Hopkin sighed benign judgment: 'Black bastard.'

Ceaseless ripples chased the length of Llyn Glas. Greyness smudged opalescent streaks low on the western horizon. Hopkin thought, dark in another hour. Two hours from now I'll be looking at Bella's face watching television. Maybe we'll have a drink in the Royal Oak tonight. Try some local socialising. Bella hasn't a friend in the world. Strange. Me neither, come to that. Born and bred loner. It's no loss. I feel sorry for Bella. Sorry for Sylvia. She's short on courage, enough to leave her neurotic husband. He knotted a yard of 3½lbs breaking strain nylon to the end of his leader, tied a Silver Butcher on the point and a small Black and Peacock on the dropper. Again he smeared the leader with Fuller's Earth and liquid soap paste.

Fishing Hawthorn Bay, he had one sneaked offer. The flyline shook. Hopkin decided the trout went for the Silver Butcher. He threw a dozen casts, searching the area of the failed take. Nothing. Just bad luck. Then his Silver Butcher hooked itself in the leafless hawthorn. Hopkin tweaked a sideways pull. The gleaming Butcher dropped among stones rimed with lichen. *Good* luck. Spey casting, he unrolled line on the water, stepped aside to avoid the hawthorn, flung high on his back-hand cast, watched his line snaking out, levelling straight above the ripple, and suddenly the wave-lapped stone beneath his right foot toppled. Displaced water bulged as it tumbled down. Hopkin fell full length forward like a post. He had to. Yet in falling he switched his rod to his left hand and flung it on the bank. Then dread closed his throat. Identity vanished. Lost breathing stupored his mind. Unknowable, he sank without struggle until his elbow knocked a submerged rock shelf. Hopkin convulsed, waving clubbed fists like a baby. Ten feet down he rolled on mud. From blackness Hopkin opened his eyes to murk. He kicked off the mud, arms flailing as he surfaced. But his fishing bag held him sloped, shoulder strap across his mouth. He saw undercut hawthorn roots twisting out and down into moss and stones. Too far. Too far away. Anguish wailed from him. Gulping water, he sank again. Boyhood learning gave him floundering breast strokes. Grotesque as nightmare he failed to surface. Fingers scrabbling ancient scree pitching into Hawthorn Bay, he clawed himself up, hand over hand up slimed rock and stones until he collapsed face down beside his rod. Seconds lingered to awareness. Retching, he hawked coffee-flavoured phlegm. Mucus streamed, trailing from his nostrils. Squirming sideways, he emptied water from his wellington boots. He wrung his tweed hat, tugged it back on his white fringed head. Huffing through stiff lips, he up-ended his bag, recovered his fly-box, spare reel, spools of nylon and thermos flask. Hopkin's body felt cased in ice cold. Grunting conviction, he picked up his rod, reeled in, fumbled the Butcher into the cork handle. 'Run,' he whispered, and 'Run!' he cried out.

Chittering, snorting, he crouched into a wobbly, jogtrot around the reservoir. Twice he lurched to standstill, lungs burning, chin on his chest, feeling shrunken within himself. Once inside the car he gurgled a mad spasm of joy. Gripped rigid against shivering, he tap-tapped his numb feet on the pedals. Driving home Hopkin roused from gawping. He muttered, 'God damn,' kept repeating, 'God damn, God damn, God damn . . .'

Desperately laconic he told Bella, 'I'm rather knackered.'

'You look awful,' she said.

'Fetch my rod and bag from the car, please.'

She yanked down the zip on his coat, groped through to his shirt and vest. 'You're drenched to the skin!'

'I fell in Llyn Glas.'

Screeching fury and fright, she rushed upstairs to the bathroom. 'Come on, soak yourself in hot water! Stupid old man, you can't even look after yourself! Hopkin, d'you hear me?'

Later, when she brought tea spiked with whisky, Hopkin was dozing in the bath. Fuddle humbled him. Naked, he felt alien to her. 'I panicked, Bella, lost my wits.'

She sucked a quick, righteous kiss on his forehead. 'Listen, you're all right. Now drink this, it will settle your nerves.'

Whisky heat seared his gullet, flared across his chest. He thought, I'm finished for this season. 'Nasty experience,' he said.

She looked down at him as if he wasn't to be trusted. His grin stuck. 'Very nasty. Um, thanks, Bella, thanks.'

'Yes,' she said, turning away, 'that's why I'm here.'

Summer's End: Snaketown

'No, I live here,' I said. 'You down on holiday?'

She stretched a white rubber swimcap over her blonde hair. 'Actually I'm staying with friends.'

'Who're they?'

'Jane and Bernard West. Bernard happens to be my form master.'

'He's clever in a thick way,' I said.

She stiffened her face.

'I'm the last of the local Eynons,' I said. 'Chris Eynon.'

She snicked the rubber tight above her ears. 'Bernard has mentioned your name, the drop-out from art school.'

'Bernard's big mouth . . .'

'Perhaps you weren't good enough. No talent.' She walked, striding from the thighs like a samba dancer. Sudsy foam washed against her shins. She flopped down like a child entranced, swaying from her waist, arms outstretched, swishing her hands through the water.

'Esther!' shouted West, jogging thirteen stone of comfortable beefiness. 'Hullo, Chris,' he said.

Snake, son of Tan-y-môr Council's chief executive, senior snake in this bankrupt, trap-minded old town of my ancestors. Hoping for tourists since the last war. Tourism, the pox of Wales. Pox of Spain. Penultimate pox of the world. Trippers. Sightseers. Bingo brigades. Lemmings with plastic money and cameras. Thirty-seven per cent unemployed in Tan-y-môr. Deadenders, moonlighters, hobblers, snoopers, whisperers, pilferers. Up and down the coast the tag sticks: Tan-y-môr snakes.

I waded into crawl stroke.

'Hullo,' repeated West. 'Esther, ah'm, Chris Eynon. Chris—Esther Willis.'

She snugged her palm against mine, wealing my wrist with her fingernails. 'How d'you do, Chris.'

I said, 'Too true, I packed in art school.'

'Why?'

'Couldn't stomach the poncing.'

West sniggered, sculling circles, knees tucked to his chest.

She frowned a single short furrow up from the root of her nose. 'I don't understand.'

'Poncing on taste, taste aesthetics'—verdict from experience, my only weapon versus custom and practice.

Her jeer rose to screeched, 'Aren't you precious!' Levering into clumsy breast stroke, her foot struck my knee.

I ploughed alongside, dived under her, rising full force, stalling her face to face. 'Hey, next time use those talons on West's balls.'

West yelled, 'Be careful! Esther's nervous!'

She thrashed about, dread in her pale blue eyes.

He trudgeoned slowly near the blonde, pausing while she stood blinking, gasping. Soon she went out to shallow water, sat down, shoulders slumped, wavelets creaming at her feet.

'She's a beginner,' says West.

I said, 'Chopsy bastards like you give Tan-y-môr snakes a bad name.'

'I've been away for three years!'

Suddenly disgusted, I pushed his face with the flat of my hand. West blustered funk.

I did my usual Sunday swim across to the rusted stanchions of West Docks. They were gone when I returned to my clothes. Feeling resigned, I'm thinking, end of August. Come the 8th of September I'll be twenty. And after autumn cometh winter, north-easterlies freezing the snot on my nose. Roll on hope and charity. Bugger faith. Bugger faith guarantees tyrants and martyrs.

Early on Monday morning, steered my handcart down Park Avenue, the Park a vandalised spread of rhododendrons around defunct bowling greens heaped with builders' rubble and scrapped cars. Genuine Snaketown milieu. I cleaned windows for three regular customers. Afterwards the back streets, rapping door knockers. At 1 o'clock, lunch in the market cafe. Slat seats and formica tabletops. Greyed old women alone over faggots and peas. Council workmen discussing cricket, racing form, illnesses. Stall-holders bantering. Sparrows chirruping up on the flaky roof trusses.

I'm a norm. Tomorrow's entrepreneur. The Thatcher dialectic. Therefore sanctioned. Perform a public service. Syndrome for

Rule Britannia. Conscience best left to salaried Christians and Inland Revenue bandits.

Now and then I'm glancing out through the window, checking on my cart and ladders parked in the cobblestone alleyway leading to public lavatories. Thieving rules okay, Tan-y-môr battening upon itself. Culture of deprivation, West Docks a shambles, two small boats plying on summer Sundays, chugging anglers to word-of-mouth marks for dogfish and congers.

Friendly enough, I raised a forkful of steak and kidney pie, saluting the Esther Willis girl parading from the Ladies. Trailing behind her, Jane West. She's thickset, cultivating a mark for herself. Esther's wearing red trousers and a glittery yellow tank top. She frowned the furrow up her forehead when I mimed breast stroke.

Half an hour later I'm wheeling out of the alley. Afternoon lull in Tan-y-môr. Solitary moochers, hands in pockets. Workless teenagers roaming in groups, alert, foraging for excitement. Tidy old folk, all eyes, all ears, searching for offers. Knackered widows and widowers with pet dogs waddling under slack leashes. Outside the market, I saw Esther on the riverbank bench. She's eating strawberries from a punnet held high in her hands like a squirrel.

I said, '*Shwmae* then.'

'Have some strawberries, Christopher.'

'Where's Jane West?'

'Dental appointment.'

'Where's Bernard?'

'Interview. He's short listed, hoping to come back here to teach.' Mouth puckered, she sucked a strawberry off its calyx. 'He's a marvellous teacher. Maths and Physics.'

'Where you from, Esther?'

'Questions, questions, you ought to be on TV.'

'I'm a data bank shark,' I said. 'Where?'

'Slough.'

'How does Jane West fit in?'

'Next month, Mister Quiz-master, Jane will stay with my family. Student exchange sort of thing. Bernard made the arrangement.'

'He fancies you, ah?'

8

'Rubbish!' She wiggled on the bench.

'Ta very much, quality strawberries,' I said. 'No offence, Esther. I can't mind my own business. Jane's near enough your age, seventeenish. Slightly butch, is she?'

'You pig!' Her smiling teeth are flecked with pink mush. 'Mr West says *Shwmae* to old Mr Elias who looks after the garden. Do you speak Welsh?'

'Hardly any,' I said. 'Two communities here in Tan-y-môr. Mostly ancient, a few modern. There were Eynons in Tan-y-môr two hundred years ago. The Wests came in the late Sixties.'

Low on umbrage, Esther peeved, 'Sometimes I hate Slough. My father's a building contractor. He's so macho! He wants me to go to a secretarial college. I think I will next year, to get away from his vicious temper more than anything else.'

Fathers, I thought, including everybody's in heaven.

'Cornwall would be a nice place to live.'

I said, 'Bloody illusion.'

'How?'

'Potters, painters, sculptors, designers, would-be poets, do-it-yourselfers messing with poultry and pigs and bees and goats, all trying to escape from the rat race. They smother common sense.'

She squinted across the bridge of her nose. 'You escaped.'

Ladders balanced ready for take-off, and I'm sniffing like a Disney hound. 'Tide's on ebb. Man-o-man, the sweet pong of mud. See you around maybe. So-long, Esther.'

She kept pace. 'How romantic, window cleaner in a seaside town.'

'You're unreal,' I said. 'I'm just making a crust.'

Esther chatted with two old Bethany Street spinsters while I worked. At 4 o'clock she's watching me rinse chamois leathers. 'That's my lot,' I said. 'Sufficient unto the day, as Adam said when he skinned the snake.'

'Ssss-hsss . . . where do you live, Chris?'

'Not far.'

'How far?'

'Never mind. Point is, I'm sorting myself out.'

'You already have! You're independent!'

I had to say, 'Look, go back to the Wests.'

'Invite me to your home.'

9

'For Jesus' sake!'

She slithered a soft kiss from my cheek to my mouth, then posed, hands on hips. 'I suspect Bernard's a virgin.'

We stared, blue and brown eyes probing. Leaning forward, we Eskimo-rubbed noses.

'Righto, girl. It's a two room flat behind the Earl Haig Club.'

'No parents?'

'Separated when I was a kid. I've lost touch with my father. He's escaping too, somewhere, from himself.'

'Your mother?'

I said, 'She's a carnivore.'

Esther yelped, 'Dreadful!'

I'm smirking like a novice cynic. 'She's landlady of the Marine Hotel.'

'Really?'

'Pure Tan-y-môr bloodstock. Come on, I have to collect some meat in the market.'

Esther pried into the fridge. She tapped paperback spines on the sideboard.

'Feel free,' I said.

She picked striped caterpillars off nasturtiums overflowing a rotting window box left by the previous tenant—West Docks ex-weighbridgeman who went ga-ga, died in a Nissen hut annexe to Tan-y-môr Cottage Hospital.

'I like your flat, Chris. It's peaceful.'

'Peace, I'm expecting it here and here,' I said, left hand over my heart, right hand clutching my forehead.

Lamb chops are sputtering under the Baby Belling grill, twin half saucepans of potatoes and kidney beans bubbling on the ring. And she's standing behind me, arms around my chest, her fingertips pianoing my ribs.

Our mouths clung.

I turned off the grill and the ring, picked her up, barged full tilt into the bedroom. Nameless as in dream we undressed each other. Lightning stroked my brain: *Sharing flesh, the beginning and end of nations.*

Yet over the soggy vegetables and crisped chops, we were exchanging chat, Esther saying, 'I'm leaving on Wednesday.'

'We'll keep in touch,' I said.

'Promise.'

'Cross my heart.'

'Cross my heart,' she promised. 'We're going to Ireland for a fortnight, staying with my father's sister in County Cork. He's so tough, guh, dumb as a rhino. Of course Jane will be with us.'

'Coffee coming up,' I said, smacking two mugs on the table.

'Say, truly now, anything at all between you and Bernard?'

'He's afraid, at least I think he's afraid.'

'Probably neuter,' I said.

Esther snapped, 'I don't know! Bernard's thoughtful, he's kind, that's all!'

'Weirdo tribe, the Wests. Anyhow,' I said, 'conniving, nepotism, square pegs in round holes, they thrive in Tan-y-môr.'

'Would you come to live in Slough?'

I poured the coffee. 'Not on, girl. But you could stay here later on, after leaving school. Borderline stuff, this. Can't offer much else either. Zero ambition. I belong here. We're all over Snaketown, marginal blokes.'

'No family, no responsibilities, nothing. You must be awfully guilty.'

I put it straight, 'Esther, I love you the only way I know how.'

She went prowling around the rickety table, intense, sloshing coffee, staining her red trousers. 'Just another eff, is that what you mean? I oaf on the beach every summer, part-time stud, full-time window cleaner?'

Sensing no option, I waited.

Esther held my face, 'Sorry Chris, I'm sorry.'

'Forget it,' I said. 'Doesn't matter. I wish I could feel sorry for myself. I resented West gossiping as though I were a freak. To me he's sort of human in bits and pieces. I'm always suspicious, but I can't feel sorry for myself.'

'Chris Eynon the egotist! You dropped out, that's why I spoke to you on the beach!'

I said, 'Good. Now I know. Esther-girl, let's take a swim. Meet you outside the Marine Hotel at eight o'clock.'

Above the hubbub in the bar, I heard my mother. 'Quiet! There's a darts match going on!'

I'm free of Sarah. No more conflict. I can tolerate Sarah Eynon. Freedom though, with scant hope. But it's enough. Ordinary Snaketown limbo.

11

Lightness tingled my skin, Esther calling, 'Bye!' to West, who drove around the Marine without a glance. She crossed the road. Her kiss slid to my lips.

'Everything al'right?'

'Jane's disgusted, but Bernard seems to think you're a decent fellow.'

We held hands, walking the potholed strip above Tan-y-môr sands. Brambles greened pebbly ridges left by forgotten high tides. The sea came swilling in, sunset sheening the water like pewter. From West Docks, bare distance sharpened uneven thumps and clangings. Scroungers collecting scrap. Slow dereliction over the years, since my father went to infants' school. My dad Gomer, loser to Sarah.

The shoreline goes eastward in wide scallops, isolated cottages whitely dotted here and there, solid houses and silos bedded deeper inland. Old pastures, fields hedged centuries ago when Wales was a monoglot, Shanks's pony nation.

Esther's moody. 'There's too much water, too much space. I feel I'm a stranger here.'

Cross-grained, I thought. Urban bird and Snaketown romeo. Patience now, patience, teaching her crawl stroke, how to breathe correctly, demonstrating in slow motion, head held level, turned with the roll-down of the shoulder.

'Relax, Esther, learn to relax. Your only enemy is fear.'

'What are you afraid of, Chris?'

'Not much since this afternoon.'

Bouncing my face at her breasts, she sopranoed, 'I'm the mermaid of Tan-y-môr!'

'Nice,' I said. 'Luring this window-cleaner to his doom.'

'Shall I?'

'Any time, my lovely,' I said.

Not many arm-in-arm couples were strolling the beach. Head-down loners patrolled the tide line. Dog owners plodded in ritual. Gloaming chilled the air.

Esther's rigidly upright while I'm towelling her. 'Have you done this before, Chris?'

'Never.'

'Where are we going?'

'Hungry?'

'I'm famished.'

'Fish and chips. Prolie fodder scoffed on the hoof.'

12

'Yummie!' She bunched her bikini and towel in a duffle-bag. 'Then your flat.'

'It'll be late,' I said.

'I'll phone Mrs West.'

Rules. Obey the rules. 'There's a kiosk outside the Marine Hotel,' I said.

Big Sarah, she's haranguing stragglers away from the pub door. 'Clear off home! Move! G'night! G'night!' Her bawl lowered, pitched laconic, 'You, boy!'

Parcel of fish and chips in each hand, I said, 'Aye, it's your son and heir.'

Esther swung her stride, the lithe slink of health. I gave her one of the parcels.'

'Who's this, boy?'

She went up to Sarah. 'Christopher's mother? How d'you do, Mrs Eynon.'

'Esther Willis,' I said.

Sarah raised her arms. 'Come inside, the pair of you.'

'Some other time,' I said. 'Esther's staying with the Wests.'

'Suit yourselves.' She turned, agile for a heavyweight woman. 'I've done my best, whatever he wanted he only had to ask for it. But show gratitude, not a word.' She hammered her fist on her palm. 'Daft ideas, boy, that's your trouble,' and she closed the door. Shoot bolts clacked home.

I heard myself: 'Goodnight, Mam.' Finished, all the wrangling, over and done with bar the scars. No rancour left. I'm clean.

Esther slurped off a corner of steaming cod fillet. 'She's awfully domineering, ph-phu-phoo, she's . . .'

'She busted his heart,' I said.

'Your father?'

'Gomer my father.'

'You Welsh people exaggerate!'

'Know what,' I said, 'your lallahs are beauties.'

Esther wobbled forward, legs straddled, laughter joggling her blonde head.

Formally as before, patting, smoothing her nape, 'Fishbone stick in your gulley? There-there there-there. Better now, *cariad*?'

13

Habit triggered at 7 o'clock, Esther murmuring to sighing as I sidled from the narrow bed. She slept with her mouth slightly open. A thin cusp like white enamel slotted above the lower lid of her left eye.

I'm brewing tea, glancing into the bedroom, rootless foreboding niggling. Where to from here? Ruts are for living in. I've found mine. Lonely sometimes, but there's no hassle. None. After tomorrow we shan't see each other . . . she's lovelier than everything else in my days, nights, my twenty years.

'Tea's ready,' I said.

Marvelling wide eyed, she came golden shinned out to the kitchen, and I'm proud as a barbarian king, passing the mug to her hand. 'Esther, I'll be on my way in a few minutes.'

'Where will I find you?'

'Market cafe. One o'clock.'

She writhed her mouth. 'Same as yesterday, such a long time ago.'

'We've shifted off the calendar. We're in time out of whack.'

'Yes, yes,' she said.

Feeling zombied behind the handcart, images of her flowed, froze, flowed. Polishing the windows of a jewellery-cum-souvenir shop, vacant face glimmering, I fretted back to honesty. Lack of destiny stirred regret. I've no sense of achievement. Here in Snaketown I'm sane. State of grace. Aggro nil. Muddling along. Dogtrot persistence. I cherish this old town. Despise and cherish the jigsaw streets, all the green-eyed, wayward, ingrown descendants of seafarers. They pull out in dribs and drabs. They drift back to Tan-y-môr. Most of them stay. They won't leave. Me neither. Less than a year ago I quit the biggest con job in civilization: ART. Mind over matter tricks. Here's where I was born. Twentieth birthday due. Born and ill-bred. Small fish in a small bowl.

The jeweller dappered out in his slippers, bald head askew—he's gnawing a hangnail. 'How's your mother these days, Chris?'

'She's okay, Mr Emanuel.'

'Handsome woman Sarah was, take my word for it. Bit of a tartar now and then. You had to use some gumption with Sarah Price, get my meaning? She was in our Seaside Follies party, great trouper, sing her heart out, good honest strong contralto, oh long before she married Gomer Eynon. Any news about Gomer? No? No. Ah well, it happens to the best of us. Indeed, yes indeed. I hear you're keeping company with Missy what's-er-name, her staying with Mr and Mrs West. Myself I can't fathom Bernard. Brilliant chap. Deep. Mr West and all, he's sharp. He doesn't put a foot wrong, certainly not. We can't complain, us members of the Chamber of Trade, we can't complain against Mr West. He does his best for us people in business. No argument about that.' Iorrie Emanuel gawped, wet-mouthed. 'What's her name?'

'Esther Willis,' I said.

'It was on the tip of my tongue. Tell me, she's English through and through?'

'Irish on her father's side,' I said.

'Smart looking girl.'

Reaching full stretch on my squealing squeejee, I thought, you rotten old turd.

Iorrie dry-wiped his hands. 'Listen, Chris, round the back when you've finished. See Mrs Emanuel as regards payment.'

At 10 o'clock I'm rattling the lion's head knocker of Morlais House, every ground floor window blanked off with marine ply on the front, corrugated sheets at the rear.

Silence.

Shouted through the letter-box, 'Mr Lewis, you there?'

Jonah Lewis creaked the door open, his nose profiled for seconds. 'Eynon! God damn, get on with it!'

Curtains shivered, Jonah spying, soft-footing from room to room in the large Edwardian house. For a while I forgot Esther. Day-dreamed, pondering the mystery of genes. Can't dodge genes. In the beginning, legendary Llewellyn Lewis, owner of West Docks, the Mercantile Chandlers Company, and Tan-y-môr's first bus service. Llew Lewis who once owned rows of terraced houses. From legend to dust, likewise the bulldozed terraces, Tan-y-môr's first and last slum clearance, wasteland left behind. Then Jonah's father, Rosser, he drank himself to death. Choked on his own vomit. Rosser's widow took schoolboy Jonah to London. They disappeared. Thirty years went by, Morlais House rented to the parish as an orphanage, until Jonah brought two Filipino women to Tan-y-môr— Snaketown by now. Jonah reclaimed his property. The Filipinos looked like twins. Months later they also disappeared.

Thereafter Jonah remained indoors. He deals with the world by telephone.

I banged the knocker again at mid-day. As always the cheque stuck half-way out of the letter-box. Seven quid.

'Same time next Tuesday, Mr Lewis?'

Silence.

'Anyhow, I'll call as usual.'

'Eynon!'

'Yes, Mr Lewis?'

'Take care, mind how you go!' Jonah's about the same age as Gomer and Sarah.

'Cheerio, Mr Lewis.'

I skimped two cut-price bookings for well-off pensioners. Pushing down dirt lanes, I arrived in the cafe at ten past one.

'Blonde girl? Nuh, no blonde been in 'ere, least I've not served any blonde,' says Gatchy the bearded handy-andy behind the counter.

I ordered rissoles, three veg, and a chunk of home-made bread pudding. Kept watch on the café entrance and my gear in the alleyway.

I'm twitchy by 2 o'clock.

3 o'clock. She's jibbed, I thought. Inquire at the Wests' house? Must be a reason why she's not here. Or let go? Not for the first time I felt like my father. So take it. Let go. Take it.

Wheeling along the riverbank footpath, swallowing misery until I felt witless, stupefied, blaming neither Esther nor myself. Staying alive brings a few highs here and there, bright spasms, the rest a goofy experiment. Dull palavering. Fair enough too, no hang-ups at all. No bother. Carry on every day without sticking my neck on the line. Fair. Safe. Why not?

Christ, I'm down, right down. This is shit street.

I'm in the Earl Haig Reading room, reminder of the Club's pre-War heyday. *En bloc* Labour committees. Welsh nationalism psyching up north, and Tan-y-môr revolutionaries arrested for singing The Red Flag on Saturday nights. I skimmed the muckload of four dailies, meanwhile listening to two fragile old dockies sharing the *Evening Echo*, dead serious, as if unravelling occult gospel.

Went through the billiard hall. Bought a pint at the hatch *en route* to the side lounge. Same faces, same family names. They all know Sarah Eynon's one and only.

16

The steward's wife says, 'That Podge West's been looking for you.'

'Bernard the Podge, earlier on,' explained Joby the steward. 'I told him you'd be here more or less ha'-past nine. Said he'd be back.'

'Believe me,' insisted Thora, 'she was seen ages before Podge came in, sat next to a fella in a blue Volvo, stopped at the crossing lights, definitely before half-six 'cause we hadn't opened our doors.'

'Correct,' agreed Joby. He's stone-faced. 'How's everything, Chris?'

'Steady, no sweat,' I said.

Thora shrugged, saying, 'They took the bypass.'

'Only bloody way out from Tan-y-môr!' Elbowing past her, Joby said, 'Take it easy, mate. When he comes in I'll let you know.'

Esther's gone. She's somewhere in Slough.

I joined a game of Brag. Lost myself in tactics until the steward came over. 'He's out in the lobby. More private.'

'Right, thanks,' I said.

Joby blurted a low grunt. 'Us town blokes, we stick together.'

West braced himself, fingers interlocked across his stomach. 'Hullo, Chris. My role in this affair has been entirely innocent . . .'

I'm rubbing a thumb down a lapel of his cream alpaca jacket. 'Man, you'd betray your own bowels.'

'It was Jane, she phoned Esther's parents. Obviously Jane has a cruel streak in her. My mother is terribly upset. Quite simply, ah'm, Mr Willis has taken Esther home. In fact she was supposed to leave tomorrow, Jane too, but that's been cancelled. Well, Mr Willis, he's rather headstrong, ah'm, he's a strict Catholic. And there it is, I'm afraid.' West snatched an envelope from his wallet pocket. 'Esther asked me to give you this. I'm merely the go-between.' He hesitated, pacing aside. 'You'll appreciate the matter is out of my hands.' Side-stepping faster, he shouldered himself through the swing doors.

There were ragged sentences:

See you next summer. Love, Esther.

Wait for me. Yours ever, Esther.

My father flipped. I told you about him. He pulled my hair.

Goodbye, Chris, until we meet again.

All my love, E.

Wilfully numb, playing Brag, holding my own, then I walked around to the flat, answering Goodnights to couples, groups, singles, a late Tuesday night mix of Tan-y-môr. Failing sleep, I rambled the beach. I'm done for. I'm beaten. Esther, she's taking it off her old man. If I had the guts I'd fight for her. I'd do anything. Anything. Bang one on him. He's stupid. He's a fanatic. If I wanted Esther . . . but I'm gutless.

So I wept, sobbed on Tan-y-môr sands, purging for the only time since Gomer went away.

Market Forces

He vanished in fog gloried by street lamps, his scoop-jawed mother grousing, '*Ych*, worst than his father Iorrie.' Tushing shallow venom, Jemima kneed shut the kitchen door.

Glan Mack felt comforably alert, moving up-hill from lush autumnal riverbank. He's swanky shouldered as cat-walk cheesecake, but he ambled toes-in, feral. His eyes have the cold swivel and fixity of a raptor. Night-time swelling his soul, consciousness barely turnkeyed dreams of his childhood. Rubbled track underfoot, he avoided sprawling stands of rhododendrons where no birds flurried the glossy foliage. Scatters of gnarled oaks above the half-cobbled yard, the one-time farmhouse prettied as fairytale.

Glan squatted. Cemetery hush. Far off little owl yelping. Very softly he sent 'Shh-shh shh-shh shh-shh,' from his tongue and palate. Small hacked phlegms cleared his throat.

By elbow and finger-touch he stepped alongside a barn, roused the old sheepdog from her kennel and kicked the grey-muzzled bitch from growling to stillness. He pulled a claw hammer from his belt. Visual memory served at the corrugated, barrel-roofed hen coop. He muffled the lock with rag, hit the underside, freed the sprung lever from the hasp, groped a roosting fowl in each hand, backed out, re-locked the door, and he climbed over the top end gate from the farmyard. The black Minorca hens hung limp. He lofted his arms to cruciform. Subdued clucks, the birds dangling inert. Then he gripped the four scaly feet in his left hand, murmuring, 'Keep moving.'

Beside a drainage ditch older than the rhododendrons, Glan ended glugged squawks with Jemima's carving knife. He's repeating, 'Shh-shh shh-shh shh-shh' while the part severed heads bleed, swishing in running water. He hefted the birds side by side. 4lbs a piece: 'Yeh.' And he shouldered them home in a bin liner.

'Glandwr!' screeched Jemima carefully.

'Quiet, s'al'right,' he said, plucking over a galvanised washtub. Feathers, giblets, feet and heads were finally squashed among newspapers and knotted in the bin liner.

Jemima slept, unaware of accepting decrepitude. Bent spine

and sepia-ed epidermis, insignia of peasantry and bluebloods. Maligned and/or revered. Later in the pantry she simpered pleasure, her grained knuckles rolling on the pimply carcases.

Glan slept until the 6 o'clock news.

'Lazy thing you,' jeered his mother, munching biscuits layered with jam between sips of strong tea. She's watching television. 'Well, well. Another young gel kill't—where's that, boy?'

'Ah?'

'Her found in a canal.'

'West Midlands.' He slurred indifference, 'She went missing few days back.'

'Aye,' said Glan.

She wheedled, 'Who they for?'

'On order.'

'Iorrie wouldn't, never.'

'Leave it,' he said.

'What about principle then?'

'You mean shit street. Leave it.'

'Gone twenty-seven, time you settled down,' vowed Jemima.

'Daresay, aye.'

She's nodding sanctimony, 'There's no respect, none at all.'

'Not much.' He mimed a chopping blow on her spine.

Jemima crept a pious face close to his, 'Nasty you are.'

'Ditto,' he said.

As if pleading justice, 'I've tended him hand and foot since he was born!'

Deborah Lazarus palmed her car keys to Glan in the Conservative Club, her silvered lips spelling, 'In the boot.'

'Ready for the oven,' he said.

She's jiving her arms, 'Our Mam will be cooking all night.'

'Dad'll be fast asleep. Me too.'

'Good girl,' he said.

Shorn blonde Deborah, eighteen, voluptuous, fourth daughter of Joey Lazarus, his twelve hours a day, six-day week *Delicatessen & Take Away* in Moel Exchange shopping precinct. Shrewd Deborah, law unto herself, quixotic pledge of her being.

The trussed chickens were in a carrier bag stamped STYLE above copperplate *Myra Mainwaring*. From the car park he watched Deborah prodding the chin of a lanky Dewinton

Technical College student. Glan squirted thin spittle as the youth reached two glasses of white wine from the counter. Deborah tap-tapped the side of her nose as the youngster turned, crossing to the snooker room.

Beneath transparent plastic in the BMW boot, two skinned hares draped on sheets of kitchen roll. Bolster of scrunched roll separated the hares from three glimmering, gutted sea bass. China bowl of brown eggs, white enamelled bowl of fresh cockles. Carton of lettuces. A jar of honey glistened under the boot light. He lodged the chickens among net-bagged onions.

While tippling white wine Deborah peeled a £50 note from her handbag. Smooth the way she tucked it in Glan's top pocket. 'Settled for our Dad's car and tonight's goods.'

He folded the note in his wallet. 'Not on, girl. I grafted repairing your old man's gear box.'

Smiling her mouth, 'Really?'

'Another twenty.'

She slurped wine. 'Right, okay. Must go now. Do my round,' the £20 in his top pocket as if by legerdemain. 'See you, Glan,' twirling her car keys like a *Country Life* tart except short-time pickup she was not.

At the side bar in the snooker room, he bought a pint of Clyne Extra. 'Say, boy, how'd you make out with Deborah?'

Stretched over his cue, the lean student skewed his head like a wryneck. 'Take it easy, man.'

'Don't be a thick bastard all your life.'

'Look, we were in school together.' The youth levered upright after potting a red, his skinny frame swaying triumph. 'We were kids from All Saints Place until my parents moved into the Villas.'

'So-long, boy,' he said.

'Hey, Glan, Glan, Mack! Deb, she passed the word. Um, my name's Meurig Rhys'—hand held out, disregarded but Meurig persisted, 'Glan, listen, um, fancy a run next Saturday? Deliver and collect for Cled Francis, the video shop in High Street arcade.'

His nape tingled.

'What d'you say, Glan?'

'Way you're shooting your mouth off, might be I'll get to bust your pretty face,' he said.

'Hundred quid in hand,' guaranteed Meurig, his snooker opponent brawling, 'What's going on, private conference!'

'Glan . . ?'

'See you later in the bar,' he said.

Where he promptly agreed.

He drove the Transit van to Southall, trolleyed boxes of cassettes into a steel-shuttered warehouse and humped replacements into the van. 'Your cheque will be in the bank,' he said to a fatly at-ease Asian woman.

'My kind regards to Mr Francis,' she inflected like a Southern Counties matron.

He located the sour-smelling shiplap bungalow after recrossing the Bridge, one padlocked suitcase and two tape-sealed toolboxes with handles neatly stacked in the porch. And a storming amazon cursing her foppish husband in mongrel Welsh. He's wilful too, droning, effing and blinding the misbegotten universe.

Mellow twilight by now.

He handed over a stapled jiffy bag from Cledwyn Francis.

'Wait,' demanded the amazon.

Glan sniggered amiably. 'You pair need to sort yourselves out.'

'Pearl!' cried dandy Vince from inside the bungalow.

She backheeled the door.

'Fetch him in for a coffee.'

Instead Pearl sneered sidelong, 'Clever bugger, nobody asked you to poke your nose in. G'wan back to bloody Moel Exchange.'

He raised a fist high. 'Lay off, spunkmouth.'

Cled Francis was stirring beef curry in the cellar kitchen below the video shop. He's forty, gorilla-armed, black hair ringleted to his round head, silver quarter moons pendant from each ear, leather thong necklace holding a lumpy gold crucifix below the hollow of his throat.

'How's negotiations, Glan-boy?'

'No trouble. What's in the luggage?'

'Ha,' replied Cled. 'Taste this,' offering the steaming spoon.

He blew, tasted, panted, 'Huhh-huhh . . . yi yi, warms the gut. Only I prefer chicken curry.'

'Bombay Taff,' says Cled. 'Stay for a meal, few glasses of

plonk?' He poured rice into a saucepan. 'Shut-shop at nine o'clock.'

'Tell you,' he said, 'those two in the bungalow off the motorway, they're crap comedians.'

Cled hooted benign exult.

He leaned on a mock Welsh dresser. 'Know what, I'd appreciate a cuppa.'

Hustling and spurting grunts, Cled plugged in a kettle, stirred the curry, fanned his hands over the rice, snatched a *Cymru am byth* mug off the dresser, aimed a teabag into it, pinged the sugarbowl and milk bottle with a teaspoon, prayed his hands to his forehead, level-toning, 'Welcome, *brawd,*' like the C. of E. amen. Then he shouted up the stairwell, 'Thuh-elm! Fifteen minutes!'

He decided, this man's all right. Pure Moel Exchange.

Thelma David's smile was a magic flux of seraph/siren. And time emptied from Glan Mack, eclipsed by food and drink, humankind's inheritance since the beginning, against sateless hunger.

He slept on a couch—Cled Francis and Thelma David are in the bedroom above the shop. Sunday noon when he left the kitchen via a door to the backyard. Nettles and brambles crowding the flagstone path to a barbed wire topped breeze-block wall. The wrought-iron gate had a trick shootbolt. He's preoccupied walking a dirt lane: Thelma the Jewess. Last of the Davids who kept the pawn-shop. Herself and Cled, they're on a winner. Videos. Wacky baccy. Tabs on offer. Like aspirins. Aitch very tidy in foil.

He foot-flicked gravel: Regular contract. I'm in. Down to me. Steady.

September into late October, ocherous sycamores towering among lichened ruins of Exchange Manor, and Jemima's gushing bliss, 'Now these are *proper* presents, lovely boy,' fanning tenners and fishing them beneath her apron. She stiffened to tableau, 'Oh, young chap came after you went mooching up the Roman road—whyn't you settle down, Glandwr?'

'C'mon,' he said.

'He wouldn't say much, Meurig something, thin as a rake, awful nice for 'round yere, nice and polite.'

'Meurig Rhys.'

Squealed Jemima, 'Rhys! We called them the *Mabons*!'

'From the Villas.'

'Used to be Chapel Street years ago. Well well, God alive. Oh yes, said he'll meet you in the Con.'

Glan sighted Meurig behind the *Echo* in the main lounge. He roofed the student's head fore and aft with the evening paper. 'Sing it true, boy.'

Meurig whispered, 'Deb's in Spain, staying out there with her Auntie, y'know, temporary. Family problem, Glan, Inland Revenue, the bastards.'

'So-long, kid,' he said.

Midway across the foyer, wearing jeans, floppy collared sweater and dark grey bomber jacket, Detective Constable Rowley held up his palm. 'I'd like a word, fella. We're making inquiries as regards Miss Lazarus. When did you see her?'

He hunched controlled bafflement, 'Who's she?'

'Twenty-sixth of last month, ninth of this month, you were with Deborah Lazarus in this Club.'

Unblinking eye to eye, 'Say, mate, mentioning Lazarus, he's a steel erector in Clyne Vale. Great bloke, genuine.'

Which peeved D.C. Rowley. 'Cut the bullshit, Mack. You a Club member?'

'Definitely, too true,' stepping his long-distance, pigeon-toed gait aside, rounding the copper.

'We're referring to Miss Lazarus from the precinct.'

He saluted matter-of-factly, 'All the best, mate.'

Muttered D.C. Rowley, 'Watch it, Mack. We'll put you in. G'night.'

Then gawky Meurig came, hoarse again, blinking distress, 'Hey, man, wait. I had the word from Cled. They're looking for Vince and Pearl. Um, Thelma too, she's pulled out.'

'Christ,' he said.

Glan Mack disappeared for ten months. Dumper driver on open-cast anthracite, he lived in a Portacabin with a bearded maintenance fitter, this gnostic, ex-Navy Irishman allegiant to his trade as a monk.

August Bank Holiday when he returned to Moel Exchange, toothless Jemima saying, 'They all went off. Gone away, the

Lazaruses. Girls all up and left like gypsies. Bankrupted. Yes! It was in the *Exchange and District Leader*.'

He said, 'Cled Francis from the arcade?'

'Him! Summoned! For drugs! Thousands! It was all in the *Exchange and District Leader*,' Jemima stroked his arm, 'Any spare money on you, boy? See, two red letters on the mantelpiece, gas, 'lectric; now they want to cut the water off! I'm at my wits' end, honest, if God Almighty strikes me dead. Please, Glandwr . . . I'm ever so glad to see you home.'

'What's to eat?' he said.

'Bacon 'n' egg, fresh tomatoes, some black puddin'.'

'I'll be in the garden.'

Where he sat on turf outside a dwarf picket fence, his bare feet dipping in the greeny river until Jemima called, drafting indulgence like a reprieved harpy.

My Uncle Dan

Having no other, Uncle Dan effectively cherished himself. Throughout most of his long life he endured the loneliness of a saint. His instinct for survival had the sovereignty of grass. He endured. He outlasted his generation. There are no words for the truth of him. Mine are impressions, speculations. Imagination wilts on the fringes of alienation of Dark Ages penury. I remember Uncle Dan as an enigma, the harmless iconoclast of my boyhood, the reject of my mother's family, unholy wanderer taken in for a week every summer. A grudge duty. My spinster schoolmistress, Aunt Mag did likewise, her obligation a week later, 34 miles away. And Uncle Dan walked the route.

He had the short-shuffling gait of a rover. He tramped the roads for over thirty years, with a hawker's licence and a cardboard suitcase display of England's Glory matches, shoelaces, tintacks, dubbin, needles, safety pins, reels of cotton, hairgrips, ribbons and Old Moore's Almanacs.

My maternal Grandfather died shortly after my mother left school. Thereafter Granny Ben housekept for successive common-law husbands. Three in all. Monoglot Welsh, nasty tempered, Granny Ben merely dratted at her grandchildren. She lived with Auntie Mag in a whitewashed cottage, the bindweed-blossomed towering hedged garden stretching down to elms on the bank of a cocoa coloured canal. In this garden I first met Uncle Dan 63 years ago, even then impenetrably hangdog, his soul (or whatever) secure, true as gravity. Granny Ben hustled him into the cottage, where he stayed hidden while his underclothes were washed and dried. Uncle Dan probably slept in the attic. It was high summer. I watched him leaving the following afternoon, shabbily grey suited, black cap flat on his head, clump soled boots scuffing the dirt lane up to the pavement, brown paper parcel under his arm: Swansea loaf, cheese, butter, screws of tea, sugar and salt, packed by Auntie Mag. Dangling from his other hand, a plaited straw shopping bag holding his possessions: tin kettle, mug, plate, knife, fork, spoon, and some rolled-up clothes.

Uncle Dan lived in spikes all over Wales and the border

counties, workhouses run by Guardians of the Poor. His bushy eyebrows overhung very small, wet glistening eyes. Reading the *Evening Post*, he held the newspaper an inch from his blunt spud of a nose. His mouth registered stillness. Speaking to my mother, he addressed her as Mary-Ann. Auntie Mag he called Margaret-Maud, his younger brother Evan-Glyndwr, patronyms of their Ynystawe home and hearth.

Why was he spurned by everybody?

My mother married a collier. They reared five children. Uncle Glyn lived with us. He was killed underground on Easter Monday, 1929. Auntie Mag remained childless until she died.

Why? Surely not because of Dan's short-sighted fumbling, his fretless inadequacy. Something else, unlovable, some innate flaw which conditioned him for a lifetime of selfness. Unselfish too, finally.

I never heard a kind word spoken for Uncle Dan. Never. My mother bullied and snapped at him. Auntie Mag treated him as a burden on her conscience. Uncle Glyn's droll humour probed lightweight malice. My father regarded old Dan as a damned nuisance. The annual visits upset my mother.

Every summer in the month of August, 'Uncle Dan has come.' Homeless roamer drifted in from God knows where, his suitcase full of paraphernalia kneed into the cubbyhole under the stairs. Deliberate, empty greetings, a curmudgeonly concern for Dan's personal welfare. Like a man rapt in dream, he turned aside from us children. We were foreign to his days. But he obeyed the ritual, the awful rigmarole. Bath first, even before a cup of tea. Low voices in the kitchen while he soaped himself. Then, without knocking the door, my father went into the bathroom with clean underpants, vest, shirts and socks, on loan to Uncle Dan for a few days. My mother finger-tipped Dan's grimy clothes into the bath-water. She dollied them. Changed the water. She hand-washed them, rinsed, expertly wrung old Dan's vest and shirt over her left wrist, piled the lot into a bowl and pegged them on the clothes-line.

Uncle Dan dunked rock cake in his cup of tea, a snack pending dinner-time or supper-time. While eating he snuffed through his nose. He made mumbly responses, fitting small talk about the family—Auntie Mag and my mother corresponded weekly, four-page letters written in Welsh. Uncle Glyn would leave the kitchen, usually to play his button accordion in the front room, old Welsh ballads, love songs. He was courting a forthright handsome young woman named Hilda, but the pit killed Glyn before they were married.

So my parents tolerated Dan for seven days. He helped out, supervised by my mother. Simple chores, washing dishes, sweeping the flagstone backyard, chopping firewood, fetching coal. It wasn't in the man to communicate, to socialise. Mornings after breakfast, he walked the village main street, unseeing, perfectly alone, heedless of people and the pub. Many villagers recognised him. 'Of course, Mary's brother. Yes, he's the black sheep.'

He rounded the back garden time after time, hands fisted in his trouser pockets, occasionally stooping to sniff wallflowers or stock. Uncle Dan the tramp, estranged adult of our childhood. We were expected to feel sorry for our mother and Auntie Mag, old Dan their liability, their worldly shame. The pull of blood clung throughout their lives. Uncle Dan felt it too, imprinted on him as a baby, toddler, boy. The rift must have occurred during his adolescence.

Physiology, psychology, these are piffling tools to measure how Dan survived, this Welsh vagabond between world wars. I never saw a smile on his face. One August his wrists and ankles were blotched with impetigo. He simply scratched. My mother doused him with calamine lotion, treatment accompanied by tongue lashing. They were contraries from the same wedlock, old Dan utterly social, a human doldrum, while she seethed with worries, dogmas, domestic campaigns, responsibilities, righteousness. She acquired intense skills. Ineptitude isolated him. Somewhere inside Uncle Dan, a quartzy lode of contentment, a core of immunity. He was dull, scrupulously *twp* enough to be absolved, yet he attended to his destiny.

Uncle Dan spent the last 28 years of his life in a Home for the Blind, the Zion of his hard, philistine decades hoofing the roads. He had a white stick and a Blind Pension in his early sixties. Within seven years all his immediate family were dead. By now his nephews and nieces were married with children. Totally ignored at Christmas-times, excluded from weddings and funerals, years and years of silence diminished Uncle Dan. Old Dan's existence lingered very tenuously in my mind. I knew about the Home for the Blind somewhere in West Wales. No more than that, without a qualm either, obviously.

When he died at 91, his nephews and nieces were grandparents of a scattered generation. Natural dispersion peculiar to industrialised Wales. Uncle Dan was buried unmourned by a single relative. Several months later, my sisters, my brother and I received copies of a solicitor's letter, the jargoned chronicle of Daniel Davies's death and Christian burial in Llanelli. Old Uncle Dan the tramp, he left each of us £45 in his will.

Before Forever After

It was tamping down, September gale rain drowning Wales, sodden donkey coats steaming in our canteen, the huge pot-bellied stove leaking squiggles of sulphur smoke, half a dozen card schools on the go; discussions, arguments all round, a rowdy, becursed, shifting quint of football, women, horses, work and money.

A group of us were playing pontoon, Strapper Cullen banker, my mate Chris down to a few tanners, his dragged-in mouth jutting his knubbly-chin—he looked like a pensioner elf. Big Strapper with the bronzy, hard-skinned tan of a buck Huron, he said, 'What's for you, Chris?'

'Turn it over,' Chris said.

Strapper twisted a black nine.

Chris returned his cards. 'Too heavy. Strapper, there's no form, no run of play, there's nothing to go by. With you it's all luck.'

'Lend you half a bar,' offered Strapper.

'When I borrow money to play cards I'll pack in altogether,' Chris said.

The navvy ganger said, 'I'll stick.'

'Me, I'll stick,' I said.

Pete the crane driver bought for a tanner. 'Enough,' he said. 'I'm satisfied.'

Strapper turned over his pair. 'Eight.' He turned over the ace of clubs. 'Nine.' He turned over a deuce. 'Eleven—boys, I can't bust.' Another deuce, Strapper grinning like an advert. 'Thirteen. Pay pontoons only.'

He collected the stakes.

The navvy ganger fisted the table. 'If he fell in our dub he'd come up with milk choc'late. Deal me out, I'm finished. I couldn't win a game of Oxo.'

'Jammy sod,' explained Chris. 'Typical. Some day he'll marry a whoor who'll drag him down to where he belongs.'

Strapper skidded a few shillings across to the navvy ganger. 'Bus fare to go home,' he said. 'As for you, Chris, win or lose you moan like a granny. Wait till you see this bird I'm knocking around with these days. She'll make you wish you were stone blind, you chopsy old tiger.'

Friendly Strapper Cullen, most favoured character on the building site. A wide open man, generous, brotherly. Everybody loved him.

The navvy ganger rattled his bus fare, walked across to the stove. I said, 'Where's she from, this gorgeous bint of yours?'

'Berw Vale. She drives her Triumph Herald over the mountain road at ninety. Perfect timing. She's perfection itself.'

'Blonde girl in a white sports car?' I said.

Strapper dealt the cards. 'Yeh. Seen us have you, Dai?'

I said, 'Rebecca Pearce. Her old man's rolling in loot. He's chairman of Berw chamber of commerce, he's on the corporation, he's got shares in Marvel-bread bakery, he's director in the chain-works . . .'

Zealot through to his marrow, Chris choked on private disgust. 'Taliesin Pearce be damned! He's a social criminal of the first water. Born crooked, lives crooked and he'll die the same.'

Pete the crane driver signalled for hush, Strapper smiling pleasantly, saying, 'Quiet now, ah, if you don't mind?'

'Dirt sticks,' insisted Chris. 'When you're my age you'll appreciate what it means to speak your mind with a clear conscience, knowing full well that you have never taken advantage of your fellow workmen. Consequently, boy, I won't have you telling me to be quiet. In my experience, size and strength don't count. What counts is the state of a man's conscience. Mine's clear.'

I chanted a little mock of praise for my old mate Chris. 'Clear as isinglass. Transparent forever. Stand aside, make way for Christopher Llewellyn, the white knight of the A.S.W!'— we're both chippies, see, side by side, concrete shuttering, boxing RSJs on this new factory project.

He said, 'Very clever, Dai. When it comes to conscience as regards expenditure of public funds, I can supply certain facts relating to Councillor Tal Pearce.'

'Rebecca's luscious,' I said. 'We were in school together, her little whass-names dancing inside her blouse the day we finished last in the three-legged race.' I sucked a few hostler noises, street-corner erotica. 'Bee-eautiful 'Becca,' I said, 'blonde as raffia, cool as . . .'

Strapper twirled his podger on a loop of thong. 'Shut up,

31

Dai.' He was grinning though, eyes pale blue as sunshine on bits of ice, the podger a blur, harmless, disappearing, dropped back into his belt.

'Cool as a menthol cigarette,' I said.

He pressed one finger on my sternum. 'You and Rebecca went to the same school?'

'All the way from infants, to itchy adolescence. She's al'right, genuine, but her father, he's pure Welsh Mafia.'

'Hundred per cent,' confirmed Chris, placing his spade ace face-up over a picture.

Pete stuck.

I stuck with nineteen.

Strapper turned over his pair. Ace of diamonds. Black queen. 'Sorry, Chris,' he said.

Chris left the table. The rain slashed down. Mack whistled us off the site at three o'clock. Cockney born, Mack showed all the brave style, but too many G.F. jobs on too many cut-price sites had ulcerated his stomach. We shared a decent bonus system on this new factory, after weeks of ca'-canny, the usual mixture of threats and syrupy sweet reason. The job flowed: steel stanchions, concrete, more steel, more concrete, steel roofing trusses, big Strapper cat-walking the top-most RSJs, black against white clouds, like a visitor from somewhere anti-gravity. Old Pete operated the crane, a droll, neckless, throwback Celt who seemed to tap into Strapper's mind.

Came one crisp Friday as we straggled towards the pay office, and Rebecca Pearce drove her white Triumph across the site.

Chris spat neatly aside. 'That's her, Strapper's piece?'

'None other,' I said.

She's wearing a leather two-piece, oatmeal colour, long blonde hair shawled around her shoulders, wolf calls and parrot whistles answering the hunting music of her twin klaxons. Cockney Mack watched from his office doorway, our happy enough general foreman licking Rennie tablet rime off his lips. Again that musical yelp from the Triumph Herald. I'm looking for Strapper. He's airbourne, slowly revolving, floating down like a sun god, old Pete in the crane cabin, lowering his jib out over the roadway, dangling Strapper above the car, joggling him forward until he jinks smartly off the chain hanging from the hook, spanners and podger jingling on his

32

belt. Without taking his eyes off Rebecca, he waved up-and-away to Pete.

A seven-second tableau, Strapper's thick brown mane bent towards blonde Rebecca, then he's loping away to the canteen for his jacket.

'Clown,' decided Chis, 'endangering himself and others.'

I said, 'See you tomorrow morning. I'm going to have a chat with Rebecca.'

'Obvious to me the girl's a parasite,' he said. 'She's using Strapper. The boy's on hire.'

Meagrely built, a really small man, but old Chris is loaded with ethics. I walked over to the Triumph.

'Hullo, 'Becca.'

'David Samuels!' She switched off some utterly shitty pop on the car radio.

'Long time no time for,' I said.

'So this is where you work.'

I asked her, 'Are you still with that dot and carry one insurance company?'

She pushed treble sized sun-glasses high up on her blonde hair, toned herself into old-fashioned Welshy, and by the Christ she looked beyond the reach of us all. 'I've climbed to private secretary. Aye indeed, Dai Sam. Awful responsible it is.'

I pinked the windscreen. 'Win this banger in a raffle. I can't afford a Hong Kong gambo. As a single man I'm taxed to five nights a week drinking club beer, and pleasant day-dreams.'

Rebecca said, 'Twenty-second birthday present from my father.'

'Four years ago he gave you a holiday in Spain.'

'I haven't seen you since, David.'

'Bitter-sweet tears flowing from her angelic eyes,' I said.

She blew a demure raspberry, subsiding to a snaky hiss.

'Tempus fugit, 'Becca.'

'The flower clock in Swansea! I remember. Whit Monday. It rained. You caught a cold. I went to Spain the following week.'

'Remember our three-legged race?' I said.

'*You* weren't concerned about the race.'

'I cannot hurl the lie back at your milk-white teeth. Tempus fugit.'

'Ha, ha, ha. Funny.'

'How do you find Snapper?' I said.

33

'John found me'—flatly under-stressing her God-given grandeur.

'Everybody calls him Strapper. He's a fine bloke,' I said.

'Handsome, all the makings of a hero. I admire him. You too, girl, I've always admired you.'

She fiddled with the sun-glasses. 'I missed you in Spain. We were only kids, but it was awfully nice.'

'Niceness is nice,' I said.

'It doesn't last, perhaps it isn't supposed to beyond a certain point.'

'Are we talking about the same thing?' I said. 'The one and only experience past all telling?'

'I don't understand.'

Who would, I thought, conceding an influx of worms in the bud. 'Falling in love,' I said.

'But it works both ways. We also fell out of love.'

I said, 'What happened, 'Becca?'

'I wish you wouldn't call me 'Becca. It takes me back to hockey sticks, the smell of liniment when I sprained my knee . . .'

'And that P.E. mistress with a voice like Humphrey Bogart,' I said.

She frowned. 'I felt sorry for her.'

'It's contagious,' I said.

'All right, Dai Sam, what are you hinting at?'

'Dead-end passion.'

'You always were a cruel boy.'

'No, I reckon there's a niche for everybody, even me.'

'Cynic, seek and ye may find,' she said.

I saw Strapper coming down from the canteen, tee-shirt and jeans bulging with the power of him, denim jacket swinging in his hand. 'Here's your spider-man, 'Becca.' To Strapper I said, 'We've been laying flowers on dead memories.'

The untouchable grin, confident as a prince under protocol. 'Forget-me-nots?'

'David's referring to the flower clock in Swansea, O ever such a long time ago.'

I said, 'Aye, tempus and fugit and so on and so forth.'

Strapper vaulted into the car. 'Watch your language, matey. Away, Rebecca, before I lace his ankles around his neck.'

She smoothly whoofed one-two-three through the gears,

and I felt myself bowing like a toy mandarin, as if my groins carried rise and fall hinges.

Mack came out from his office. 'Strapper's found himself a real classy skirt. Wouldn't mind myself. She's a goer, stands out a mile.'

I said, 'Her old man's a tycoon.'

He freed his tongue from a juicy puddle of alkaline. 'Don't say. What's his line of business?'

'It's a Welsh disease, ancient as these scab-faced hills and valleys.'

'Come off it, Dai.'

'Our inheritance from times of tribulation,' I said. 'If you can't beat 'em, turn cannibal.'

Mack lowered his head, his shiny all-welded shoes reading ten to two, the empty smile of a prig failing to comfort his hagged eyes. 'I'm worried. See that last line of trusses. Tricky situation. Jib's too short. Worse, I'm seven weeks behind schedule. Can't expect my scaffolders to hang scaffolding on sky-hooks. What we'll do, track back, swing that last truss in from outside. Use ropes, coupla ropes. Strapper can do it, him and Pete. They work good together.'

I drew my wages. Mack and the navvy ganger were still out on the site, Mack waving his arms, trying to prove his case to the wrong man. Pete the crane driver was homeward, sleeping on a Western Welsh bus. Big Strapper and Rebecca were clocking ninety over the mountain road to Berw Vale.

Next day Saturday, half-day, thank God. We were up on the second deck, toggling beam-side shutters around a RSJ, old Chris venting his brand of Socialism, with Strapper and Rebecca included in a selective purge when the revolution came. I'm his sounding board, less than half his age, plus double his immunity to consequence etcetera, etcetera. We've argued politics, morality, economics six days a week for two years. Like Robert Tressall of Hastings, he's truly bent to buggery by his craft. Times change. Back-stabbers belong everywhere. We inherit chaos. It's unconditional.

'For example,' Chris said, 'take a muscle-bound moron like Strapper Cullen. Double-time every week-end since his firm came on the site. Before he's fifty he'll be worn down to a shadow, what with Tal Pearce's young bitch after him and all. Steel erectors, I've seen more intelligent men sweeping the roads. Glorified labourers, that's their status, glorified labourers.'

'You're afraid of heights,' I said.

'Listen, Dai, there's more than one kind of nerve. Put him up on a platform in front of five hundred trade union members. Could he explain the pros and cons of negotiation? Could he enlighten the rank and file, the backbone of our society?'

'Your father should have named you Jesus,' I said.

He pulled his elvish face. 'Check this shutter with your level. I'll toggle the wire.'

I suggested, 'Take five, man. We've done our whack until tea-break.'

'Where d'you learn that attitude? You youngsters, you're bankrupt as regards scruples. It's all grab, grab, grab. How you'll manage when the hard times come, I do not know.'

We levelled the shutter.

'They can pour this beam first thing Monday morning,' he said. 'Now, as I was saying, there's such a thing as common decency. They were rolling about, her squealing like a stuck pig on the bank outside my allotment. Full harvest moon last night, remember. Midnight, them two bathing in private water. Privilege again, Tal Pearce pulling strings so's his daughter and that big moron can swim in Berw Lake, a body of water which serves for domestic purposes under certain emergencies. The likes of that girl are taking the cream off the backs of the likes of you and me. What I'd do is draft her into skivvying for a few years. Laundry work and dirty dishes. She'd earn the right to flash around like some loose slut because then, Dai, *then*, personal experience teaches the lesson. If society makes profit off a girl's body and nothing else besides, she conducts herself accordingly. Cheap in her own eyes. Follow my meaning?'

'You're a bloody dictator,' I said. 'Becca works for an insurance company.'

'Only parasites flog insurance. Vultures they are, profiteering on public and private sorrow, not to mention property.'

I hammered a 2½" nail, fixing the lower beam-side to the soffit.

He said, 'I'll remind you about that nail when we come to strip this shutter. She'll tighten up when they pour.'

'Yes, Jesus, but in your company I can afford to be careless once or twice, surely?'

'Better ease her off the soffit, Dai. Do it now.'

'Okay, Jesus,' I said.

'Neither does it pay you to sneer at a man old enough to be your father,' he said.

Strapper leapt off the RSJ, clean over my head as I prised the shutter away from the soffit with a nailbar. He laid the three foot spirit level on the palm of his hand, watching the bubble. 'Hullo there, pimper,' he said to Chris. 'Did you get an eyeful last night?'

Chris stiffened up, clenched for self-defence. 'Careful what you're saying. There's a witness standing right behind you.'

Strapper gently wielded the spirit level, royalty bestowing grace, tapping Chris on each shoulder. 'I'm entitled to know, old matey.'

'And *I* should like to know who gave you permission to swim in Berw Lake? That Lake belongs to the corporation. Furthermore, for your information, what I witnessed by sheer *accident*, I wouldn't repeat to a living soul.'

I had to say it, 'Old fork-tongue.'

Strapper said, 'I'll come to you, Chris, if there's any gossip.'

Undeterred, Chris raised up on his heels. 'I'll cope with anything you can dish out.'

'I'm not threatening you, old matey. I'll leave that to Mr Pearce.'

'Him! I'd step over Tal Pearce if he was curled up in the gutter.'

'Who owns your house?' asked Strapper.

'Never you mind who owns my house!'

'Mr Pearce,' said Strapper.

I chipped in, 'Well-well-well-well,' sing-song style indicating mood and nous.

'Yeh, he's the owner,' affirmed Strapper, and he jumped up off our scaffold, balanced on the RSJ, the tight cheeks of his buttocks high above his long legs as he walked across to the last line of roofing trusses.

'Happy thought to suit the occasion,' I said. 'Strapper might become your landlord some day.'

'She's got him for stud, pure and simple. It's bloody wicked. Little bitch like that, she'd match a poof better than a bloke like

Strapper Cullen. She's whooring around, Dai, that's what she's doing. Look, I'd be the last man on God's earth to create animosity. As for yourself, it's dead rotten when two workmates can't exchange a few confidential items. I'm off down the ladder. Call of nature. See you in the canteen. Tea-break in a few minutes.'

A marathon arguer, old Chris kept the topic going, the navvy ganger sitting outside us in the canteen, eating half a cooked chicken.

'Puritan,' I accused, 'you're a dog-in-the-manger puritan, with no authority at all to pass judgment like some spunk-bound old shag-bag. Offer me a Woodbine—I forgot to buy fags before coming to work this morning.'

'You'll learn, boy. Wait until you're married, reared kids, hair dropped out, no teeth left, then you'll shut your mouth. You'll think first instead of throwing insults. Here I've been trying to explain pollution, the possibility if either Strapper or that sloppy girl had a dose of syph or something. Time you realised a country is only as good as the people who live in it. Ever read *The Citadel*?'

'I'd drink 'Becca's sweat,' I said, stalling the ganger on a thick bolus of meat.

'It's in *The Citadel* you'll find an example of pollution such as we've never experienced.'

'I'm more familiar with the Song of Solomon,' I said, straightaway spouting another little beneficial chant: '*Thy navel is like a round goblet, which wanteth not liquor; thy belly is like an heap of wheat set about with lilies; Thy two breasts are like two young roes that are twins. Thy neck is a tower of ivory; thine eyes like the fish-pools of Heshbon, by the gate of Bathrabbim; thy nose is as the tower of Lebanon, which looketh towards Damascus.* Mind passing that cigarette now, please, Christopher.'

He munched his lettuce and tomato sandwich—lettuce cut around midnight the night before. 'As a life-long agnostic, the outcome of serious thought, I nevertheless respect any man's religion. In a democracy . . .'

'It's poxy,' I said.

Delayed response, nicely balanced between unction and righteous scorn. 'Navel like a goblet, huh, out of all proportion to common sense. Exaggeration beyond reason. Rubbish, boy, romantic rubbish. That's the trouble, today's youth won't face reality. Real issues upon which decisions have to be made for the betterment of mankind. Solomon's got fuck-all to do with us building that factory out there. Try Solomon on Mack. Try Solomon on those scientists who leave their bags of urine floating around in space. I'll tell you the plain gospel for the man in the street. It's economics, always has been since we dropped down from the branches. Even a stupid fella like Strapper Cullen appreciates the power of a quid note in his hand. Wouldn't surprise me if he's knocking out thirty-odd a week.'

I said, 'Jealous?'

Give in to Chris, he's dauntless. He lit my cigarette, his pursy mouth set tidy. 'Take a so-called Socialist writer like Mister George Bernard Shaw. He left umpteen thousands. Some of our hypocritical Labour leaders are financiers in their own right. By comparison Tal Pearce is just a potcher, yet we've seen his corruptive influence in Berw Vale politics. I think it's shameful, that young pusher in her bloody sports car, chucking herself at a semi-skilled worker. It's enough to make a good man spit blood.'

I said, 'Bile is what I feel like throwing up.'

The connection skewed, went wrong; Chris wasn't listening, muttering to himself, 'Too true, boy, too true.'

'You're putting my holy ghost through a mincer,' I said.

He looked around the canteen. 'Where is Strapper?'

'Out on site with Pete and Mack.'

He smirked nastily. 'Some principle, working through tea-break.'

'We did the same last week, stand-by while they poured that column on number two deck.'

'Emergency, Dai. Anything goes all to balls on the site, us tradesmen land in the pickies.'

'Mack's in trouble,' I said. 'They can't swing in the last truss. He wants Strapper to bring it in with a couple of ropes. How does she look in the buff?'

Chris scowled ten years on his worn face, the grunt escaping like an air block in shoddy plumbing: 'Ah?'

''Becca Pearce,' I said.

'Oh, al'right so far as I could see. White, exceptionally white, I thought. Goes with her being a blondie, I suppose.'

'*Duw-Duw*,' I said.

He said, 'Aye.'

We were back up on our section of scaffold when he found another little burst of spleen, vowing, 'I should have stung her backside with the airgun I use for killing rats in my compost heap. Teach her a lesson.'

Far up above our heads, a scaffolder was singing 'Your tiny hand is frozen'—choir tenor, undoubtedly. It was Indian Summer weather, spiritual in a way, Berw mountain in the distance, changed to rust, fawny-grey, dark blobs of hawthorn cringing ready for winter; black leghorns scratching in the yard of a condemned (progress being what it is) smallholding below the new factory, a yellow 'dozer ripping out great arcs of bramble behind the smallholder's two up and two down cottage. Smells everywhere. Green stuff dying.

Right.

'Chris, Mr Jesus,' I said, 'much sadism in your family?'

'None at all. I come from good, honest Welsh stock. There isn't a trace of mongrel blood in me.'

I said, 'You look pure, too, especially in profile. Any love-children in your family?'

'They're no disgrace. Mind, I believe in discipline, decency all round, not love thy neighbour and at the same time brain-wash them till he can't think for himself. Ever see a bishop humping a tool-bag? Ever see a parson emptying ashbins? They're the biggest shower of bastards in our Western society. Fascists to the core, every man jack of 'em.'

'She's very white then,' I said, because against a man like Chris, tactics are justified. The slow-motion surrealist gambit.

He gave me one of his sincere scrutinies, signifying word of honour. 'Dai Sam, take my advice. Find yourself a lovely open-minded Welsh girl, and marry her. To be quite frank, boy, there's a strange kink in your mentality.'

We moved across the scaffold, began fixing another soffit while I told him the story about our Whit Monday in Swansea. The flower clock, the rain, how I sheltered in the Gents, Rebecca in the Ladies, and about the ravaged old bloke with one arm who talked to himself in one of the cubicles. Grumble-grumble behind the bolted door: 'Gerroff, this is my seat. I was here first. This is my seat.' That lunatic flower clock, the minute hand jerking around like armageddon camouflaged by Walt Disney. I gave old one-arm the price of a Woolworth's meal . . . but it rained all day.

Chris remembered the bombing of Swansea. Changed forever since, not so friendly.

'Tempus fugit,' I said.

'What?' he snapped, as the burping roar of Pete's crane cut out. We turned, a gasping moan ascending from the site, Strapper Cullen deflecting off a RSJ, falling all-shapes, the visible bounce of his body on the ground floor concrete. Seconds ticked out, glacial, then frenzy, men racing towards ladders, flying down scaffolding like monkeys.

He looked like a goner for sure, blood seeping from his ear, his nostrils, the greyness of death on him.

Chris took charge. He issued the orders. Mack phoned for an ambulance. Men sprinted to the canteen, brought their coats; Chris draped them over Strapper. Pete was crying, down on his knees, crying, 'Strapper-boy, it's me, Pete. Can you hear me?'

Chris cuffed backhanders against his chest, jarring the grief out of him. 'Dai, come here. Take care of this man,' he said.

Old Pete broadcasting how the swinging truss clouted Strapper on the shoulder. Chris said, 'Shut it—Dai, shut him up. This isn't a case of negligence. Act of God.'

I dragged Pete through the crowd, Chris yelling, 'All you men, stand back! You (to Mack), keep everybody away.'

Mack followed the navvy ganger round and round the ring, arms spread out, blabbing, blah-blah-blah. And big Strapper, he looked to be dying. Skull fracture, fractured spine, pelvis crushed. He fell on his spanners and podger.

Still dangling from the crane jib, the truss spun very, very slowly, barely whiffling the hanging ropes.

All this happened before.

A year later we were second-fixing in the administration block, the only two chippies left on the job. Clean craftwork, inside, no frozen hands and feet from north-east winds. We weren't Mack's blue-eyed boys either. First on, last off, the seniority rule.

Another October day, blustery, the lifeless smallholding, empty cottage vandalised, naturally, our timber canteen dismantled, taken away, replaced by green sward landscaped down to the roadside. Contemporary planning. For every new factory, a few square yards of turf, token allegiance to the chlorophyll which buries civilisations.

We were hanging beech-wood doors. Flush panelled hardboard doors down on the factory production floor, of course, again perfectly natural That's life. Chris was contented, pushing his steel jack-plane, drooling over the beautiful tight grained timber. He sniffed shavings like an addict—it's on the wane though, the servant/master hand of man is alien to concrete and plastics. Craftsmanship is doomed.

I lifted the *Morning Star* out of the rear pocket of his overalls. The date clicked: October 23rd. I said, 'It's a year to the day since Strapper Cullen had his accident.'

'Bad day,' Chris said. 'Youngster like that, hardly in his prime, ruined for life.'

'Fate,' I said, 'bastard fate.'

'True, Dai. I can't contend otherwise.'

We offered up the door again, Chris inside, me outside. Perfect fit. I didn't hear Rebecca's footsteps, her quiet voice snapping the dream between my ears. 'David?'

Irascible as a starved virus, Chris shouted, 'Hold onto the bloody door!'

I said, 'Wonderful to see you, 'Becca.'

'Introduce me to Mr Llewellyn,' she said.

We lifted the door away from the jambs.

She was transformed, facially harder, her bobbed hair untidy, less outright blonde, her girl-shape lost under a black PVC windcheater, all slanting zips and press studs, a dingy sweater, old jeans and scuffed jackboots.

'Want me? What for? What's the trouble?' demanded Chris, intolerance deepening the crow's feet around his eyes.

'My husband would like to speak to you, Mr Llewellyn.'

'Husband? I don't know him. Who is he?'

'John Cullen. I think you might possibly see him from that window.'

We looked down. Big Strapper all right, standing hunched over a pair of alloy crutches. Parked at the kerb behind him, one of those three-wheelers for disabled persons. And behind the three-wheeler a ropey looking Bantam two-stroke, with a tatty crash helmet perched on the saddle.

Chris affected *bonhomie*. 'Congratulations. How is he?'

'John insists on speaking to you personally. Won't you come down to the road?'

'Glad to, Mrs Cullen.' He grabbed my arm. 'Dai, c'mon, we'd better go together.'

'Certainly, you too, David,' she said.

Exactly the same Strapper Cullen, heavier, confident as ever, his short-reached handshake making Chris wince.

'Reason I'm here, I want to thank you for looking after me when I took my big tumble. While I was in hospital, old Pete told me how you organised things.' Strapper patted his jacket pockets, teetering a little. Rebecca darted forward, placed a cigarette between his lips, lit it for him.

'Ta, love,' he said, smiling, her face calm, lowering, their cheekbones touching, a brief nudge of affection. 'Anniversary of the day!' he said. 'Know something, Chris, I'm *born* lucky. Rebecca married me while I was still wearing a plaster cast.'

'The worst is over,' she said quietly.

'Over,' repeated Strapper. 'My lovely, we can't fail.'

'John swims every afternoon in the sea,' she said.

'Well done, boy, well done,' approved Chris.

Strapper chuckled pleasure. 'I'm like a drunken crab until I get into crawl stroke. Hey, love, give them our address. Listen, Chris, we bought this six roomed bungalow down in Pembroke. Pay us a visit. Stay a couple of weeks. Any time.'

She handed Chris an addressed envelope from Strapper's wallet. 'Bring your wife, Mr Llewellyn. We shall be happy to have you stay with us.'

Chris mumbled. He didn't know what to say.

Rebecca buckled on her crash helmet. 'It's a long drive home, dear. I think we'd better get started.' She opened the car door, Strapper flopped in sideways; she tucked in his useless legs, collapsed his bright alloy crutches and stowed them in the boot.

We shook hands again. Rebecca said, 'You're a good man, Mr Llewellyn. Goodbye, David.'

Two kicks on the Bantam and she was ready.

'Cheerio, Chris,' bawled Strapper. 'See you, Dai, So long for now!'—Rebecca riding on ahead, slowly, Strapper zig-zagging the tiny three-wheeler, his horn blaring Bhaap-bhap-bhap-bhaaap, bhaaap-bhap-bhap-bhap-bhaaap up the road.

I said, 'That's what I call guts, him and her.'

Chris squared his shoulders, ground out his feelings like dogma, 'Yes, boy, they do make a man feel small, they definitely do.'

July Saturday in 1940

'Jesus saves,' promised Mr Everett serenely, his sharp dark eyes watching the Home Guard shuttling into ranks on the village square. Behind him in the doorway, his wife held her pinafore up to her nose like a suspicious harem lady. Mr Everett hawked without spitting. Double-handed, he pressed a bible to his sternum.

Corporal Price tolled the school bell until Sergeant Lewis bawled in his ear, 'Get on parade, you daft bugger!'

Excited boys and girls darted among the Home Guard—nineteen men with one Lee-Enfield rifle and a clip of bullets. Lieutenant Barney Bryant carried the rifle slung across his back. Barney, the colliery under-manager, was middle-aged, swarthy, ruffian grained like a Hollywood Mexican.

Sergeant Shink Lewis, ex-Welsh Guards '14-'18 war, stamped himself upright. 'Make a suggestion, sir?'

Barney nodded.

'Horses from the stables, sir. You and myself. Reconnaissance.'

Corporal Price waded through the ranks, pushing kiddies, demanding, 'Quiet! Everybody shurrup for instructions from Mr Bryant!'

'Now there's trouble,' said Mrs Everett from behind her pinafore.

Corporal Price partly evaded the forearm smash to his chest. She was a heavy, earth-mother woman, her fist wagging at the Corporal's chin. 'Keep them flamin' 'ands to you'self, or you'll cop one of these. Bloody blaggard as you are.'

'I'm only trying my best, missis, honest!'

'Ye-es, I know. They all say that.' She elbowed through the Home Guard, children trailing behind her to the pavement.

'I'm only trying my best,' appealed Corporal Price.

Barney signalled him forward with his forefinger.

'Report to the officer,' ordered Sergeant Lewis.

Corporal Price pointed north, Cefn Nant-y-Bwlch rising to a massif of towering buttresses above the village. 'Up there, Mr Bryant! They was seen coming down!'

Barney scowled his grey streaked eyebrows. 'Fetch the boy.'

Mr Everett stepped aside, allowing his wife to push out their

44

twelve-year-old son. 'Speak the truth, Isaac,' warned Mr Everett.

Isaac dangled a wilted bunch of buttercups. 'I was picking these by the Frogs' Pond, for my Mam.'

Corporal Price wheedled aggressively, 'You must tell Mr Bryant what you saw.'

'As the aeroplane went over the mountain they came down up there,' said Isaac.

'Parachutists!' shouted the Corporal.

Sergeant Lewis leaned forward. 'How many, boy?'

'Few,' Isaac said. He waved his hand gracefully. 'They just floated down.'

'See, Mr Bryant! German invaders! Definite!' blared Corporal Price.

Isaac Everett ran indoors. Mr Everett thrust his bible at Mrs Everett. Bleakly solemn, striding to the window, he prayed, 'Yea, though I walk through the valley of the shadow of death, I will fear no evil: for thou art with me; thy rod and thy staff they comfort me.'

Mrs Everett closed the front door. She lingered behind her husband at the window.

Sergeant Lewis regarded his men. 'Private Miskin, forward at the double!'

Joe Miskin held his 12-bore at point of balance. He cherished the shotgun, barrels recently blued at the cost of a week's wages. 'Ne'mind the bullshit, Shink,' he said quietly.

Lieutenant Bryant nudged Joe's arm in a friendly way.

'Miskin, what's it like up there, back over the rocks?'

'Bare as a badger's all the way for miles. No path. Don't follow the telegraph poles else you'll come out on top of the quarry . . .'

'Above Dinas itself,' said Barney.

Joe hefted his 12 bore. 'Want me to take a dekko, Mr Bryant?'

Barney shook his head.

As he sauntered to his place in the ranks, Joe muttered. 'Up your pipe, Shink.'

'Wait. Come here, Miskin,' said the Lieutenant.

'Borrow two saddles from the farm. You,' he said to Corporal Price, 'fetch two reliable horses from the stables.'

Smiling tightly, Sergeant Lewis hustled another man to help Joe carry the saddles.

Corporal Price brought two huge horses with feathery fetlocks, docile nags on the colliery surface for hauling timber and supplies. Insulated by know-how, Joe saddled the horses. His privilege. He cursed everybody who tried to interfere.

Mounted up on the square, Lieutenant Bryant rose in the stirrups. 'Stand easy, men.'

Slow and massive in the warm mid-day, the dobbins set off on the green parish track up and over Cefn Nant-y-Bwlch.

Mr Everett, fists hugged to his armpits, sang harshly, *sotto voce,* *'We're marching to Zion, beautiful beautiful Zion, we're marching upward to Zion, the beautiful city of God.* Those potatoes are boiling over,' he said to his wife.

In the kitchen, Isaac held a single buttercup under her chin to find out if she liked butter. 'Good boy,' she said. 'At least you won't grow up like your father.'

Isaac couldn't read.

The Home Guard hunkered in groups or sat on the curb. Wives brought cups of tea. Saturday dinner-time emptied the square, barring Corporal Price. Eyes fixed on Cefn Nant-y-Bwlch, he ate a cheese and beetroot sandwich. Joe Miskin had jog-trotted up the Nant gully, short cutting every loop in the winding, droughted stream. Finally, steadily, he criss-crossed on high rock ledged to the summit. Scuttling along on all fours like a sheep, he cleared the skyline. Joe scanned the rolling tops. Heat haze confounded distances, the green-blue of molinia grass blurred against a great shimmering weight of horizon.

'Parachutists my arse,' said Joe. 'Sweat for fuck all.'

Shotgun slanted over his left arm, he walked to a low outcrop of lichened boulders snouting through stunted heather. Here, squatting in comfort, he gazed across a flat, ragged acre of peat. Skylarks and pipits skulking in songless July, silence filled itself with insect humming. A split second too late, Joe squashed a horsefly on his wrist.

Scarcely hoping to flush snipe, he moved rightwards along the tussocked shoreline of sun-baked peat. Then he saw it, silvery, snagged in a channel on the far side. Joe kneeled, whispering a catch-phrase, 'Aye-aye, up in the morning's the game.'

Silence. Stillness.

He raced full-gallop across the spongy peat, bundled up the

46

small parachute and its flare canister, and went squirming through the long grass on his belly, just a couple of yards, turned, skewing on his elbows, and again he surveyed the mountain top.

Nothing, only thin, feline mewing from a buzzard soaring beyond eyesight. Joe skirted right around the naked peat. He found two more parachutes in the boggy watershed of Nant-y-Bwlch. Down in the gully, he cut off the canisters, heeled them under soft, dry shale, and stepped off ten paces to his marker, a dead rowan. Grunting for breath, he then crouched through a culvert beneath the colliery screens, climbed the wall of his backyard, and he hid the parachutes behind some corrugated sheets in his father's coal shed.

Mr Everett frowned at his meatless dinner. His wife fretted, 'We can't even manage corned beef these days. It's awful.'

Mr Everett gawped very briefly, forked a potato and rolled it in the weak gravy, saying, 'Trust in the Lord.'

'Will they catch them Germans?' asked Isaac.

'You being bad with your back, under the doctor all the time,' said Mrs Everett to her husband.

Chewing remorselessly, Mr Everett stiffened sideways, squeezed pain in his eyes, quick flicks of his head confirming he was a sick man.

'Will they, Mam?' repeated Isaac.

'We couldn't be any worse off than we are,' she said.

'Mam?'

'We'll have to wait and see, Isaac.' She stroked his hair. 'Finish your dinner, there's a lovely boy.'

Mr Everett carried a crust of gravied bread to the window. Biting and chewing, he nasally hummed, *Washed in the blood of the Lamb.*

Billy Eddy Crump swung himself delicately out to School Street corner, a Woodbine dripping ash on his white silk cravat. Billy's insignia, the Woodbine and cravat. His second cousin, Charlie Daniels, said, '*Shwmae*, Billy. Germans landed up there on the top of Cefn, so they reckon.'

'Any signs?' enquired Billy.

'Not so far. Sooner them than me, without weapons to put up a fight.'

47

Billy hobbled heel-toe, heel-toe in his cracked glacé leather shoes, his puny shoulders shivering. 'Should be signs by now.'

They shared fragility, Charlie's the consequence of rheumatic fever as a collier-boy. Born hunch-backed, Billy carried desperation in his tiny bones.

'Everett's youngster saw them from the Frogs' Pond,' said Charlie.

'Have one of these,' offered Billy.

Charlie steadied his trembling head and hand to light a cigarette. 'Bit backward, that kid,' he confided.

'Say no more. Shame too, pity for him,' said Billy. 'Where's Joe Miskin? He can tramp these mountains in his sleep.'

They saw Joe crossing the square with his shotgun, and five hundred yards away on the parish track, Barney Bryant and Shink Lewis riding the big horses. Billy and Charlie remained on School Street corner, while Corporal Price went banging at doors, yelling for the Home Guard to come out.

'False alarm, Billy.'

'Seems like it, Charlie.'

Clamour rapidly waned on the square as Barney and the Sergeant dismounted. A parachute and canister were draped across the withers of the Sergeant's horse. Barney jounced a few times from the knees. Handing the Lee-Enfield to Sergeant Lewis, he said, 'Dismiss the men.' He turned to Corporal Price. 'You take care of the horses. Thank the hostler from me.'

'Right, sir. Sorry sir.' Indignation lifted falsetto in the Corporal's voice. 'That boy, he should get a tanning in my opinion!'

Lieutenant Barney Bryant thumbed disgust, slammed the door of his car and drove off.

Joe Miskin softened his threat with grinning. 'Shut it, Pricey man, don't be a mouthy old bastard all your life,' the butt of his 12 bore gently prodding the Corporal's ribs. 'Listen, Pricey, do us a favour. These saddles, take them back to the farm. Okay?'

Tugging resentfully, Corporal Price led the horses to the stables. The Home Guard crowded around Sergeant Lewis. Grimly amused, he showed them the silk parachute and its flare canister. Billy Eddy Crump and Charlie Daniels strolled up from School Street corner. Billy fingered the quality of the material. 'Shink, I wonder if there's any more of these on the mountain.'

48

'Very likely. They wouldn't drop just one.' The Sergeant was cynical. 'Mission failure, so they chucked out the evidence. Understood?'

Charlie murmured to Billy, 'I'd do the same if I was a Brylcream boy.'

Billy sank his chin behind the white pout of his cravat. 'Ways and means. It's human nature.'

'Praise the Lord,' announced Mr Everett from inside his living room window, adding. 'See who's at the door!'

Joe Miskin threw a wink at Mrs Everett. 'Here's a tanner for the boy. 'Nother thing, tell your man to come to our house later on. There's a rabbit waiting for him. I downed a couple in the woods last night.'

She cupped the sixpence in her palm. 'Yes . . . yes! Thanks, Joe, thanks ever so much.'

Mr Everett jabbered, 'God bless you, God bless, God bless.'

'Aye, right. See you then,' said Joe.

The warm summer day cooled to evening. While the Home Guard were drilling on the football field, Sergeant Lewis's parachute was stolen from their HQ room in the Miners' Institute. Joe Miskin sold his three parachutes in the village pub. As the landlady pointed out to her barmaid, 'For knickers and petticoats. Best silk! Think of the saving on clothing coupons.' The barmaid (Sergeant Shink Lewis's daughter, grass widowed at twenty-three, her husband in khaki) bargained herself for a few square yards. And on Sunday morning before chapel, Mr Everett stood in the middle of the square, bible under his arm, watching a party of searchers, men and youths roving across the summit of Cefn Nant-y-Bwlch. Out of evil, he thought, out of evil cometh good. Halleluiah.

A Hero of 1938

The pony raised his head from the trough on the double parting, mild eyes gleaming like spoons in the soft flare from Bryn's cap lamp. Bryn fingered the gristle of the pony's ear. 'First shift of the week, Joey.'

Lowering his bucket-ugly head into the trough, Joey's sensitive snorts larrupped the chaff.

Bryn hunkered, resting with some collier-boys, Percy Naylor timing five minutes of his cased Ingersoll watch, then they went on together, another hundred yards before turning left into Percy's heading. Heavy-boned, lumpy-shouldered from grafting, holding under the shank in low seams, Percy was a Forest of Dean man married to a Welsh woman built like a cask. They had no children. They weren't chapel-goers. They made no enemies. Mrs Naylor kept chickens. Most evenings Percy walked two ageing Airedales across to the Miners' Institute and once around the football field.

Percy hacked and shovelled coal back to the top of the road, where Bryn filled the trams—three by eleven o'clock.

'Grub up. Dab my number on the bugger,' Percy said.

Bryn chalked 773/3 on both sides of the tram.

Percy ate cheese sandwiches with a flagon of cold, milkless tea, reflective, dreaming about coal, timber, 3 yards of rails, sleepers and road nails.

'When d'you reckon they'll knock through to the water, Percy?'

'No tellin' on that.' Percy rubbed his baldness. 'Once't thee heers um shout, put thee fuck'n clo's on.'

'Won't take us a few minutes, we'll be out on the double parting,' Bryn said.

'Up the Four Deep an' all! Gerrout on the main!' Percy gargled the last of his tea before streaming into the dust between his boots. 'This body of water drownded the oul Gelli.'

'Miles from here, the Gelli level, over the other side of the mountain. 'Nigh on ten years back, same water fer Chrissake.'

'I was only a kid in school,' said Bryn.

Percy wagged a long, dark grained hand, dismissive.

At twenty-past eleven the haulier came, a squat man riding crouched on the hitching plate behind Joey. They tumbled the empty while he turned the pony to shackle onto their full tram.

Bryn pretended not to see Percy palming the haulier two florins. Percy Naylor had a good name for paying trumps. Hardest collier in the Four Deep. Best trumper.

Leading out the pony, the haulier bawled, 'Fifteen minutes! Bollock it in!'

Pulling out slips of soft coal from the top of the road and shovelling fast, they filled the tram. Bad policy, keeping a haulier waiting. When he came with their fifth tram, Percy said, 'This un'll do us till ha'-past one.'

Bryn stroked Joey's nose.

The haulier crowed mocking delight. 'Gwyn Dando's bored fifteen feet into the coal! Sheer slavery!'

'No option else,' said Percy. 'Dai Hughes the ouverman down there?'

'Earlier he was.'

Joey steamed sweat, nuzzling through greaseproof wrapping for Bryn's leftover possey sandwich. 'How's your sweet tooth, Joey?' he whispered.

Morosely calm, Percy vowed, 'I'd plant a medal of paper an' shit on Dai's chest.'

Whooping like a primitive warrior, the haulier clouted a glancing first punch across Joey's rump, 'Gerrout of the way, Bryn-boy!'

Joey pulled, the haulier leapt on the hitching plate, and the tram rolled out of the heading.

Bryn said, 'He's a mad waster. There's no need at all for him to hit the horse.'

As they pushed the empty forward, Percy explained, 'S'only fuck'n chops wi' him. Lissen, strip the clod off up'n the left side. Mind to pack the gob wall tight.'

He grinned at Percy. 'We scrumped all the easy coal for our last dram.'

Percy grunted indifference.

'Fifteen foot by hand with an auger takes some doing. He's a strong bloke, Gwyn Dando.'

Another grunt from Percy.

'Will they keep the water down with that new pump on the double parting?'

'Better do. Us'll be on the parish till they's open us across't frum this district.'

Percy climbed into the face, stooped over his bent knees,

51

arms hooped out wide, breaths hissing from him as he lowered himself at full stretch to hack under the seam. Using a heavier mandrel, Bryn started peeling off nine inches of hard, shiny slag layered above the 4'6" of clean bottom coal. Conversation ceased between them. Bryn worked conscientiously, packing the muck a yard from the coal, walling a compact pillar up to the roof. Every Friday outside the colliery office, Percy handed him ten bob trumps on top of his wages. Good collier, good trumper, although Percy refused to join the Miner's Federation. Bryn was eighteen, six feet tall, lithe, fast moving. He didn't care about the Fed, either. Working in the Four Deep meant sticking up for yourself. Only trams and yardage counted. Make sure every man-jack took the message, otherwise some lackey official would send you afternoons or night shift, or some dog rough crib where poor sods were struggling on the min. Decent blokes maybe, but hopeless colliers. Bryn regarded himself as privileged. In three years he'd be driving his own stall. Straightaway then, cash down for a brand new Rudge 500 ccs motorbike. Do sixty over the mountain roads, easy. Brecon inside the hour. Easy.

Far off down the coal face, he heard dull whumps of a sledgehammer in Tommy Griff's heading. Old Tommy or his step-son Gwyn Dando fixing up a post. They filled thirty trams a week, six less than journeyed down to the weigh-bridge under Percy's number.

The shout came before 1 o'clock, a collier waving his lamp at the mouth of the heading. 'Watah! Watah! Everybody out!'

Percy rolled over and swung to his feet like a bear. 'Ne'mind them tools! Leave um!' He scrambled past the tram, his false teeth clicking. 'Get thee fuck'n clo's on!' trotting jerkily, snatching up his flagon, tommy box, waistcoat and jacket, turning to Bryn, blurting outrage, 'C'mon, c'mon fer Chrissake! Shift thee fuck'n self!'

They jogged out of the heading. Scores of bobbing cap-lamps were trailing up the double parting. Gwyn Dando came alongside, shoulder-arming his stepfather, helping him, old Tommy Griff refusing to panic, pausing to hawk a dollop of coal-dust-stained phlegm from his throat. 'Supposed to break through on top of my road,' he protested to Percy. 'Came down from the rib instead, see, just a trickle at first.' Tommy spat again. 'No shape on those surveyors in the office. My boy boring test holes on top of our road—since when, Gwyn?'

'Fortnight ago, Dad.'

'Blame tha' Dai Hughes the overman,' said Percy.

Tommy's righteousness panted husky tenor. 'I was yards an' yards off point! There's no bloody sense!'

'They'm na' worth fuck-all,' snarled Percy.

'About eight yards up the rib from my test hole,' said Gwyn.

'Wrong point altogether!' cried Tommy Griff.

Dai Hughes and two firemen were tallying colliers, hauliers, day labourers and boys on the double parting. Dai had quiffed, grey-streaked eyebrows, his nose a thick meaty blob above the red glistening, black-rimmed lips of a tobacco chewer. While shouting orders he remained bent forward, hands clutching his thighs above his kneecaps.

'Keep moving! No messing about down here! Everybody up the Four Deep!' Cordially aside, he greeted Tommy Griff and Percy.

Tommy said, 'Well, there it is. My boy couldn't give you any more warning. All the men out?'

'Of course they are, Tommy.' Dai laughed, slewing his bent shoulders to and fro. 'Ianto Bevan left his coat hanging on a gob wall, two quid notes from the Outing Club stuck in the top pocket.'

Percy Naylor clumped away. 'See to that' fuck'n pump, Dai.'

The overman straightened himself. 'In due course, Percy. Besides it's *my* responsibility as you know full well.'

Percy muttered, 'Worst luck, be fuck't.'

Dai aimed a forefinger. 'None of your interfering, ah, if you don't mind?'

'Let's make our way out,' said Tommy Griff.

Dai nodded, 'Aye, once I've started the pump I'll be right behind you. See you in the cabin, Tommy.'

Bryn counted thirteen ponies nose to tail, chains clicking, leathers squeaking as they plodded up the Four Deep.

'Joey on in front?' he asked the haulier.

'Nah! Daft bugger bolted before I could shackle up in Gomer Preece's stall!'

'Where is he now then?'

'Down there! Dai Hughes said to leave him be.'

Bryn elbowed the haulier's throat, pushing hard, banging him against the side. 'You rotten bastard!'

He sprinted back to the double parting. 'Dai, I'm going to fetch Joey. He's in the dark.'

'You'll do no such thing.' Dai thumbed sharply. 'Look, see how fast it's making. There's no chance, Bryn, no chance.'

Water swilled gently like thin ebony cream around the sleepers at the bottom of the double parting.

'Don't fret, Dai, I can swim,' Bryn said.

'Stop this boy!' shouted the overman.

Bryn evaded the fireman. From standing shin deep in water he flung his jacket and boots at them. 'Take care of these!'

The firemen raved. 'He's off his bloody tump!'

'For fuck's sake, Bryn . . .'

'Bryn, you come back here!'

Dai Hughes carefully paced on sleepers to a concreted sump-hole beside the tram-track. He squatted, watching the water rising, covering a bright steel, perforated canister bolted to the end of the pipe line connected to the new pump. Scurrying back to dry ground, the overman yelled, 'Start the pump!'

Bryn ploughed on, legs dancing to balance fierce sculling with his hands.

Third stall to the right off the straight.

Black water shone level, coiling a yard below the roof. Turning into Gomer Preece's stall, he firmed his cap-lamp.

Must keep my light. Must, or else . . . forget that.

'Joey! Hee-yaar Joey!'

Airway. Right hand off Gomer's. Where to? Old workings?

He turned, floundering from thigh deep to waist deep in water. His feet searched the bottom.

No sleepers. No rails. Old workings.

'Joey! Jow-heee!'

Not many posts about either. Left to go ruin.

Bryn came to a heavy wooden frame supporting hanging sheets of brattice-cloth.

Airway for sure.

White fungus lay plastered on the timber. The brattice-cloth wafted, bulging towards him. He pushed through, wavelets slapping at his chest. For the first time fear crawled inside Bryn, conquered by rage.

Bloody hell! I'll swim back out on breast stroke!

'Joey! Joey!'

By the Jesus Christ, this is it.

Ten yards in from the brattice-cloth, he found Joey lodged sideways, up-sloped like a dog on its haunches in the narrow airway. Rapid whinnying shuddered from the pony.

'Aah, there you are. Silly old bugger you. Come on, we gotto get out from here.'

Reaching for the bridle, a slide of pulpy underwater shale impacted, sucked around his legs to his knees. Lifting and thrusting, stamping down the shale, he climbed towards Joey's head. He grabbed the bridle.

'Easy now, easy does it. You and me, Joey, we'll be out on the Four Deep in no time. Ready? Here we go.'

Bryn heaved on the bridle straps.

Jesus Christ, he can't turn. His arse-end's trapped.

The pony squealed, his front legs thrashing. Shale rained down off the sides of the airway.

'Woa-ow, mun, woa! Steady on, Joey, steady now, steady.'

Bryn searched the roof for breaks. It looked safe. Solid rock. He groped along the pony's flank.

His hind legs are buckled under him.

'Joey, there's only one way. Brute bloody force. Like this.'

With his socked feet braced against the right hand side, he dragged Joey's head across and down. Slurried water gritted in Bryn's mouth. Suddenly Joey's squirming front legs collapsed. A great boil of water surfaced. Submerged to his nostrils, the pony lunged. Still gripping the bridle, Bryn went tumbling backwards as Joey's hind legs levered upright, free.

'Right, we've done it! Steady then, we're alright!'

They surged through the brattice-cloth. Bryn heard his cap-lamp snicking against the roof. He trod water, allowing the pony to turn out of the airway into Gomer Preece's stall.

'You first, Joey. Lead the way.'

He stabbed short-arm breast strokes, slowing behind, Joey crashing forward in low, hesitant leaps, his neck strained out, ears flattening at each plunge of his head. They turned left again. Now they were out on the straight heading. Bryn estimated the distance. Fifteen yards between stalls made forty-five yards. Add another twenty yards out to the new pump. Black water glimmered like silk, eighteen inches from the roof.

No lights. No bloody lights. They should have waited for us on the double parting.

His trousers swagged heavily, sapping power from his legs. Bryn clung to a roadside post. Unbuckling his belt, he kicked off his trousers. He shed his waistcoat.

'Keep going, Joey! We'll make it!'

But he crawled to the new, low-droning pump on his knees, gulping for air in spasm, all his mind centred on survival.

We'll make it. Keep going.

Joey shook himself, lumbering towards the lights: Dai Hughes and the two firemen. They came running back down the Four Deep. As they lifted Bryn to his feet, the pump's electric motor cracked, whined and cut out. Crotch deep in water, the officials gawped at each other.

'Let's move, let's move,' urged the overman. 'Seems like it's finished for good down here.'

Mucus dribbled from Bryn's nose and mouth. 'Is Joey al'right?'

'Safe, boy, safe!' Dai Hughes swayed nearer. 'Hey, there's more guts in you than any man I've ever seen. Where's his boots? Put his boots on. Can you walk, Bryn?'

'I'll manage.'

All in a tight bunch, they waded out to dry ground.

'He's knackered,' the fireman said, yanking at Bryn's boots, lacing them, the other firemen thrusting Bryn's arms into the sleeves of his dry jacket.

Bryn sagged, 'Aye, just about.'

'Why? 'Cause you saved that bloody horse!' insisted the overman. 'One each side, men, that's the idea, help him up the Deep. Right, we're away.'

Two hundred yards up the Four Deep incline, Joey stood waiting in darkness. They shackled him to an empty tram on the level main, a quaggy mile of tee-head tram-track out to the mouth of the drift. Sitting in the tram with the officials, Bryn slumped over his chilled legs. He fell into a stupor.

Most of the colliers had gone home. He saw Joey being led to the stables. When Percy Naylor barged into the cabin, Bryn lay huddled, drowsing in the purring heat of a blazing fire, a surface worker's overcoat wrapped around his legs. Percy stroked sky, hurried cuffs on his shoulder.

'I give thee best, son. My missis, she'll fetch some clo's frum thee oul lady. You'm a good un, butty.'

Bryn slept.

Comrades in Arms

Soup kitchen summer of 1926 and they were penniless.

'Redvers, let's join up.'

'Might as well, aye.'

'No option, man.'

'I'm with you, Lemmy. Nothing much at all for us in Blaen-du these days.'

'Mouth, that's all I'm getting indoors,' vowed Lemuel Nelson. Redvers Gillard mangled venom under his breath. 'Me too, from the old lady.' A haggard fury, Mrs Gillard ruled her brood like miscreant destiny.

So Lemmy and Redvers left Blaen-du. They signed on for 12 when the South Wales Borderers were sworn to maintain British Empire red anywhere on the map. Tall, wilful Lemmy, strong boned, half-brother to six sisters, his peacock eyes glittery inside Asiatic cheekbones. His wide mouth and prognathous jaw spelt wilderness. Redvers came midway in the Gillard family of four boys and three girls, the lads bare-fist bundlers in the dirt lanes of Blaen-du. Louche conscience fitted Redvers' eighteen years. He belonged nowhere in his heart.

While they soldiered for the Crown, bullying, rifle-butting, subduing factions, zealots, dervishes, in India and Egypt, few people in Blaen-du thought about Lemmy and Redvers. They were part of an exodus forced by Depression. A generation of teenage girls became skivvies for the cloning middle class of Britannia while gaunt men begged, went on tramp.

In June 1938 Privates Nelson and Gillard returned. They were well-fed, hefty, marching from the station in tweed jackets and grey trousers, their suitcases filled with exotic mementos: underwear-wrapped vases and ornaments, silk shawls, bangles, brooches, rings, engraved wallets, tiepins, cufflinks, knives, cigarette cases, keepsake rupees, piastres, milliemes and sepia snapshots in fret-work frames. Two disciplined Regulars, survivors of malaria, prickly heat, brothels, and bonded by weal and circumstance, their parents long since buried, never to be remembered with daffodils on Palm Sundays.

Lemmy and Redvers lodged with married sisters. Lemmy's half-sister had four children and a TB husband dying in

Talgarth Sanitorium. Redvers' brother-in-law was a Methodist lay-preacher and colliery night watchman. He despised the ex-soldier.

Anyhow, they were back home, shoulder to shoulder in Bothi Number 2 pit cage, armed with new round-nosed shovels bought in the colliery stores. Night shift labourers, lowest of the low, but Lemmy and Redvers were neither meek nor arrogant, only tactfully obedient. Lemmy hacked and shovelled much for an old repairer who had worked in Blaen-du pits from the age of thirteen. Redvers took orders from roadmen and repairers on the main line, simply shovelling debris into trams.

Summer flowed into autumn. Now and then moodiness, bleak fatalism beyond reach afflicted Lemmy and Redvers. Their village contemporaries were married, settled, insular, dominated by filling out coal, Friday wage packets, rearing children, darts, skittles, football results, pigeons, loyalty to the Lodge. Beer and sex redeemed the ex-soldiers. Triumphantly boozed, they felt immune to consequences. With supreme confidence they swapped feckless women, widowed, abandoned or outcast by fate, who gossiped their unsung joys and miseries in the Dunraven Arms snug.

While Adolf Hitler preached his master race lunacy, guaranteeing Old Testament disaster, Lemmy and Redvers planned shifts off for day-long boozing sessions. Between afternoon stop tap and evening open tap, they cronied with flagons of beer in a ferny dingle above Blaen-du's grace-and-favour bungalow, where lived the colliery cashier, a greyly-terse Company autocrat married to a roly-poly breathless, vindictive woman. After these non-stop bouts, Lemmy and Redvers eked out, lingering over scrumpy and dog-ends, because naturally they were on the bare Min. Absurd, the notion of overtime or allowances for night shift labourers.

Winter crimped and rusted the bracken hills around Blaen-du.

Redvers moved in with 'Becca Rees. Slapdash 'Becca, almost old enough to be his mother. Once her GWR ganger son arrived without warning, motor-biking from Cardiff Docks. Sprawled asleep on a wooden settle after Sunday dinner, the ganger's boots and fists left Redvers KO'd with black eyes and bleeding lips. Monday night, comedy on the main line from pit bottom, Redvers bragging the ups and downs of his affair with 'Becca Rees, how they went at it first time behind the colliery stables, thunder and lightning, slashing rain, their feet squelching in slurried clay. Redvers riding his luck while it lasted. He stayed with 'Becca after her son returned to Cardiff Docks.

Lemmy Nelson courted Cranwen Parsons, a bosomy widow with two children in Elementary School. Three nights a week at 9 o'clock, en route to collect his lamp at Bothi Number 2 pithead, he visited Cranwen. Their pleasure on the hearth mat, shared without promises. They slept together on weekends. Saturdays he bought chunks of beef and slabs of fruit cake. Saturday nights with Cranwen, they clapped encores in the pub concert room. All in all, Lemmy's good life. For the time being he felt nicely tamed, at ease. Her kiddies loved Uncle Lemmy, banker for pennies, singer of slow songs: 'Show me the way to go home', 'Marta', and 'Standing by a church-yard in the city', his finale with dramatic mime.

Came the benign summer of 1939, when Cranwen changed her mind due to blonde Jilly Hughes, the pub landlord's daughter. Fifteen year old Jilly, working in Blaen-du Co-op. Well-developed for her age as they say, Jilly wore stillness, a kind of magical, passive surety. She wasn't very pretty either. Her heavily boned nose a solemn prow, her mouth pouty, fretless, her eyes greenly glacial. Innocent Jilly until the day she served Redvers with ten Woodbines. He dated her for Sunday evening, Jilly stiffly murmuring, 'So long as we're not seen.'

The Co-op manager came full flurry in his long white dust coat, sleeves precisely quarter rolled.

'These ten Woods on 'Becca's book till Friday, y'know, Mrs 'Becca Rees, where I'm in lodgings.'

Dolorously Shylock, the Co-op servant warned, 'Mind you pay now, Mr Gillard.'

'On my life,' promised Redvers, 'same as every Friday since I left the mob.'

Jilly stared at Redvers. She winked rapid flicks of her left eye. He thought, 'Close ranks, hold steady.'

From sanguine habit he included Lemmy, two ex-South Wales Borderers strolling a Sabbath evening, approaching the dingle slantwise across Pen Arglwydd mountainside, no sign of the girl and Redvers prepared to leave things be. Just another lost cause. But Jilly appeared in the cool gloaming, blameless as Eve by England's Glory matchlight, curious to see what they had, touch, feel for her own sake without cheat or swoony palaver.

'You'll be al'right,' urged Redvers. He placed his hand over her mouth when she whimpered. 'Ssh, girl, please don't make any fuss.'

In his turn Lemmy sympathised, 'Don't worry, love, let yourself go, c'mon, enjoy you'self.'

Explained Redvers, 'Me and Lemmy, we've had our fair share of such experience.'

'Well-aye, abroad see, girl,' confirmed Lemmy.

From Redvers, 'Best keep quiet about it though, if I was you. We don't want no trouble in Blaen-du. Same goes for you and all.'

'God alive, I'm not that *twp*.' Jilly tidied her blouse and skirt. 'S'long then. I'm only allowed out till ha'-past ten. Honest, the rows I get off my mother. God alive, I'm not a kid any more.'

'You're the goods,' said Lemmy.

'Lovely, real lovely,' said Redvers.

From the brow of the dingle they watched her disappearing, reappearing ghostly as she walked past the lighted bungalow.

'What d'you think, Lemmy?'

'Nice bit of kief, not bad at all considering.'

'She wanted it.'

Redvers said, 'Obvious to me when I first set eyes on her.'

Lemmy flogged the back of Redvers' neck with a bracken stem. 'You bloody Welsh whoormaster.'

Redvers tried a leg scissors on him. He failed. They rolled apart.

'Tomorrow,' said Lemmy, 'we'll have a day in the Labour Club. Finish the night in the Dunraven.'

'Righto, you're on, mate.'

The cashier's wife told the pub landlord's wife. Proven facts witnessed from her windows. Half-eight when Nelson and Gillard came across Pen Arglwydd. Quarter to nine when Jilly climbed up to the hollow. Gone ten it was, Jilly again passing the bungalow, hurrying home, and exactly twenty-five to eleven before those two rodneys, rotten they were, laughing and effing and blinding, proper no-good pair ever since they stepped out of khaki.

Lemuel Nelson and Redvers Gillard were jaunty, cheerfully drunk when Barry Hughes ordered them out of the public bar.

'Hey, lay off, man, don't bugger us about,' said Lemmy. 'Me and him, we're good customers.'

Barry was suffering, his wife upstairs, slapping and cuffing their daughter, spoilt for life, ruined by these two bastards. Hysteria tenored his bawl, 'Off these premises! You're banned *sine die!*'

Silence then, Redvers sniggering, deliberately clacking coins on the counter, 'Hughesie-boy, pull us a coupla pints.'

'Up the Borderers,' intoned Lemmy like a dreaming regimental chaplain.

Mrs Hughes screeched, her head jigging through the hatch behind the bar. 'Chuck 'em out! They forced our daughter up there on Pen Arglwydd, took advantage of her they have! Fetch the policeman!'

Babble spurted around the room.

As if polarised, Lemmy and Redvers sidled towards each other. They were grinning like masks, feral.

'Assaulted Jilly!' cried Barry Hughes.

Grizzled old men dry-spat aside, all grunts and rankle.

'Bloody pigs, nothing but pigs. You fellas, put the boot in.'

Hard young colliers flexed their shoulders, relishing the prospect of being a big fish in the small bowl of Blaen-du.

'Gerrout from yere else your feet won't touch the ground!'

'Too bloody jonnack!'

'Say the word, Barry, they'll be dumped on their arses!'

'Wasters!'

'Out and out wasters!'

Suddenly Redvers softly howled, winding up then down to crouched shuddering as if small explosions were firing inside his body. Lemmy howled, desolate, rabid, nerve tingling. Clutching each other's wrists, they howled, twitched, hopped in slow, baroque two step.

The tough young men edged forward, fists ready, muttering, 'Jesus Christ.'

'Watch out for Gillard.'

'No bloody sense in this.'

Then erupted bedlam, frenzied legerdemain, Lemmy and Redvers pelting glasses, bottles, ashtrays, bar stools, chairs, tables. Lemmy clouted Jilly's father, felled him with a flagon. Redvers slammed the hatch across, bruising Mrs Hughes's forehead. Lemmy skimmed framed photographs of football teams, boxers, NUM committees, brewery adverts. Redvers hurled double-handed, rows of bottled beers and silver-plated tankards and fistfuls of money from the till. Customers crowded out through the doorway. The door banged shut. The bar was empty.

Lemmy and Redvers shuffled around, switching from clockwise to anti-clockwise, yipping, heads rolling, stripping off their clothes. Naked except for shoes and socks, Redvers leapt up on a table. He spun, head askew, moaning, waxing to hissing ecstasy. Naked Lemmy padded to and fro, spasms jerking his mouth. He smashed a brewery mirror with his fist. He urinated zig-zags on the cold stove. Redvers found twin-tone moaning, circling on the table. Lemmy crashed a bar stool, snapped off two legs and kettledrummed a tin tray balanced across his thighs, his eyes slitted, throatily keening, wordless, a primal dirge. Redvers spun circles, drool glistening his chin.

The hatch crept open. Baffled villagers spied on Lemmy and Redvers. A toothless Great War veteran whispered judgment: 'They've gone doo-lally.'

Crouching below counter level, the giant Blaen-du constable sneaked into the bar from a trap-door to the cellar. His black truncheon skittled Redvers' legs. He struck again as Redvers toppled, a fast stroke on the temple, the sustained round-arm swing hitting the back of Lemmy's head.

Mrs Hughes scrammed their faces while they were unconscious.

Ends compound beginnings, trivialising logic plighted to the enigma of existence. In Redvers Gillard's case, direct from Swansea jail into the army. Made up to full corporal during the retreat to Dunkirk, he vanished before reaching the beach. Presumed killed in action. Forgotten Redvers Gillard—true to all mankind under the ablation of Time.

Lemuel Nelson returned to Blaen-du from Swansea Jail. Cranwen Parsons was living comfortably with a middle-aged, loveless, genteel colliery fireman earning good wages. Spurned by his harrassed, ashamed half-sister, Lemmy slept that night in the Institute boiler-house. Two days later, destitute in Brecon town, he rejoined the army. At the battle of Alamein, Staff Sergeant Nelson won the Military Medal for outstanding courage in the face of the enemy. Honourably discharged in 1946, he brought home his Polish refugee wife, this heavyweight woman a counterpart of himself. But they were stoically humdrum, vitality on the wane.

Lemmy found his civilian niche, pit-head labourer loading trams with posts, sleepers, rings, rolls of brattice, drums of oil. After nationalisation Ela worked in the colliery canteen.

In 1967 Blaen-du pits were closed, since when the village began dying, broached on three sides by Forestry Commissions conifers. Dark sitkas shroud the bulldozed collieries. Vandals set fire to the deserted Workmen's Institute. The football field disappeared under builders' rubble, household debris and a scrap merchant's barbed wire fenced yard. A smart red brick Forestry Commission office occupies Blaen-du's bowling green.

On pleasant afternoons senior citizens Lemmy and Ela dawdle the red ash lane alongside the one-time cashier's bungalow. Friendly Jilly Watts calls from her front garden, 'Hullo Lemuel, hullo Ela. Nice day again.' Jilly is married to Brendon Watts (BSc Forestry, Bangor), a purposeful man from Essex who wears a green slouch hat. He's Head Forester with the Commission. They have no children. Late now too. Of course too late.

Reaping the Sown

She was in the sidecar, her green eyes dreaming when he steadied into the right hand bend. Dilwyn Tamplin applied a correct safe squeeze on each brake. The combination slid outwards, hissing over the diesel stick. He snatched more throttle to clear the bend. Gravel spurted as they tumbled. The sidecar wheel spun free. Myfanwy was unconscious, hooped forward. Dilwyn hawked vomit, his collarbone cracked, scraped skin burning from his knee, down his calf to his ankle.

"Vanw!' he cried.

Spilled petrol stank the warm air.

Dilwyn opened the sidecar bonnet. He hooked his left arm around her. Myfanwy's head lolled, smears of blood faintly reddening her blonde hair at the angle of her jaw. A fine pencil-tip of blood welled from the lobe of her ear. He saw the ear-ring wedged between her shoe and the twisted rubber mat in the side-car. The road stretched empty, glistening under the hot sun. Black road, bare green hills, blue sky, dark blood seeping into his boot. He hauled her to the verge, his right arm dangling useless.

She regained consciousness irritably, mildly cursing. Dilwyn flagged down a BRS lorry. He held her on his lap, the driver promising, 'Few minutes we'll be there.'

'That patch of oil threw us across the road,' Dilwyn said.

'Your bike's al'right, mate. Straighten the kickstart and the footrest.'

Dilwyn felt bad. 'My wife's three months pregnant.'

The driver whewed alarm. 'By the Christ, real sodden luck.'

At the Infirmary, he watched a porter wheeling Myfanwy into Casualty. Then another porter dumped him in a wheelchair, insisting, 'Just relax, I'm taking you for X Rays.'

Two hours later he went to see Myfanwy. She ignored his arm in a sling, humbling him with, 'You look a proper wally in those trousers.

He said, 'These? Given to me. My jeans are in shreds. This shoulder's the worst. I've fractured the bone.' He touched her stomach. 'I've been worried about you.'

A Sister came in, radiant false teeth smiling distrust. 'You will have to leave now, Mr Tamplin.'

64

'She's three months pregnant,' he said.

'Confirmed, yes. Thank you. Out now, please, Mr Tamplin. Wait in Reception.' The door whumped shut behind him.

He heard Myfanwy saying, 'Don't boss me around!'

Cripples, pensioners and schoolkids were queueing at the counter in Reception. Ambulances and cars shuttled to and from the ramp outside the entrance. Through the window, he saw conifer trees marching slantwise above rows of terraced houses. Dilwyn let his chin sag. Dozing, he looked like a wounded partisan, bandaged right leg outstretched, crash helmet cupped on his left knee, his right arm slung up to his chest.

'Dilwyn Tamplin?'

'Here,' he said.

Elbows propped on the counter, the receptionist wagged her index finger at him. 'You can go home now. The ambulance will take you. We'll be sending Mrs Tamplin home tomorrow. It's our procedure after concussion, twenty-four hours observation.'

'I'd like a few words with my wife,' he said politely.

'Not allowed. She's under sedation.'

In the ambulance he sat opposite another pregnancy. Huge woman, grained pores in the creases of her neck.

'Bless 'ew, s'no worse'n 'avin a tooth out. Look'a me! My fifth!'

'You're strong,' approved Dilwyn.

'Course I'm strong. Gotto be these days.'

The ambulance stopped.

'Cheerio, missis,' he said.

She nudged him as he climbed down. 'Take care, love.'

His father-in-law met him at the back door. 'Where's my daughter?'

''Vanw's al right. We took a bit of a spill.'

Retreating to the house, Cledwyn James bawled, 'What a mad-brain swine you are!'

'Shut it,' warned Dilwyn. 'I'm working fifty hours a week in the furniture factory to keep this roof over our heads, so belt up. Anyhow, it's none of your business.'

'We'll soon see about that!'

'One of your fits coming on?' asked Dilwyn.

'Ignorant bastard!' Cledwyn backed off until only his head,

eyebrows jerking, hung around the parlour door. Soon afterwards he began playing the piano and singing 'Macushla'. Cled James the pub tenor, pathetic old widows and cronies buying his beer every weekend. Dilwyn despised him. The coward punched his wife. Mrs James with her long brown hair, still handsome but helpless. She'd given up the ghost. Taken too many beatings. Cled the one-time epileptic flopping about on building sites, sang 'Macushla' in the parlour. When Myfanwy arrived home the following day, he was singing 'What a Wonderful World'.

Myfanwy said, 'They tested my brain same as before I left school. Remember I fainted in morning assembly? The anaemia? I'm okay now though.'

'Always have been, *cariad*,' praised her father.

Mrs James hugged her, weeping relief. Over her mother's shoulder, Myfanwy dibbled out her fluted tongue at Dilwyn.

Like father like daughter? Never, no chance, he vowed to himself, ''Vanw's normal. She's tough.'

Five Sundays after the accident he repaired the kick-start and the footrest. The big Honda roared, drumming the corrugated sheets of the garage. Dilwyn marvelled, relishing the power of his machine.

Sun-bathing on the lawn, Myfanwy said, 'I'm bored. Let's take some sandwiches and a flask.'

'Right then, I'll sort out the clobber, you make the sandwiches.'

Thirty miles into hilly country, Dilwyn found a narrow valley where small waterfalls poured over ledges shaggy with hanging moss. They stripped off. Myfanwy unleashed quiet shrieks, standing shin deep, swirling water with her fingertips. Experimentally brave, he dived into the pool, swiftly in and out, a breath-stopper.

She giggled, prancing around him. 'You've shrivelled!'

'It'd shrink the tool on Cetewayo,' he said.

She rubbed his penis over her rounded tummy. 'Mine whenever I want, my dicky-di-doh.'

Suddenly, water dripping from his hair wrinkled her nipples, spinning him along thoughtless wonder.

She said, 'Lay down, I'll be jockey.'

'I'm shivering, girl!'

A dipper careered upstream, shot whistling aside, skimming over the waterfall.

Myfanwy's fingernails, scrabbled welts on his chest. She slid to and fro, her blonde hair shawled over her face.

"Vanw . . .'

'Hush for God's sake.'

She moaned to sighs. Presently she arched herself, backwards, resting on his thighs, her toes flexing in his armpits.

He sighted her along his torso. 'You al'right?'

'Yeah, only you go too quick.'

'Not that time,' he said.

Two jet planes crossed high under the blue, vapour trails fading. Gulls were wailing lower down the valley where the brook ballooned out, filling a marshy lake. Dilwyn saw a tiny oatmeal-coloured frip land on her flank. It vanished. Scrapey snores rattled in Myfanwy's throat. Wriggling himself free, he tidied her sprawl. He covered her with towels and their leather jackets. Dilwyn felt light-bodied, calm. Slowly windmilling his right arm, he acknowledged a painless grinding, the shoulder scrawny, bonier since the tumble-up.

He was toasting cheese sandwiches when Myfanwy awoke.

'Smells nice,' she said, standing over him. 'Hey, my ankles swelling?'

'Only your belly, 'Vanw.'

'My boobs are bigger.'

'Might be a girl.'

'Fair enough.'

'Dil, d'you think I'm over-sexed?'

He nodded wisely.

Settling on his lap, she ate a toasted sandwich. Still chewing, Myfanwy grabbed his testicles. 'I know I am,' adjusting herself, bearing down, panting. 'Wait for me, Dil, wait, wait!'

'I can't!'

She gagged, whimpering, 'O Jesus . . .'

He felt defeated. 'I'm not made of stone.'

'Stay still then. Leave it in.'

Burnt sticks fell apart, his Boy Scout fire dying away, greying to ash under the dropping sun. Shade sliced up the narrow valley. Greens darkened. The pool's foam swilkered like advertised suds.

Myfanwy argued, 'It's always the same.'

'We'll *learn*, 'Vanw.'

She turned, facing him, hunched, her legs spread. 'Selfish, that's your trouble.'

'Be fair, girl.'

'I feel sicky.'

'We'd better get dressed,' he said.

They stopped at a pub on the way home. Myfanwy shone female health. Dilwyn said nothing. She made him feel guilty. After two glasses of lager she excused herself. He sat there, smoking, resting easy now, chogged by sequences of lifetime. Sunday night, first week in August. Autumn around the corner. Winter. Christmas. New Year. Confinement on 9th January, give or take a couple of days either way. 'Vanw, she'll take it in her stride. We'll find a place of our own. Away from her father and mother. Next June I'll be twenty-one. Old enough for a mortgage. Flog the Honda combination. Buy a scooter for riding to the furniture factory. Aye, little pop-pop two stroke shitting the plug. Spare plugs in the toolbox.

Empty. He bought another pint. Ten minutes since she went to the bog. Dilwyn strolled out to the paved yard behind the pub. 25 watt bulb above the GENTS. Summer stars speckling matt sky—the twitching universe meant nothing to him. He passed a stack of beer crates. "Vanw!' he called. 'Myfanwy!'

A gaunt tottery woman appeared from the LADIES.

He said, 'Anybody in there? Blonde girl wearing a black leather coat?'

'Nobody in there at all.'

'Thanks,' he said.

'Don't mench.'

Back in the bar, he took thin sips of beer. He looked in the lounge, he checked the car park.

"Vanw!' he shouted.

Customers were leaving the pub. Stop tap. The lights flicked off-on, off-on.

Dilwyn returned to the yard. He heard her laughing, lurching out from behind the beer crates, the man's hand reaching for her arm, a burly chap with thick greying hair, urging, 'This way, kid, through the side entrance. My car's parked in the lane.'

Dilwyn ran. 'What's the matter?'

Quite gently the man levered his forearm against Dilwyn's

chest. Carefully jovial, he said, 'No problem, mate. Drop too much. I'm in charge of the young lady.'

'Lay off, she's my wife!'

'Aah, righto. Um, excuse me. Goodnight both.'

She sang gaily, 'Goodnight George!'

'Who's he?' Dilwyn said.

'Foreman in dispatch where I used to work. Nice fella really.'

'What were you doing behind these crates?'

Myfanwy skewed her head, mouth twisted, sucking air for a husky scream. She gnawed at the flesh of his hand, hysterical. Safeguarding himself, Dilwyn cuffed her, *whap*, a reasonable back-hander.

'Go on, do it again! See if I care!'

'Whoor,' he whispered, pitying her as if she was suffering more than she could bear.

She dry-spat aside. 'Huh, as if you didn't know. Piss off, leave me alone.'

'I'm taking you home.'

'Get lost.'

He dealt her another cuff, lighter, slack wristed. 'That's my baby you're carrying. Now shut up. No more chops. No more, right? C'mon, jump in the sidecar.'

'I could spew over you,' she said, following him through the pub and out to the car park.

Less than a mile from home he turned off the road, steered the bike in bottom gear along the trodden pathway of an abandoned railway embankment, then downhill on tarmac to a lychgate in the cemetery wall. Engine off. Lights off. He lifted the sidecar bonnet.

'Out.'

'Whaffor?'

'Something you ought to see, 'Vanw.'

'Morbid,' she sneered.

He pulled her from the seat.

They had to climb over the lychgate. Faint pallor chilled the cemetery. A slender cusp of moon held the dark round whole. He led her to his father's gravestone. 'Look at this.'

Howard Tamplin. Born 2nd December 1950. Died 14th June 1978.

Dilwyn douted his cigarette lighter. 'My old man,' he said. 'The drunken waster, he left my mother soon after they were married. Come here, I'll show you her grave.'

He counted nine cypresses beside the driveway, turned left, counting gravestones. 'She's here. This is where they buried my mother.'

Flame gushed from his lighter.

Sadie Tamplin, beloved wife of Howard. Born 10th April 1953. Died 2nd November 1965. N.P. CALLED HOME TO THE LORD.

'Nineteen sixty-five, the year I was born,' he said. 'They both died young, him from boozing, her from cancer 'cause he broke her heart.' Quaking from loss, Dilwyn yet felt heroic, pleading, 'Believe me, 'Vanw, if you think I'll allow you to go whooring around, you're mistaken. Definitely.'

She complained miserably, 'I can't help my feelings.'

'Listen! Feelings? Control your bloody feelings! Human beings are not like animals in the jungle!'

'Have some patience, Dil.'

'No! It's being responsible! If ever I catch you chasing after any bloke, I'll lay you out cold. As a matter of fact I swear to it.' He placed his palm on the gravestone.

'Take more than threats from you,' pouted Myfanwy. 'I'm not afraid of anybody, never have been.'

'*Spoilt*, that's why, spoilt by Cled James!'

She snuggled up to him. 'What d'you expect? I mean, be honest. Put yourself in my place. All I want is, well, y'know, satisfaction. Only natural for a girl my age.' Snuffling at the side of his neck, tearful, she whined softly, nibbling love bites up to his mouth.

Dilwyn forgot the hasty, furious coupling alongside his mother's grave. They were chugging across the embankment. He had no memories of Sadie Tamplin. One image remained of his father, a crump shouldered man, very thin, narrow eyed in a soundless grin. Howard Tamplin, cider drinker. There's no reason why I should suffer, decided Dilwyn. None at all. After the baby comes next January we'll have a normal married life, just 'Vanw and me. Both of us need patience. Her nerves are raggedy, must be, otherwise she wouldn't cry so much.

'Dil!' she screeched, 'I'm peeing myself!'

He de-clutched, braked to a standstill, the Honda idling perfectly. Like brochure tourists they were limned against stars on the railway embankment, Myfanwy scuttling through the headlight. He thought, one thing for sure, she doesn't pretend. 'Vanw's genuine.

They lost the baby on Guy Fawkes' night. Dilwyn crouched, gaping under the arms of the midwife. He glimpsed their flaccid, mis-shapen son. Myfanwy wailed. The midwife pushed him out of the room, advising righteously, 'Start another one straight away. Nobody's fault. Accident of nature.'

Myfanwy named the mite Cledwyn after her father. Every evening for three days she vented hysteria, Dilwyn appealing, 'Shh, 'Vanw, please. You didn't even set eyes on him.'

Myfanwy howled, Mrs James nursing her, rocking her like an infant in the bed, while Cledwyn watched television down in the kitchen, hands pressed to his ears, the volume blaring full pitch. He dipped into the rent money to buy her chocolates.

Dilwyn went to the Citizen's Advice Bureau. He wanted a flat or a maisonette. The pensioned-off civil servant telephoned the Housing Department. Tishing regret he pushed his notepad across the table: *D. Tamplin, 613 on the Council Housing List.* 'Only a medical certificate would give you priority, in particular tuberculosis or blindness, but you're both young and healthy.'

Dilwyn nodded, 'Of course we are.'

At the end of January his 'cold on the chest' became bronchitis. He collapsed at his bench in the furniture factory.

Cledwyn James protested, 'We can't look after you. You should be in hospital.'

'Ye-es,' chimed Myfanwy and her mother.

Dilwyn endured, anguished on a camp-bed in the box-room, Myfanwy bringing his meals or shouting from the bottom of the stairs, 'Take those antibiotics!'

One fevered night he saw a pale slender woman at the foot of the bed. She beckoned, smiling forlornly.

'Mam, I'm awful bad,' he said.

Fixed in his gaze, he saw her diminishing, beckoning.

'Mam . . .'

Fever blanked out everything.

But he recovered. Four weeks later he overhauled the Honda. He de-coked, adjusting the tappets, changed the oil, charged the battery and sold her for £450. Cash in his wallet. She was worth £550.

Dilwyn made another deal in the factory. One of his workmates had a two-berth caravan, guaranteed immaculate condition. Dilwyn paid £400 for the caravan, £50 remaining at

£10 a week. He worked overtime, evenings and weekends. The caravan was paid for before his twenty-first birthday.

'We're away,' he said to Myfanwy. 'Start packing. There's a Transit coming to collect our stuff. It'll take us about three trips. Kitchen cabinets, chairs, pots and pans and so on. Your mother can keep the bed.'

'Sandy Bay or Happy Valley would be nicer, Dil, instead of that mucky field.'

'Talk sense, girl! Where'll I find a job down at Porthcawl? We'll be independent in our caravan. What's more I've bought a scooter, 125 ccs, one owner, needs some bits and bobs for the road but she'll be ready in a fortnight.'

The field belonged to Tommy Thompson, a butcher who also owned a vintage Daimler and traded in ponies, everything except the Daimler inherited from his father. Twice married, twice divorced. Tommy was forty-seven, a compulsive Don Juan with a witless old mother reduced to futile bewailing in a nursing home. Instead of visiting, Tommy sent her flowers and food parcels.

'Look, I don't fancy one of those chemical lavs,' said Myfanwy.

'They're safe by law,' stressed Dilwyn. 'Hygienic.'

Myfanwy was again three months pregnant when she took a part-time job in the delicatessen counter in Tommy Thompson's shop.

'Ever so interesting, Dil. Besides, there's no telling what I might be able to fiddle.'

He warned her, 'Don't try any such thing.'

Summer rolled on. A bonanza summer for Tommy Thompson. Myfanwy had a key to his flat above the shop. Blooming into her fifth month, she travelled to Shrewsbury Flower Show with her paramour. They stayed all night long, worldly Tommy teaching his good-time bird a few soft porn ploys in their hotel bedroom.

Dilwyn worked his Saturday shift. Late afternoon and he opened a window in the caravan to clear the smell of kippers. Water, he thought, ready for 'Vanw when she comes back from visiting her relatives—she actually had two aunts, uncles and cousins in Wellington. Crossing the field with a five gallon polythene bottle, he saw the Daimler nosing down a clay lane behind Thompson's stables. The ponies were far off, blobs of black, brown and white on a hillside. Dilwyn filled the bottle, turned off the tap wall, then he heard her voice floating calmly, 'Bye-bye, see you later. Nine-ish.' The big car droned away beyond earshot. Dilwyn squatted behind a water butt. He saw Myfanwy rounding the stables. She entered the caravan. Reggae music thudded from the radio.

I swore on oath too, he thought, blinking tears, grimly shouldering the heavy bottle across the field.

White as milk in front of his shaving mirror, she sprayed anti-perspirant over her body. 'Hiya, Dil. Marvellous flower show. Pity you had to work this weekend. Kippers for dinner? For God's sake whyn't you buy a decent meal in a cafe?'

He switched off the radio. 'If you wasn't carrying that baby I'd smash your face. You're nothing but a slag.'

'O ta very much. Mind telling me what you're on about?'

'Thompson the butcher, you slag.' Fist raised, he shouted, 'I've had enough!'

She giggled, arms and thighs akimbo, hula-ing.

Dilwyn swung the bottle, sloshing pints of cold water over her. Myfanwy screamed, vast gaspy screams spluttering to laughter. Bent double, legs spraddled, breasts hanging, she laughed, racked herself, then dropped to the floor, convulsions jolting her limbs. Slow tics pulled down the left side of her mouth.

''Vanw, 'Vanw, take it easy! You'll do yourself an injury! Think of the baby!'

Dilwyn laid her on the bed. Stillness came.

He closed the window, drew the curtains. 'Sleeping?' he whispered.

'I wish I was dead.'

'Don't say that.'

'They ought to shoot me.'

'Shh now, girl.'

'What time is it?'

'Ten past six.'

Her eyes stared, pale green, sightless as glass beads. 'Something's wrong with me, Dil.'

'Nerves. You'll be al'right, 'Vanw.'

'Something, whatever it is.'

'Go to sleep.'

'I wish I was dead,' she repeated serenely, her soft lips palping as she breathed into sleep.

Dilwyn's turmoil verged on ecstasy. Should he fetch the doctor? Or 'Vanw's mother? Wanting to escape, he dreaded loneliness. Memories of boyhood piled back at him. Drafted from one foster mother to the next for years, living in hostels, strict rules, locked doors. Worse perhaps than being tied to 'Vanw. Proof, he thought. First get the proof. More proof. How though?

Dilwyn set the alarm clock for 8 p.m. He pushed his scooter out onto the road, he tickled the carb. She fired on the second kick. Great little machine. Slicking up through the gears, he purred along at 25 mph into town. Sausage, egg and chips followed by a Guinness raised his self-esteem. He rode the lane to Thompson's stables, parked the scooter in one of the stalls, and climbed up into the loft.

The alarm rang promptly. Unaware of himself, he counted off seconds, muddled the count before reaching two minutes, waited, his mouth drying as she appeared in the caravan doorway, tousled, naked under a counterpane, scratching herself, querulous: 'Dilwyn!'

He wanted to hold her tight forever.

8.35 p.m. Myfanwy stepped down fully dressed, a sunflower-yellow maternity-smock tented over her fawn trouser suit. She caught a town bus.

Dilwyn skidded and bounced the scooter across Thompson's field, raced after the bus, held back fifty yards from each stop, and finally he watched her entering the door alongside Thompson's butcher shop.

At last, he thought, this is it. She's rotten.

He lingered on the pavement, worrying. Find another site for the caravan. Find another girl. Start fresh with another girl. Why not? Some girl, decent, straight, honest.

Muttering for courage he pressed the doorbell. Distracting himself, he hurried to the scooter, freed the prop-stand, re-set it at a sharper angle, and turned to face Tommy Thompson.

'Hullo-hullo. Hull-low, Dilwyn. Anthing I can do for you, lad?'

'Seen 'Vanw, Mr Thompson?'

'Hasn't she come home from Shrewsbury?'

Dilwyn yelled, ''Vanw!'

The butcher gritted authority. 'Be quiet. I'll have the police on you for creating a disturbance.'

Like a sacrificial wench, Myfanwy swayed out from the flat above the stairway. She posed, hands on her hips, her face a smiling mask of innocence.

'Come inside. Have a drink,' offered the butcher.

'You're welcome to that slut. She's stone crazy,' Dilwyn said. 'Good luck all the same. Myself, I know when I'm beaten. So-long, 'Vanw! Don't forget that baby's half-mine!'

Drought ended the summer. Chill nights shed heavy falls of dew. Dilwyn Tamplin lived alone, his caravan propped on bricks below the rusted gantry of a derelict steelworks.

October roared into November. Hailstones, gales, floods, frothy brown torrents churning down mountainside gutters. A sense of vacancy comforted Dilwyn, emptiness within himself lulled his fears of loneliness. Other people wrought confusion. Neglecting regular meals, he bought a carton of crisps. Often at night he ate crisps in darkness, huddled under blankets on his bed. And he communicated with his possessions. Simple statements, references, as if they were mortal. His witnesses. One night the roof blew off his sentinel box lavatory, so he flattened a secret place among great arcing tangles of brambles. Whole days passed in fretless oblivion.

Scrupulously acquitting himself of a bad time-keeper, the furniture factory manager made Dilwyn redundant. Dilwyn celebrated. He painted the scooter white, all-over white from headlamp to rear light, then he bedded the wheels in six inches of concrete. He felt virtuous. Safe inside the caravan, he watched children who came to play on his super machine.

The year fell into winter. Short grey days, north-east winds soughing through fissures in the mossed walls of the old steelworks. Dilwyn snuggled for warmth. He roamed hedgerows, he gathered kindling in the cemetery. His parents, Howard and Sadie Tamplin, they belonged elsewhere. They weren't in his mind. The sexton gave him a bag of coke, but pneumonia laid him low. Two days of silence were broken by a scavenging scrap merchant who peeked through the caravan window. He saw Dilwyn curled on his bed.

Myfanwy visited once while he was in hospital. He felt drained beyond hope. She flounced gaiety. O yes, their baby girl was ever so pretty. Name of Amanda. Did he like Amanda? Amanda Tamplin. And no, she didn't have a regular bloke so why bother about a divorce. Unless he wanted a divorce? And O yes, as for Tommy Thompson, at least she finagled something out of him. Radio cassette recorder. Her father was recording his favourites, 'Macushla', 'Goldmine in the Sky', 'Calon Lân'. While she blurted these bits of news, Dilwyn lowered himself, drifted away, found peace.

'Hey, Dil, wake up!'

Coma protected him, his skinny hands resting on his chest as if in effigy, his unknown mother, Sadie Tamplin, absent, the unction of Intensive Care his end.

Natives

Levi Jones swung away from the bar, a mindful slew on his stiff right leg. He returned to the table. 'Referring back,' he said, holding out the tray, Martin and Felix taking their drinks, 'it's my opinion we have been discussing the modern disease. There's too much yap about balance of payments, productivity, mobility of labour, royal commissions examining this and that, it's a disease of the soul.'

Felix said, 'I've had politics up to here.'

Martin said, 'The rot set in when they closed Fawr and Fach collieries.'

'We're left-overs from the regime of King Steam Coal,' said Levi. 'But listen, the best human stuff comes from roots, from inheritance. Put bluntly, a man can't, he *can't* renege on the way he's made, his birth-given packet. Where people don't belong, that's where they go doo-lally. Therefore, boys, culture, civilisation, these are ours until Upper Coed-coch becomes totally extinct.'

Martin spoke to Felix. 'He's still librarian in the Institute, knocked down about eight years ago.'

'Time has reduced this village,' conceded Levi. 'The old cramp of time, in conjunction with economics, the great falsehood, the gospel of men who worship privilege. We are governed by twenty-four carat fakes disguised as civil servants.'

'Rubbish,' said Felix.

'Profitability,' argued Levi, 'comes before people. Whole families have left, drifted away from Wales forever. Every time a house falls empty, the council start demolishing.'

Martin said, 'Train service killed by Beecham, bus service every three hours, our doctor emigrated to Australia, my grandchildren travelling eight miles each way to school . . .'

'We are living in a ghetto,' pronounced Levi.

'One pub, used to be five,' said Felix.

Levi grimaced, firming his false teeth. 'Boys, truth is we're on shifting ground, similar in miniature to the biblical Jews except there's no redeemer, no flesh and blood God's-son guaranteed to unite the masses. We need a big name figure, a kind of phoenix ready to spurt up from our ashes.'

'Politically powerless we are,' said Martin.

'Cultured decadents,' explained Levi, 'short of a prescribed saviour.'

'We're well past middle age, we're on compo and hardship allowance,' Martin said.

Felix added, 'Knocking back scrumpy five nights a week, beer on Fridays and Saturdays.'

Levi raised his glass. 'We are the immovables, financially deprived, dauntless, capable of social sweetness, murder by degrees, slow suicide, humility, even visions. Anything at all on the graph of human behaviour.'

'Bar earning a living wage,' grumbled Felix.

Martin said, 'Being disabled, the three of us on the books in Hobart House, London S.W.1.'

'Sacrificial victims to the old black diamonds!' crowed Levi. His friends nodded.

'King Coal, the rotten waster,' said Felix.

Levi rolled three cigarettes and fingered a single match from the ticket pocket of his jacket. 'Aye, Upper Coed-coch has been renamed Isolated Area by our county planning experts. Consequently the Forestry Commission has taken over. Surface pillage succeeding subterranean rape.'

'Mountains around here,' said Martin, 'they'll be like the Western Front when these trees are cropped.'

Felix went into a controlled bout of coughing. Then he apologised, 'My sixty per cent dust from hard headings down the old Fawr Nine Deep.'

'Me, I'm seventy-five per cent pneumo,' said Martin.

'We shan't witness the millennium,' promised Levi.

Martin looked angry. 'Nor roam the mountains on Sunday mornings. You need a can-lamp and knee-pads to crawl under the bloody Christmas trees.'

Levi dipped a finger in his beer, swam it humming around the rim of his glass. 'Economics, the name of the game.'

Martin coughed, paused, steadied his breath to mutter, 'The daft sods.'

Felix suggested, 'Let's shift from this corner. Sing-song out there in the back room.'

Levi launched into chicane prophecy. 'By the year two thousand and eight, every infant will slot-fit instant social service before he's off the breast, his poop conduited to manufacture manna, his water piped to produce energy from the earth's magma, and at the end, at the very end his processed corpse will magic blossoms from gravel!'

'Talking like the bible again,' said Felix.

Levi lowered his head, presenting tanned baldness, whispy eyebrows and the blue scarred ridge of his heavily boned nose. 'My prerogative, Felix. I'm one of your stall and heading examiners who filled out coal on a diet of Spinoza, Immanuel Kant, Nietzsche, Voltaire and Charles Darwin, with Walter Whitman and Johnny Keats for afters.'

'Some fuckin' collier,' vowed Felix. 'C'mon, let's see what's doing in the back room.'

'He dropped in clover after his kneecap was busted,' said Martin.

Levi sniggered like a schoolboy. 'Twenty years in the Institute library, franking the date on Westerns, Thrillers, Ethel M. Dell, Conan Doyle, Rafael Sabatini, Jack London. H. G. bloody Wells and Charles bloody Dickens. Righto then, we'll join the entertainers. As from tonight universal literacy is a curse, a cancer spread by Fleet Street.'

They left the public bar.

There were less than a dozen customers in the large back room. Friendly atmosphere, greetings, the compo and hardship allowance trio settling at a table near the serving hatch.

Martin whewed disgust. 'This used to be the Singing Room, crammed to the doors every Saturday night.'

'Blind Goronwy tonking the keys as usual,' said Felix.

Goronwy played 'When the blue of the night meets the gold of the day', with Mrs Charles crying tremolo fragments from her small mouth.

'Fierce, she's a fierce old bird,' Levi said, remembering Crad Charles, killed, crushed between fallen rock and timber, circa 1959.

'Her and Mrs Sen-Sen James, they've messed up a few marriages,' said Felix.

Levi tutted amiably. 'Mrs Sen-Sen looks fey, a lady born and bred not to lift a finger to help herself. Black hair from a bottle greying out from the crown of her head. She's well matched with Mrs Charles, they're close, spur and stirrup since burying their husbands.'

'Fawr pit widows both,' said Martin.

'Queens of deception,' said Levi.

Felix humphed a noise in his nose. 'Young Billy Tash could do with a bath.'

'Scrap merchants make their contribution to the community,' contended Levi.

'Glenda put the snaffle on him good and proper,' said Felix.

Levi supplied details. 'She's the brainiest woman in Riverside Terrace. Glenda used to fill in Billy's income tax forms. One morning last summer he found her what they call *en déshabillé*. Billy, well, his eyeballs came out like gobstoppers. And then, boys, human nature. Short jump and long hop to their wedding before the end of the taxable year. Glenda's old enough to be his mam.'

'True,' agreed Felix. 'She's older than Jesse Mackie'—Jesse was sitting with Billy and Glenda.

'Orphan,' said Martin. 'Underpaid labourer for Billy Tash since Billy went into collecting scrap.'

Levi hoiked himself upright in his chair. 'Jesse never knew adolescence as a time of pomp and arrogance!'

Martin and Felix pretended they were deaf.

Goronwy played 'Sixteen tons and what do you get, another day older and deeper in debt', encouraging Hopkin Morgan, who cuffed Whitey, his pale grey alsatian. The animal dropped couchant like a dog-faced sphinx. Hopkin sang 'Sixteen tons', stanced in profile, occasionally shovelling imaginary coal.

Felix called, ''Core, encore!'

Martin was clapping. 'Not bad for a man who never filled a dram of coal in his life. Oil-boy and haulier since he was a kid.'

'Pack of dogs these days and he's on his third wife,' said Felix.

'Sound Coed-coch stock,' maintained Levi. 'Head of a druid, muscles bulging below his armpits, chest like a barrel, hands like grappling hooks, and now he's redundant, probably never work again.'

Felix scowled. 'Bloody Hopkin, he'll thrive where the crows' beaks'll drop off.'

Pamela Pryor (BA Aber.) came to the serving hatch. She bought a bottle of stout for Blind Goronwy.

Levi said, 'Evening, Miss Pryor. Visiting Mam and Dad for the weekend? Nice too. If there's one thing I admire it's families sticking together.' He saluted Idris and Maisie Pryor. '*Shwmae*, Id! Hullo there, Maisie!'

The Pryors smiled, tucked at their table by the piano.

'I'm driving back tomorrow night,' said Pamela.

'Smart little car, Fiat,' said Martin.

Felix winked at the scholarship girl. 'Ask Goronwy to give us a number.'

She swayed a little, reflective, left knee dipped, her tummy sagging. Pamela taught English and History in a Surrey boarding school.

Felix recommended, '"Your tiny hand is frozen", that's Goronwy's favourite.'

Pamela sighed, 'Goronwy is a lovely old character. Excuse me.' She walked to the piano, poured Goronwy's stout, then went to every table, collecting glasses on her tray, and returned to the hatch, innocently imperious, beckoning to Levi, Martin and Felix.

Martin said, 'Straight beer, please. Ta very much.'

Goronwy lifted his thin, true eunuch's tenor through 'Your tiny hand is frozen'. He followed this with a chorus piece from *The Desert Song*.

Martin said, 'Something I'd like to do, buy drinks all round. I couldn't afford to, not even when I was on yardage down in the Red Vein district.'

'Why bother! You can't make any such comparison,' declared Felix.

'Neither is she at all like her father,' Martin said. 'Idris Pryor's a tight man, always was.'

'Similar to her mother,' said Felix.

Levi prolonged his, 'Aaaah.'

They stared at one another, brief, silent, glinty scrutinies.

From Felix, 'Aye.'

Martin, 'Well, yes, same as Maisie when Maisie was Maisie Beynon.'

Levi, 'Undoubtedly.'

Goronwy spun around on his stool, plump face utterly impassive, his blindness shielded, sunk in rolls of pinkness. He spun again, pudgy fingers roving, tinkling 'Rock around the clock'.

Stan Rees and a blonde woman began dancing.

'Go-go, that's your real go-go,' said Felix.

Rising from the table, Levi waggled his stiff leg. 'Old style, boys, handed down from Africa! Or from Iolo Morgannwg. Come on, have a go-go!'

They trucked awkwardly to the beat. After the dance Maisie Pryor hurried across the room, a trim woman in her late forties. She said to Levi, '"Lonesome road" please, for our Pam.'

He made the announcement. 'Ladies and gentlemen, by special request, "Lonesome road" from Martin Davies and Felix Mathias! Give them a big hand!'

Male voice party baritones, they achieved Gregorian purity, singing directly at each other, solo phrases given each to each, balanced, the harmony of instinct.

Mrs Charles and Mrs Sen-Sen James sent high piercing squeals above the applause. Pamela Pryor brought three whiskies from the hatch.

'Years ago,' Felix said, 'we were near enough perfect. Right, Martin?'

Levi intervened. 'Water under the bridge. On short notice you boys did very well.' He caught Pamela's wrist. 'See, Miss Pryor, time goes by. My butties are out of practice. Can we expect a number from you?'

'Contralto,' said Martin. 'I remember this girl in a school concert. St. David's day it was.'

'Oh, I wish I was back in Upper Coed-coch,' confessed Pamela. 'It's depressing where I am now.'

'Aye, the *hiraeth*,' said Levi.

'*Hiraeth* won't pay the rent nor keep grub in the pantry,' said Felix.

Martin carefully pummelled himself on the chest. 'Hold on! Got it! "Greensleeves"! I'll pass the word to Blind Goronwy.'

'Oh, no no no!' Suddenly Pamela's pleading collapsed to enigmatic composure.

Martin waited for her at the piano. He held up his arms. 'Quiet one and all, right 'round the room, please! Thank you!'

Pamela sang 'Greensleeves'.

Said Felix, 'Her head's screwed on the right way, different from Maisie at her age.'

'Meticulous, despite the fact she's half pissed,' said Levi.

Martin downed his whisky. 'Strong contralto. Sheer quality.'

Felix chuckled delight. 'Us three, we're all of us half pissed.'

'As we are *entitled*,' stressed Levi.

Their heads close together over the piano, Goronwy and Pamela quietly chanted snatches of 'Myfanwy'. Stan Rees had his hand up the blonde's skirt. Billy Tash gave some money to

Jesse Mackie. Glenda seemed lost in daze. The widows Charles and James were watching Stan and the blonde. Hopkin Morgan eyed the clarity of his seventh pint, and lowered it to a third. The dog Whitey remained motionless. Idris and Maisie Pryor smiled at themselves.

Goronwy lifted the lid of the piano. 'It's in there somewhere! My Joseph Parry music sheet!'

'"Myfanwy!" "Myfanwy!"' yelped the widows.

'In public,' muttered Felix. 'Stan Rees better leave that girl alone or she'll spew her guts up.'

Levi raised his fist, 'Boys, rapture is on the loose tonight! Blind Goronwy and Miss Pamela Pryor are about to unlock the paradox of paradise! Entrancement of the species! A throbbing pore in the flesh of flux! Aye-aye! Reality grinds behind the gargoyles of our humdrum dementia!'

'Husht, man,' said Martin.

Miss Pryor and Goronwy sang 'Myfanwy'.

'Up, Wales,' growled Felix.

'You bloody cynic,' Levi said.

Martin added a rider, 'Fel, don't be a shit all your life.'

Goronwy banged hard for silence. He turned his blind head. 'We call upon Levi Jones for a monologue!'

Stan Rees came over with his blonde. 'How about it, Levi? Give us "The green eye of the little yellow god".'

'"If!"' shouted Hopkin Morgan.

Felix and Martin said, '"If."'

'"Dangerous Dan Magrew!"' screeched the widows.

The blonde's mouth hung open. 'Well a' bugger me, let 'im make up 'is own mind for Chrissake.'

Stan threatened her. 'Watch you language in company.' He grinned at Levi. 'Take no notice, she's been on the vodka and lime since seven o'clock. Tell you what, Levi, recite "The green eye of the little yellow god" and I'll buy you fellas a pint.'

'"If,"' insisted Martin.

Stan's grin fell sour. 'No offence.' He steered the blonde away. 'C'mon.'

Levi limped across to the piano. 'Ladies and gentlemen, some Rudyard Kipling. These days old Rudyard is seen as a bit of a flag-waver before Britannia turned constipated on her throne. I must ask you to make allowances. My memory is not so good. I might get stuck here and there.'

83

'He's on form,' said Martin.

Goronwy spun delicate chords, pacing Levi's elocution. Afterwards he recited 'The green eye of the little yellow god'.

Martin approved. 'Nice performance, Levi. You held 'em in the palm of your hand.'

Stan Rees refilled their glasses.

Eira came into the back room, Hopkin Morgan's third childless wife. The alsatian trailed her to the piano. Blind Goronwy celebrated Eira's faded reputation, playing 'Blue moon'.

'Torchy girl from days gone by,' said Levi. '*Duw*, the scorched christs and creamy lucifers of long ago, long before they even sank the bloody pits.'

'*Blue moon, I see you standing alone*,' sang Eira, her arms reaching out to Hopkin, his stubbed teeth grinning pride.

Sprawled at her feet, Whitey dreamed along his nose, sensitive quivers plucking the roots of his cocked ears. Jesse Mackie went to sit beside Mrs Sen-Sen James. His forearms were on the table, each side of his pint. As Eira pecked a thank-you kiss on Goronwy's forehead, Mrs Sen-Sen went to the hatch for a Scotch egg and a packet of crisps for Jesse.

'Eira's over the hill like the rest of us,' said Martin.

'Liberation, emancipation,' cried Levi faintly. 'Freedom from anxiety and remorse. We're aeons from the jet set, light years from lotus delirium!'

'Quiet, man, talk sense,' warned Felix.

Martin said, 'Hops affecting his culture. He'll sleep downstairs tonight, on the couch.'

'Stiff as a poker come morning,' said Felix.

Levi pulled up the leg of his trousers. Howling softly, he slapped his misshapen knee. 'Boys, Charity blows her snot in the bandage off the eyes of Justice!'

Goronwy played '*Calon Lân*'. Everybody sang. Billy Tash followed Glenda to the serving hatch. She bought a bottle of brandy. 'Goodnight, Mr Jones,' she said. 'Goodnight, Mr Davies. Goodnight, Mr Mathias.'

'Party?' enquired Martin.

Billy slid the bottle into his pocket. Glenda's features squeezed disdain. 'It's for Billy, he's not feeling well.'

'Touch of the 'flu I think,' Billy said.

Glenda edged herself in front of him. 'And besides, he works outdoors in all weathers.'

Levi held up his open hands. 'Say no more! The man who succeeds in business starting from scratch, he deserves nothing but the best!'

'So long as you don't cast sneers, Levi Jones.' Glenda's eyes were green, glacial. She caught Billy's arm, leading him from the room.

Mrs Sen-Sen bought three hot pasties wrapped in doilies. Jesse Mackie sat between the widows. They mothered him competitively. Eira bought a pasty for Whitey. Maisie Pryor and her daughter visited the Ladies. Stan Rees and his blonde were kissing. She drooped limply in her chair, eyes wide open, empty as sky.

'Whoor-master, he's nothing but a whoor-master,' growled Felix.

'Ordinary greed,' muttered Levi.

Out in the public bar, the landlord rang his handbell.

'Can't be!' Martin said.

Felix drained his glass. 'Bloody-well is! Last orders. My turn.'

They rose together with fresh pints as Goronwy hammered the opening chord of the national anthem. But the widows and Jesse Mackie wound up the night, singing 'We'll keep a welcome in the hillsides'. Blind Goronwy was leaning on two pillars in the Gents.

Levi, Martin and Felix stood near the door. They shook hands with everybody. Outside the pub, moonglow chilling the forested hills, they huddled for a few minutes, talking, then strolled home, still arguing, comparing, marking boom-times, tumults, struggles, the rising and falling histories of Upper Coed-coch.

Left Behind

Cadwgan and Nita Pugh lived in Railway Terrace. He was shaped like a neutered oriental wrestler, stomachy, bow-legged, neckless, arms hooped like staves, his black hair healthily greasy under a pepper and salt dai-cap. Awkward enough when sober, Cadwgan now and again exploded bouts of fury, rampage fuelled by mixing whisky and beer in the Dunraven Arms. He had the non-stop courage of a Neanderthal saint. What's more, in marrying Nita he took on a flinty woman. Their corner house overlooked our village, seven short side streets pegged to left and right off a few hundred yards of main road. Glamorgan village of bittersweet memories, pensioners chuffing nostalgia, familiar tales, the long hot summers of '21 and '26, strike days of bazooka jazz bands, soup kitchens, pitch-and-toss, ratting terriers, tip scratching, whinberry picking, TB families, pot-bellied toddlers with the glazed eyes of malnutrition.

So there they were in Railway Terrace, childless, edging towards middle age, difficult as neighbours, a cranky couple best left alone. Maybe children would have brought routine shambles, forgiveable mess into their lives. Cadwgan cleared his stents of steam coal in Golau Teg pit; Nita scrubbed Siloh chapel, which also served as the Infants' School. Every Saturday evening they came down to the Dunraven Arms. Tall Nita stern as January, she drank in the snug. Cadwgan stayed in the bar. By stop tap the pub rang with slushy Ivor Novello ballads, *hiraeth* strained from Williams Pantycelyn hymns, and febrile songs from Hollywood. Fist fights flared in the public bar. Needle fights ended out on the pavement. But Cadwgan and Nita were left to scrap each other, theirs the privilege, insular, peculiar to themselves. Boozed or sober, Cadwgan had the beating of every man in Golau Teg pit. His fights with Nita were trimmed, strictly ethical. He pushed and scragged, even butted her, lightly side-flicking his bumpy forehead like a front row forward. Nita swung a bottle, scythe-wise, overarm, underarm. She was fearless, had to be, feeding and bedding with Cadwgan. He rarely put her down. He'd kick the bottle to smithereens, wipe her face with his sleeve, and he'd say, 'C'mon, Neet, let's make our way home. Wait, gel, steady now, steady. Lemme get a proper holt on you,' stooping under her height, half carrying her up the road to Railway Terrace.

They were primitive, a senseless pair, tactfully avoided even while pretending not to ignore them. Nita interfered, she quarrelled with harrassed mothers bringing tearful infants to Siloh. Cadwgan prided himself on mining expertise, sweaty techniques for manning a conveyor face. Coal-butties endured him, Cadwgan being inevitable, like bad weather. Golau Teg officials bluffed around him. Bandy Cadwgan slashed into his daily stent, incapable of dodging hard graft, the shiny steam coal his endless enemy.

Blacker than imaginable, it happened one July morning: Cadwgan Pugh smashed under a roof fall in Number 4 face. Smashed beyond humanity. We dug out his remains, crushed bones and flesh scraped into a blanket and sent up to top pit in a hay-sack.

It was early in the shift. Colliers were shovelling loose water-bombed coal prepared by the night shift. Our conveyor charge-hand came at twenty past seven, Idwal's rigmarole, everything normal. '*Shwmae*, boys,' from Idwal. 'Any problems? Righto, get stuck into it.'

Everything normal, 'bacco chewers taking their first plug of the day, every man-jack with ten bloody tons to throw on the belt.

Idwal scuttled down the face, shooting off his hippo mouth as expected of him. 'Ballock it on, lads! If they close the Golau Teg we'll be flogging our houses to the NCB. Next move they'll cart us *en bloc* to some long-life pit in the bastard Midlands.'

Cadwgan scratched his stomach. 'Coal Board,' he said, 'ask me they're a worse shower than private owners.' He propped his shovel against a Dowty post. 'Be back inna few minutes.'

I said, 'What's on, Dwgie?'

'Want me to drop it by yere!' and he crouched a low, neat vault over the conveyor belt.

This was early in the morning. We hadn't raised sweat.

Now, whether or not there's some everlasting Lord God, some high redemption for Cadwgan's death is of no consequence whatsoever, the death itself too cruel, alien to any justice since the unknown beginning, let alone the bled-white history of filling out coal. By the same mark, if there's some time out of mind Lord God, he undoubtedly said, *Let there be carbonised vegetable matter*—to prove how poxy Nature really is. Peace on earthers spout delusions, drool about rapport with the birds and the bees, but Nature herself has to be man-handled, forced, controlled, exploited, and coal-getting's the essence of it, less than a short spit away from deep sea trawling. Human nature takes some forcing too, else we'd still be scratching fleas off each other's backs.

Fourteen colliers in Number 4 face, plus a conscientious youngster on the conveyor tip-end. When Cadwgan leapt over the moving belt, he went under broken ground. Night shift men had crashed the roof to pack on (nearer the coal seam), following behind afternoon shift men who had jugged the conveyor forward, who in turn followed day shift colliers who worked off the coal stents. That's the sequence. It's logical, a production planner's psalm, a Coal Board beatitude. The broken roof slanted up to fifteen feet, Cadwgan Pugh probably not yet relieving himself, this massive slab of rock slamming down out of millions of lightless years, without warning, smashing him. Time. Old Cadwgan merely had enough time to be there, unbuckling his belt, and perish.

Shouts floated down to our tip-end youngster, telling him to switch the power off. The belt stopped running. Squeeze, this was a big squeeze. We listened to the roof pounding, coming closer, cracking like guerilla warfare. Stones fell, blue pennant whining and powdering. We were twelve cap-lamps bunched near the coal, protected souls, steel-flatted roof above our helmets. Guaranteed suicide the other side of the conveyor belt.

Idwal came trotting on all fours like a grounded ape. 'Where's Dwgie Pugh?'

'Back in there,' we said.

'He's copped it then! Sure to! Get on the phone! Under manager, am'blance man, I want 'em both in here!' Idwal bawled loudest, spreading phony authority. One of the older colliers recommended a Cadbury's chocolate medal the size of Idwal's head. The charge-hands in heavy industries having nothing to lose but commonplace lunacy. Idwal crept over the belt, inching his limbs like a fox in a kitchen.

'Daft bugger you,' said the old bloke. 'Use some brains while you still got the chance.'

Idwal came back under the steel flats. We waited, hunkered in safety for about an hour, the squeeze climbing, easing away, lifting harmlessly into higher ground. When we started digging for Cadwgan it was like attacking a landslide, working in to the central slab of rock, our old bloke muttering, 'That's where Dwgie is, he's under the lot,' cursing, 'Christ Almighty, by the Jesus Christ Almighty.'

Golau Teg emptied the day Cadwgan was killed. Every man walked out. Night after night in the pub, his life story went the rounds, villagers who'd grown up with him from childhood, witnesses to his earliest fist fights, who remembered his spells in Swansea Prison, and his unpredictable, sudden marriage to Nita. Slow-supping, crumped-up old men named his mother: Sarah Ann Pugh. His father remains a mystery. They rumoured Cadwgan's father, and that was all.

Cadwgan was significant, true, a minor marvel, extremely natural. You have to heed extremity. Nita Pugh never saw his shattered meat and jumbled bones. They sent her a screwed down coffin from the Miners' Hospital. During the funeral service in Railway Terrace corner house, the full team from Number 4 conveyor crammed shoulder to shoulder, ingrained pit grime oozing inside our shirts and underpants. Two decrepit Siloh deacons were badgered into paying their respects. Easier to bend with the wind than refuse. They were afraid of Nita. Guilt festers from cowardice, so they paid lip service to Cadwgan, bull-headed Dwgie the opposite pole to all their scoured dreams and pie-in-the-sky hopes. The Methodist minister came, snaking out soft handshakes, his smile a raft of unction wafting on professional friendliness. He riffled through his Authorised King James, nudging himself sideways to the head of the coffin, and he prompted the killed-collier's lament: 'Lead kindly light', Nita gripping herself upright, flat-backed as a slab sawn post, silent. We sang for Cadwgan.

'Thank you, thank you one and all,' the minister said. 'Now we are gathered here to bless our brother, Cadwgan Pugh, taken by the Lord in the very prime of his life. But, my friends, I would remind you, the Lord moves in mysterious ways his wonders to perform! Yes, oo-oh ye-es! As we are told in Ecclesiastes chapter nine, verses eleven and twelve'—chin uplifted, the minister sightlessly flickered his eyes at Nita's stained ceiling, expertly *hwyl*-ing the text he did not have to read: '*I returned and saw under the sun, that the race is not to the swift, nor the battle to the strong, neither yet bread to the wise, nor yet riches to the men of understanding, nor yet favour to the men of skill; but time and chance happeneth to them all. For man also knoweth not his time: as the fishes that are taken in an evil net, and as the birds that are caught in the snare; so are the sons of men snared in an evil time, when it falleth suddenly upon them.*'

'Amen, amen,' bleated the aged deacons.

Tenderly closing his bible, the minister held it praying in his hands. 'Truly, friends, here in the midst of sorrow we are faced with the infinite power of the Lord. His terrible power! Consider! Why, only last week Cadwgan walked the streets of our lovely old village. Splendid to behold he was! We would have laid a premium on his health and strength! But! Remember! A man knoweth not his time!'

'Amen,' quavered the deacons.

The minister bowed his head. 'The Lord giveth and the Lord taketh away.' Pause, catarrh fouling his throat. 'O heavenly Father, gather Cadwgan Pugh to Thy-ever-open, ever-charitable heart, for Thine own name's sake. Amen.'

From the deacons, 'Amen, amen.'

'Succour his bereaved wife Anita, together with these comrades who mourn his passing over to the other side, these loyal comrades who toiled with him in the very bowels of the earth.'

'Amen!' cried the eldest deacon—ex-Golau Teg overman, a genuine tyrannical waster during his reign underground.

'For it is not granted, Lord, that we learn thy wisdom from here to eternity,' conceded the minister.

Nita flung out the rods of her arms, blurting, 'Come to the finish now, please.'

He smiled his half-and-half smile. 'Patience, Mrs Pugh,' his head lowering: '*The Lord is my shepherd, I shall not want . . .*' our schooldays' chant picked up, aimed murmurously from the shabby parlour in Railway Terrace, tall Nita staring dry-eyed, bleak, standing in the doorway, thirteen stifled men turning out into the fresh air, relieved, grouped around, watching the bearers hump Cadwgan's coffin down the front steps to the hearse.

Nothing extraordinary, soft summer drizzle seeping from a milpuffy sheet of sky as we drove to the cemetery.

'Ashes to ashes and dust to dust,' promised the salaried Christian. He moved away for us to Indian file past the grave hole, glance down at Cadwgan's box—Cadwgan the men sent to oblivion in Number 4 conveyor face—the undertaker's quiffy head craning towards the sexton, both whispering, nodding, exchanging the old Gehenna chat, then we climbed back into the cars for home. First stop, the Dunraven Arms.

Ordinary July day, traditional burial, death itself the certain damn on every single life spurting intelligence, awareness, brightness, sensibility foreign to that loveless primeval slurry. But in the grieving all the rules are made for breaking. The way Nita grieved. Saturday evening as usual she stalked down to the pub, dignified, lean as a rail, trap-mouthed, the hardness of her worn too deep for betrayal. At eleven o'clock they were singing 'In the sweet by and by, we shall meet on that beautiful shore', men and women with their arms about each other, sometimes harmonising to tingle the nape hairs, more often discording to hurt the archangels, the landlord gone rather stony, his sociability fallen to dregs, holding his nose, flushing a lav with his right hand. Another Saturday night well spent, togetherness and booze, proper to Welsh mining villages, to metropolises, to clock-run multitudes everywhere.

Nita Pugh went off alone to Railway Terrace, swayed up the main road, raw-minded, bankrupt past all telling. Shortly after midnight, using her personal key, Nita locked herself in Siloh chapel. She set the place on fire. Panelled to the eaves with varnished pine, quality timber from the heyday of the Methodist Revival, the entire building erupted. Windows burst out. Slates exploded. There were less human remains in the ashes of Siloh chapel than we sent up in the cage from Number 4 conveyor face.

Grief, grief is a carnivore at the heart. Grief is the fate of anyone left behind.

Time Spent

Doctor Gammon dogs-eared the buff envelope. 'This report confirms the X-rays. Set your mind on it, Lewis, you are finished in the pit. You're one hundred per cent. Neglect, man, sheer neglect. I've sent scores of colliers to the NCB medical board.'

Lewis Rimmer crossed his legs. He had wide, upward tilting eyes, dark, vulpine above the bony ridge of his white-glazed nose, tight skinned like his forehead. Forehead and anchor boned jowl trapped him: a man estranged by passions. 'I'm fifty-seven,' he said. 'They can't expect a bloke to change his job at fifty-seven. All I've ever done is work on the coal, driving headings in Fawr pit, been driving headings for nigh on thirty years.'

The Doctor tutted impatience. 'Let's be frank. If you don't leave the coal face you won't reach sixty.'

'By the Jesus . . .'

'Here's my advice. Live outdoors as much as possible, cultivate an allotment, grow vegetables, flowers, then you'll increase your chances of lasting to a good age.'

Lewis jigged his foot. 'My pigeons keep me occupied. Where'll I find a job though, ah?'

'Forget about employment. See your lodge secretary, see him today. He'll put you in touch with the compo. sec. You are entitled to full compensation.'

From the doorway, Lewis said, 'Crime in my opinion, shoving a man on the street. Goes against the grain with me.'

Doctor Gammon aimed his forefinger. 'Lewis, you are finished in the pits by *law*! The Coal Board dare not employ you after serving fourteen days' notice.'

'By the Jesus . . . so-long, Doctor,' he said.

Head sunk, hands fisted in his jacket pockets, Lewis walked the wet pavements. Pen Arglwydd mountain towered behind shifting drizzle. He crossed the road to the chemist shop. Alert behind the counter, her lips stretched, the girl said, 'Good morning,'—glancing at his prescription—'Mr Rimmer.'

'Bit of chest trouble,' he said, staring at her, thinking, nice piece, aye, guaranteed banker for the old through and through stakes. She makes my Bessie look like a bag of slurry tied 'round the middle. 'What's the damage, gel?'

A shivering spasm wriggled her shoulders. The rawness of his ugly face, his huge, black-nailed, gripping fingers. Ugh, stupid old miner. 'Seventy pence, Mr Rimmer.'

'Reckon 'Nye Bevan's turning in his grave,' he said, grinning, slapping his sides.

'Mmm, I don't know what you mean.' She heard the soft rustle of maple peas in his jacket pocket. 'Please take a chair. I shan't be a few minutes.'

A talkative group of matronly women filed in, ranged themselves along the counter. Lewis fell away into himself, his foot jigging, sight and hearing emptying away. The girl re-appeared, still smiling, lost for Lewis, vanquished. He left the shop without thanking her for his tablets.

Drizzle thinned to creeping mist across the massive frontal nub of Pen Arglwydd. As he came out of the corn chandler's store, Lewis saw his bus leaving the curb. He decided to walk home. Take it steady. Nothing spoiling in the house. His pigeons were fed and watered. Bessie's morning job. Least she could do, by the Christ, after living off his back since she clicked for William. Just gave birth once. Barren ever since. Therefore waste. Swill chucked down the drain.

Single paced, unamazed, Lewis paused at a street corner, shuffled a narrow half circle, muttering, 'Well-aye, short cut.' He climbed the up-and-over footbridge, sulphur-tasting smoke flooding above the full trucks. Lewis crouched, held onto the handrail, coughed, coughed, his heart hammering. Down on the pavement again, he cursed his weakness. Then he cursed having to walk home. He came to a road bridge, Melyn brook flowing below, black as enamel. Leaning on the parapet, Lewis cleared his chest, 'Chhhhachhh,' and he spat into the brook. He examined the tablets, swallowed one, and dropped the plastic bottle into the water.

Resting for a while, he wondered if he should bring his tools out from Fawr pit. If a man can't use his tools best forget about them. Never do a bad turn when you can offer some bugger a good turn. Let one of the night shift repairers have them, buckshee, some poor sod on bare wages.

Lewis coughed again, down to hissy grunts. Hundred per cent, he thought. By Jesus. Men are pegging out with fifty per cent. I'm miles from that state. Rough chest first thing in the morning, short of breath until the circulation starts moving. Good Christ almighty, fifty-seven, packing it in at my age. Doesn't make sense. Bloody hell. There're colliers in Fawr close on pension time, old plodders clearing their yardage every shift. Me, bloody scrap-heap. Doctor Gammon, his mouth about gardening, he's never done a day's graft in all his natural. Him sat there on his arse, telling me what to do.

Before leaving the bridge, Lewis spat a gobbet of coal streaked phlegm into Melyn brook. Fretting about his age and the pneumoconiosis, he raised his head, breathed deeply, held himself firm, striding, but ache fired his shoulder-blades, his ribs, so he relaxed, hands in pockets, chin out-thrust, sight fixed on the coming and going of his toecaps. A six foot man in his prime, the curvature of his spine lowered him six inches, the curve prominent, hard packed under the shiny serge of his long, double breasted jacket. His shoulders and sleeves were stained with wiped-off pigeon droppings.

There were three glossy caravans propped in a line behind the roofless smithy of derelict Number 2 pit. Outsiders, he thought. Bloody NCB, they bring in these outsiders to dismantle while our own men are signing the dole. On impulse he walked past stacks of pit props, thrown higgledy-piggledy, rotting reminders of pit closure. 'Shwmae,' he said formally, repeating, 'Shwmae,' the three young wives nodding, smiled posed together, smoothing frocks and pinafores. He strode clump footed through the colliery office, a square, echoing building. Looters had stripped doors and windows. Long slits of daylight glimmered beneath the eaves. Everywhere the smell of urine and sheep droppings. From the office he walked to the top pit stables. Mildewed horse collars hung on spikes driven into the walls. Ruination, he thought, nothing but ruination. He followed railway tracks to the end of the colliery siding. Red rusted truck buffers were bolted to mossy baulks of timber. Turning left, he picked his route between ancient greening slag heaps back to the main road.

Bessie Rimmer had her hands in chicken meal, a heavyweight woman, grossly slack-bodied like a primordial Venus.

'What'd he say, Lew?'

'I got it al'right. The full dose, hundred per cent.'

She said, 'Lord above.' Her fingers ploughed through the meal. 'Want me to write to our William, tell him about you?'

Lewis sat near the fire. He rested his heels on the hob, his long, dark specked hands dangling from the arms of the chair. 'Leave it be. The boy's minding his own affairs.'

'*Duw*, hopeless you are, Lew Rimmer. Should have gone for a board ages ago. No, stubborn, think you know everything better than anybody else, go your own way regardless. Now see what it's come to! D'you ask Doctor Gammon about a fortnight in that convalescent place on Gower? Don't suppose you did. Couple of weeks rest is what you need, for def'nite!'

He said, 'Your fowls are waiting for that mash. Come straight back and lay some grub on the table.'

Bessie went out and through the kitchen door. She met her neighbour in the dirt lane, Esther Rees, spinster, the school cleaner.

'Hundred per cent he is,' Bessie said.

'Oh, shame,' sympathised Esther.

'Should have known it himself, yes he should have.' Bessie hugged the pan of steaming chicken meal. Her mouth pouted resentment. 'My Lewis won't be told. Always out to prove himself diff'rent, nothing at all like anybody else God ever put breath into. From now on he'll have to knuckle down, stands to reason with hundred per cent dust.'

Esther sloped her head, sighing resignation. She was forty-nine, tall, lean as a distance runner. Bessie marched down the lane, pale grey whiffs of steam rising from the chicken meal. Esther rotated from the waist, her head perched, watchful, blue eyes watery, lips puckering, ageing within the defensive wedge of her cheekbones and chin. She lifted her empty ash bucket off the backyard wall, 'Tch-tch-tch,' and hurried indoors to inform her son—Lewis Rimmer's son, Bernard. Of course Bessie knew about Bernard Rees, but all that happened a long time ago. Not worth bothering about any more. Bernard was thirty-two, a bachelor, two years younger than Bessie's son, William.

Lewis rested, unaware of resting himself. He sat without thinking. The sideboard clock chirruped, stroked twelve pinging chimes. Roused, Lewis jabbed the firegrate with the sole of his shoe, sparks and dead ash spluttering into the hearth. He huffed while climbing upstairs. From the landing window he looked to see if Bessie was in the lane, before entering the small bedroom, William's bedroom until he left home to join the Army. Lewis used his fingernails to lift out a length of floor board. His secret place. Counting the money, mumbling, each note was passed from hand to hand. Seven hundred and eighty-four pounds. My sweat, he thought, carelessly piling the notes on the plaster lathes between two joists. He felt no excitement.

The back door rattled. Lewis clumsily tip-toed out of the bedroom to the lavatory, pulled the chain and fiercely slammed the door.

'Use some bloody elbow grease on the bowl of the lav,' he said.

'Fancy anything special to eat?' asked Bessie.

Lewis grunted, slumped in his fireside chair. 'I'm off my food, gel.'

'Obvious an' all, after what Doctor Gammon said to you this morning. I'll be down his surg'ry later on, find out regarding that place on Gower coast. Years an' years you've paid the NUM without so much as a pint of beer off of 'em. There's facilities for compo cases, Lew, laid on for the likes of you'self.'

'Aye,' he said, 'and leave you to look after my pigeons.'

'Pigeons! Health comes before pigeons!'

'You mind your own business, Bessie.'

'Suit you'self, if that's how you want it.'

'Right, that's al'right,' he said calmly.

Bessie persisted. 'You drove our William away as if he was a total stranger. My own son! Seems to me you haven't got any feelings left at all, only for them blasted pigeons. Fat lot of good they'll be after . . .'

'Shurrup!'

'You can't frighten me no more.'

'Shut it. Just lay some food on the table, and shut it.'

Bessie waddled to and from the pantry with cheese, pickles, cold ham, tomato sauce, bread and butter. Elbows on the table, Lewis began eating while she brewed the tea. By the time she sat down, Bessie felt uncomfortably flustered. And her toes were itching. Slipping off her shoes, she rubbed her toes with her heels, hard, rubbing and rubbing. The torment and ecstasy of her itching feet.

'You wash your hands after mixing the mash?' he demanded quietly.

'Course not, 'tisn't as if I've been messing with filth.'

'Sit still then, you're fidgetting like a woman with the piles.'

'My toes are burning hot!'

'Guh, you're the bloody limit.'

'As if you cared about anybody 'cept you'self,' she grumbled.

Lewis chewed methodically, false dignified as an old captive lion.

'How much is full compo these days?' she inquired, friendly now, leaning towards him.

'No idea, gel.'

'Be enough for us two I expect, Lew. We'll manage.'

'I daresay.'

'There's our William, he'll send us a few pounds if ever we run short.'

'I shan't take a penny off the boy. He's got a houseful of kids.'

'William's earning big money,' protested Bessie. 'Any case, he's our son. It's his duty.'

Lewis levered himself away from the table. 'Duty, no such thing,' he said indifferently. He opened the back door, pleased to see bright sunshine drying out the damp morning. 'I'm off up to the loft. Lissen, gel, fetch me a couple of cartridges from the drawer.'

His shotgun hung in the cupboard beneath the stairs. He greased the action with smears of lard, cleaned both barrels and slotted in the cartridges.

'Lew, how long will you be?'

He hefted the gun at point of balance. 'Be back at three o'clock.'

'Can't I write a letter to our William?'

'No.' He shook his head. 'Scrub the lav, Bessie, don't forget.'

His pigeon loft stood on a green mound sheltered by willows. The school playground fence ran below, some fifteen yards of clay-blotched turf between school and fence. There was a turnstile gate, hub of half a dozen footpaths winding the lower hillside. Lewis climbed the shallowest gradient. He released his pigeons, forty birds, reds, blues, dark and light chequers, mealies, grizzles, a bunched swarm, primaries whirring. They swept out free, wider, higher, turned, plumed and twisted headlong over the village, climbed, hurtled

97

towards the mountain, their colours winking like shell fragments against the green background. Lewis watched them, his private delight, his own expert joy. They were a part of himself. Closer to his heart than Bessie or Esther. His birds, and driving headings in Fawr pit.

He scraped the loft, sprinkled nest boxes and perches with anti-lice powder, then he carried fresh water from a cask at the back of the lean-to roof. The pigeons were roving in unison under ragged white clouds. Lewis sat beneath a pollarded willow with the shotgun across his knees. He gazed along the distant horizon of the hills. 'Stay away from my birds, johnny-hawk,' he said, lowering his bent shoulders against the tree. He watched his flock performing. The shotgun symbolised his youth, when falcons stooped from the sun, downing his beloved homers. Years gone by. Now peregrines very seldom wheeled above the valley.

The flock drifted over-head, swung up-wind, disappeared over the mountain. Lewis closed his eyes. Thoughtlessly he went, 'Ssss-huhssss-ssss-ssss.' through his teeth, a cold sound, tuneless, like wind pressing itself through a cracked window-pane. He was resting himself.

The pigeons returned, swishing a tight trajectory around the willows, vee-winged, legless, knobbled beaks and glinty, popping eyes. They plunged upward, flight line broadening, heading for the shadowed face of the old quarry. They flew yet higher, seeming mechanically driven, speeding like flecks of hail over the mountain top. Lewis laid aside the shotgun. He coughed, cleared his chest, ending on throaty sibilance until he spat phlegm.

Esther called, 'Lew!'

He moved gawkily stiff-legged to the edge of the mound. She beckoned from the turnstile gate. 'Come on up,' he said.

'Can't, not now. Busy in the school. Lew, your Bessie told me about the report from Doctor Gammon. Won't they give you a light job?'

'Not down the pit.'

'Well, what have you got in mind, Lew?'

'Don't know yet.'

'I've told my Bernard. That's only fair, isn't it?'

'Why not . . . aye.'

They were linked by silence, her thin elbows held horizontal, clutched by her fingertips, forearms pressing her skimpy bosom. 'Pity too,' she said. 'Bye-bye for now, Lew.' She gave him a subdued little wave and hastened into the school building.

Lewis propped his shotgun in the loft. There were slatted flight runs each side of the aisle, the aisle itself littered with scrapers, a hammer, skewed handsaw, tins of nails, stunted cane brush without a handle, and a small sack of maple peas. Above the shotgun were two shelves of medicine, powders, artificial eggs, earthenware nesting bowls, broken rings and a Flit gun.

He returned to the pollarded willow. Old longings stirred, disturbing his dryness like the peckings of feeble squabs. Lewis sat up, wrists on his knees, hands dangling. He remembered Esther, the cool girl of seventeen. Cool, helpless, useless—his desperate, wild rage. She'd sickened his guts. Was it worse, any worse than this, the X-rays, the medical board, the final evidence: hundred per cent dust? She stayed cool, always. Bloodless Esther. Daft, her and Bessie, both daft. Young Bernard, he followed his mother. Tall rope of a bloke, no strength in him anywhere to do anything. Lewis flapped his hands. 'All of it's bloody senseless, the whole lot.'

He cursed quietly to himself, stream upon stream of cursing. Incoherence waned to misery. He drooped back against the tree. She meant nothing. Bessie, nothing. William, nothing. Bernard, nothing. It's me, Lewis Rimmer, fifty-seven, that's all, fifty-bloody-seven. Man for man I've filled more coal than any collier in Fawr pit. Now this. Here I am. What's my next move? How carry on? What's next? Jesus Christ.

He glanced around for his pigeons. Bare sky, two carrion crows winging down, down below the high level rim of Pen Arglwydd. His dark eyes blinked, kindling memories, falcons shot on the mountain, hours spent waiting for johnny-hawk to cop in to roost. Warm, dusky summer evenings hiding in a den of fallen boulders, puffing Gold Flake fags inside his folded cap, blowing the smoke down between his knees. Long, long time ago. It's well over twenty years since I climbed Pen Arglwydd. Can't manage it now. Finished. Christ, aye, I'm finished. What shall I do? Gardening. Huh, mess about like some old betsy. Not likely. I'd sooner jack it in altogether.

He heard his pigeons, the frantic clap of pinions as a bird

tumbled against telephone wires strung from the school down to the road, wires dotted with split corks. Lewis cursed. Plodding slantwise down the mound, he cursed the wires. Aware of his violence as he banged into the kitchen, Bessie left him alone.

At four o'clock he whistled the birds in, fed them, and carried his shotgun back to the house. Bessie replaced the cartridges in a drawer of the sideboard.

On Monday morning the manager visited Lewis's heading. Behind him came the overman, safety stick tucked under his arm. 'Lew,' said the manager, 'I've got some bad news.'

Lewis sent his young butty up into the low face—a narrow layer of rider coal and shale. They were driving through to a virgin seam. 'Pack the right hand side, boy. Make sure you wall it up properly.'

The men hunkered beside a half full tram of rubble. 'I know all about this bad news,' said Lewis.

Elderly, with blue scars freckling his left temple, the manager unclipped his cap-lamp. 'I'm down for ten per cent myself. Early stages.'

The overman said, 'Take it from me, Lew, these quacks don't know everything.'

The manager scowled. 'Wait now, wait. Regarding Lewis, there's no question of error, and there's damn all I can do about it. Not a damn thing. Understand, Lew, my hands are tied. Truth is, Lew, your fourteen days' notice is in my office.'

The overman squirted tobacco juice. 'First hundred per cent case since we worked the old Four Foot seam through to the boundary. Real hard coal up there, hard as the hobs of hell.'

Lewis spoke to the manager. 'Job on the screens would suit me.'

'Impossible, only wish to God I could put you somewhere on top pit. If I can do anything for you, Lew, let me know. Anything at all outside the colliery. And listen, try not to worry. The man isn't born who can cure worry.'

Lewis watched their cap-lamps retreating from the heading. He shouted to his butty. The youth jumped down into the roadway. Lewis continued prising rock from the blasted roof. Behind him, his butty filled rubble into the tram. Bent over his shovel, the boy said, 'So you're going on compo, Lew.'

'You're all ears,' said Lewis.

'Last night, mun, I heard it in the club last night.'

'Never mind what you bloody heard.'

'You're hundred per cent, right? That's what they reckon.'

'Let's see that dram filled,' Lewis said. He knew the arguments in the club. Lew Rimmer's finished. All the slashers travel the same road to Coed-coch cemetery. Pig-headed Lew, never wears a mask when he's boring holes. Tight-fisted money grabber, won't wait for the dust to clear after shot firing. Big Lew, he's packing muck in the gob walls when you can't see your hand in front of your eyes. Typical slasher. They all go the same way. Silicosis or pneumo. Loaf around on street corners until they're only skin and bones. Nothing but skeletons by the time the undertaker comes to measure them.

Conscious of damaged pride, of his reputation in Fawr pit, Lewis elbowed out his gaunt arms, hung his whole weight on the crowbar, pressing evenly. The long slab of rock cracked on, then he shuffled backwards, prised again, arms outstretched until the rock crashed down. Lewis broke it with a sledge-hammer. His butty lifted the stones into the tram. Lewis moved forward, he swung a heavy pick, ripping back the sides of the road. Soon he had a pile of rubble in front of his working boots. Stepping up on the loose stones, he struck ahead with his pick. Pride again, remorse, smothered grunts, his spoiled self-esteem turned vicious, aiming the pick, his body angled away by instinct, teetering, the soft-jointed stone sliding soundlessly out from the side where he'd been ripping, falling edge-wise on his outflung forearm, breaking the bone.

The youth dragged Lewis around the tram. Frightened, running out, around to the next heading for help, he kept hearing the muffled crack of bone breaking, and Lewis blaspheming like a lunatic.

For two days Bessie endured a brooding husband. Lewis slept and ate in the armchair near the fire. Unshaven, sullen, he remained there with his feet set straight on the coconut fibre hearth mat. She fed and watered his pigeons. Early on the third morning she heard him cursing in the hallway. Bessie pulled the soiled double breasted jacket across his shoulders.

'Be careful, please, Lew,' she said.

Humbled, the plaster cased left arm swung up to his chest, he walked the dirt lane, moving stiffly, jerking along, Esther

Rees watching him from her kitchen doorway. He climbed the mound in sharp zig-zags, the humped shape of him alternately profiled. Poor Lew, she thought, letting himself go to rack and ruin. Distaste wrinkled her nose. She closed the door and returned to ironing Bernard's white shirts.

Lewis freed his pigeons, he cleaned out the loft, scraping laboriously, wheezing breath through irregular, dry clickings of his false teeth. He felt tired, inwardly softened, sluggish in his blood. Something had drained out of his system, seepage finding outlet while he waited behind the tram with his numb arm held to his stomach. He sat on the wooden steps outside the loft. Down-valley, he could see the smoke stack above Number 2 pit, the railway footbridge and far off, hazed by morning sunshine, the dwarfed spread of terraced houses, shops, stone-built chapels and pubs mapped each side of Melyn brook. His tiredness succumbed to alien contentment.

Images of Bessie flowed, from her gamin childhood to nubile adolescence to the hulking slovenliness of her middle age. Soft sniggers warmed Lewis's throat. After a while he filled the food hoppers, brought fresh water into the loft and he shut the wire screen entrance door.

He walked down in a state of infantile euphoria. Bessie cooked breakfast. He mocked her chickens. Bantams laid bigger eggs.

'My life,' she vowed, humouring him, 'I haven't seen you like this since I went pregnant on William. Anyway, my fowls show more profit than them bloody racing pigeons. Now look, I'm doing my shopping this morning. Mind how you go with that arm of yours.'

'Old gel,' he said, 'never panic over Lew Rimmer. There's no need.'

Alone in the house, he sat on the lavatory for an hour, broken circulation deadening his shanks. Lewis giggled, stamped his feet on the landing. Giggling induced coughing, a harsh, prolonged bout toppling him to his knees. Time went by. He crossed to the small bedroom, raised the floor board and stuffed seven hundred and eighty-four pounds into his pockets. Downstairs again, Lewis emptied the tea caddy, a sweeping fling showering tea grains around the kitchen. He crammed the notes into the caddy.

Very slowly in warm mid-day, he climbed the green mound

to his loft, shotgun held balanced, carried at arm's length. His birds were down. Lewis carefully stepped among them, he named his favourites, praised their courage and suddenly, gently, he shooed them all way.

Stooped in the aisle, cursing, pressing off the safety catch, blindly cursing, his broken arm hanging, clenching the mouth of the double barrel between his teeth, Lewis gagged curses as the trigger slicked back under his thumb.

Time went by. The pigeons came floating down. A few copped on the roof of the loft. Crop puffed out, a dark chequer cock made deep rich cooings, strutting around a grizzly hen. She responded, nibbling his shoulder feathers, her wings partly opening on the instant as she rolled slightly sideways beneath his tread. They frisked apart, the dark chequer volplaning into the loft, where he gobbled two maple peas spilt from Lewis's pocket.

Ben, the T.V. Playwright
and his wife, Lottie

'My insomnia.'
  'Take a pink tablet for God's sake,' Lottie said.
  'Too late now. I'm going downstairs.'
  'What time is it?'
  The alarm clock churred softly on the bedside table. 'Half past four. Dawn's just coming up.'
  She embraced his thigh. 'Love me?'
  'I loves ya,' Ben said. 'What would you like for breakfast?'
  'Bacon n'egg.'
  'Right, call you at eight o'clock.'
Spectacles perched low in the gristle of his nose, Ben drank two saccharined coffees in the kitchen. He dog-eared the BBC envelope. Here's evidence, he thought. Achievement, break-through into the media after fifteen years of fluxing between cause and effect. Ordinance of life. Seven books, silent worlds, seven hundred thousand shapes from the grid of my ID. Pied magic. The old Sisyphus slog towards mapping Ben Rees. Eks marks his centre. Trove hinterland. Each book a failure, ultimately flawed. Language makes losers.

He jotted statements on the BBC envelope: *Juh-heez-zuss Kerriste, appurtenant of failure. Failure expressed as universal. Endless sin conducts permanent guilt, equals bearable comfort.*

Time thinned, went skew. Came the familiar puzzle. He argued, 'Where did that come from?'

Ageing crawled the kitchen walls, sensitised a waning horse-fly bite on his neck. Ben scratched.

The splinter principle in creation—he wrote it down, rolled himself a neat, loose cigarette and wondered about the unknown couple chosen to sound his dialogue, image the symbols on television. Actors? He turned over the envelope. *Facts make acts. Factors make actors make acts from facts. Then he wrote: Lalopath's epitaph: Inn meye farther souse arm men knee man shuns ∴ eph phoph.*

The postman knocked while Lottie flexed and pruned her lips, unaware of confronting strangeness in the hallway eagle mirror. She opened the door, her opaline mouth blurting, 'Ta very much. It's for my husband, his television play.'

'Great,' approved the postman. 'Me and the wife'll have a dekko at that. Cheerio, Mrs Rees.'

'Ben!' she yelped.

'Rehearsal script,' he said. 'Look, Prysor Rhys . . .'

'Rr-hees, same as us, almost!'

'Omen,' said Ben. 'This actress, Ethel Houghton, she's English.'

Lottie crowed excitement. 'My lipstick tidy? I'm late!'

'Director,' he read, 'Peter Davies.'

'Welsh,' insisted Lottie.

'We'll soon know. I'm meeting him in Cardiff this afternoon.'

'Kept you awake all last night.' She nibbled his ear. 'S'long, my love. I'll miss my bus.'

'If the door's locked you know where to find the key.'

'Okay! 'Bye, darlin'!' She sped past the window, her breasts jiggling, the profiled moment seizing his throat, stiffness clinging at the root of his tongue.

'Peter Davies,' he repeated, thinking, yet another exiled Celt crafting a niche for himself in London. Power, authority, tycoonery, fame, they drain from Wales like sewage pours into the sea. The route away from roots—mine, too, it's time I left this cloth-cap land of my fathers. Claim on race or creed amounts to perjury. False assets set arses. Easy feelings, gut comfort spreading like psychic cataract.

Before mid-day he fell asleep over his work table, viscid dribbles crystallising on the back of his hand. Panic, lumbar twinges the instant he straightened his spine. He galloped lop-sidedly to the railway station, flopped in a corner seat with the script on his lap and remained motionless, stupored for an hour.

In Cardiff, the hotel receptionist jerked her arm like a traffic cop, her tone limpid, the tall young man parading willowy, Cavalier haired, a catalogue advert quickened on purpose.

'Ben Rees?'

'How d'you do,' Ben said.

'Peter Davies, and let me say how delighted I am to be directing your play. It's beautiful, really is, a beautiful piece of writing.'

Ben shuffled quarter circles. 'Shall we have a pint in there, the back bar?'

Peter Davies sipped sherry. He unwound lucid clichés, shorn sesames of politeness.

'I think it has unity,' Ben said. 'What I mean is, growth from start to finish.'

'Absolutely.' Peter smiled winsome detachment. 'Of course we'll have to cut, yes, um, six pages, six minutes. It's by far the most reliable formula.' He flipped open his rehearsal copy to page 23. 'Here. Rather extraneous I suspect, coming so late in terms of dramatic continuity.'

Hunting defensively inward, Ben lost sight of the young TV director. He laid his fist on page 23. 'Six minutes you said?' Peter nodded, smiling his immunity smile. 'If I cut six pages from here,' Ben said, grinning, 'to page twenty-nine, how do we introduce, I mean how is anyone to know about the girl being in the pudding club?'

'Bring her confession forward, end of scene one,' said Peter.

'She's already in a state of crisis, rejected by her family.'

'Add strength to the plot, I should say.'

Ben said, 'Much too bloody much.'

'Well, it's no problem. Have you met Prysor Rhys?'

'I haven't.'

'He's ideal for the part. Surely you saw him in *No Smoke Without Flame* last week?'

'The serial? I can't take serials,' Ben said. 'They clog my insides.'

Peter tilted his romantic head, finger and thumb prupping his lower lip. 'Actually I directed the pilot for *No Smoke Without Flame*.' He talk-talk-talked about techniques, styles, roles, trends.

Ben felt ancient. He thought, why? Me and this trained length of nobody's shite. 'Whisky?' he asked. 'Can I fetch you a whisky?'

Peter swam his hands, bland refusal widening the gulf between them. Ben swallowed short whiskies and half pints of beer.

Peter said, 'We were most fortunate to have Ethel Houghton. Charming person. You'll like her, I'm sure. 'She's heavily committed.'

'TV plays?' Ben said.

'Stage.'

'How old is she?'

'Ah, I see your point! Really, Ben, she's a remarkable actress. Portraying adolescents is Ethel's forte. One suggestion, if I may. At the first read-through, do refrain from criticism. You see, we are all inclined to be nervous in the presence of the author. First readings.'—Peter wriggle-giggled—'are often quite insane. Nerves, Ben, you understand.'

'You won't be alone,' Ben said.

Peter smoothed his eyebrows, stroked the bridge of his nose. 'Production-wise, the nitty-gritty problems emerge during rehearsals. Essentially it's straight-forward. The story-line has enormous power.'

'How are we going to lose these six minutes?' Ben said.

'I suggest you meet our script editor. Monday morning? Good. Elevenish? Good-good. He admires your work immensely.'

Ben said, 'Ten to one he hasn't read any of my novels.'

'Neither have I! Be patient, old chap, give us a little time.'

Journeying home with the script on his lap, Ben fretted. He thought, that velvety long-shanks came down from London for a chat and a few drinks. He slid the photographs out from the script: Ethel Houghton and Prysor Rhys. Hard, the girl, hard eyes. She looked fit to cope, match any lad with more between his legs than between his ear-holes. The Prysor Rhys portrait slanted feyly across the glossy paper. Pretty. 'Pretty young fella,' Ben muttered, rousing a schoolboy from behind his comic.

'Say somethin', mister?'

Ben rotated his index finger against his forehead. 'Nattering to myself.'

'Whaw, bad sign. My Granny's the same, talks back to the telly all the time. Proper scream she is, my Granny.'

'I daresay you'd like to be on television,' Ben said.

'Aye, why not. Big money.'

'I've written a TV play.'

'Honest? Whassit about?'

Ben winked. 'A boy and a girl living here in Wales.'

'Some luck, meeting you on this train! When's it coming on? I'll tell my Gran, she's mad on plays.'

Ben said, 'We haven't started rehearsals yet.' He showed him the photographs.

The boy whawed again. 'I've seen *him*! *No Smoke Without Flame*. Who's the girl?'

'Ethel Houghton.'

'Any more photos?'

'There aren't any more, just these two.'

The boy stared at him above his comic. 'Oh aye,' then he hid himself.

Fickle disciple, thought Ben. He scrutinised page 23, hissed anxiety, rolled himself a cigarette, stood at the window to ease his beer-tight belly, and grew into quiet pride. From tichy beginnings, gargantuan endings. Maybe. Drifting from reality, mindless, he watched the flowing landscape until the train stopped.

The boy nudged him. 'S'cuse me, mister.'

'Cheerio, all the best,' Ben said.

He worked throughout the night squeezing bits out of the text. The six minutes haunted him. He incited Lottie to screaming attack, trying to fob off his resentment on her. Self to self, Ben felt less than his wife.

Monday morning they were up at five o'clock. He caught the earliest train to Paddington. London roared under heatwave. He walked Praed Street before taxi-ing out to the studios, his rehearsal copy in a black briefcase belonging to Lottie's schoolteacher brother. The script editor met him in the reception hall. His office was up on the third floor. A rigid faced secretary with shining blonde hair brought them coffee. They lunched at one o'clock.

'Kafka's *Castle*, this place,' wheezed the editor, a dry stick Scot, grained compromiser from years in radio and television. 'We fiddle slots for makers and fakers.'

'Sounds corrupt,' Ben said. 'This play of mine, it's like a baby held to its mother by the string. Just the string.'

The Scot grimaced. 'Nice metaphor. You expect too much.'

'I'm concerned. It's my work.'

'Drama isn't literature, unquote. Don't waste subtlety on the box. I recommend cutting scenes fourteen and nineteen.'

'Why?'

'Indulgence, man, the self-indulgence. Let scene nineteen begin on page forty-one.'

Ben said, 'I am not self indulgent.'

The Scot grinned his false teeth. 'You're a bugger for high prose.'

'I'm in good company, historically.'

They returned to the office. After another hour the blonde coffee-bringer began typing Ben's revised script. Scenes fourteen and nineteen were excised. Ben conceded the hatchet job. He warmed to the Scot. Drama wasn't Eng. Lit. Right, relax, stand by, wait for the read-through.

Peter Davies introduced him to Ethel Houghton and Prysor Rhys at the end of August. Naïve enthusiasm lifted him at the first reading. Then came misfortune: Ethel Houghton collapsed from nervous exhaustion. Pepped up too long, decided Ben, hindsight wise from his reliance on soneryl. Rehearsals stopped. The actress went abroad to recuperate.

He drafted another play for television, melodrama, rowdy crises hinged on parochial politics and philandering. Scant encouragement brought Lottie in for part reading, a new experience for both of them. They ranted face to face, echoed the house, enjoyed themselves. Satisfied, he locked the script in a chiffonier drawer, the foolscap pages suspiciously meagre above the thick quarto bundles of his novels. Still, it was finished for the time being. Slackening off, Ben screwed out a batch of hopeful titles for his next book. He drank heavily, the extent of it governed by Lottie's tolerance. Winter killed off autumn. Ben reached obsession, lack of any routine driving him along on his eighth novel. When he left his work table he didn't know what to do, how to use himself. Most evenings he supped a couple of slow pints in the local pub. Lottie joined the ladies darts team. Ben fattened. He vowed to get himself fit, spend the summer burning starch out of his system. Early in February he unlocked the chiffonier drawer. Like an oven, Ben spurted bright language, bright ideas; he chopped to and fro, revising the new play and building his novel.

Peter Davies halted him with a telegram. The first play was in the can. Possible transmission in April. Splendid production. Everyone delighted. Ethel and Prysor send warmest congratulations. Ever, Peter.

Lottie said, 'We'll have to do something.'

Ben lowered himself at his table.

'O, the rotten young waster,' she said.

He wound a sheet of paper into his machine. 'I'll stop it.'

'Means lawyers and so on.'

'The blind, ignorant bastard!'

'Mm, he should have let you know,' Lottie said. 'Want me to come to London?'

'Ah?'

She said, 'I'll come with you. We'll spit in this Peter Davies's face.'

Ben laughed.

'Lovely,' she cried. 'Ever so lovely to hear you laughing.'

'Lottie, the truth is I'm stupid. I'm innocent.'

'Of course, trapped like a monk inside these four walls. It's what I've been saying for years.'

'Aye, I know that too.'

Ben tapped out an enquiry to the dry stick Scot. Was he happy with the production? Near perfect, damn good television, replied the script editor. Would Ben like to see a preview? Expenses on Auntie.

They travelled 1st Class, Lottie wearing her Christmas gift fur hat. A quietly civilised journey. She gripped his wrist in the small TV theatre. Six times during the next hour, Ben stood up, shouting, 'Alien!' or 'Cheap!' or 'Not my work!'

At the end Ben wore the look of a man absolved from punishment. They trooped curved corridors to the producer's office. Peter Davies turned from closing the door as Lottie, palms cupped around her mouth, accurately planted spittle on his face. He wailed contralto, gasping down to nausea, Lottie reaching hooked fingers, tugging his long wavy hair until he fell to his knees.

Shock stunned the editor and the producer, pinned them standstill like spooked mules.

Ben felt safe.

The producer hugged himself. 'Impasse,' he pleaded, 'We'll come to some mutual arrangement. Please calm yourself, Mrs Rees.'

Lottie jeered, miming Ha-ha-ha-ha.

'I'll write to every critic,' Ben said, 'every newspaper, every journal, the damn governors themselves. This bloke here, this slick boy Davies, he deserves the worst. He's a polluter. I won't have my name anywhere near that play.'

110

Said the Scot, 'I never thought I'd live to see the day. Art for art's sake! Climb down, man, be sensible.'

'Quiet, *you*,' Lottie said. She caught Ben's arm. 'I've done my best to put the silly sod in his place. Let's go home.'

On the morning of his forty-ninth birthday, they were bickering amiably across the breakfast-table, when the postman arrived. Recorded delivery, for Lottie, her signature, her summons for assaulting Peter Davies.

'Marvellous publicity!' She gagged on rarebit and joy, yellow flecks of cheese spraying from her wide mouth, tears tickling her nose until she exploded sneezes. Lottie's healthily aggressive joy. Relieved she sang, 'Morning, darlin'. Bye-bye, see you!'

She ran past the window.

Ben hooped over his work table. He sent a letter to the producer, offering terms, sanction, his name to the play if Peter Davies dropped the prosecution. Peter Davies agreed, swerved from righteousness by the £8,000 spent on production. So Ben's play was transmitted one rainy night in May. His pub friends decided it was crappy. Better entertainment in *High Chaparral*. Brief eulogies appeared though; *The Times* and *The Guardian* acclaimed a genuine talent, a new voice, fresh, original.

Ben retreated from his eighth novel. Stuck on disgust he boozed steadily, lasting the pace all Summer, across the threshold to forgetfulness. A bad summer, tenderness frosting between himself and Lottie. But he came back, as before, as always, to the dual breaking and making of language on blank paper. He had no choice.

Titty-bottle hearts—he wrote
comfying
echophrasiac old
tongues
inside
these
H
E
A
D
S

111

Shit souls in situ
                              —he scrubbed *burping*
            slurping
         love sans love
            from
            turned
            down
              M
              O
              U
              T
              H
              S

Designer, he thought. Taffy artificer.

'Ben!' she called from the foot of the stairs. 'This play we practised last year, want me to post it off?'

He said, 'Thanks.'

'Registered mail?'

'Of course.'

He watched her striding the flagstone path between tattered stalks of wall-flowers. 'Lottie!'

'So-long, my love! See you dinner-time!'

And he stood there, humbly serene, palm raised like a breech-clouted tribal chief until she disappeared behind the never-cut privet hedge.

November Kill

As if talking to himself, 'More guts than sense in this bitch,'
Miskin said. Hunkered over the belly-up bedlington, he
caressed her ribs with his knuckles. Lady wheezed sighs,
slaver glistening her teeth inside slack lips. Miskin had three
hunting dogs, two rough-coated brindle lurchers, Fay and
Mim, and the slaty-blue bedlington.

Beynon's terrier, Ianto, was a long-jawed black and white
mongrel.

Miskin's small, clenched mouth accentuated the bumpy
profile of his broken nose. He screwed two short vertical
furrows up his forehead. 'We'll cover Dunraven Basin this
morning.'

'Good,' said Beynon, who had the closed face of a weary
spectator. Tall, lean, deliberate in style, he squatted beside
Miskin. 'Saw you coming out of the Club last night. Any luck?'

'She's solid asbestos,' said Miskin curtly.

'Thought so.'

'Come off it, how would you know?'

'I've tried Glenys.'

'Real kokum you are, Beynon.'

'You were slewed,' Beynon said.

'Same as most Saturday nights,' conceded Miskin.

Beynon levered himself upright. 'Set? Let's go.'

Miskin thwacked his trouser leg with a thin stick. 'Come in,
dogs, *in*.' The lurchers fell to heel with the bedlington.

Beynon clipped a lead on his terrier.

'Train the bloody animal,' jeered Miskin.

Beynon winced mock alarm. 'Ianto's like me, he's
uncontrollable.'

'You! There's more temper in a dishrag.'

'I'll frighten the crap out of you one of these days,' said
Beynon.

'I'm pooping already!'

'Take it easy, Miskin.'

They grinned, gently grinding shoulders, appreciating a
bond without malice.

Eight o'clock Sunday morning, quietness everywhere, two
milkmen bypassing each other in whining electric floats, the

113

village main street otherwise deserted. On ahead, Pen Arglwydd mountain jutted up at the November sky, a stillness of dark, bare cliffs intergullied with heathered ledges. Scree slopes gave way to invading bracken. Below the rusting bracken, patches of marshland, mole-tumped pasture, scatters of gnarled oaks, relict oaks older than the village, older than the national anthems of Mighty Albion. Alders lined feeder streams running into Nant Myrddin. Silver birches were spreading eastward, seedspill from a large stand of blackening, dying trees.

The young men followed Nant Myrddin up-river to a sunless, rock-walled gorge. Above the waterfall, half a square mile of sphagnum and rushes. Striding on tussocks, they moved out to dry ground. Now and then, Miskin puled soft repetitive whistling through his pruned lips.

They rested above the craggy amphitheatre of Dunraven Basin. A frizzled silhouette of conifers curved the Basin summit from end to end. Far distant behind them, the flat crown of Pen Arglwydd clung as if suckered to cold blue sky.

Miskin said, 'Lend me your glasses.'

A hidden, grounded raven sounded triple honk calls. Another came peeling over the conifers, swung down, rolled anticlockwise, flapped straight out, hard primaries soughing like bellows, out and out, followed by its honking mate. The big black corvids left the Basin. Down below, acres of glacial bog shone deceptively green.

'See anything?' Beynon said.

Elbows on his knees, binoculars steadied, Miskin breathed 'Naah,' from between his palms. He returned the glasses. 'Take a look at the '83 bury, or maybe it was '84—remember?'

Beynon focussed on ancient, fallen rocks underneath a nearside buttress, weathered blocks like collapsed cenotaphs skewed among tons of rubble. At the lower edge of the rockfall, a few hummocks of trampled, peaty soil stippled with posy-size clumps of heather. 'Cubs, Miskin. They're anywhere in Wales by now.'

'Any-bloody-where,' agreed Miskin.

The couchant lurchers were side by side as if on show, like stylised hunting dogs in Egyptian frescoes. Lady rattled a snarl at the black and white terrier.

'She's cranky, worse than my mother,' Beynon said.

Miskin flicked his thin stick, lightly rapping the bedlington's rump. 'Shut it, you nasty sod.' Then he tished a kind of resigned dolour. 'Your mother and mine, Beynon, they're a cowing pair.'

Beynon shrugged.

'Ten years my father slogged his goolies off to give her everything she asked for, the slut.'

Beynon said, 'My father likewise. They're all over though, men with more ballocks than brains.'

'Where's your mother these days?'

Beynon thumbed west towards the conifered skyline. 'Shacked up with some bloke in Swansea. Insurance agent. She's his tax allowance secretary.'

'Mine's in Spain, running a cafe with this guy she's supposed to have met on holiday. He's loaded.' Miskin spat aside and scythed the withered tuft of whinberry where it fell with his stick. 'They didn't rear us, Beynon. Me, I saw more dinner-times than cooked dinners.'

'Yeh, true,' said Beynon.

Miskin wagged his fist. 'I was only nine when she decided she'd had enough. After that, nothing, not a word. She vanished. Now, last Christmas, she sends me a poxy card from Spain.'

Hiding his face, Beynon scanned Dunraven Basin through the binoculars. 'I was seven.'

'Why, Beynon?'

'No idea. My father clamps up, he won't talk about her.'

'My father hit the booze. No shape on him till recent. Sits on his arse all day watching television.'

'C'mon, let's move,' said Beynon. 'We're pitying ourselves like two old betsies in a surgery.'

They slanted down from the north corner into Dunraven Basin. Rutted sheep tracks creamed with hard sills of peat, skirted around lichened boulders. Steep pitches of blue-grey shale slurred underfoot.

'Here goes,' said Miskin.

The bedlington scurried into the fox bury. Soon she surfaced, went sniffing alongside Ianto, watched by Mim and Fay, their tails wagging in slow counterpoint.

Miskin spoke softly, 'Take Mim and your dog. I'll work across from up there.'

Beynon held Mim's scruff. 'Good bitch, Mim. Stay now.' He waited while Miskin climbed to a sheeptrack winding midway around the cirque. Then they kept parallel, rounding inside the vast bowl of Dunraven Basin. The dogs hunted systematically, the lurchers higher, leaping ledges sure-footed as goats, Lady and Ianto nosing holes and crevices.

Miskin came down at the far end.

A buzzard hung like an emblem above the horizon, standing still in the updraught. Harsh *kaark kaark* calls from the two ravens, weaving low over the glacial bog.

Miskin rubbed mucus off his nose. 'I thought we'd raise one this morning.'

'We've seen some good chases this time of year,' Beynon said.

The lone buzzard drifted back over the skyline. A mallard squawked. Beynon spied through his glasses. He saw the drake shooting up from the narrow glittering stream emptying from the bog. The ravens planed and wheeled.

'Something's down there, Miskin.'

'Great. You sorted that out all by yourself.'

'Mouthy bastard,' said Beynon equably. 'Hey, reynard . . . left hand side of the brook, on that stretch of mud.'

'Glasses!' Miskin snatched, he hissed through his teeth, sighting the fox trotting its side-long gait, front and rear legs inswinging, four pads straight-tracking in the peat-stained silt, then rippling tremors of rushes and tall, fawny grass blades snaked diagonally across the bog. Light-footed over cropped turf and up to scree spillage below a gully, the fox climbed swiftly, skittering over stones like a squirrel.

Miskin pushed the glasses at Beynon.

Beynon said, 'Ta.' He sharpened the focus, thereafter he supplied a commentary: 'Long in the leg, sure to be a dog fox. He's in perfect nick, white tip on his brush, black on his ears, white on his breast. Man-o-man, he's a beaut. What a pelt, aye, wrapped around the neck of a girl by the name of Glenys. Bet you a pint he's heading for the same old bury.'

Miskin gulped snickering. 'Much too far away to send our dogs after him,' he said.

Beynon said, 'Four hundred yards.'

'More like five.' Staidly polite, Miskin accepted the glasses. 'What's he doing out and about in daylight, ah? There, you're right enough, Beynon, he's just gone to ground.' The dogs milled around Miskin's legs. He flipped neat backhanders. 'Quiet!'

Beynon put Ianto on a lead.

Miskin leashed the bedlington with a choker. 'Okay, let's bolt the bugger.'

The fox-hole angled down through raked stones. Lady whined, ceaseless shivers quivering her slingy body. They searched for another exit from the bury. Miskin looked worried. 'There's no place for him to bolt. This little bitch, she's onto a pasting.'

'Send Ianto in first,' Beynon said.

'He won't go far, too big around the chest. Fox'll chop his face to ribbons.' Miskin stroked the bedlington. 'Steady, gel, relax.' Reluctantly, muttering concern, he slipped Lady into the hole.

Ianto bayed like a hound. The brindle lurchers weaved to and fro on tiptoe, wetly black noses twitching, ears full-cocked from their sheepdog sire.

They heard the bedlington barking, a rapid burst followed by growling. 'Christ, she's in deep,' vowed Miskin. Kneeling, he poked his head into the hole. 'Shake him, gel! Meat off him!' He sat back on his heels. 'She's cornered him. It's a block end.'

'Put Ianto in,' said Beynon.

Ianto howled underground for fifteen minutes.

'Call him out, Beynon.'

'Right, he's this side of the bitch, can't get on, and he might make things worse for her.' Beynon shouted at the hole, 'Hee-yaar Ianto! Hee-yaar Ianto!' The terrier came scuttling out, one of his front paws bleeding and a flesh graze on his shoulder. 'Good dog, good dog,' Beynon said.

The November Sunday waned to lifeless evening. Miskin and Beynon shared cheese and ham sandwiches. Without animosity, they argued pros and cons. At dusk they left the Basin, Miskin cursing, effortlessly cursing the bedlington bitch.

'Take it easy, we'll dig her out,' promised Beynon. 'Hard graft, but we'll do it.'

'She's in deep, man.'

'I know, I know.'

'Listen, Beynon, tomorrow morning: mandrel, round nosed shovel, hatchet. We'll need a hatchet to make the place safe.'

Beynon said, 'I'll bring a crowbar and a bowsaw. Plenty of timber on top. Those bloody Christmas trees.'

Miskin nodded grunts.

Short-cutting on lower ground, returning to Nant Myrddin, they reached their home village as the first white frost of winter rimed roof slates.

'Half-seven, early start,' said Miskin.

'See you,' agreed Beynon.

They felled three sitka spruces, trimmed the six-inch boles and chuted them down grassed gullies to the fox bury. The lurchers pounced, jostling around the hole, kneed and clouted by Miskin. He listened at the cavity. Very faintly, the snarly growling of the bedlington. 'Beynon, she's in deeper than last night.'

Beynon said, 'Sounds like it.'

Miskin organised the work, his authority from five years at the coal face. Taking turns, they hacked and shovelled surface debris, starting a vertical dig above the trapped fox—Miskin's calculation. By late afternoon they were prising out big stones with the crowbar, from the jumbled bulk of the old rockfall. Interlocked layers of blue pennant sandstone governed the shape and size of their hole. When they were a yard down, a massive, inclined slabstone. Miskin stamped on it. He flung curses.

Mim, Fay and Ianto snoozed, curled on the trampled soil outside the fox bury.

'We'll be here tomorrow,' said Beynon.

'Maybe. Depends on that bastard gravestone.'

'Work around it,' Beynon said.

'No option, man!'

'Anyhow, she's still alright down there.'

'Sheer bloody guts.'

'We'll dig her out, Miskin.'

Evening came, chilling the sweat on their bodies. Their ragged hole was like a shell crater. Props and stayers held the slab of rock. As they trudged home in darkness, Beynon heard Miskin groaning misery. 'Take it easy, butty,' he said quietly.

By Tuesday night they were twelve feet down, hauling up rubble with a bucket and rope. Less often now, Lady's growling sounded hoarse. She responded instantly, feebly, when Miskin yelled at the mouth of the bury.

On Wednesday morning they felled four more sitka spruces. They fixed horizontal timbers across the dig, with props and heavy wedges at each end. Beynon relied on Miskin. He felt safe doing his stints down below, levering his weight on the five foot crowbar, heaving stones up on the cross timbers.

Mim, Fay and Ianto were thirty yards away, tucked on a wind-trapped mattress of dead molinia at the base of a buttress.

'Weather's changing,' Miskin said. 'Time for some grub. Catch hold.' Gripping wrists, he helped Beynon out of the hole.

Beynon hated failure. And he felt troubled for his mate. 'Miskin, what d'you say we sink a few pints in the Club tonight. Do us good, right?'

'Nuh.'

'We're much closer to the bitch. She's not far below us. Tomorrow she'll be ours.'

Miskin argued, 'Listen to me! If it rains the sides of this bloody crib are likely to start slipping!'

'So we shift the bastard muck again!'

Miskin thrust his hand into the fox-hole. 'Lay-dee! Lay-dee! Hee-yaar bitch!'

She barked for seconds, then silence.

Miskin chewed a sandwich, 'Weakness, Beynon, she's weakening.'

'But she's safe. We'll get her out.'

'Too bloody true,' said Miskin.

'That's settled then. Tonight we'll have a few pints.'

Hospital charity dance in the Social Club on Wednesday night. Beynon and Miskin sat in the snooker room. Very soon, as usual, they speculated about their runaway mothers.

Miskin: 'She never felt anything for me when I was a kid. As for my old man, he was on a loser from the start.'

Beynon: 'Before my old lady went off, she treated my sister and me as if we were nuisances in the house. What do they call it, maternal instinct? It's a load of bull.'

Miskin: 'D'you think all women are the same, I mean selfish?'

119

Beynon: 'Christ knows. They go their own way like cats.'

On and on, the same unforgiving rancour, the same helpless groping for motive, a reason to shed guilt, absolve themselves and their mothers.

Beynon said, 'My old man's a worrier, he's a clock-watcher taking tablets. Duodenal ulcer according to the quack. Knock it back, Miskin. My turn.' He crossed over to the serving hatch with their empties. Happening to glance above the hooded glare on a snooker table, he saw Miskin brooding, his powerful shoulders humped forward, chin pressed to his chest. Beynon thought, she's been four days without food and water. It'll break Miskin's heart if Lady dies underground in Dunraven Basin. He'll quit. Sell the dogs. No more weekend fox-hunting. By the Jesus, we'll have to dig her out tomorrow.

Miskin raised his full glass. 'Cheers. Before stop tap we'll manage a few more.'

Beynon watched the beer glugging steadily down Miskin's throat. 'Bloody sump you are, comrade.'

They were cheerfully drunk leaving the Club, moodily determined next morning, wading through sodden, crimping bracken. Drapes of mist scudded across towering Pen Arglwydd mountain.

'Showers forecast, dry this afternoon,' said Beynon.

Miskin hooted disgust. 'It'll tamp down all day over in the Basin.'

Beynon said, 'Sure to, butty.'

9 a.m. at the fox bury, Miskin ducking his head into the hole. Silence. 'Lay-dee! Lay-dee!' Far-off husky whining from the bedlington. Silence again. The lurchers and Ianto cringed away, sensing viciousness. Miskin raged despair.

'Hey man, take it easy,' warned Beynon.

Sheltering from the rain, the lurchers and the long-jawed terrier clumped themselves together on accumulated sheep droppings below a cavernous overhang at the foot of a buttress.

Using the head of his mandrel, Miskin tapped protruding boulders in the sides of the fifteen foot crater. 'Sounds okay so far. Nothing loose.'

Sweating inside oilskin coats and leggings, they continued hacking out stones, rubble and clay. Rising wind lulled the downpour to sheeting drizzle driving around the bowl of

Dunraven Basin. It was 1 o'clock. They fed the dogs and themselves. Miskin kept three faggot sandwiches in a canvas bag.

Beynon cooled a pint of tea in his big flask. He said, 'I'll dig for a spell,' clambering down on the cross-timbers. He listened, his eyes tightly shut. 'Lady! Hee-yaar bitch!' Then suddenly, he punched up his arms, shouting, 'She's below us! We're right on top of her!'

Miskin swung down like an ape. He elbowed him away. Beynon spread-eagled himself against the sides of the pit. Balanced on one knee, Miskin placed his ear close to the clay-slimed rubble. Low snoring, like someone sleeping in another room.

'Lay-dee!'

She yapped briefly. The snoring seemed to come in fading spasms.

'Careful, Miskin!'

'God dam, Beynon, shurrup! I know what I'm doing!'

'Alright, alright,' Beynon said.

The wet rubble concealed another tilted stone flat as a table. Scrabbling with his fingers, Miskin clawed down, searching for the edge of the stone. It was a foot thick, lodged in the sides, immovable.

Beynon climbed up across the cross timbers. Miskin filled the bucket, Beynon hauled the rope, flung the debris, lowered the bucket. They worked for less than an hour, until Miskin saw clay-water whirlpooling down a cranny below the underside of the big stone. Delicately, slowly, Miskin corkscrewed the crossbar at a shallow angle into the fissure. The water swilling away. Like jigsaw trickery, the bedlington's snuffling, mud-smeared nose appeared. Miskin's yell screamed to castrato. 'She's safe!'

'Thank Christ,' muttered Beynon.

'Those sandwiches!' cried Miskin.

The lurchers and the terriers came bounding down from the overhang. Ianto threw his echoing hound baying. Miskin clubbed when she sprawled into the pit, her hind legs flailing in sliding rubble. 'Get away! Out, gerrout!'

The brindle escaped, curvetting zig-zag leaps on the timbers.

But Lady was still trapped under a crack between two stones bedded like conrete lintels. Beynon squeezed the width of four fingers in the slot. He strained a grin at Miskin, 'Three inches, mate.'

Miskin spoke to the bedlington while dropping her pieces of faggot sandwich. 'Good bitch then, good bitch. You're in the way, Lady. I can't bash these stones if you stay there. Use some sense now, gel, back off a bit, back off the way you came in.' Frustrated after several minutes, he stood up, ranting, 'It's like talking to that bastard shovel!'

'Take it easy,' Beynon said.

'For fuck's sake you've been saying take-it-easy take-it-easy since last bloody Sunday!'

'Shh't, leave it,' Beynon said, head bowed, not looking at Miskin. 'You're blowing wind and piss, you're hysterical, like my old woman, like yours an' all.'

They laughed at each other.

Miskin slid his hand edgewise into the crack. He fingered Lady's head while Beynon wrenched on the crowbar, creeping the stones another inch apart. Exhaustion slumped Beynon on his backside. Miskin had pulled her out. She wriggled. She snorted ecstasy. Her floppy ears were scagged with cuts, tooth-holes through her upper lip, clotted blood on her feet, clay matted in her fur. Miskin mumbled, cradling the bedlington in his arms, 'You daft bloody thing you, bloody daft, daft . . .'

Beynon let the shakes drain from his limbs. 'She's stinking of fox,' he said, probing the cavity with the crowbar. 'Aye, he's in there. Lady killed him.' He picked shreds of fox fur off the chisel tip of the crowbar. 'Definitely, she finished him.' He slumped down again. 'I'm knackered.'

Miskin said, 'Thanks, butty.'

They climbed out. Lady lapped the lukewarm tea, then Miskin carried her all the way home, shovel, mandrel and hatchet roped across his back. Beynon carried the bowsaw, crowbar and bucket, a steady plod in cold drizzle, trailed by the brindle lurchers and the long-jawed terrier.

Spoils of Circumstance

Agnes blaring, 'Certainly I remember!'

'You laughed,' he said.

'Nothing's funny after all these years.'

'Twenty-seven.'

'I know!'

Doug said, 'Long time.'

'Typical.'

'What d'you mean?'

Jerking up two fingers, 'Blame yourself for a change.'

'Too much guilt between us,' he said.

'Much obliged, Doug.'

Strolling the same red ash lane, autumn tingling the late Sunday afternoon, but now FOR SALE posters, back to the land misfits advertising Cae-mawr Lodge. The gazebo a black tumbledown. Scrapped cars scattered daftly surreal on the brambled hayfield. Once, driven by libido and storm rain, they had fiddled a window latch, sneaked into the gazebo, slept wrapped together on the wooden floor, escaped from squealing rats during the night, Agnes weeping, scream-weeping.

He said, 'At seventeen you were rather hysterical.'

'What did you expect, dragon like your mother?'

'You wet yourself from laughing.'

Dolour anguished her eyes. 'The past is dead and gone.' They crossed the ruined hayfield, Agnes saying, 'Central heating before Christmas. I insist.'

'Gas.'

'Of course gas. Coal fires are ridiculous, filthy and expensive.'

Said Doug, 'Workmen were laying gas pipes under the path between Cae-mawr and Trefnant Infants' School.'

'Two thousand, four hundred and fifteen quid. Seven radiators, boiler, Royal gas fire, the one I showed you in the pamphlet. Ever so smart. Teak finish and chrome.' Licking her thumb Agnes pressed a tiny fluffed scag in her skirt.

Doug Prior stroked his nostrils. Her mindless stance stirred futile loss of maiden thighs.

'. . . nineteen, twenty! Ready or not I'm coming!' shouted a boy sloped over the rusted bonnet of a wheelless tractor.

Children crouched doggo in nooks.

Complained Agnes, 'Comfort in my home, that's what I want. Some mornings I feel dreadful.'

'Let's try the old footpath,' he said.

'It's fenced off.' She wheeled slowly from watching the children. 'Doug, you're a brazen fool.'

They rounded patchwork chickenwire fences. Two mongrels slavered in the next allotment, and white geese marched idiot stately outside the Lodge backyard.

'Where'd you reckon you're going?' She had the clenched face of desolate hobbledehoy. 'Private down to the river.' Her arms limbered outwards, returning a goose to the flock. 'No trespassing.'

Doug held out his palm. 'This path used to be a right of way.'

Agnes fluttered mealy-mouthed, 'Do you mind really?'

Bleak indifference from the townee girl. 'G'wan, bugger off.' She turned side-on, squalling, 'You bloody deaf?' and swayed slow-motion like a couturier's drudge back to the Lodge.

Righteousness moaned from Agnes.

'There,' he said, 'nice to be pure Trefnant Welsh.'

Resentment skewing her jaw, 'Don't you make fun of me.'

The wayward goose honked as if shocked, then foraged its yellow bill through clumps of sedge.

He thought, Aggie's trapped in her shell. Mollusc stranded in drought.

The ancient parish track vanished in marshland and bogged stands of alders.

'My shoes are leaking! I'll be down with bronchitis again!'

'Every winter,' said Doug.

'Nag nag nag. You, too pure to breathe you are. Bad conscience. Insomnia for God's sake.'

'It comes and goes,' he said.

'Worry! Doug the worrier!' Spindly as a desert nomad she bobbed heels-toes on a sunken boulder, incongruously vivid, frizzy grey hair and radiant false teeth, gloved hand cupped to her ear. 'I can hear Trefnant River.'

He remembered dropping into the man-deep gas pipe trench. Girl shrieks pealed encore inside his head. Instant havoc in November darkness. Aggie screeching glee. Then three weeks clumping a plaster cast on his right foot.

124

She's scowling witch-bitten insight. 'Ghost walking over your grave?'

Disgust freed his tongue. 'You laughed when I broke my ankle.'

She licked a cat-smile. 'Ye-es ye-es.'

'Blind fate. Like our marriage.'

'Ow, what a sha-ame.'

Doug thought, neurosis has no mercy.

A flat-roofed factory squatted on the site of the Infants' School. Seamless elephant grey and sheet glass. Behind the factory a one-time hazel dingle overflowing bricks, plaster, broken tiles, rotten battens from the demolished School. Gloaming softened rusting bracken blanketing uphill from the river bank.

At the footbridge a retired policeman still powerfully raw-boned, gimping under a roped bundle of willow sticks.

'How d'you do, Mrs Prior—Mr Prior.'

Agnes minced politeness. 'Hullo there, Mr Conybeare.'

'Mind your step, dangerous planks. Kids, that's all they do these days. I'd larrup the sods.' He propped the bundle upright, levered it along his other shoulder. 'These'll dry out for my runner beans next season.'

She dawdled, leaning over the handrail. Whirlpools spun behind stanchions. Two planks were half sawn and hacked at each end. Streaks and dents glinted on countersunk holding bolts. He wondered why. Vandalism, shorthand for judgment.

'Never kids,' vowed Agnes. 'Some madman.'

Again, 'Why?'

'Revenge twisting his mind. Lots of men carry grudges.'

He tempted bodyweight on one of the planks.

Says Agnes, 'Don't be silly.'

'Treacherous after dark. Reminds me of long ago.'

'Stop feeling sorry for yourself.'

'Mine isn't contagious,' he said.

Crossing over to street lights, 'We're marching to Zion' comes soaring innocently from the Salvation Army congregation, their dilapidated Citadel braced inside scaffolding, Agnes hugging herself, hurrying into Number 3 Nythfa Close. The Rayburn stove purred heat but she jigged the sliding bars, distracted, grumbling her spiel, 'Every decision always left to me. Always Agnes in this house. Furniture, carpets, wallpaper, shopping, back and fore, back and fore. Well, *now* I want central heating. Two thousand, four hundred and fifteen. We can afford it. Winter's coming. I've had enough misery. I'll make supper. Put the dishes to soak—Where you going?'

Doug said, 'Car battery needs charging ready for the morning.'

'If you had a garage my kitchen wouldn't be like a pigsty.'

'Good point,' he said. 'Convert the front room into a drive-in. No family, no problems.'

Crudely, 'Of course, your mother was a breeder,' and converted to wheedling, 'Garden shed then, Doug? Nice attractive garden shed?'

Miniature gazebo, he thought. Enhance our civilized lifestyle.

She's watching him top up the battery cells. Fancy-dressed children are rattling the knocker. Glittery-haired little fairy, little boy somewhat dago.

'Please help Mari Lwyd'—Mary Lloyd they kept saying, for 50p.

Eating cold pork pie and relish with her cup of tea, Agnes says, 'I'm aches and pains right throughout. Must have a hot bath. Ach, the stink in here. Poison acid. Open the window. Shut the kitchen door.'

Eight o'clock Monday morning. Glassy crinkles of ice on the windscreen. He fixed the battery in the car. Agnes is sleeping, kayoed by valium.

Dead battery when he left Trefnant Council Offices at five o'clock, and Chief Executive Edgar Sealey prowled sanguine with municipal clout.

'Trouble, Douglas?'

'Battery's flat,' he said. 'Won't hold a charge.'

'Phone the yard. Mention my name.'

A van driver brought jump leads. 'Okay, once she fires keep revving 'er. Listen, Mr Prior, I c'n let you have a batt'ry for seventeen quid. Brand new, twelve month guarantee. Int'rested?'

Doug trailed him for nine miles. His schoolboy son dumped Doug's battery on a heap of scrap. 'See, brilliant with 'is hands,' whispered the van-man. 'Kevin-lad, put this one in Mr Prior's car. Aye, righto, Mr Prior, cheque will do me very nice.'

Twenty past seven when he parked outside the house. Aggie's note tented over the electric kettle: *I'm in bed.*

Her breathless shout, 'That you, Doug?'

The sheets are up to her eyes.

He said, 'Bronchitis?'

Between gagged whimpers she wailed, 'Weakness, awful weakness! I'm burning!'

'Aggie, you've had these feelings before. We mustn't panic.'

'No strength left in my body.'

'Shh,' he said, 'you'll be all right. What have you eaten today?'

'Crackers, burnt they were, and a pizza . . .'

'From the freezer?'

'In the microwave.' She's convulsing little by little, hacking fever coughs under the sheets, until she dragged her bedclothes down below her chin. 'Some warm milk, please, Doug. Send for Doctor Singh in the morning.'

As usual he slept in the box room. Omar Singh arrived after surgery. He's scrupulous, cocked head snared in his stethoscope, rapid flicks dismissing, mystifying diagnoses. He rolled Agnes over, listened some more, straightened her again, thumbed back her upper eyelids, examined her fingernails, her throat, patted her hand and tucked her in.

Singh's small mouth unpruned itself. 'Bit of inflammation on the lungs, nothing for us to worry about.' Huffing friendliness, he leaned over Aggie. 'Only lie quiet, missis, rest in bed, must lie quiet.'

Doug inquired, 'Inflammation and what else?'

Past crises came willy-nilly: bronchitis. Arthritis. Conjunctivitis. Quinsy. Shingles twice. Peptic ulcer. And *specialists*. Aggie's first, second, final miscarriage. Begetting ended by surgery. Bale on Agnes and Doug, married at eighteen, wounded within ten years, careless at thirty, at forty enmity, remorseless, mutual.

Break free, he thought, as if the impulse manslaughtered consequences.

Instead, however, Wednesday morning on the phone, dictat from Edgar Sealey. 'Your immediate priority, Douglas, look after Mrs Prior.'

By the weekend he's merely drawn towards booze. Agnes is easier, mending with Singh's bumper course of antibiotics and a plastic tub of multiple tonic tablets. Enough to backbone Eve in the chauvinist fantasia.

Saturday evening she says, 'Bye-bye,' jabbing through

127

channels, their television transferred upstairs by a moon-lighting Council electrician.

Formal dancing after bingo in the Nonpolitical Club. It's 9.15 on the clock above the bar, a committee stalwart urging, 'For Jesus' sake, Doug, you'll be struck off the books, banned *sine die.*'

'Sorry, forgot,' he said.

'No excuse, man. Look, you want to be legless by stop tap? Slow down then, go steady.'

So he paid his dues, cordially interrupted by a Nythfa Close neighbour, blonde giantess Letty Greenaway. 'We heard Agnes is rather poorly.

'Right,' he said. 'Pleurisy.'

Letty's forty-ish, confident, quick beyond reach.

Nous up front, Letty's the nonpareil inveigler. 'You understand, Douglas, we don't like to interfere.'

Insurance broker Archie Greenaway pulls weight in Trefnant, a sporty wheeler-dealer possibly bowling in the alley down below pavement level, therefore, 'Archie playing skittles?' he said.

'He's in Brighton, actually, y'know, business conference. They lay it on regardless in Archie's racket. I came along with Moira, mm, better than staying indoors on a Saturday night.'

Doug looked for Moira Gwynne, regal old whist shark, survivor of three marriages. She's waltzing with another committee-man.

'Dance, Letty?'

'Why not, Duggie!' her smile healthy, bland as summer. Only his feet are out of synch.

'Careful, mister, we don't want to make an exhibition of ourselves.'

Courtesy surfaced. 'Say, Letty, how's everything these days?'

'Fine.'

'Good, good, *good.*'

'You?'

'Word of honour, as regards Agnes and myself,' he said, 'we sort of quit years, yeh, years ago.'

She tished priestess enigma.

Bending faith, hope and charity, he argued, 'Nobody's fault either.'

Letty blew a contralto, 'Well well!'

Now he's intrepid on putty knee-joints, 'Know what, Letty, come Pancake Day nineteen ninety-four I'll be forty-six. Not bad for a Trefnant pen pusher.'

Her grip clamped his wrist. 'Steady.' Standstill, eye to eye. 'You are loaded, my dear,' a controlled shove planting him on a chair against the wall. She drifted slantwise into the next chair.

Moira and the committee bloke are looming overhead. He's sarcastic. 'Look who's here. Doug Prior from our Environmental Services Department. Once upon a time your old granny used to bleed Christmas cockerels in the gutter below Sidings Terrace.'

'Quiet, you!' The toecap of Letty's shoe skidded off the committee-man's ankle. Doug felt joyful in secret. 'Douglas has come to the Nonpol to relax from personal trouble. Yes, Mrs Prior, she's very ill.'

'Poor dab,' soothed Moira.

Another Victor Sylvester tape plink-plonking through the hall.

'Dance, Letty?' he repeated.

'I'm taking you home.'

'Early yet.'

She swanned her wristwatch under his noise—Moira and her partner are gliding like skaters.

'Meet me outside the lobby in five minutes.'

He thought, Archie's maroon Jag.

Then, 'Wait here,' behind Number 11, the only walled garth in Nythfa Close. The Jag droned like machined eternity. He felt lucky-charmed until doomcrack on three pints and two whiskies. Letty floated through the headlights. Doug saw the gaping cave of Archie Greenaway's garage. She slewed in at a creep, switched off eternity and they are parading on spongy lawn. He's plotting words for his mouth, left unsaid by fearless void.

'Grill for supper,' she says.

A front space in his mind requested, 'What about Archie?'

Letty flung hauteur like a grace and favour madame, ball and chain earrings bobbling each side of scornful, greeny eyes. 'I shan't see the *mochyn* for four days, Tuesday night as a matter of fact.'

'Oh.'

'I've lost respect for him.'

'Me too,' he said, 'for Agnes.'

'Mm, common knowledge in Nythfa Close,' agreed Letty. 'Awful strange, isn't it? I mean marriage, the transaction of marriage. We make mistakes, terribly important things that leave us miserable afterwards.'

Parroting familiar hurt, he said, 'Worse, desperate.'

Letty glowed charm, 'Now, Duggie, feel free. Bathroom through there, second door.'

Elsewhere in the house two clocks chimed plangent 10 p.m. discord. Large poster Blue-Tacked to the bathroom door: Trefnant Amateur Dramatic Society presenting *West Side Story* in the Freemasons' Hall. Next, his scalp seethed fiery from hitting the lavatory cistern. In the wall cabinet split mirrors it's alien civil servant D.M. (Moelfryn) Prior nodding, nodding, but he can't liven his face.

Letty's humming a no-tune deciphered to 'I Did It My Way' while gammon rashers, eggs, sliced tomatoes and mushrooms are sizzling. The unWelsh bloom and Juno hugeness of her amazed his damped-down machismo. Slow but sure he's stretching a new skin.

Arm hooked around his shoulders, 'You look like an orphan,' she said.

'New experience this.'

'You mustn't fret, *cariad*.'

From nodding to negative, 'I don't think I am.'

Letty's arm tightened vast as destiny. 'Our lives are our own.'

Braving too hard brought on stammering. 'Under the circumstances I . . . I . . . it's natural, natural to feel awkward. Sort of. Furthermore, um . . . thanks, thanks for inviting me to supper.'

'Heavens above,' gurgled Letty.

Fuddle and the big grill laid him out warm in Archie Greenaway's kingsize bed. They are safe in rapport, time out of mind, all the rest of the world extinct—being Doug's alternative to bragging romantic jackalese, hindsight blurbing agape.

Letty's forty-one. Doug Prior forty-five.

'Lovely,' the last he heard until, 'Papers!' echoed from the letterbox.

She opened the window curtains. 'Coming! Hang about!'
Melodious, decided Doug, like Tarzan's mate.

This Sabbath mid-morning full of yesterdays and
unknowable tomorrows, blue-gowned Letty deftly lobbing the
Observer onto a sideboard. She plugged in filter coffee and
Radio Wales, some banal dumbo promoting twangy old
Hoagy Carmichael's 'Stardust', Letty pitching her deep
contralto in his ear—swanky hugger-mugger performance
slow foxtrotting to 'Stardust' in Archie's double-glazed
kitchen-cum-conservatory clogged with fuchsias and Busy
Lizzies.

'Coffee's ready,' says Letty, her grin waxing gamine. 'Ring
Agnes, spin her a tale, use your imagination. In for a sheep as
for a lamb, that's my opinion.'

He said, 'No alternative.'

Came Letty's edict. 'There's no love lost. When Archie picks
up some girl he's always doing business or playing cards with
his mates. Takes a slag to make Archie think he's a stallion.'

He envisaged nine front doors away, Aggie huddled close to
the Rayburn, dunking chocolate digestives.

Her voice grated venom. 'Shows how much you consider
me when you're out enjoying yourself. Stupid from drink
while I can hardly lift my head off the pillow. Three times I
phoned the Nonpolitical Club. Nobody knew where you were!
Drunk, they said, Dee ahrr yew en kay!'

Aggro for aggro, 'God damn, I went for a walk, didn't want
to disturb you.'

'All night long! Where are you, Doug?'

Deliberately, 'Damn it, I *was* drunk. Spent the night in a
railway carriage behind Trefnant station. Almost perished! So
what!'

Outraged, she's choking on tea and mush.

'See you soon, Aggie.'

'Selfish.'

'Shan't be long. Calm down, Aggie,' he said.

Letty's spying over her coffee cup. 'Tell me, why are you
afraid of Agnes?'

'Afraid for her. She's helpless.'

'You feel responsible?'

'Aggie's incurable. She's suffering. All told it's a cruel story.'

'Pity her if you must. She won't forgive you.' Letty stretched,

131

writhed her shoulders, supple, witfully feline. 'Shall I see you again, Duggie?'

Temptation's anthem in his old-fashioned heart of hearts. Free love. Free love means Aggie and Archie must share the same ignorance.

Letty's reaching hand ruffling his nape hairs. 'Unless you'd prefer to go somewhere away from Trefnant?'

The power and corn goddess glory of her—anxiety buggering the NALGO card carrier, so, 'We'll have to be careful,' he said.

Solemn as troth from nuzzling necks Letty suggested, 'Our cottage in Carmarthen. Next Saturday. Stay the night.'

Confusion freaking reality, Doug's shouting, 'Where, girl, where?'

Hooting delight, 'Big girl too! Never mind, Duggie-love, let me show you on the map.'

Brochure with the map. It's fifty-odd miles away in hinterland Carmarthen. Archic Greenaway's picture-postcard retreat: *Tŷ-bwllfa*. Beautiful scenery etc.

Tŷ-bwllfa kept buzzing his braincells like static. Muffled to her cleavage, he said, 'Meet you there next Saturday evening, near enough seven o'clock.' Promise flawed by years of funk, proven after skulking roundabout to Number 3.

Agnes comes scarecrowing downstairs, unkempt, woollen bedsocks waggling on her feet. She collapsed on the couch, singsong lamenting, 'Ow-what-a-rotten-waster.' Doug laid a blanket over her. Her palping lips slackened in mysterious-as-always sleep.

Relentless aftermath under his paid-for roof in Nythfa Close. Night-time came. Agnes sighed, shivered herself awake. She's feebly spooning chicken soup. Aggie's bereft, worn down without hope.

As before.

Spent-out.

After she went to bed he stared at blackness in the box room, minor Trefnant bureaucrat stormed in limbo, ideas moiling, the daunting amok of circumstance, of failure.

Max Thomas

He wore the firm's duffle coat like a high-class doxy. Gambler Max, with his spread-lipped-talker's mouth, his glinty, far apart eyes, his mastery of building trades jargon. Max Thomas had wit, style, the leggy, chesty swagger of immunity. Green slouch hat raked like a bandit, he dominated Nebo site—our foreman carpenter who couldn't handsaw down a chalk-line in hardboard. Useless on the tools, Max relished authority. The G.F., the foreman brickie and the navvy ganger were his puppets, ruled by equally subtle and brazen intrigue. Max had nerve, he made mistakes, converted them into profit. He was an educated liar, a diplomat neutralising umbrage. He drilled full blame for the big deck shambles right into the agent's heart. Pig of a man, this agent, pig on two legs. We called him Amos Pig. Snort and rut and grub were stamped on him. Boar's neck, the swollen body of a Large White baconer, the hidden, glaring eyes of a wart-hog, the splayed gait and wobbling dewlap of a sow in farrow, Mr Amos was swinish all over.

The Nebo contract meant two hundred council houses and a concrete footbridge over a railway. Clean site, most of the houses occupied. Chippies, brickies, plasterers, painters, labourers, they knew every fiddle in the bonus system. Sensibly, on bonus, you make just so much, not too much or the targets get slashed. From digging footings to glossing sashes to ultimate redundancies, the bonus targets on every site are slashed. What I'm saying is, you can't dodge Time and Motion, those matricidal and patricidal gits spawned by Progress, twins inherited from days gone by, days far worse. Ask any old grafter in the building trades. Long, long before *The Ragged Trousered Philanthropists*, the all-weather hordes who built palaces, towers, aqueducts, portals, esplanades, highways, cathedrals to the glory of bedlam Jehovahs, and castles to the virtue of maggot bait. On no account risk, trust bland smilers, explainers like Dr Bronowski and Sir Kenneth Clarke. They extol round ends from duff means, principia circus, older than crucifixions. And as regards Government Training Centres for craftsmen, they're the dirtiest corruption since William Morris played dipsy-do, prettying the stand-still crap of guild ethics.

People, coming and going, they wipe the sweat off with blueprints of civilisation.

Nebo site, gimcrack council houses plus the footbridge to Nebo village, where steelworkers' families lived in cramped terraces designed by Queen Victoria's heroes of laissez-faire. But how did Max join the A.S.W? Who proposed, who seconded him for his Class 2 union card? Nobody knows. Obviously we admired Max. If Glamorgan was evacuated, given over to rearing reindeer, with a tiny complement of Lap herders, Max would keep his hands clean tallying births, fodder, bounties, social services, entertainments. A man with a grin instead of a grouse is *safe*. Of course we appreciated Max. He elevated humdrum folk, he made us feel important.

I worked mates with Elvet Evans. We pitched out-house roofs and handled not very much first fixing, because Elvet lived a few doors away from Max. It was a formal finagle. Max booked in the hours; we split the bonus five ways, Max collecting his fifth every Friday night in the Cymric Club. A nice steady system, foolproof all the way to the up and over footbridge, when Max—*no,*—Max, Amos Pig, Elvet and myself, we were mutually responsible for the deck collapsing. Responsible in principle, except principle in industry is hard to nail down, and harder to define with Sermon-on-the-Mount sincerity. From napkins to old age pensions, good citizens survive on snippets of truth.

There were flights of concrete steps (utopian planning: mothers with prams walked a mile to level crossing gates) climbing up to paired stanchions on each side of the railway track. Bolted to, linking the stanchions were eighteen inch RSJs.—rolled steel joists. The flat deck measured thirty-three feet long, by nine feet between the webs of the RSJs. We laid the deck in three bays, stop-ending with twelve inch boards, ply, greased, slotted to stand over the reinforcement mats. The ply would strip away easily from green concrete, leaving neat grooves for finally tying-in, making good on expansion joints —unavoidable, this lowly technical stuff.

Okay then. We were fixing pans, decking out the first bay, when the agent ordered Max to cut down on timber for the whalings. He also recommended six by one inch bearers across the top of the Acrows. Crazy man-pig, that Mr Amos. Ordinary shuttering timber as bearers!

We argued with Max. Dour Elvet, he seldom argued, but now he insisted, 'This goes against the grain so far as I'm concerned, 'cause it won't be safe. Too dangerous unless they pour the bays separately. By separate I mean giving the end bays a week to harden off. Pour the middle bay last of all.

His unsoiled palm spread like a blessing on Elvet's chest, Max said, 'Look, this is only a piddling little job, therefore, taking everything into consideration, let's do what the Pig wants for peace and quiet.'

'It won't be safe,' warned Elvet, who had the reverse vision peculiar to flawless concrete shuttering. 'The whole deck'll be hanging on skew-nails, and them six by one bearers'll either go bust or sag like a clothes-line.'

'Hush-up, man, listen,' coaxed Max. 'You're talking like Frankenstein fed on bread-and-dripping. It'll be safer than my wife, and she's been knotted three years come next Mari Lwyd night.' We sniggered, Max saying, 'After this first bay, lay the other two according to the Pig's idea. Agreed?'

More arguing. I said, 'There's a mile of work in this bay yet.'

'We're humping these pans about like Chinese coolies,' said Elvet.

'Enough!' vowed Max, grinning like a dago. 'The pair of you, you leave me with a nastier taste in my mouth than Shoni-Bad-News.'

Shoni was our A.S.W. card steward on Nebo, a short-bummed jabberer, trade union spokesman as manufactured by free collective bargaining. Max paddied Shoni to a nicety. They were friendly enemies.

Next morning we started on the second bay. Steel-fixers followed tight behind us with reinforcement mats. The whole job was scrambled beyond reason. Common-sense fell apart. Amos Pig came over from the site office, time after time he climbed the steps, gushed miniature-cigar smoke, threw dollops of phlegm and waddled back to the office. He should have been there, underneath, when they poured the bays a week later.

Scaffolders erected a ramp from the big mixer to the top of the steps. A long, gradual ramp, Amos Pig's pinch-penny ploy, muscle power instead of hiring a hoist. It was raining when they started the pour, constitutional rain, the fine drizzle you learn to live with below and at the heads of all the valleys. One foot on the ramp's safety rail, elbow on his knee, Max hustled the labourers pushing bogies of wet concrete. Jovial Max, clever—himself incapable of knocking up a rabbit hutch.

'Pike it in, my lads! Good man, Ossie, we'll have this first bay finished before tea-break. We'll finish the whole bloody deck by grub-time!' Super-manly Max, encouraging the labourers, a liar of integrity, promising, 'It'll be cushy for the lads this afternoon. You can bank on my word!'

'It better be,' said big Ossie. 'I'm not rushin' like a daft bott for bugger all.' He and his mate up-ended the double-handed bogie, sloshing concrete around the punner's rubber boots. Joey Snell did most of the punning on Nebo site. A fastidious young bloke, Max elected him for tricky jobs. Joey had the patience of Jonah and the daunting, fumbling diction of pedigree breeding. He was very careful, a supreme potcher, worth his weight on any site.

The concreting sped along, Max in his element, watching steel reinforcement mats and oiled pans disappearing under the thick grey flow. Joey and Ossie tamped the first bay (first *poured*, actually the farthest) level, leaving it glistening smooth to harden off. The drizzle continued, cloud sweat guaranteed for days here in ancient Gwalia.

They started pouring the middle bay after tea-break. Max covered his round of the site, then he came back to the ramp. Every kind of site foreman is fascinated by a biggish concrete pour. Aesthetic taste perhaps, or maybe, more likely, the plain three-dimensional lust of emancipated troglodytes. Something foetal on the prowl. Amos Pig and the G.F. visited a few times. Max stayed, morally in charge, anchored, foot resting on the safety rail, cajoling, cracking the cunning whip over the navvy ganger and his men. The bogies were tipped up, hauled back over the mats, turned about, trailed at arm's length down-hill to the concrete mixer.

The middle bay looked ready for tamping off. Joey asked for one more bogie load. He punned scrupulously with his sharpened piece of batten (we weren't building the Severn Bridge, for God's sake), running cement fat down the shutters and around the RSJs, to set creamy smooth on the soffits. He slightly raised, shook the mats over-lapping into the third bay, allowing rich fat to ooze through, under the stop-end board. Ossie and his mate pushed their bogie forward, tipped the handle, and Joey yipped his tenor, 'There, that's plenty-plenty for this one! No more now, no more!' Some day Joey Snell intended being in charge himself. He'd squeeze the pips from conscience, you could tell from his attitude. Proven fact, Joey's commitment to excellence, leading to lance-jack prestige, the few pence an hour extra.

Ossie and his mate returned, passing Max at the top of the ramp. Max said, 'Woa, Ossie. Give Joey a hand on the tamper.'

'By the Jesus,' grumbled Ossie, 's'always me.'

Joey was alone, reaching for his end of the tamper (a scaffold board rigged with handles) when the entire deck fell through. Joey swooshed down, out of sight in wet concrete. Tearing timbers squealed, pans clanged, reinforcement mats flopped, fell away, melted into the grey slurry like a commando's nightmare.

'Get on the phone!' yelled Max. 'Ambulance! This looks like a hospital case!'

Ossie's mate set off full gallop to the level crossing signal box. Big Ossie, he hung spread-eagled, a gorilla dressed in yellow oilskins on the inter-locked reinforcement mats. We leaned over the edge of the ramp, Max screaming, 'Climb, man, climb!'

Ossie climbed. We had him safe, twitching, shocked but safe.

First glance and you'd swear Joey had vanished. Just a great splodge of wet concrete, pans, splintered boards, fully extended Acrows flung all shapes, long grey streamers dripping off the hanging mats. Out of this mess, Joey slowly emerged. Stretched flat on his back, he sat up, staggered upright, lumpy grey from head to feet, and he sat down again. Max *laughed*. Nothing like a person, young Joey Snell, merely a creature, mindless, senseless. And Max laughed—we heard him.

'Send for Amos Pig and the general foreman,' Elvet said. He nudged Max. 'Straight away.'

'Later. Keep your mouths shut. I'll do the chopsing to Amos Pig.' Shouting, waving his arms, Max had twenty men down on the railway track before he moved from the end of the ramp. He performed. It was impressive. Luck saved Joey. He fell through a fraction behind the mass of concrete, slapped into it hard on his backside. Dazed, unhurt, a charmed youngster, Joey was drunk from shock and bruises. Max organised. He knew every man by his Christian name. Four stalwarts carried Joey into a council house. They bathed him. Meanwhile Max directed the navvy ganger to beg clothes for Joey from the council house tenants. Then he sent for the agent.

Amos Pig came down the track, our G.F. dithering at his heels.

'Mister Amos!' yelled Max. 'Mister Amos!' The gang stood around, dumbly supporting Max, his bawling righteousness. Inquisitor on the rampage, Max blazed conviction like a tin chapel Baptist preacher. 'I hope you're satisfied Mister Amos! This accident almost cost Joey Snell his life! Look at the span, I'm asking you, Mister Amos, look at that span!'

Amos Pig dipped the sole of his right shoe in concrete slurry. He shuffled, head bent as if pondering some cosmic formula.

'We can't afford to skimp on this kind of work!' cried Max. 'Mister Amos, you can't ignore proper specifications as laid down by civil engineering!' He caught the agent's arm, urgent, appealing, dragging him to the house where they were soaping concrete off Joey's body. 'See for yourself, Mister Amos, see the result of sheer negligence . . . this man's life at stake.'

The G.F. sidled after them like a brow-beaten puppy.

Elvet said, 'He's got 'em where he wants 'em.'

We began salvaging timber from the wreckage. Joey went off in an ambulance. British Railways sent out a crew, low-paid humbles in their carnival safety jackets. Nebo labourers were barrowing concrete off the track, dumping it in a brook— ecology means much the same to a navvy ganger as to any Crown minister, until some informed party stirs the brain cells. The Nebo crowd were cursing Amos Pig. We listened, stepping forward now and again for lengths of timber as they shovelled into the heap.

'That Joey Snell,' said Elvet, 'he might suffer after effects in years to come.'

'It was the first bay pulled down the other two,' I said.

'If you say so.'

'We warned Max.'

Elvet skidded another broken board onto the pile. 'Mucked up job from start to finish. Tell you why. Seven by two bearers on the first bay, right?'

'Right,' I said.

'Who shoved up the Acrows?'

'We did.'

'Aye, without making allowances for the six by one bearers under those other two bays.'

'By Christ,' I said.

Elvet spat disgust. 'Correct. The point is, Max takes care of Max Thomas. You and me, we look out for ourselves.'

Fear and guilt marry deep in the gut as sure as compassion moves the bowels. Again I said, 'It was the middle bay dragged down the other two.'

'Without doubt. But listen, Amos Pig and Max, they decided to pour the whole deck in one go. Their mistake. Somehow though, we gained a bloody inch over a distance of twenty-two feet.'

God Almighty in heaven, I thought, favour all foremen in the building trades. You need the soul of a crocodile, the steam engine blind-sight of a rhino, the guile of Louis XI, the turntable wisdom of Solomon. You need to be like Max Thomas.

Nice Clean Place

'Spare us a Woodbine, kid?'

The kitchen-boy cum porter wheeled in his Sunday best 6/11 brogues. 'Don't smoke.'

Brief death-rattle disdain from the crease-jowled, blue-uniformed Great War prisoner, two compatriot derelicts slumped alongside on the bench, inert as babes in the summer warmth.

He felt becalmed, 'Sorry, mister,' thinking, there's a state to be in, supposed to be heroes.

Below Chepstow bridge the bile green river rolling, coiling ceaseless. He squirted spittle over the parapet. Then alertly confident Clayton studied the café window notice: Egg, sausage and chips, pie and chips, fish and chips, so 'Fish and chips, please,' he said, 'with a cream bun and a cup of tea.'

The slattern waitress scratched her nape with a red pencil. 'Cup three-ha'pence, mug tuppence.'

'Mug for me, please.'

As another Great War prisoner hecked on his stick to the counter. 'How bist thee, m'dear?'

'Bad back all morning, Percy-love,' said the woman, miming lumbago. She served him Franklyn's tobacco.

Clay watched the pavement, met Jonas's glittery dark eyes above the longhand menu, dogsbody gardener/handyman Jonas mouthing, 'Pictures?'

He nodded, 'Right.'

'Second house, meet you outside.'

Clay saluted, 'Righto.'

They were midway sons of seven children, two large families from Glamorgan valleys separated by mountains, pulled to the same Wye-side hotel by *South Wales Echo* adverts. Sharing a vernacular too, these raw-boned teenagers, flat bellied and gauche. Round faced, tawny-haired Clay Cullen and Jonas Reed with a fleet left-corner mouth tic. Clay and Jonas, suckled during the '21 strike.

Seven o'clock when they queued past the ticket booth, swing doors thudding whump behind them, torch-beam at their feet. 'This way—this way,' from the usherette. *S.O.S. Coastguard*, mad inventor film with Bella Lugosi, trademark malice smiling his sinister face.

But they relished the film as America by rote.

Murmurously singing 'Carolina Moon' sotto voce on the last bus to Tintern, where Clay and Jonas strolled around Beechgrove Hotel to a small shiplap bungalow with two truckle-beds, criss-crossed bamboo-legged table, hand basin under a cold water tap, and clothes hooks each side of a 3' x 2' window. No heat, no light but one candle, the youths gossiping about guests, toff anglers with chauffeurs and wives who looked like catalogue women. Chatting in darkness until, 'G'night, Jonas.'

'G'night Clay-boy.'

During the night Jonas Reed disappeared.

'Such people are uncivilised,' accused Mr Rampard, owner of Beechgrove, rotundly middle-aged with glossy, brilliantined hair.

Said Clay, 'We were in Chepstow last night, no word from him at all. He pinched my other pair of socks.'

Mr Rampard tished disgust, the back of his hand waving dismissal, 'Go about your duties.'

Mrs Fuller vibrated judgment, 'Birds a' feather stick together,' her outflung pudgy pink fingers up-ending Clay's teacup. Thereafter she read his mid-morning tea leaves.

'What shows here for certain, this crop of luck.' She chuckled gargoylean amnesty. 'Lucky young tyke. Wonderful good fortune. Bounty out of the blue. You got a second name?'

'Myrddin.'

The cook hooted dowager scorn, 'No matter!'

'I could do with some luck,' he said.

Warned powerful Mrs Fuller, 'Be grateful! God's will be done! Move boy, out of my kitchen!'

Frilled lace at her cleavage and cuffs, the refinedly glamorous forty-four year old spinster receptionist beckoned, 'Here, Clayton, Mr Rampard wants to speak to you in his office.'

'I went to him first thing as 'gards Jonas Reed.'

'You'd better hurry.'

'Aye okay.'

'Straight away, Miss Minty.'

He saw the river gillie's woolly grey head outside the Hotel entrance. Distant below tree-top foliage, Tintern Abbey sunglazed, lifeless, and mysterious beyond Clay's nous, Mr Rampard behind his desk.'

'Were you in the lounge yesterday?'

'Once before lunch. My half-day starts 2 o'clock.'

'Before lunch eh?'—Mr Rampard utterly sphinx.

'I fetched *The Times* from reception.'

'Really?'

'For Colonel Hargreaves.'

'Where was Colonel Hargreaves sitting?'

'No, standing over by the window.'

'Smoking?'

Clay grinned friendlily, 'I smelt cigars.'

Mr Rampard interlocked his fingers across his paunch, raised them above his head without touching his hair and brought side-by-side fists drumming bomp-bomp on his desk. 'I am referring to a large packet of Gold Flake cigarettes beside the wireless cabinet.'

'Don't know what you mean, Mr Rampard.'

'Are you a thief, Clayton?'

'Never, on my mother's life!'

Mr Rampard huffed dolour. 'Do you have any money?'

He counted 7/2 from his trouser pocket. 'Recent I been trying to save a bit.'

Mr Rampard carefully chinked sixpence on Clay's retreating palm. 'Go home. Pack your bag and see Miss Minty.' Eyeing his Ingersoll watch, 'You will be paid up to mid-day.'

'I didn't take those fags from the lounge! Jonas Reed, the dirty waster, he's the one. Must 'ave sneaked in through the cellar.'

'Leave these premises, find another occupation,' ordered Mr Rampard. 'Mrs Fuller will prepare some sandwiches.'

The gillie overheard his muttered, 'Shit on it! Shit, shit, shit!' as he scuffed a gravel footpath around to the bungalow. 'Hoi there, watch your language.'

'Not you, man,' said Clay. 'I've just copped the sack for bugger all.'

'Well, boy, they comes and goes.'

'Somebody pinched fags from the lounge.'

'He won't wear that in Beechgrove,' vowed the gillie.

'I never set eyes on those fags. True what I'm telling you. Any road, so-long.'

The gillie flapped his pepper-and-salt checked cap against his thigh, 'Look out for yourself, Taffy.'

Twenty-five minutes later in the kitchen, 'Shameful, quite

shameful,' the cook pleading unfelt remorse, handing him two brown paper wrapped parcels, 'Some special salmon kedgeree on Hovis in there; sponge cakes with Royal icing in there. O Clayton, great good fortune before my eyes, as God's my judge.'

'Thanks,' he said, then, 'Awful mouthy you are, and you're a liar. So-long now.'

Aghast as pantomime the cook hugged herself on faint screams.

To Miss Minty he repeated, 'Thanks,' pocketed the £1.4.6d. 'Mr Rampard, he's making a big mistake. Jonas Reed was too fast off the mark for him. Myself, I wouldn't steal a penny off nobody.'

Miss Minty slitted her eyes and mouth and dry-wiped the tip of her nose, watching him lugging his belt-lashed, flaking cardboard suitcase down the drive. He sat on the suitcase in the wide, grass tufted forecourt of Tintern Abbey. Obedient sightseers trailed to and fro. Feeling rancour more so than defeat, he ate two of Mrs Fuller's Royal iced cakes. Two left for the kids, his little brother and toddler sister. He opened a sandwich, dibbled his tongue on the alien filling: salmon kedgeree—for the old lady and the old man. Gone to a scarecrow, Rupe Cullen. More meat on a two-yard rail.

Came the bare legs of two girls wheeling bikes, English the slangy way they talked: 'Beautiful, ever so beautiful,' and 'I say, Deborah, my Sturmey-Archer's marvellous,' and 'Snapshots over there under the arch.'

He thought, hope I bump into Jonas some day. I'll bust his teeth out. Rotten swine of a bloke.

When, 'Hoi Taffy,' said the river gillie, 'Mr Rampard's been talking on the phone. They picked up Jonas Reed in Mountain Ash, his auntie's house. Mr Rampard says for you to come back up to Beechgrove.'

'Half a mo' . . .'

'Genuine, fella, you're restated . . . re-*in*-stated. Extra two bob a week on your pay.'

Clay swung his basin chin, he finger-scrubbed across his chest, clearly speaking his mint conviction, 'Just decided, I've had a gutsful. Don't fancy being a bloody lackey for Mrs Fuller and Miss Minty. Mr Rampard neither, come to that. Next week I'll be eighteen. I'm joining the Army.'

The gillie up-tilted his cap, light pale grey ringlets escaping under its peak like a smothered nimbus. 'I served seven years on deck in the Navy. Take a tip now, once you're wearing khaki the Army's your mother and father. What I'm suggesting, make the best of it.'

'Ta,' he said, hefting the battered suitcase. 'Nice place this Tintern. Nice and clean. Up there in Beechgrove Hotel though, they're a bunch of scrapers, proper ass'ole scrapers.'

'Got trainfare?'

'Enough,' he said. 'So-long, all the best.'

The gillie tugged down his cap. 'Mind how you go, son.'

Clarion Boys

Rick Taylor borrowed the cheapjack 6' x 4' tent reeking of linseed oil. No groundsheet. Cycling capes and Army blankets sufficed because Rick and Lew Cullen are hard enough teenage fetch-and-carry workers in Moel Exchange brewery. They train and turn about, biking roads in the three Glamorgans. Lew's dream is foolishly arrogant. He'll wear a Tour de France yellow jersey.

They pitched on a campside alongside the river Wye.

'Spuds, corned beef, bread, butter, milk, tea and sugar,' decided Lew. 'Unless you fancy luxuries.'

'Such as?'

'Cakes, bloody delicacies. We're only here overnight.'

'I like cooked dinners,' says Rick. 'Pudding and custard for afters. Anyhow, I prefer coffee.'

Shopping in the ancient spa town, flatfooted Lew goes thwap-thwap in heel-less cycling racing shoes.

The corner-shop grocer married his eyes, 'You chaps from the camp?'

'We're in the 25-mile event tomorrow morning,' said Lew. 'I'll have a pound of corned beef, please.'

Rick's forefinger signalled the shop assistant. Middle-weight brunette, her mouth inquiring 'Yes?'

'One of those (cartoned sponge cake), three pounds of new potatoes, smallest jar of coffee, two pints of milk—Lew, cheese?'

'Caerphilly or Cheddar?' said the girl.

Rick cheerfully fisted his left palm. 'What you reckon?'

'Mature Cheddar. Eight ounces?'

'Suit us,' said Lew.

She had heavy upper arms, dimpled elbows, long fingers on the toggle slicing the wire through lump cheddar.

'Just over, do you mind?' she said.

Rick grinned, 'Expert you are, girl.'

Lew called, 'Ask her about glucose.'

Her head rolled rightwards, 'Up the street, Davy Daniels the chemist.'

'Glucose for our bidons,' Lew explained to the grocer.

Who sterned his mouth, 'Bidons?'

'You know, man, alloy water bottles.'

The grocer smirked, 'Anything else?'

Rick and Lew shared expenses to a penny.

'I'm the clinking and clanking rider,' peeved Lew, lobbing out cutlery, saucepan, miniature kettle, enamel plates and mugs from his saddlebag. 'Right, all right, *you* carried the tent and blankets.'

Lew scraped potatoes while Rick hunted for firewood. Early evening when they fed, faultlessly halving corned beef, potatoes rolled in butter and the sponge cake. Lew hunkered over syrupy tea, Rick likewise over sweet coffee. As Lew began a bragging spiel about Sunday's time trial, Rick elbowed him, 'Husht a minute.'

A Landrover crawling off the road: 'Your attention please!' The driver tap-tapped the mike. 'We have an announcement from Paragon Wheelers. Terrible tragedy, my friends. Very tragic. Two of our members were killed in a car crash. Couple of hours ago now. Yes, two excellent prospects for the future. Edwin Bailey and Ivor Marsh. Both killed. Therefore, friends, as a mark of respect we are cancelling tomorrow's event. Thank you one and all.'

The disappearing Landrover left aghast babble on the campsite.

Lew repeated, 'God Almighty, God Almighty.'

Rick nodding, 'Aye, Edwin and Ivor, strong as lions.'

Lew stuttered tenor whines high in his nose. 'Faster than me last season! Who'd have thought!' Distraught for seconds, 'Listen,' he said, 'Paragon Wheelers, they're *organised*.' Crossed wrists pressed to his chest, 'Not like our bullshit Moel Exchange Clarion.'

Rick withdrew unburnt sticks from his Boy Scout fire. 'Suggestion,' he offered. 'Being as the race is off, let's meander, sup a couple of pints.'

Lew waggled his slack thigh triceps in both hands.

'I'm with you, c'mon.'

Back on the old town pavements, 'In here'll do,' says Rick, carefully shouldering towards the Blue Moon public bar. 'Two pints of draught Guinness, missis.'

Veering away from the jocund, palavering Saturday-nighters, after stop tap they ate fish and chips on a bench outside the 16th century churchyard. Familiarity sanctioned cross-talk, Rick saying, 'Awful cruel about Edwin and Ivor,' to

146

Lew's 'Nice bit of cod that,' and 'Last season I was pipped by eight seconds for third fastest in the 50 over Waun-glas Flats.'
'By Edwin and Ivor?'
'Nah, Billy Purvis. You wasn't even on the card. You busted your thumb in work.'
'Don't remind me,' said Rick. 'Through to the bone.'
They sprawled contented.
Lew kindled his dream, 'I was feeling on form an' all.'
'When?'
Miming stooped over handlebars, 'For tomorrow morning.'
Lew winced regret, 'By the Christ.'
Rick said, 'No matter. Let's stroll.'
A kissing gate lowly groaned as they sidled into the burial ground. Night of wan glimmers under enormous yew trees. Lush mossy spongy underfoot.
'Witching hour,' murmured Rick.
They walked on, full-bellied, beery-confident. Suddenly careless and gritty, Rick snarled, 'Wake up! Wake, you bastards!'
Came alien silence, Lew appealing, 'For God's sake, boy.'
Rick doubled-up over sniggering. 'They're not bothered,' he said.
Lew argued, 'Know what, you're a pure savage.'
'Sure, sometimes,' conceded Rick.
They slept dreamless in the mottle-stained bijou tent until the harmless stun of voices roused Rick. He poked his head through the tent flaps. Their propped bikes were still chained, padlocked together. Young men and girls were carrying kettles and plastic bottles of water from a standpipe. Lovely morning, he thought, 8.15 a.m. on his wrist-watch. Then abrupt surprise locked his benign gaze. He untied the flap tapes and thrust out his head, left arm and shoulder. Twenty yards away a man wearing a deerstalker hat was in the river, white froth bubbling at his throat.
'Lew, there's a bloke in the river!'
'Ah?'
'Fisherman. He's turning. His head's under!'
'Bloody hell!'
Rick said, 'I'll get him out,' running in his singlet and pants, flinging into a racing dive, thrashing crawl stroke and he ducked under the rod-flailing angler. They moiled about. Hefty Rick grabbed his collar, kicked off gravelly bottom, kept

going, scissors-kicking to the far bank. Line trailed down-stream, the spread-eagled angler holding his rod as if crucified. The deerstalker remained on his head.

'You'll be okay,' guaranteed Rick, hauling the man up off his hands and knees.

Middle-aged, he had the calm, pale face of indoors. He gusted long breaths, grimaced fearless and shook hands. 'Thank you. I lost my footing.' He sat sideways, reeling in line, emptied his waders and his bag. 'Lost my damned senses too. I used to fish this stretch thirty years ago.'

'You'll have to go home, change clothes,' said Rick.

He stood tall, flat-backed, grey woollen stockings folded at his knees. 'Edward Winton,' reaching a handshake again, the softly firm hand of a woman.

'Rick Taylor,' he said.

'Address, Rick?'

Rick stifled grinning. 'Leave it, mister. I'll nip back across the river. We're in a tent. So-long now.'

Lew was bawling, 'You all right?'

He waded thigh deep into his foaming crawl and pelted up the turfed slope.

Edward Winton waved, smiling.

'All the best,' shouted Rick.

The fisherman slapped his wet hat against his leg in self-mockery.

Watching Rick towel himself inside the tent, Lew Cullen vowed, 'I'd never attempt what you've just done.'

'I could do with a big feed,' says Rick. 'We'll hit the roads this afternoon. Easy does it today.'

'There's no rush,' agreed Lew. 'Who was he, the bloke you saved?'

'Proper gent. English.'

Lew shivered his body. 'He's lucky the Wheelers' event was scrubbed this morning. Edwin's and Ivor's families are suffering.'

Rick said, 'Yeh, for definite.'

All day they dawdled, amiable as tourists. Side by side crossing Brecon Beacons under summer starlight, Rick supplied descant to Lew's drawling 'I did it my way'.

Just off the road a darkly clumped, straggly herd of sleeping mountain ponies. Lew skewed aside, braking to standstill.

Straddling the crossbar, he's righteous as John the Baptist quietly intoning, 'Wake, you bastards.'

Rick triggered his bell, trings pealing the night. He's serene, too: 'Steady there, boy.'

Lew eased himself back into the saddle. 'Too bloody true,' he said.

Lew's Old Man

Eddie Wynn elbowing through a gang of men on top pit.
'Lewis Bowen?'

Who said, 'What's up boy?' Strong minded Lew, he's thirty, married, no kids.

Eddie's jigging his shoulders like a bouncer. 'I'm your new butty behind the cutter.'

'Oh?'

'Reason being the under-manager took me off afternoon shift.'

'Why's that?'

'I tangled with a few blokes,' says Eddie.

'None of my business,' from Lew.

'Arguments, see, Lew, just mouthy arguments. Wasters, they shopped me.'

'Right then, keep your nose clean. Carry these.' Lewis gave him the bag of sharp cutter picks.[1] 'Every morning you'll be taking a set of blunt picks to the blacksmith's shop. Collect them every night.'

Eddie learned fast. He's eighteen, leggy, hunky-chested, impudence glittering his eyes. Small brown eyes tucked above the root of his lumpy nose. Eddie thinks he's tough. Truth to tell, he's more clown than blaggard.

Eight years Lew has been driving the Longwall coal-cutter. Nights regular. Young Eddie's a genuine grafter behind the jib. It'll take Eddie more than he can afford to spend the cheeky aggro in his system. Lewis isn't bothered. Enough on his plate. When there's no machine-cut coal for day-shift colliers, nine times out of ten Lew cops the blame. Outright greedies, some of our Welsh colliers. Tories wearing cap-lamps. Know-all buggers born and bred here in Moel Exchange.

This single grudge in Lewis, namely his old man, Dai-Rees Bowen being a fanatic. Awkward. Old Dai-Rees, he sticks by religion. Deacon in Bethesda plus fireman by night, therefore a muggins in the eyes of colliery management.

Lewis goes his own way.

'Come off it,' says Eddie, 'your old man's straight as a die.'

Lew knocked out the tow-post.[2] 'On account one-time he played flanker for Wales before I was pupped.'

'Yeh, definitely. Never a bad word agenst Dai-Rees in my Club. For why should he chuck his weight about.'

'You're brilliant, kiddo. I don't want your opinion. Make sure that tow-post is safe.'

Eddie dragged the tow-post up the face. Always the same shout, 'Take the strain, Lew!'

Hand on the control chipper,[3] Lew's creeping the steel rope around the haulage drum. He can't fault quick Eddie. Boys behind the cutter, they come, they go. Then he waited for him to drop back, shovel gumming[4] behind the Longwall.

It's a Monday night. First shift of the week and they're three-quarter way up Number 2 face. Roof pouncing like shell-fire. Three, four stents down the run, lids snapping off posts like carrots. Squeals and creaks of breaking timber. Best steam coal in Number 2. Broken ground though, dog-rough conditions for a fortnight. What a bastard shambles. Forest of posts in every stall, barely space for the cutter to pass. Eddie's shovelling, his left shoulder edging along the gob wall.[5] He's relying on his eyes and ears to protect his head, arms and his backbone. Now and again he's scooting up front, dodging flakes of rock spewing out above sagging coal.

'Bloody crib this,' he says.

'Stay here,' Lew said. 'Let her plough through on the chipper.'

Eddie laughed. 'You're in charge butty.'

At the end of the pull, same procedure. Lewis lugged the electric cable up the face. Eddie dragged the tow-post.

'Grub next stop?' says Eddie.

'Harry Hughes's stall,' he said.

Except trouble came. Old fashioned Moel Exchange bedlam. Back down the face, nothing but ruination. Not Lew Bowen's problem at the moment. He's chipping her dead slow. By inches. How many volts in the Longwall? Enough power to gut the human race. Lew held up the chipper. The chain cleared itself around the 4'6" jib. Hot duff mixed with stink of burning steel.

'Aye, no argument, fucken picks are burning,' says Lewis.

Eddie taps his shoulder. He's bent double, yelling at Lew's eyeballs, 'Knock her off!'

Lew cut the motor. They ape-walked away from the Longwall.

Eddie's sarcastic. 'There's a clever man. Now listen! Just listen!'

151

It's all on the move. Squashed coal and muck skidding off the steel clad machine. Roof cracks grinding, pressure sending tiny gouts of greyish powder floating innocent as salt. Blue pennant ground to dust.

'Find us a decent hatchet,' said Lew.

Eddie picked the lock on Harry Hughes's toolbar. Fiddled it with a knife horseshoe nail. He's sniggering to himself. Young Eddie enjoys listening to colliers raving about wage-men borrowing their tools. Custom and practice rules in emergencies.

'They should be grateful,' contended Lew. 'We timber faces while they're snoring next to their wives. Commonsense colliers, they won't take offence. Sooner a busted Woolworth's lock than the top of the road fallen in.' Lew spat aside. 'Golden rule: Keep the top of the road safe.'

Eddie's chopping a 6-foot post to size when big falls down the face sends them running. Worse, they're coming closer. Lew's worried about the cutter. If she's buried, his fault again. Still, no matter, forget it. Stressing inside his head: First and foremost I'm here to look after myself . . . and Eddie Wynn.

Sneaky as burglars they returned to the top of the road.

Eddie's whispering, 'See that lot!'

Side by side, staring hard, they watched roof coming down, lids[6] on posts slowly spreading like chewed matchsticks. And pounding, real heavy pounding throughout Number 2.

Says Eddie, 'Me, I'd rather be in Exchange Labour Club.'

Heedless Lew, nodding, 'Four-and-a-half-foot posts we need.'

'Where from, for Jesus' sake? Only a few six an' a half footers piled on the side back there.'

Lew said, 'Dram-full out in the supply road.'

Eddie's nudge caught him off balance, 'Hey, talk bloody sense.'

'Boy,' he threatened, 'go easy or you'll be up top pit and you won't raise your lamp again either.'

'Chopsy bastard,' says Eddie, doggy fawning, grinning his wet mouth from his teeth. 'Okay, Lew, I'll find a haulier, bring the dram in here. Fetch your old man an' all, if you like?'

Lew said, 'If this face isn't timbered sharpish she'll fall in up to the bloody moon.'

Eddie grabbed his arm for another short dash over the sleepers. Storms of duff blowing up the face. Big squeeze a mile underground while close on three thousand souls in Moel Exchange are fast asleep.

Eddie's jogging away to find a haulier. 'Shan't be long, Lew!'

Squatting on his heels, Lewis effortlessly pondered ends and means, dead-end dreaming until three lights turned off the main heading into Harry Hughes' stall. Haulier leading his pony with the tram of 4½-foot posts, young Eddie and fireman Dai-Rees.

Cadger all his days, Lew cut the haulier a chew of Ringers.

'Ta very much, Lew,' and he takes his pony back out to the heading.

Lewis's old man stands about eight yards away from the Longwall. 'Rather nasty,' he says in his humble, dauntless way.

Eddie's gloating, 'Too fucken true.'

Dai-Rees clicks open the brass case of his pocket watch, sort of talking to it, 'Couple of hours to knocking off time, and ah'm, twenty-five yards up to the stable where you jib out. Say half an hour to load her onto the ah'm, trolley.'

'Can't be done,' said Lewis.

Eddie's acting hysterical, pummelling the flat of his hand with his fist.

Serene as far-off water, 'Yes it can,' says Dai-Rees Bowen.

Lew threw dollops of spit as if it's poison. 'Want us to get killed, ah? Want me and Eddie to get killed?'

Dai-Rees shakes his head. That's all.

He's nobody's bloody father, decided Lewis.

Then they're hustling away again. Another fall. Maybe ten, fifteen trams of muck.

Eddie's howling, 'Ferret couldn't go down that face!'

Thin fine dust spinning through cap-lamp glare, powdery, drying the insides of their nostrils. Lew's taking shallow breaths. He's thinking, guaranteed pneumo stuff. Since starting as a kid from school, I've seen all kinds of mad things in this pit. Crazy hauliers booting ponies and banging them with sprags. Screwball officials—my old man, he's abnormal. Brain-washed managers—one finished up in the asylum. Piecework dumbos slogging knee-deep in water. Injured men crying for mercy—none about down here. Beaten men cursing the world. Obvious, Lew, *go steady, go steady*.

Dai-Rees does some dratting under his tongue. 'Seems to me it's moving up the face.'

Young Eddie's giggling, wobbling his legs like a comedian pissed out of his senses.

Shuffling like a boxer smearing his bootsoles with resin, Dai-Rees says, 'Help me with these, Eddie-boy.'

One, two, three 4½ foot posts hooked under his left arm. Canting sideways, he draws Harry Hughes's sledgehammer and mandrel off the toolbar. 'Lewis, cut me some lids by the time I come back.'

Lew jabs his fingers against his father's chest. 'Don't be so bloody daft!'

'Lay off,' says Dai-Rees.

'Wait! Let it settle!'

'Out of my way, please, Lewis.'

'By the Christ Almighty!'

'Mind your tongue, boy. Cut some lids.'

They followed him. Then backtracked slow-motion a few yards, watching Lew's old man sledging up those posts on top of the road, the squeeze whimping, chunks of rock raking down like coffins, pulverising the coal. Dai-Rees kept lurching about in the face. No time to fix lids, just hammer posts up under the breaks.

Lew started chopping. He's careless shaping the lids, simply slicing off a couple of shavings. All sweat and snobs behind the tram. *Safe.* Eddie's on the run, flinging 4½ foot posts and lids into the face. And Lew's expecting a shout from Eddie. By any reckoning Dai-Rees is bound to suffer. Fighting the squeeze single-handed, but he's flesh and blood like everybody else. Lewis feels sickened to his bowels. For every family crisis, 'Trust in the Lord' from Dai-Rees, Mattie Bowen ignoring him, coping off her own bat. Long-headed Mattie, she always treated Dai-Rees like patient mothers regard cranky children.

So Lew's sweating and raging, God damn and blast, God damn and blast!

Until the shout, 'Lew, your old man's bleeding!'

God damn . . . 'Where's he bleeding?'

Eddie's pawing his hand down over his right ear.

Lew sprinted. Dai-Rees is way up the face, ten yards past the Longwall cutter. The whole roof has lowered since Lew switched off the power.

'Come on out! No timber left!'

'In a minute,' says Dai-Rees.

'Come out! We've emptied the bloody dram!'

Sweat souring Lewis's mouth, but thank Christ the squeeze is lifting, pouncing into the higher ground, easing away. He goes up to the Longwall, hidden under muck and mashed coal. Couple of tons, Lew muttering, 'Bugger all.' First, shovel through to the pommel.[7] Once my hand is on the chipper, I'll gamble she'll plough herself clear.

Wishful thinking of course, Dai-Rees saying, 'Leave her be where she is.'

Why? Because he's dabbed zigzag rows of posts tight to the coal. Lew's old man, he saved Number 2 from Harry Hughes's stall up to the return heading. But listen, prima donna colliers and day-wage blokes, they'll be working hand-cut coal for a week. Slow, slow work, timbering with cogs and flats as they fill out stents to straighten the face.

All of a sudden Dai-Rees pokes his head closer to Lew's cap-lamp. His ear, it's hanging like meat scrag, blood pouring down the side of his neck, reddening his shirt and waistcoat.

'I suggest you jib out[8] and change the picks. Be careful,' he says. 'Ah'm, what I'll do, make my way back to pit bottom.'

Lew's bawling, 'Jesus Christ, man, why'd you have to take it on all by yourself? Bloody stupid thing to do! You could have brought in half a dozen repairers! Know something, you'll be the talk of Moel Exchange!'

'Haa, gossip.'

'Who d'you think you are?' accused Lewis, old Dai-Rees's righteous attitude sickening him again, so now he's bull-raggling his father, 'You expect me to *respect* you?'

'Hush, Lewis, hush. I'm more concerned about your mother. Better explain to her. Tell Mattie I'm all right. Understand, she mustn't get upset.' Shrugging like a haggler, saying, 'Understand, Lewis?'

Well, come 7 o'clock Tuesday morning, Lew's old man is leaving the First Aid room on top pit, with layers of bandages clumping the side of his head. Stepping into the ambulance, he says, 'Remember, tell your mother there's no call for panic, none at all.' Secretive as Bopa he's mouthing into Eddie Wynn's earhole, 'Good on you, lad.'

Dai Rees-Bowen lost most of his right ear. Ladder of raw cuts down his cheekbone. Scarred for life. Touched by madness, he went beyond reason. He staked himself.

As Lewis said to his mother, 'I can't fathom *why*. Bethesda mania perhaps, some kind of dipsy-do.'

Mattie Bowen simply raised her hand. 'Dai-Rees doesn't want to hurt people. It's the dread in him. Your father's been through all that.'

'Mam, last night he was humping his own gravestone.'

Like bitter frost she says, 'Be quiet. Go home, son, live your own life.'

'No option,' said Lewis. 'So-long, Mam.'

Mattie Bowen raised and dropped her hand.

[1] *Cutter picks*: Stubby, angled, approx 3", the squared ends bolted like painted teeth in the chain travelling around the jib of a Longwall coal-cutter.

[2] *Tow post*: Fixed raked to the roof, steel haulage rope from cutter shackled to its base. Rope laps on drum housed nearside in Longwall as the machine operates.

[3] *Chipper*: Small hand lever governing pace of Longwall.

[4] *Gumming*: Coal ground to dust (duff) by cutter picks.

[5] *Gob wall*: Dry-stone walling of shot-fired roof muck, back-filled with slag and debris, repeated and extended as coal is extracted.

[6] *Lid*: Timber cross-piece fixed on head of posts.

[7] *Pommel*: Connects power (electric cable) to Longwall.

[8] *Jib out*: Straighten jib from 90 degrees to remove/change picks.

King of the Fo'c'sle

Tankie's bawling, 'Gerrup there, Ginger!' climbing the ladder behind him.

On deck it's handlines to the galley. Black night all wild in a Force 9, biting sheets of rain, loose gear grinding, swinging, 'Aaachch' croaking from Ginger and Tankie laughing, 'Keep movin', yous Welsh git.'

Shinbone scraped fiery—but Emlyn Jones is Cochsant Welsh through and through, ancient village in Powys crammed higgledy-piggledy since Roman times. Cochsant boy to Merchant Navy fireman five years ago. Tonight they're off the north coast of Ireland, homeward bound on *Red Sunset*. Light ship from Tangiers, so she's slip-slopping like waterlogged dunlopillo.

Tankie, he's Irish/Cypriot, born and bred Scouse, Steenie Lees his true name, gut fearless as Jesus parading on water. *Tankie* due to reputation, meaning hardknock brawler. Yet he's a real black gang mate. Of course, speak as you find. Obviously.

Behind Tankie on the handline, Pete Ramsay, orphanage reared, one-time fairground dogsbody. Pete's quirky tempered, Walton Jail on his record according to Billo Slaney. Billo's their trimmer down below, another Scouser, scrawny, sloping mouth under a small budgie nose.

As they rushed into the galley, Tankie's whooping, 'Faaque dat!' Gale wind is still blurring Emlyn's ears as he pulls up his wet trouser leg. 'Lump of timber smacked my shin.' He thumb-smeared a run of blood seeping into his sock.

Says the cook, 'I'm out of anti-septic. Vaseline and this'll do the job,' ripping off a strip of clean towelling. He bandaged Emlyn's rawed shinbone.

The galley boy served Tankie enough grub for two men. Because there's fifteen stone of him. Sometimes on the quiet, you'll hear Tankie praising his twin sister. She died within minutes of taking breath.

Easy in the warm fo'c'sle, big Tankie double-handed eating his supper, heedless now, ideas concentrating him—he makes Mr Universe seem like twopennyworth: 'Oil-burner next trip. Meself, I've 'ad me lot of raisin' steam. *Red Sunset*, she's ready for scrap.' Lips wiped on his sweat-rag, he's nudging Emlyn, 'Whatsay, Ginj?'

'Righto, oil-burner. Bloke on the shovel slogs his goolies off saving enough to get married.'

Pete sneered, 'She'll make more on her back.'

Tankie snickered through his nose.

He crooned 'Jezebel' under the shower, tremolo tenor for all his macho bulk, curly black hair plastered flat around his football head. Like a giant imp he squirted a bar of soap from his hands.

Pete dodged, guarding his privates. 'Lay off.'

Tankie says, 'Whassamarrah?'

Huffing long dribbles under the downpour, Pete says, 'Yeah.'

Tankie's kidding, 'Yous fornicated bastard.'

'Yeah-yeah-yeah,' says Pete.

Emlyn's lowering into sleep when Billo comes fidgeting like a ghost. When Billo climbed into his bunk his snoring ruined Emlyn's dream-time centred on Bronwen Hughes. A Powys lovely. They're engaged. Soon though he's gone into mindless sleep, until the shout floated down: 'Tankie, Pete, Ginger, Billo.'

8 a.m., god-forsaken seas hanging up there, whitewater shredding like steam. Corpse-coloured winter sky, Red Sunset wallowing, wallowing, and Chiefie at the foot of the ladder. 'Well done, chaps. Keep her steady.' He's checking pressure gauges over and over, always gabbling to himself.

'Chiefie's on the brink,' says Emlyn. 'Too conscientious. He's in the wrong job.'

Tankie spat indifference.

Emlyn warned him, 'Hey, Chiefie, put your head down man. You're in a state, panicking over nothing at all. Go on, put your head down.'

'Chiefie'll blow off his faaquen clock,' says Tankie to Pete Ramsay.

Pete's a sampler of style and skill, flinging coal, sparks fizzing through a level layer of black-bedded over red-roaring embers. He says, 'Billo slept on the rake last night.'

Tankie swigs from a flagon of water. 'Tell yous, me an' Billo's in the Beaumont Club, paid up members us two.'

'I'd scrub the bastud,' says Pete.

'He's beat, too knackered to wash hisself.'

Snarly from Pete, 'What about the itch?'

Tankie clowned, scratching his armpits and crotch.

Emlyn kept nagging the chief engineer, 'You'll do yourself no good.'

Snapped back to common sense, Chiefie went up to his quarters.

'T'ree days from now we'll be in the Beaumont,' says Tankie, winding a little jive in his greasy jeans and St. Michaels singlet.

'More like four,' Emlyn said. 'I reckon I'll be on the night train. Aye, great.' In split seconds he's eye to eye with Tankie. 'We'll keep in touch for our next trip.'

'Bang on, Ginj.'

'Pete, you with us, oil burner next trip?'

'I'm taking time ashore,' says Pete.

'For how long?'

'Twelvemonth maybe. Depends.' Pete's brows are screwed down, his thrust lower lip shining pink, the lip of a chimpanzee.

'Thievin' an' poncin',' says Tankie.

Queerly polite from Pete, 'Come agen?'

'Faaquen thief,' says Tankie.

Pete switches to bumkin brogue, 'Aa-hi dean mess abah-ow-wi' pee-igshit,' and he's jigging on tiptoes like a quarter-staff bloke from Robin Hood, shovel held slantwise across his body.

Tankie gleamed sweat, glare shining his grinning teeth. 'You'd nick flowers off yous oul lady's grave.'

Pete sprang as he struck, clouting Tankie on the left shoulder. The shaft of Pete's shovel snapped like a fresh carrot. Tankie crumpled, he fell on his backside.

A Wrigleys tablet spurted off Emlyn's tongue: 'For Christ's sake!'

Hissing came from Tankie. He swayed upright, his huge bent arm pumping his left shoulder up and down, up and down.

Stay out of it, decided Emlyn. None of my business.

Pete back-pedalled, leapt to the ladder. Tankie embraced his legs, hauled him away from the rungs, fastened to him like a bear, Pete kneeing and butting. Big Tankie's forehead hammered through, smashing two gold teeth from Pete Ramsey's dentures. He's lying half-curled, retching. He's quivering to unconciousness. Tankie barrowed Pete into the bunker, tipped him out, left him there, a steep coal-slide slurring down, guaranteed to bury Pete's head. And frantic as a terrier Billo scooped into the sliding coal with his shovel.

Suffocation left Emlyn's throat. He's into action, dragging

159

Pete away. Honestly, Billo saved Pete Ramsey's skull, at worst even the rest of his days.

'Okay, dat's okay,' says Tankie. Kind of trance on him, quite gentle, call it grace, the way you see mourners up off their knees after praying.

Emlyn lost his temper. 'Bloody madman you are! He's bound to chuck the book at you for this! Oil burner? No chance!'

'Clean 'im up,' says Tankie to Billo.

Later Chiefie comes mumbling down the ladder. He's scurrying mazy circles in front of Pete's boiler. Where's Pete?'

'Caught short,' says Tankie, miming the chain-pull. 'Gone forra crap.' He's been stoking both fires while Billo and the cook are washing blood off Pete's face up in the galley.

Like royalty waving to the gauges, Chiefie cries out, 'Watch the pressure!' As usual he's shinning back up the ladder, some private Satan forking his rump.

Pete spent time searching for his gold teeth. He found one. Meanwhile Tankie and Emlyn fired his boiler turn and turn about.

Billo Slaney signed the chitty for Pete's new shovel.

Sullen, awfully deliberate the way he marched starko to the showers, caked blood on his swollen mouth, his eyes slitted inside pulpy welts. Piece of comedy then, four black gang men reaching for the mixer taps as Chiefie came in a crouching run.

'Damn-damn, the system's out of order! Hot water in the galley. You'll have to use buckets.' Whinnying squealed from Chiefie's soundbox, breaking to, 'Sorry, chaps!'

Tankie swaggered mockery, 'Faaquen sabotage.'

Chiefie wobbled a double-take, squinting at Pete. 'Hullo, what's happened?'

'Slipped on the ladder, busted me face a bit.'

Trotting away, the chief engineer threw a sharp cold wail.

'He's a wreck,' said Emlyn.

Tankie flicks a salute. 'Good on yous, fella.'

Pete's tiny eyes are black enamel like in the head of a snake. 'Pete or Peter, take your pick.'

'Yi-yi, sure, right on, Pete.' Tankie giggled, twisting himself into a lopsided hunchback, red blotch mapping his left shoulder. He's heaving to full height, great chest, arms held clenched like a museum example of Greek sculpture.

No spite at all, 'More bollocks than brains,' says Pete.

Captain Leighton Mars-Graham came down from the bridge. He's outside the galley. Emlyn's inside, bandaging his shin. And listening. Stern on account it's expected. Mars-Graham tells the second engineer, 'Find it and fix it.'

The second's a versed bullshitter. *Marine engineer*, him. More windbag than sea-farer.

'Where's Chiefie?' inquires the Captain.

Grafting his corner, the second says, 'Stripping off panels with the first mate. Chiefie thinks it's above the showers. In my opinion, Skipper, it's the colorifier, there's a faulty line from here'—pointing at the galley. 'Corrosion, either corrosion or scaling.'

'Ask the donkey-man to lend a hand.'

'He's off watch, Skipper.'

'Well now, young Jeremy, Archie Greg was on this freighter before you lost your bloody milk teeth.'

'I'll turn him out, Skipper.'

But firemen and trimmers lugged buckets of hot water from the galley for four days and nights, during which time every man in the fo'c'sle is a proper deep-sea lawyer.

Said Emlyn, 'Slick and a wipe like peasants. We're back in the years of Captain Morgan. I'll remember this trip when Bronnie and me are on pension.'

Sarcasm from Pete, 'Yer dog collar's choking, Taff. Marriage don't last, they won't let it, they'd sooner pick up Social. When my missis split she went short timin' on the Social. They ain't beholden same as was. No way. We don't count in their eyes.'

'Bronnie and myself,' he said, 'we'll stay together. First though, we're buying our own house, definitely.'

Pete's a world prophet, 'The man ain't born who'll best a woman.'

Tankie stays hidden, stooging behind his dark Irish/Cypriot eyes. Teasing him, Emlyn said, 'Any girl waiting for yous in Liverpule?'

'Few, 'ere's a few.' Tankie spun a cigarette, conjuring it up to his mouth. 'Dis piece, what's she at?'

'Works in a crèche, Bronnie does. Child-minder see, only mostly they can't even talk Welsh. The *Saeson*, they're paying thirty, forty thousand quid for ramshackle cottages, plaster fallen down, ferns poking out from the chimney stacks. Next they claim improvement grants. New roofs. New doors and windows. Extensions. Yellow pebbledash. Fancy patios. Caravans in the garden. Scrambler bikes racketing about everywhere. Peace and quiet gone forever.'

Without fret, Tankie says, 'Ginj, yous faaquen thick up in dem mountens.'

'Perhaps we're small-minded,' conceded Emlyn. 'Don't forget, remember, we were there first. Our country, our language. You *Saeson*, nothing but mongrels you lot are. Excuse me, I don't mean you blokes personally.'

Tankie's gurgling the tea in his mug.

That night Pete slept on the rake. Face and hands washed, he tucked down in his bunk. Billo the trimmer, he slept on the rake. Tankie soaped himself with hot water from the galley, followed by cold sluicings from a hand basin. Emlyn felt his blood too thin. One at a time he carried two buckets of hot water. He resented coal-dust and sweat griming his skin. Furthermore he abandoned Chiefie. Sod him. Instead he accused the second engineer. 'You couldn't hold down a job in a pickle onion factory.'

'We're doing our best, Ginger.'

'Brilliant,' he said. 'Ask the Skipper for a medal.'

There's a clean dry scab flaking off his shinbone. He'll history the scar to Bronwen Hughes.

Mushy snowflakes shrivelling like suds on deck when hot water returned to the showers. End of February. They washed each other's backs for the last time. Suitcases and dufflebags were packed. Off duty crew lined the rails while a harbour pilot crept *Red Sunset* to berth. Every man hungry for land, but it's a grey Liverpool under drizzly rain when they stepped ashore. Queue outside the company burser's office. Banter, chitchat, bullragging to do with booze and crumpet. Familiar strangeness at the end of every trip. Fivers bunched in his fist, Tankie jigs along the queue, yipping like a carnival Redskin.

First Emlyn sent a telegram to Bronwen: *See you in the morning. Love Emlyn*—righteous Tankie spying over his shoulder as if entitled, 'Any road, Ginj, yous din't sleep onna faaquen rake.'

'Pretty near it. I was tempted.'

'Jeezus Chrise,' says Billo. Billo's wearing a maroon leather jacket, collar wing buttoned high across his Adam's apple, and a black leather cap with ear-flaps buckled on the crown of his head.

Pete's faking *bonhomie*, jabbing vee signs like a clock-work politician. 'Tarra, might bump into you sometime.'

Privately to Billo, 'Fix you up with Dorothy,' Billo standing hunched, 'On my oath.'

Tankie warbles his tremolo, 'Hang about! We been shipmates five months. Let's eat, 'en we'll call in the Beaumont.'

Emlyn's patting his bulging wallet pocket, 'Four months and twenty-three days.'

Then Tankie's crowding them into a transport cafe, 'Emlyn-Ginj, here we goes!'

They're flushed in the Beaumont by nine o'clock. Smallish Club, shabby, cream gloss peeling off the walls, Scousers effing and blinding regardless, dart board at the far end, MEN ONLY snooker room beyond the bar, off-set lounge for newspapers, cards, dominoes.

Slurping whisky through his gapped teeth, Pete says to Billo, 'C'mon, giss that old number, hi-um, "Red sails inna sunset".'

Billo curled his lips like a clever lurcher. 'The man's pissed awready.'

Pete started, '*Red sails inna sunset,*' Billo chiming in, '*way out onna sea,*' and Cymro to the marrow, Emlyn's obliged to offer his light baritone, '*O carry my loved one home safely to me.*'

Vowed Emlyn, 'I shan't sign on that bastard ship again. Come ten o'clock I'll be in a taxi to Lime Street station. Drink up, boys, my turn. Hey, Tankie . . . Tankie? Where's Tankie?'

Pete thumbed aimlessly, 'Very likely gone to splash his boots.'

Billo pretends bomping the table with his fist. 'Leave be, kid. Jest fetch the drinks.'

Emlyn thought, Roll on tomorrow. 'Four double whiskies, please,' he said to the Beaumont stewardess. 'See a big-big bloke, missis? Club member he is, aye, Steenie Lees, huge, gi-gantic.'

Billo called, 'Ginger!'

She's a wheezy middle-aged roly-poly, gasping inside squashed bosoms. What she says Emlyn can't fathom.

'Taist actchally, s'lla question of taist. Yayce yayce. S'owvah de odds, ow indaid, spesh, extra spesh.'

Try again: 'Steenie Lees. I'm looking for Steenie Lees.'

'Billo Slaney, this Taffy genwin?'

Pete's firming his sea-legs crossing to the bar counter. 'Bank on Ginger Jones, never once't slept onna rake. Naw once.' Shielding his yellow-blue bruised eyes under his hands, Pete's romantically see-sawing his elbows. 'Ginj, giss "Red sails inna sunset", you knows through the words.'

'Missis,' insisted Emlyn, 'where's Tankie. I'm after his address. Honest, arranged between him and me before we came ashore.'

Slow as tears, Billo and the stewardess winked at each other.

'Down to yous,' she says.

Billo's snicking Emlyn's shirt front with his fingernail, 'Lissen, kid, go easy.'

'What you on about, Billo?'

'Tankie's shiftin' the muck off his chest.'

'Ah?'

Irritation rived Billo's skewy mouth. He says to the podgy woman, 'Ginger's awright, straight up now. Coupla minutes, any objections?'

She tap-tapped the side of her nose. 'Dere's me pryvaisy. Awf'llay-awf'llay 'portant.' Quick malice flared her eyes, 'When's the last time yous a punter, mister bee ess?'

Billo humphed.

Anyhow, having paid for the whiskies, Emlyn said, 'Tankie's with a bird.'

Nasty tutting streamed from the Beaumont madame.

'Having a bunk up,' he muttered to Billo.

Pete downed his whisky. Now he's sipping Tankie's.

'Coupla minutes?' repeated Billo.

As if reminding herself she droned the rune, 'P'liteness first t'ing. Yayce, p'liteness. God p'liteness. *Knock. Knock-knock.* Tayke time fer duh fayvour. Show rispect. Mustn't int'rupt. None 'ullaballoo. Tayke time.' Suddenly she's ratty, 'Oi, Taffy, keep yous mouth shut.'

He's nodding, 'Righto, missis.'

'Shan't be long, Pete,' says Billo.

Pete lurched face-to-face with the shinamalink trimmer. He fingered two notes from his sheaf, cuffed them in Billo's hand and touched the top of his leather cap. 'Next Saturday night. See you. I'll be on me way.'

'Okay,' says Billo.

Pete hefted his dufflebag, brand new briefcase from Mombasa tucked under his arm.

'Good luck, Pete,' said Emlyn. 'Take care.'

'Likewise, Ginger. Tarra.'

Mysterious in his Scouse mind, Billo four times folded the notes and zipped them in a pocket of his maroon jacket. 'Let's go, Ginj.'

When she opened the door, giggles bubbled from her. Emlyn turned away, 'Sorry, my mistake.'

Billo's complaining, 'Jeezus Chrise.'

Tankie's stretched out on a double bed, another girl child straddling him, bobbing herself, all gawp, her eyes staring unbeknown as marbles, and Tankie's bellacking, 'What-the-faaquen-'ell!'

Stupored Emlyn, thinking. Time to go home. He barged past Billo inside the doorway. 'So-long, Tankie, Dirty waster you.'

The stewardess squirmed smiling until it stuck.

'Two small whiskies, glass of lager, glass of bitter,' says Billo. Emlyn's at their table, suitcase between his knees.

Billo suggested, 'Look, takes all sorts. I've knowed Steenie since he jumped Borstal. Way out on his jack. Yeah, kid, tellew straight, Steenie copped some 'ard times. Faaquen cruel.'

Gripped on whisky shivers, Emlyn thought, Be quiet, Billo.

'Can't 'elp hisself for Chrissake.'

Emlyn swallowed beer.

'Ferget it,' coaxed Billo. 'Dere's lots worst.' He shiggled his open palm between them, 'Such poxy luck.'

Dull ache swarming inside Emlyn's chest, 'I looked up to him as a man. I took him for normal. Bloody normal!' After a hopeless grunt and growl pause, 'He ought to be put down like a mangy dog. Where I come from they'd lay in wait and boot the daylight out of him.'

As if pestered, Billo swanked his meagre shoulders, 'Dat's a faaquen problem?'

'You're talking shit. Tankie could pick any decent girl.' Emlyn pulled out his suitcase. 'I'm off, Billo. Goodbye, mate. Take care.'

They shook hands.

Drowsing snug on the mail train from Lime Street, Emlyn lolled awake for happy-go-lucky seconds. Saint David's Day. Then he slept solid as if blessed, arms folded across the wad in his wallet pocket.

Rosebud Prosser

If was stiffening cold. A driving north-east wind carried stinging dust from derelict Hafod colliery. The rusted winding gear, screens and railway siding squatted inside a triangle of slag tips. Fine location for council houses, ideal environment, all sweetness and light. Off at a dog-leg from the siding, Sebon Lakes are full of caked slurry. Two small kidney-shaped lakes, once the tranquil roach pools of boyhood generations, NCB filter beds for twenty years, abandoned when they closed Hafod. Here in South Wales, we have been civilised by utility pollution and sincere blight.

Three hundred council houses, forty-eight-year-old Ivor Prosser, the foreman carpenter, green slouch hat slanted above his peacock eyes, thin wide mouth below a dago moustache, and the swagger of vanity. Vanity slippery as terrazzo.

'Dai Sam, how's progress up there?' he shouted.

We were fixing ceiling joists and noggins in a block of four houses. From the wall plate I saw him down below, his gloved hands fisted in the pockets of a company donkey coat. Slag dust tamping off the brickwork, hissed all day like seeds.

'We're on target unless you interfere,' I said.

'Dai, I need your labourer!'

Still in his teens, a drop-out from Newport Art College, our labourer had the attitude of a self-trained loner. 'Ivor,' I said, 'you can't take Musketeer away now, not after he's done all the hard graft on this block. He's been humping four-by-twos since we came on the job this morning.'

'Emergency!' yelled Ivor. He crab-walked, straddling himself across a narrow conduit trench in the frozen mud. 'Wocky's unloading cement! For God's sake listen to me! Essential we unload that stuff before knocking off time!'

I said, 'Find another bloke.'

'Point blank refusal to co-operate! No damn principle! Me and you, we travel in the cab with Wocky!' He spun away from the wind, threatening, 'Al'right, Dai Sam, no more favours!'

The following week we were roofing. Four chippies sharing bonus. Casual Musketeer, he dropped my hammer down a wall cavity. We lost money while I blindly fiddled and failed to hook the hammer with a length of wire. I had to leave it there, a fine-clawed, nicely-balanced hammer. From Musketeer came, 'Sorry, Dai. Hey um, how much do I owe you?'

'Too much,' I said.

But thank God the north-east wind eased. Human nature is caricatured by extreme climates.

'Snow forecast,' Wocky said, gearing down for the climb up Heol Gwyn mountain. On crystal mornings you can see the Bristol Channel from the top of Heol Gwyn, glimmering flat in the distance, twenty odd miles away. Originally a Shanks's pony track, Heol Gwyn rises two thousand feet above sea level, with horseshoe and hairpen bends each side of the barren summit.

'Ha, snow, good for the soil,' Ivor said. He blabbed exaggerations and lies about horticulture. The Prosser family were indoctrinated by a grandfather who worked for settlement Quakers during the Depression.

Behind us in the lorry, twelve blokes were huddled under a plastic canopy. Every day two lorries grinding up and over Heol Gwyn. Red lorries, yellow canopies.

Slam your foot down, it's quarter to eight,' urged Ivor, delirious, the way big fish madden themselves in small ponds.

Wocky dry-spat disgust. 'Shurrup. My wagon, this. I'm responsible. You, you couldn't drive a pram.' Blunt Wocky (Cynlais) Eynon, a born-and-bred industrialised Celt.

Ivor grinned indulgence. 'Where were you drinking last night, Cynlais?'

'Same place.'

'Where though, man, where?'

Wocky elbowed him. 'Don't keep on. Shift over a bit. I can't get at the stick.'

Ivor crowded me against the cab door. Wocky pushed into high as we cleared the brow, slid into a cutting between low drystone walls holding back peat bogs, then we began the long twisting run down hill.

At five-to-eight we piled out of the lorries. By ten o'clock the first flurries of snow sprinkled Hafod slag tips. Next day the same, sudsy flakes wandering from a gun-metal grey sky. Sleet froze on Heol Gwyn. Council workmen sprayed rock salt.

Thursday morning, Wocky promised, 'We'll get it today.'

Ivor laughed, gay as a bandit.

Anyhow, the world turned white by lunch-time.

167

'There it is,' Wocky said, dummying a half-nelson on Ivor to make him look up at Heol Gwyn. 'Means we'll have to go round-about. Across Sebon Common and up the other valley. Forty miles. Hour and a quarter each way.'

'We'll make it over the mountain,' insisted Ivor. He grabbed my arm. 'I'll pay this Dai Sam to gallop behind us with a whip.'

Wocky sneered, 'Your mouth's in the wrong fuckin' place, mate.'

'Hush't, don't panic. I'll sort things out with the general foreman.' Ivor's promise guaranteed nothing. They were still arguing an hour later, the G.F., the firm's agent, two card stewards and Ivor Prosser. Of course, the G.F. and the agent didn't have to cross Heol Gwyn before putting their feet under the table.

All in all a shabby housing contract. Brickies, chippies and labourers came and went like shy, troubled birds. Sure sign of a cut-throat firm.

So, at ten-past-three our lorries pulled away from outside the site office, through a few inches of snow, winter's soft blanket fall, which tilted, came slashing horizontally as we climbed Heol Gwyn.

'Them wipers pack in and I'm beat,' said Wocky, leaning forward, twitchy-eyed, snowflakes ragged as wet cotton sedge smudging across the windscreen.

'Mush! Mush!' cried Ivor.

Sullen Wocky, he said, 'Clever waster you are.'

Lighting his slim-line pipe, Ivor sucked and whoofed tobacco smoke. 'Men, listen, we ought to arrange a Saturday night on the beer. Just the three of us.'

I recommended the Footbridge Arms.

'Right! Bring some birds in. Through and through in the snug,' boasted Ivor.

Wocky huffed, muttering to himself, 'By the Jesus Christ, hark at him.'

We were crawling now, up into blizzard weather, Wocky on his feet, reaching out his arm, clearing the windscreen with his cap, Ivor shrinking from the draught, pipe jiggling in his teeth, his collar drawn up to the slouch hat.

Vicious umbrage from Wocky. 'Where's the bloody road? I can't see the marker stones.' Pause: 'Come on, Charlie, c'mon-c'mon.' Charlie drove the second lorry, tailing us, blurred as a war machine in the white welter.

'Footbridge Arms next Saturday night,' confirmed Ivor. 'Let me tell you from personal experience, there's no price to leisure time. Regardless of expense, every man should have his fair whack.'

'Whattew smokin', old socks?' asked Wocky.

Ivor sang, *'Everybody loves Saturday night, everybody loves Saturday night, Everybody everybody everybody everybody, everybody loves Saturday night.'* He had a ringing high register baritone, his slim-line pipe ratt-tatting West Indian rhythm, doing lieu for a bongo pebble rattler.

'Not bad, mate,' begrudged Wocky. The wipers jerked to and fro. Wocky stayed in bottom gear, steering around the first horseshoe bend. 'I gave you proper warning, Ivor. We're the only dull bastards travelling this road.'

Ivor snuggled between us. 'Cynlais-boy, never let it be said your father reared a jibber.'

We rounded the horseshoe, bedlam howlings coming from inside the canopy, our fellow workers caught in a chute of blizzard, then we climbed below high buttresses, sheep tucked like hibernators at the foot of the rocks. Another slow turn fed us head-on into the blizzard. We were two hundred yards from the cutting on top of Heol Gwyn when a small herd of mountain ponies fanned out, ghost shapes trekking down to lower ground. Wocky tished sympathy. 'Poor buggers.'

Ivor braced his forearm against my neck, peering out and yipping like a cowboy. More yelps came from under the canopy. The shaggy ponies trudged heedlessly.

'Wouldn't mind me a ramping big stallion,' Ivor hooping himself, jockeying, stroking the insides of his thighs. 'Ride to hounds like the spunk-faced aristocracy. That's the life for Ivor Prosser.'

'You'd fall off a feed bag,' said Wocky.

'I'll be riding some lush bird next Saturday night!'

Wocky said, 'Your missis, she'd dose you with Paraquat.'

I felt goose pimples—this crazy banter from the building trade as we nosed into a snowdrift. Wocky reversed, inched forward, stuck, reversed, rammed at the drift, snarling, 'Right, gerrout and walk.'

Ivor's charisma went absent. Lips stretched off his choppers, eyes bulging fear under the brim of his green slouch, he looked like a peon doomed to bullets in the stomach.

I opened the cab door. It was arctic all right. Men were dropping off at the back of the lorry, staying bunched, hop-hopping in the lee. Charlie came, followed by his passengers. Six foot three Charlie bent double, crouched in the swarming headlights of his lorry.

Wocky shouted, 'This is it! I knew! Nobody'd listen to me!'

'Two bloody coffins on wheels,' said Charlie.

Ivor scuttled into the gang, donkey coat clutched to his throat. He choked on panic. 'Every man for himself!' Barging through the crowd, he rested his forehead on the tailboard, 'I'm bronchial, Dai. Can't breathe. It catches me in the tubes,' but he raised his arms like a preacher, 'every man for himself!'

Ivor's inane bravado.

The snowdrift inclined sharply, filling the cutting between the drystone retaining walls. There weren't any heroes. We lost direction. Musketeer rambled, wailing for help, chest deep in bog and snow. Hands grabbed him, hauled him back to the main ruck. We were blinded, every man-jack floundering legless, the blizzard sucking air from our lungs. Bear right, I kept saying to myself, remembering the left-ward oblivion circling of lost souls. Genuine cannibal, the human heart.

Ivor Prosser suffered. He moaned. He chittered. All the time stumbling, falling, moaning. One grizzled old pipelayer stopped, turned his back in the blizzard. I caught his arm, pivoted him around—he was mumbling, maybe praying, in Welsh, the hearth language of his childhood. '*Diolch*,' he said, his cold lips at my ear.

We linked hands, tall Charlie in front, then Wocky, Ivor, the rest of us strung behind, the awkwardest crocodile since Homosapiens rose up off all-fours, down through the Eskimo weather, downhill two miles from the blizzard thinned away to gusts. Again the soft, threatless blanket fall. We chatted, shared cigarettes, enjoyed each other like citizens converted to peace for evermore. Except Wocky Eynon. He swore the lorries would remain trapped for days.

They were, too.

Saturday night with Wocky in the Footbridge Arms, for the fourth successive weekend we befriended Olive and Megan with vodkas. Bland Olive and brash Megan. We didn't expect to see Ivor. Cars were chaining cautiously up and down the slushed valley. Half way up to Heol Gwyn, the council abandoned a snowplough until daylight. Dumps of rock salt were empty. In the crowded lounge bar, love buds were ripening favourably by ten o'clock, when Ivor shouted from the lobby, 'Dai Sam! Where's Dai Samuels?'

He was wearing a fawn duffle coat with mock bone toggles, green and brown checkered suit, primrose yellow pullover, blue pinstripe shirt, pale silvery tie and oil-shining hair accurately parted along the side of his head. 'Found this boy in the Royal Hotel,' he said, parading Musketeer into the lounge. Musketeer wore elephant corduroys, zipped boots, khaki ganzi with suede elbow-patches, a Spanish guitar draped down his back, and the benign, lorn face of a folksy troubadour. In his triple-ringed left hand, a glass of rosé wine. Musketeer nodded without smiling.

Squeezing himself between Olive and Megan, our foreman carpenter mimed strumming. 'Righto, kid, let's hear from you.'

'Oh yes, please,' Megan said, coaxing.

Ivor flashed his gay bandit's grin. 'Listen, gel, you with Dai or Cynlais? No matter, what are you drinking?'

Megan frosted him, Olive doubling the snub, leaning across the front of his natty pullover, whispering to Megan, 'Here's a scraper from God knows where.'

'I think he's wearing a toupée,' said Megan.

Musketeer sang slow, dirgy verses about fields, hedges and dewponds disappearing under motorways. Musketeer's tied, mournful style, effective yet somehow unreal, like artificial insemination. I forgave him for dropping my hammer down a wall cavity. Half starved in his soul, that young Musketeer. I saw his name once, on a pay docket: Billy Rowlands.

Afterwards the lounge bar crowd made some decent harmony, mixing pop and ballads until stop tap. Buffing up his charm, Ivor failed to impress Olive and Megan. While he sang 'Persian Rosebud', Musketeer stroking chords, searching for the tune, the girls went to the Ladies' place. Unique baritone, Ivor Prosser, the sad, foppish bastard.

We filed out into the cold night, Megan and Olive pulling each other away from Ivor. Schoolgirlish romping. He fawned like a poacher's long-dog, Olive slapping at his hands, Megan

171

chogging a wristy smack on his head, a beautifully timed accident as she tugged into her overcoat. Wocky had phone-called a taxi, Ivor reduced to pleading by now, all teeth, moustache and gleaming hair. 'Room for one more?'

'Not on, can't take five,' said the taxi driver.

Wocky slammed the door. 'Tarra, Rosebud, see you Monday morning. Mind your feet!' the nearside tyres squirting slush at Ivor as we left the kerb.

Megan whaowed. 'That fella Prosser reminded me of a vampire.'

'I wouldn't trust him at all,' agreed Olive.

'Me neither! Never!'

'Slyness in his eyes,' said Olive.

Megan heaved a throaty squawk, Wocky nudging her, 'Cut the bloody inquest, ah? If you don't mind?'

I said, 'What happened to Musketeer? He disappeared after Ivor's 'Persian Rosebud'."

'Lovely boy,' sang the girls, twin toning like Zulu descant.

Megan stressed to Olive, 'Ever such a clever boy, *quiet*, really lovely.'

'Mm,' said Olive, coolish, the Mm for politeness.

They had a flat above Pegler's Stores. Steady batchelor girls on television assembly, unworried about settling down with meal-ticket husbands. They heated pre-packed chicken curries for supper. Wocky helped Megan wheel her single bed into the living room. As usual, for the fourth time, sometime during the night he left Megan. Wocky went home. Late Sabbath morning toast and tea for three, relaxed chit-chat, the flat gently washed over by non-stop scrape-scrape tinkle-tinkle radio music from next door.

On Monday Wocky drove a hired van, grumpy behind the wheel, sogged from all-day Sunday boozing. We travelled the round-about route across Sebon Common. Snow-bound Cymru. No sign of thaw. A dozen men were crammed on the floor of the van like convicts, the same in Charlie's van.

'How did she perform?' asked Ivor.

'You're the arteest,' I said. '"Persian Rosebud", terr-rrific.'

'By damn, I'm the man should have taken her home.' Ivor pumped phallic uppercuts, howling, 'Oompah oompah!'

Wocky's eyelids were swollen. 'Rosebud,' he said, 'anything

the matter with your missis? Doesn't make sense to me, old tiger like you chasing around like a whoormaster.'

He cracked short laughs, loosely clasped his hands to his stomach, shoulders hoisted like a trouper solist, tidily arranged himself and broke out on 'Persian Rosebud'.

Communal singing then, all the way to Hafod colliery. Unnatural on a bitter January morning.

Outside the canteen shed, Wocky unlocked the rear door to let the men out, at the same time cursing the white hulk of Heol Gwyn mountain.

'Dai,' explained Ivor, anxiously knotted to confession, 'between you and me now, confidential, right? My wife's retired from cooking school dinners. Yes, she, her and myself, we got married late in life, consequence being as regards certain matters, y'know Dai, it's a question of respect. No alternative. It's separate beds. See what I mean?'

I said, 'You should have had voice training thirty years ago.'

He aimed his pipe like a pistol. 'It isn't for me to brag, others have mentioned exactly the same thing.'

'Water under the bridge, Ivor,' I said.

Perversely manful, jigging up on his toes, his alibi sounded like destiny. 'Circumstances! Widowed mother! Trouble was Dai Sam, I waited until my mother passed away before getting married. Good to me, my old lady, a saint in her own right.'

'Some mothers are way out, fantastic,' I said. 'Can you spare us a man this morning? We'll have to clear snow off the scaffold and the wall plates before we drive a nail in.'

Ivor cupped his hands around his mouth. 'Wocky!'

Wocky grinned. 'What's the trouble, Rosebud?'

'Look, Cynlais, borrow a shovel from the concrete ganger. Help Dai Sam and his mates for half an hour.'

'No problem, Rosebud,' Wocky said. 'Anything else, Rosebud, apart from those two lorries stuck up on the mountain?'

It was inevitable, Wocky tabbed him for the rest of his life: Rosebud Prosser, foreman carpenter.

Protocol Spin-Off

'Rampant as always,' he says, 'and it'll take more than revolutions, martyrs, blood on the streets etcetera. Another thing, ancient people such as the Welsh are past masters.' Rupe Maindy tongued his lips to moisten the butt of his cigar before lighting the other end. He whoofed out controlled puffs as if performing an act of grace—these are my birthday cigars. Old Rupe's a gawky pensioner with small, lava-black eyes, nubbly chin, his mouth splayed wide under a blue-flecked, bony ramp of nose. His reputation varies from wayward comedian to stubborn nit-picker, but he's sociable, he's a mixer. Rupe can laugh at himself.

I said, 'Surely you respect someone like Nye Bevan?'

'Another broken rung on the ladder,' says Rupe. 'Once, long ago, changing trains at Reading for Cardiff, big Nye ran past me on the station, fifty guineas' worth of black pinstripe on his back. I'm lugging a cheapjack suitcase. Nye was probably going to his farm in Berkshire. Not bad, from door-boy in the mines to gentleman-farmer. I'd been away at sea for months, stoker on a coal-burner. Gib. first, then North Africa, through the Med. to Cairo, on to Aden, back through the Med. to Liverpool. That ship, she rolled like a dub in jelly. *Next* time I saw Nye was in Hammersmith Hospital. Me, I'm keeping two homes going, clocking up to sixty-five hours a week as a plumber's mate. Nye, he's Minister for Health under Harold the Fixer.' Rupe vowed approval. 'Lovely smoke this, rolls 'round the sponges like camphorated oil.'

'I'm yuppy twice a year,' I said. 'Christmas-times and birthdays.'

Rupe flung a quiet shout. 'Good on you. How old?'

'Twenty-eight today.'

He brought two shorts from the bar. 'Little chaser to celebrate.' The gulped whisky wriggled his shoulders. 'As for class distinction, there's no cure. We all come from the womb, we all wind up in dust. In between we disguise ourselves.'

'How long were you in London, Rupe?'

'Depends when you're referring to, Glyn-boy. Y'know, I used to migrate back and fore like the wandering Jew.'

'When you saw Nye Bevan.'

'Couple of years that time. Trouble was, my wife and me, we'd struck a bad patch. Couldn't stomach the sight of each other. In-com-pat-ible. Cruel adjective, means delusion *written-in* to illusion. So one morning I pulled out. We had two kids in school, our eldest daughters, fine women they are, healthy, strong minded. Every week I sent Tillie what I could afford. She managed. I lived like a monk. She's gone now, February 1983. Bless her, Tillie-my-one-and-only, regardless, taking the rough with the smooth. What's a man to do when there's civil war going on in his house?'

'Don't know, Rupe.'

'Tillie couldn't leave the kids, therefore it's up to me.' He shushed long-drawn bubbles of spittle squeezing between his clenched teeth. 'I landed in Paddington without enough for bed and breakfast. Real tester. No money. No job.' He burped through smoke. 'You ambitious, Glyndwr?'

'Sometimes,' I said.

'Curse of the species,' he says gently. 'Older than bread.'

'You're the salt of the earth, Rupe.'

Neat as a swot, he quoted, 'Sermon on the Mount, Matthew chapter 5.'

'I didn't know that either,' I said.

'My dad was a Pentecostal. Decent chap, basically ignorant. He reared seven of us on the bible. Human nature hasn't changed in two thousand years. Two millennia of di-dap-doh, the Holy Ghost camouflaging fear with faith.'

I said, 'How did you cope, skint in London?'

'Shop window advert settled my fate. I found lodgings in Notting Hill, with a Geordie skivvy who'd married a Cockney twice her age. Breakfast every morning, all meals on Sunday. She let me have a week's lodging on strap, pending my first pay. Sub actually. Following day I'm with the maintenance crew at Hammersmith Hospital. Organised class structure of course. Chief engineer, Second engineer, then all the trades. Chippie, brickie, electrician, painter, pipe-fitter, plumber, three boilermen on shift work, two Paddies responsible for drains and sewers. At the bottom, labourers, fetch-and-carry blokes. Doddle of a job compared to stoker on a coal-burner. Poor money though, naturally. You had to fiddle to make a living wage. We kipped overtime down in the ducts, or played cards. Up above our heads, men, women and children were being

175

treated for all sorts, medical students learning to doctor, researchers studying bones and blood and giblets. Hammersmith Hospital, it was a world apart.'

A tout came selling tickets for the weekly draw.

'No thanks, we've bought ours,' lied Rupe.

I nudged him to empty his glass.

He surveyed the public bar. 'In every club you'll find dead-enders who've claimed their niche. They don't want disturbance, no aggravation, just get nicely slewed seven nights a week. Can't fault it if your life's a pain. There's sod-all besides. They've jibbed against taking and dishing out orders.' He prolonged another wet Shhhh. 'I lost a stone in two weeks. Cheapo meals in transport caffs, spuds, cabbage and Spam, hungry most nights going to bed. Aye, easier on my conscience than fighting Tillie.'

Rupe Maindy, ready-made guru with a Open University degree. He studied History before the reign of Mrs Thatcher.

'Cheers,' I said—this is our fifth pint.

'Likewise, Glyn-boy?'

Prodding him, I said, 'Two years plumber's mate.'

'With Charlie Alder, who fancied himself as a tap dancer. Charlie'd be dancing *Me and my shadow* across the top of a huge boiler cooling off for overhaul, still too hot to lay your hand on. Then he'd leap onto a gantry in darkness at the back of the boilerhouse, fantastical, like that Russian ballet dancer who went schizo.'

'Who?'

'Something *inski*.'

'Inski, Rupe?'

'Ndijinski, none other,' confirmed Rupe. He hooted once from high up in his nose. 'Fame leaves a mark.'

'For which he paid the price,' I said.

'Coincidental, boy. Reminds me, the morgue attendant blew his nut in Hammersmith Hospital. He seemed a typical chopsy Londoner, cheerful until the crack of doom. Except one day George went berserk.'

I had to ask, 'Why?'

Rupe's frown deepened two clefts rising from the root of his nose. 'Glyndwr, we are *all* addicted to the medicine of hindsight. Charlie Alder had some inkling, reckoned he heard George quarrelling with a corpse while wheeling him into the morgue. This smidgen of news from Charlie before the event itself. You see, on Saturday afternoons George's mother used to come trotting with his lunch. Dumpy little chatterbox woman. All the maintenance gang knew her. Poor dab, she reared a monster. He clawed out her hair, scragged her clothes, he booted her unconscious. They took George away from the morgue in a straightjacket.' Rupe's mouth twitched on the rim of his glass. He swallowed a quarter pint. 'Anyhow, she recovered in the Hospital. Then, eventually, Nye Bevan came to officially open a new nurses' dormitory. Architectural cockup by the Prince of Wales's standards, ah'm, he'd be on his nanny's lap at the time. Massive multi-storey block of concrete and glass opposite Wormwood Scrubs Prison. You'd see pale faces looking out from behind the barred windows. There were rumours. Some of the nurses putting on amateur strip-tease shows. Rumours, mind, rumours.'

'Harmless enough,' I said.

'Without proof,' insisted Rupe. 'There's no going back either. Feelings govern memories. Sometimes we rummage inside our heads for traces.'

'Your two sightings of Nye Bevan,' I said.

'In particular the consequences,' says Rupe. He scuttled his hands in mime at arms length. 'During the week before Nye came, there were a dozen men dangling like spiders outside the dormitory windows, cleaning off snobs of compo and paint, and contractors laid a new stretch of tarmac roadway around the workshops.'

'Come on, the usual bull,' I said.

'For the hero of Socialism,' says Rupe. 'Only we weren't allowed to see him. Charlie Alder, he knew every duct under the Hospital, all the pipelines, hot, cold and steam. 'Here we go, Taff,' he said. 'Bring me toolbag.' We crossed underground from a lab where . . . *experimenters*, they injected rats and mice, aye, underground to the back of the dormitory, then up fire escape ladders to the second floor. Stretched out flat in a corridor above the main hall, we had a bird's-eye view of the reception. They were on the dais, ranged in order of status. Entire hierarchy from Matron to governors, consultants, specialists, almoner, Chief engineer, Second engineer. Out on the floor of the hall, senior Nursing staff, admin. fellas from the front office, and run-of-the-mill politicians. Tables laid end to end along two walls, a buffet spread fit for royalty, crown caterers for sure, serving the Honourable Nye Bevan from Tredegar, Mon.'

I suggested, 'There's a name for it, Rupe. Protocol.'

'Glyn-boy, every soul in Britain was on rations.'

'Oh,' I said.

'My mate Charlie, he's whispering, 'Faaque me 'ooray, some faaquin' nosh down 'ere. Faaquin' Taffy geezer like you-self.' When Nye stepped forward to the lectern, Matron posed like a middle-aged carnival queen. Nye pushed his hair back a couple of times, blurted his famous stammer at the start, rolled out a short speech about modern accommodation for the nursing profession, and while everybody clapped Matron led him smiling along the row for handshakes. Fifteen minutes later Nye was sitting behind his chauffer in a Daimler, gliding around the workshops and back to Whitehall . . . or wherever.'

'Job and finish, as in the construction industry,' I said.

'Shambolic,' crowed old Rupe.

I said it again, 'Protocol, that's all. When you went up for your cap and gown, you obeyed protocol.'

Rupe huffed, 'Huh-uuhr uuhr,' like a bad case of asthma.

'You had no option.'

'Custom and practice,' he agreed.

'There then, it's natural.'

Rupe sniped under his breath, 'Versus barbarism.'

'Nonsense, man.'

'Makes us feel safe.'

I stressed, 'Protocol makes us feel we *belong*.'

'Virtuous,' grinned the old guru, 'right down to rag, tag and bobtail. You haven't heard the whole pantomime yet.'

'Carry on,' I said.

'Consider Nye Bevan as a disgrace to the brotherhood of man . . .'

'By Christ, Rupe.'

'Him too.'

'No!'

Rupe's hands are fisted side by side on the table and he's into preaching, memorising stuff because he's stone-cold like a robot. 'His suffering arrogance down the ages, prescribing guilt and the comfort of redemption for the sentient hominid. His boggling control stroke, that we are beholden to His unknowable Sire, since when countless have perished in His name, or surrendered in artefacts of the infant psyche, in cathedrals, churches, tabernacles, chapels, monasteries, nunneries, in corrugated iron shacks on the outskirts of commerce and privilege, where the already beaten station themselves to the dumb hereafter.'

'Wait,' I said, 'that sounds bloody foreign, it's a ridiculous way to talk.'

He leered mischievously. 'On par with what happened after Nye Bevan visited Hammersmith Hospital. The dormitory was already fully occupied. Beautiful girls, serious girls, hard-faced girls, West End high-lifers playing the glamour market.' Pause, Rupe musing slack-mouthed. 'Late Forties, early Fifties, can't remember the year.'

I protested, 'So! You're an *atheist*!'

'Turncoat heretic,' says Rupe. 'There isn't a joyful J. Christ in the annals. My round, boy.'

He poked long-shanked, stoop-shouldered across to the bar. Lucinda the barmaid convulsed at his quip, upper lip curled back off her baby-pink denture. The club steward stifled sniggering, his chin tucked.

'Ta, love,' says Lucinda. 'Cheeky old thing as you are.'

'Al'right, Rupe?' inquired the steward.

'My Celtic blood is rising,' boasted Rupe, flaunting a rickety swagger with our pints of bitter. He split a few more tablespoonfuls jiggling them down on table mats.

'Slewed?' I said.

Irritation slitted his glinty eyes. 'Merely celebrating cause and effect. Twenty-eight and three quarter years ago you were *enigma*, the centre of fusion, the beginning of Glyndwr Davies, destiny mysterious as the universe. Well, here's to you, boy.'

We tinged glasses. I said, 'Now, let's hear the rest of it.'

'Righto.' Rupe triggered his right hand forefinger. 'Maybe Nye had a sex problem, nothing extraordinary either. Human *is* as *does*, yes, right throughout. Angels do not procreate. The issue remains, Nye Bevan, a teeny weeny Christ blind to the consequences of protocol.'

'No more religion, if you don't mind,' I said.

'I remember your grandparents carrying their Sunday bibles. The chapels were crammed with believers. *Hwyl* poured from the pulpits of Wales. As the fourth son of a devout Pentecostal father, it's sad witnessing the levelling of *Iesu Grist*.'

I said, 'Rupe the turncoat.'

Delight suddenly gusted from him, adjusting by degrees to serenity. 'Sanctioned heretic in all truth, although sometimes in the small hours I'm inclined to be poop scared of dying.'

'Really, Rupe?'

'Aye, the dark lasts forever.'

My tongue felt useless. Goose-pimple spasm prickled through the flush of booze. Old Rupe spying sideways under the streaky grey of his tufted eyebrows.

'Y'know,' he says, 'after Nye left in his Daimler, the reception broke up, leaving a clique of non-Hammersmith Hospital guests sipping glasses of wine, pretending to be important. I humped Charlie's toolbag back down the ladders. We surfaced in the experimental lab. At the end of our shift, Charlie held a conference in the ablutions place. He gave a guttsier spiel than Bevan, result being we formed a delegation. Charlie Alder spokesman, Howard the chippie, a painter named Leo, and a pipe-fitter named Edwin. Myself, I'm only Charlie's mate. We went to the Chief engineer's office. The Second engineer was secretive, a nonentity who kept his nose clear, unlike the Chief, who'd stick his neck on the line. The men trusted him. He told Charlie's delegation, 'Take the lot, if it's still there.'

'Take what?' I said.

Rupe hissed snakily. 'In the hall of the new dormitory, Nye Bevan's modern accommodation for the nursing profession. Nye forgot the bread and scrape-it years of his upbringing in Tredegar. Nye stole ideas, then he created a different kind of dross. The blinkered vision of leaders, statesman working the same pitch as Old Testament fathers.' Rupe failed a sweet reason smile. 'Small episode, boy, Nye up on the dais with the Hospital elite, awfully small, trivial in the mythology of democracy, but it's locked in my heart. Yes, all those exotic sandwiches, the crackers and cheeses, de luxe pastries and biscuits, the sugary fruitbits, the silverware, the serviettes. A Buckingham Palace feast.'

I said, 'Nye Bevan stole ideas?'

'From long-headed utopians in the Miners' Federation, when they were organising themselves against the coal owners,' explained Rupe.

180

Lucinda thumbed the bell behind the bar.

'Last orders. Knock it back,' I said.

Says Rupe, 'Somebody else whipped the left-over bottles of wine. We ferried the grub across to the workshops on two trolleys borrowed from the laundry. Getting dark by now, the Second engineer sweating his eyeballs, begging us to hurry-hurry-hurry. Leo the painter handed him a cake on a serviette, it was icing topped with glacé cherries. 'Shove this in your gob,' he said. Blunt individual, Leo the painter.' Rupe drained his glass. 'I pushed the trolleys back to the laundry, while Charlie and his delegation sorted out the loot. Share and share alike to all the workshops. We were eating dainty sandwiches and pastries every tea-break for days.'

More fuddled than amused, I elbowed through to the bar counter.

'Sink these sharpish,' advised the steward cordially.

'No problem,' I said.

'Hey,' says busy Lucinda, 'Mr Maindy's idea! Turn this club into a private brothel for Methodist and Baptist deacons, seein' as they've been demolishin' the chapels right, left an' centre, as we all know for a fact!'

The steward chipped in, 'Good solid buildings, the stone chapels. Genuine craftsmanship.'

'Gone dead though,' argued Lucinda. 'Nobody's bothered about 'em at all!'

The steward glanced up at the wall clock: 11.50 p.m.

Back at our table, I saluted Rupe, 'Cheers, old mate.'

He says, 'Happy birthday, Glyndwr. To put your mind at unrest, in 1937 I felt I was in charge of my destiny.'

'How come?' I said.

'We were twenty-one in 1937.'

'You and . . ?'

'Tillie.'

'Sorry, didn't realise. Drink up. Only a few minutes to go.'

'Aye, time, time, time marches on.'

'I'm no damn *fatalist*,' I said, tutored by six and a half pints of best bitter, plus the midway chaser.

'Here today, gone tomorrow.'

'Bloody rubbish, man, bloody clichés.'

'They endure, like protocol.'

Members passed by in singles and groups, heading towards the lobby.

'Howbe, Rupe.'

'*Shwmae*, Rupe.'

'G'night, Rupe.'

'Be seeing you, Rupe.'

'All the best, Rupe.'

'Hullo there, Rupe.'

'Take it easy, Rupe.'

'So-long, Rupe.'

They sent me flicked winks and casual nods.

'You *know* every bastard,' I said.

'Wrong, boy. I'm just a reflection,' his grin coming and going, creasing his battered face. 'Same old dream, Glyndwr: brotherhood of man.'

And Lucinda bawled, 'C'mon, getta move on!'

Home Comforts, Besides the Convenience All Round

Boys being what they helplessly are, we imagined roles for Mildred Taylor, the lavendered reality of our carnal budding. We cast her in situations of erotic fancy with Pip Pearce, who taught General Science. Tunnelling libidos like tormented moles, we laid small, hot bets, simpling her whole life and times. Mildred Taylor *was* beautiful, utterly, earnestly lovely with a crystalline soprano voice that trembled her soft white throat. Entering our classroom for singing practice, she personified the opposite of utility female, of bosom and loins. Our Miss Taylor shone. She was rare, ethereal, too perfect. Her dainty hands and feet were mesmeric flickerings, ineffectual perhaps . . . how were we to know? She wore flowered frocks, her dark hair cherubim-curled, scented for rousing puberal madness. Pretty girls worshipped her, plain girls envied her, sullen girls brewed malice, muttered liturgies of disaster.

One afternoon she fainted at the end of the last line of 'Flow gently, sweet Afton', while leaning over Albie Charles, who sabotaged every singing lesson.

'I tickled her bum,' Albie said.

Pip Pearce carried her out to the staff room. Tall, tweedy, smarmy, treacherous as migraine, wavy-haired, hard-eyed, you'd see him flashing his choppers at Miss Taylor, his rugger shoulders immaculate for symmetery and pose. They were lovers, we were dead certain, fast couplers on a par with any two outside the dull hell of compulsory education.

I whispered to Albie, 'Shurrup, keep your trap shut.'

'Guh, 'fraid,' he said.

Then Pip Pearce charged in again. You! Get out. Wait for me in the cloakroom.'

Therefore Albie did it, brought on the swoon, otherwise Pip wouldn't have swung at him, sick-squealing, 'Dirty little swine, you dirty little swine,' his horizontal karate chops landing on Albie's ribs.

Albie went home with a letter from the headmaster.

Next morning at eleven o'clock, Albie's old lady and his brother came strolling across the school yard. 'Righto, Mam, leave him to me,' Albie's brother said, swaying slow, Pip

183

Pearce dipping the same way, soul-trapped as a rabbit, into a fast left-hook.

Miss Taylor wept, secretly sobbed all day, her violet eyes grieving, flinching from Albie like you see in dingy old paintings of spectators at the Cruxifixion.

And now only last Whitsun I met Albie Charles for the first time in seventeen years. He jumped out from the yellow Landrover, yelling, 'Hey, for God's sake!' a cigar aimed at my mouth, his big, meaty hand dragging me into the Queen's Hotel.

I said, 'Great to see you, Albie. Right in the money by the looks of it.'

'Two large whiskies,' he said to the barmaid.

She dibbled her lips with her tongue as if she'd flog him two of anything.

'Money,' he said, quietly incisive, 'boy, last year we cleared five thou. I've just pulled a contract for laying two miles of kerb. That's what I'm in, asphalting and laying kerbs.'

'Where?'

'Anywhere, anywhere at all.' The barmaid counted his change. 'Ta. Say, what are you having?'

'Um, drop of gin. Ever so kind of you, Mr . . ?'

'Albert Charles, love, Albie Charles, born and bred in this little town. What's the tariff here in the Queen's? See, I'm around for a few months, swanning to and from Bristol till next winter. Look, bring the manager, okay?'

'Here's to days gone by,' I said.

He sniffed his whisky, muttering, 'Thank Christ.'

I said, 'This particular couple of miles, where are they?'

'Your new council estate, the lot, plus the run out to the motor-way.'

'Pondorosa,' I said. 'We call Hafod Estate "Pondorosa", from that crap show on telly.'

He grinned, fatly-complacent. 'Things don't change much over the years. They build a new housing estate, but Hafod isn't good enough, the locals tab another name on it.'

'Married yet?' I asked.

'Hah, awkward bastard,' he jeered genially, his finger and thumb doing a slow-motion castanet for the barmaid. 'Same again, my dear. Keep the supply handy.'

I left him chatting up the manager.

Less than a minute after I closed my front door, Hester reached for her cracked glacé handbag. 'If you can guzzle whisky when there's five weeks rent owing, I can borrow a few bob to visit my father. I'm entitled to! Good-bye!'

She slammed the door.

'Stay with your old man, don't bother to come back,' I said, not even hoping any more because after seven begrudged years of quibbling you suspend all hope, quit everything except the habit of tit for tat. In marrying Hester I took on one of those daunting Electra girls. Tomorrow, I thought, I'll see Albie out on Hafod Estate. He's successful. Something might rub off.

But I dithered, avoided the issue until Saturday, riding a cheap conviction that Albie's firm wouldn't be working a six day week. I could have seen him any night in the Queen's; pride's a canker when you can't jiggle two silver coins in your pocket.

My wife said, 'Albie Charles, ugh, him, dragged up he was.'

'You haven't set eyes on Albie since we left school,' I said.

She sneered, 'I'm worried sick.'

You fish-blooded nun, I thought, before asking, 'Remember the time he tickled Mildred Taylor in singing practice?'

Hester stalled, snorting endless resentment, her down-cast mouth clamped on it.

Husk-head, all mine under licence.

'See you around dinner-time,' I said.

'Scrag-end stew!' she protested. 'I don't know, we're existing worse than refugees. This isn't what I was brought up to, never on your life.'

'Your generous old man might throw us some surplus caviare,' I said.

It's a slanting climb up to Hafod Estate, the higher Clearway edged into ferny hillside, travelling a shallow curve around the mountain. After dark, traffic headlights veer away, reversing to red tail lights as vehicles take the steep S bend which clears the summit. I walked in mid-morning sunshine, the Estate glittering. Saturday kiddies and summery women were out on the trot, husbands potching in their first-crop gardens, cheerfully automaton breadmen, milkmen, insurance men, H.P. collectors, and dogs. Neurotic dogs everywhere, barking off the tops of breeze-block walls. Typical Glamorgan

185

mountain clay gardens, ochrous, cold quilt covering the best steam coal in the world. Idling up through the Estate, I heard her greeting before I saw Miss Taylor, beckoning dignified as royalty on the new front lawn of her three-roomed bungalow. Not all that old, really; she'd be thirty-sevenish, wrapped in a flowery frock as always, exquisitely Dresden, her complexion dreamed out of the beauty closet of her sincere soul.

'Well indeed, how pleasant,' she cooed. 'Another of my pupils. Come inside, I have a surprise for you.'

Albie was studying the *Sporting Life*. He wore a poncy dressing gown and red leather slippers. A red polka dotted cravat poutered beneath his blunt chin. And bald, Albie, smooth-white bald as a bladder of lard. He ripped the *Sporting Life* in half, humphed disgust as he heeled himself away from Miss Taylor's dinky little writing bureau. 'Out of bounds, boy,' he said. 'I thought you lived the other end of town.'

'He does, Albert,' her gently-levering arms bringing us together. 'Now, shake hands like gentlemen.'

'We've already met. Listen, Millie, how about some coffee?' he said, stuffing the torn racing paper into his pocket. 'Heavy night last night. I had my C. and P. experts from Bristol.' Albie exaggerated the shakes of his right hand. 'Look at that, can't steady my fingers. Eyeballs like sheep's currants in the snow, can't see properly. Fetch the coffee, Mill, ah, if you don't mind?' He went back to the bureau, sheafed some loose pages, puffs and grunts escaping from his tight mouth.

She twitched between pleasure and guilt, creases serpenting the bland forehead below her dark hair. 'I understood it was a formal dinner, token of goodwill in your business. Surely?' She touched his cheek with the tips of her fingers. 'All right, I'll make the coffee.'

He grinned, watching her tripping out of the room. 'Some bird. She sat up most of the night waiting for me.'

'What's going on then?' I said.

'Going on! I'm just the paying guest. We bumped into each other a fortnight ago. See, I'm criticising the service in the Queen's, so Mildred makes the offer. Full room and board. Suits me, home comforts, besides the convenience all round.' Albie palmed his stomach. 'I'm heading for alcoholism, don't fancy it either, seen too many clever bastards hit the bottle and land in the shit.' He worried through the loose pages on Miss

Taylor's bureau. 'Trouble is, boy, her ideas are different from mine. She knows nothing about pressure.'

I said, 'How about fixing me up with a job?'

A shaft of sunlight swooped across his baldness like a straightened aureola. 'My pleasure. You'll be labouring. It's piece-work, good money once you harden to the graft. Another thing, don't lose any time or you'll be up the road. Can't afford sentiment on this contract. It's all tight, real tight.'

'Start Monday morning?' I said.

Albie nodded, sunshine starring the buffed ivory of his dome. Miss Taylor's curtains pinkened the room. It was peaceful, charcoal drawings of prancing stallions hanging each side of the window, two tall bookcases full of book club best sellers, a round dining table, flower-print cushions ribboned to Queen Anne style chairs, embroidered cushions correctly scattered on the settee, below a flying wedge of terracotta mallards geometrically plaqued to the wall. A fan of pink-stained teazel stalks sprayed upwards inside the fire-place.

When she brought the coffee I remembered my drab, anguished Hester, her wearing rancour, her wifely uselessness.

Albie shook out three pills from a plastic phial. 'Revivers,' he explained.

'Do be careful, Albert. One hears so much about harmful drugs.'

'Never panic, I'm no gutless fool,' he said, swilling them down with coffee. There was a stoniness on him, a kind of bloodless indifference. 'Pip Pearce still on the staff?' he said.

She stared at nothing, the white of her eyes not quite so moon-glowing. 'Phillip Pearce? Well, you know, he couldn't settle down. Phillip transferred to a small country school, in Devon I believe. Yes, north Devon. His parents left soon afterwards. Mm, how long ago it seems.'

Albie said, 'That's life. Water under the bridge. That's the way it is. He wasn't a bad fella, old Pip Pearce.'

'He dealt you a real lamping one time,' I said, stupidly forgetting Miss Taylor serenely perched between us at the table.

Albie scowled, left his chair, focussed the same scowl on his business papers. 'Right,' he said. 'Eight o'clock Monday morning. Bring your insurance card.'

'See you,' I said. 'Thanks for the coffee, Miss Taylor.'

Her chin trembled innocent delight, the way she sang for us when we were kids, pouring her soprano into 'Flow gently, sweet Afton'.

Later, over the scrag-end stew, I told Hester about Albie lodging with Miss Taylor. She wasn't interested. Hester nagged, threatened to stock her wardrobe instead of paying our rent debt. They'd perished, all her school-time memories were squashed under the weight of her father. He ruined Hester's childhood. Ruined her, his lorn child. My stultified wife.

Summer spent iself, contrary as usual in up-and-down Glam., but autumn brought golden, windless weather, sappling poplars planted to beautify Hafod Estate taking on rusty tints, decay creeping slow from the highest tracts of hillside bracken. Albie's firm employed two gangs of men. The top-gang were kerb-laying down a slip road from the Clearway; the second gang worked on Hafod Estate. Houses were still going up. Slum clearance families swarmed in. More dogs, cats, plastic footballs, airguns, pigeons, napkins, transistors galore. When the children returned to school after their long holiday, Hafod Estate folded quiet. I worked with Albie's top gang, always behind the concrete mixer, consequence of rowing with the ganger. This charming navvy despised slum clearance families. Naturally enough they had a sad percentage of crocks and cripples among them: bad chests, stomach ulcers, rheums, skewed genes, game legs, weak minds, burnt nerves. He'd taken a strong dose of white-man's toxin, this cranky avant-garde navvy, so I shovelled into the mixer and humped kerbstones.

For weeks on end we saw Albie belting along the slip road in his yellow Land Rover. Then came the first hard night-frosts. Both gangs were concentrated on Hafod Estate to finish off the contract.

Saturday evening, November the fifth (the date guaranteed to stick), a huge staked Guy flared paraffin flames in the backyard next to our house. Lower down the terrace some lads were launching sky rockets, tangentially though, instead of vertically, aiming them at next door's Guy. Speaking truthfully, I'm partial to a stint of chaos. Chaos ferments the tired old dough of homo erectus, keeps it on the rise.

Hester called from the kitchen window. 'S'long, I'm away now. I'll be home tomorrow night.'

'Enjoy yourself,' I said. She spends well-nigh every weekend with her father. Military Medallist from Tobruk, her widower dad, ex-Sergeant-Major to boot. Fine hero. Messed-up his only daughter.

The lads from lower down began tossing jackie-jumpers and bangers when Albie arrived. It was like a tiny edition of warfare, these fizzers suddenly banging off, taming the autumn stars to tenth rate.

'You should know why I'm here,' he said, lighting his cigar from the glowing remains of a firework. 'Job's almost finished, but listen, boy, if you come to Bristol with me I'll make you up, put you in charge of a small gang. All the extras. I can't be fairer.'

I said, 'Much obliged. I'll stick it out here. We may come to terms some day, Hester and myself I mean.'

'We've all got problems,' he said. 'Right then, c'mon, let's sink a couple in the Queen's. I want you to do me a personal favour.'

Miss Taylor was waiting for us in the lounge bar, tenterhooked as a maiden aunt behind a tall orange juice, too much of her real age showing, pitiful, a loose lemon-yellow coat hiding her secret belly. On the second round of drinks I called Albie across to the counter. 'You didn't tell me she was pregnant,' I said.

The barmaid had survived, ceased to appreciate him. She signalled a friendly little flutter of the fingers to Miss Taylor, who strained a return smile that left her defenceless. Mildred Taylor looked stricken, wrecked on biological ignorance.

Albie brought his mouth down to my eye level. 'Here's what I'm asking you to do for me. Monday morning after I pull out, call in the bungalow. I'll arrange it with my foreman. Make her understand I won't be coming back. Two reasons. First, there's my wife and three daughters in Bristol. Second, we're starting a long contract out Keynsham way. Means I've got to be on the spot. Wait, take it easy, boy, take it easy. Listen, I'm paying for everything, see, everything. After the nipper comes along she'll collect a nice lump sum through the post.'

I said, 'Why bring me into this?' the barmaid's ears inching closer to clinch what she probably suspected. 'You can't expect me, Albie,' I said, 'to take on the responsibility.'

'Christ,' he vowed, 'al'right, I'll tell her.' His fist softly bumped the counter. 'Know what her trouble was? She'd never sampled it before. Never. Hard to credit, that, couldn't believe it myself at first. I reckon she's cried every night for two months, give or take a few here and there. By the Jesus, she's like a drain, cry-cry-cry night after night.'

Fireworks were cracking off outside the Queen's and somebody lobbed a Thunderflash into the public bar. Women screamed as expected. It was a provocative atmosphere.

'Your wife,' I said, 'what's she like?'

'One of the very best.' He emptied his glass. 'If she comes to hear about Mildred, huh, I'd sooner settle for a bed of stingie nettles.'

'Afraid of your wife?' I said.

'No-no . . .'

'Yes-yes,' I said.

The barmaid served him a double whisky. Albie sniffed it, emptied the glass, bought himself another beer, grunted a kind of private righteousness against destiny, and, 'Lead the way,' he said.

Miss Taylor nervously plucked her curly-whiffed hair, the delicate ovals of her nostrils red-raw as the inflamed poop-holes of sickly babies. I noticed some of her eyelashes were stuck together, as occurs when stye pus crystallises during sleep. Poor Miss Taylor, she looked hag-ridden. Contractor Albie, he pulled thuggish faces at a fresh cigar, his match-hand glinting a thick gold ring on the statutory bloody finger, Miss Taylor's face emptying, dredged beyond hysteria.

'That,' she quavered, 'means you are a married man.'

'Speaks for itself. Aah, listen, Millie, I fully intended informing you about my wife . . .'

'Take a walk,' I said. 'Wait for us in the lobby.'

Albie shrugged like a bit-part actor, swerved up from his chair and strolled out, grossly immune in his Dak business suit and dove-grey hat.

Miss Taylor winced herself smaller inside the lemon yellow coat. Time spayed out of whack while she struggled to find the child-like composure of her youth. She smiled. 'I'm not a vindictive person. It isn't my nature.'

'What will you do, Miss Taylor?' I said.

'I am quite capable of looking after myself. Circumstances

being what they are, I must make plans for the future.' The smile sputtered out as faint remorse. 'As for Albert Charles, may he rot in his own wickedness.'

'Buy yourself a wedding ring,' I suggested. 'Nobody'll be any the wiser, I mean we can place one of those In Memoriam notices in the local paper, bury Albie somewhere the other side of Severn Bridge, bury him forever. More important, Miss Taylor, consider the financial aspect. The man's afraid of his wife. He's harmless. We've got him over a barrel.'

Panning her violet eyes, she murmured, 'Aren't you a cunning devil.'

'Hester trained me,' I said.

She stretched almost a pretty smile. 'Strange, the girl was absolutely tone deaf.'

I said, 'Aye, true, true. Ready now, Miss Taylor?'

'Perfectly ready.'

'All that remains to be cleared up,' I said, 'is how much he's prepared to pay. We'll have it in writing, my signature as witness, just in case.'

Giggling relief, dimples plucking each side of her mouth, she confessed softly, 'Phoo, I'm glad it's all over. Tonight I shall sleep in peace.'

Here's proof, I thought. Innocence conquers experience.

Standing on the pavement outside the Queen's, she ignored Albie, her small hand cheekily wriggling the funny bone of my elbow. 'You must bring Hester to tea next Sunday evening. Promise.'

'Bank on it,' I said. 'In the meantime I'll discuss details with Albie. We'll draw up a statement.'

Tinkling like a girl, she hurried across the road to a Hafod Estate bus.

Albie trod on the butt of his cigar. 'What's all this about a statement, boy?'

'Safety precaution, Albie, confidential, as regards your wife.'

'How much?' he said.

'She insists on bringing in a lawyer, blood tests, evidence from her diary, loss of income in due course . . .'

He kicked the flattened cigar. 'I'll talk her out of it. Few hundred made out to the kid, that's my limit.'

I said, 'Three thou as a starter—I'm quoting Miss Taylor— then thirty-three and a third per cent until the child is sixteen.'

Adrenalin cued a flood of spittle to his mouth. He couldn't speak.

'You're still young,' I said. 'Only my age. Too young for a heart attack. You might as well hear the facts first as last.'

Then, 'Bitch,' he snarled, lowered his head and booted the front tyre of his Landrover like a lunatic. Strong man temporarily out of his mind. A spectacle hard to forget.

We buried him fictiously a month later, via notices in two newspapers. Mildred's son was born under Aries, the true amalgam of his mother and Albie. Fixing fate for a plump, gurgling baby happens to the Holy Ghosts's prerogative, but as the child's godfather I predict wolverine tenacity tempered by angelic sweetness. I prophesy total commitment balanced by loving kindness. He'll be unique, a phenomenon out of ancient Cymru.

The Foxhunters

Climbing Pen Arglwydd through stalky tracts of heather, they reached the scree line before heat came into the August morning.

'Let's take five,' Joe said. 'Queenie, here bitch, come in. Down, gel, down, ease the weight.' Couchant on her swollen belly, the oatmeal-coloured lurcher roved her head, dark eyes glazed, spasms twitching her black nostrils.

Joe Phelps and Shad Elias smoked thin, hand rolled cigarettes. Shad squinted at sunshot windowpanes far below, terraced rows of their home village, looped like a horizontal U inside a spangle of four collieries, the main valley road aimed straight out from its green-sided mouth. Two greens: shorn hayfield opposite the pocked turf of a children's playground. Leftwards they had a three-mile vista, the far mountain under conifers, steeping sharply down to derelict allotments. Nearside the valley shallowed, row upon row of houses, small shops, pubs and chapels broaching the gradual slope. Rightwards from Pen Arglwydd, overbearing mountains flung up tightly above Blaen-du village, the four pits resting Sunday-quiet, a stationary red bus pegged askew of the village square. Pencil tendrils of pale-grey chimney smoke hung, wavered, disappeared.

'Nice morning,' Shad said, grinning his puffy mouth. 'All the flayed whoores and bent rams of Wales are snoring, jammed fast in the aftermath of last night's lust.'

Said Joe, 'Boy, you're nothing but a cowin' preacher.'

Shad's big brindle lurcher wagged his thick tail, using his rump to buffet the third lurcher, a sandy-coated young dog named Butty. Joe grabbed the pup's scruff, clamped him between his legs, 'Hold still, you'll knock yourself up.'

The brindle, Duke, took a light backhander from Shad, sniffed around the old bitch and slouched off a few yards, facing up-hill, powerfully splay-legged, tremors shivering his flanks. He yawned full gape, ending on a squeak, shook along his length and sat on his haunches.

Rear leg cocked, the Jack Russell busied himself, licking dirt from his groin. Joe removed the terrier's skimpy collar, 'You don't want this, Nails, not if you go to ground over in Garreg-fawr.'

193

'Correct,' Shad said. 'Neither do I feel like digging him out today.'

'My old lady's of the opinion you've got a lazy streak in you,' said Joe.

Shad's grin emptied itself. 'Your old lady ought to be a lady-in-waiting.'

'Come agen, Shad-boy?'

'To some fat-arsed cannibal queen, your old lady being the only woman I know who'd give etiquette the dignity of a monkey pit.'

'Aah, be quiet,' says Joe. He held Butty enraptured, his coal-grained fingers scatching inside the pup's ears. Nails continued licking himself. ''Tis nice after last week's rain,' he agreed, 'specially last Wednesday. It tamped down while that thunder was on.'

'Couple of months from now they'll be running up to spawn,' Shad said. 'Catch any good ones in the river this season?'

Joe spat clear of his ex-WD boots. 'River's worse now than before the club took over. Ask me, we're stocking for those blokes down the valley. That's where I'll do my fishing next year, down there.'

'Everything's a massive balls-up,' remarked Shad mildly.

Joe said, 'Leave it, man, leave it.'

They climbed again, winding along narrow sheep paths, foot-picking up gullies, the dogs tracking out, nosing behind whinberry clumps on rocky ledges, covering ground methodically. Shad's brindle lurcher leaping to higher ledges, working like a robot. When they reached the summit the dogs fell to heel. Rolling mountain top under naked sky, invisible grasshoppers churring, ceasing like engineered mysteries. A late brood of crows rose from a dead sheep, the eyes, tongue and intestines ripped out. Small maggots speckled the soiled wool.

'We might see a this year's cub on the move,' decided Joe. 'Remember last August, way over the top above the waterfall?'

'Queenie flung him a couple of times,' Shad said. 'Aye, decent chase fair-do. He could shift too, for a young fox.'

'Almost full grown. Be ideal for Butty, easy one like that.' Joe put a leash on the pup, 'Stop your bloody galloping. Your father had fits when he was your age.'

'Greater love hath no man,' muttered Shad, swiftly lifting his instep under the brindle lurcher's ribs as he made to roll in the sheep carcass. 'I know you're acting natural, Duke, but you'll pong the house out.'

'He shouldn't be indoors at all,' argued Joe.

Walking downhill on the northern slope of Pen Arglwydd, Joe processed a quiet, tuneless 'Tarr-rrarr-rrarr, tarr-rrarra,' from his wide-lipped mouth. Anciently-sunken mossed scree underfoot, with stunted oaks, rowans and hawthorns. Lower down, rough pasture abruptly ended on the lip of a glacial gutter. Deep pools boiled froth, the gutter dipping laterally across the landscape.

Joe hunkered with the pup lurcher between his thighs. 'Try your glasses, Shad, just in case we miss a clever reynard breaking away before we cross the river.'

Shad unclipped his binocular case. He scanned the jumbled escarpment of Garreg-fawr. Dark, man-high crags outcropped beyond a fringe of willows on the far side of the gutter, skirting a hill of rocks thrown all shapes and sizes, fixity from remote chaos, silent under heat shimmers. Odd, grasping hawthorns tufted green in the black welter, giving Garreg-fawr the deceptive fragility of oriental paintings.

'Nothing,' said Shad, then, 'Haa, no, *can't* be!'

'What?' demanded Joe.

'Loving Jesus . . .'

'What, man?'

'There's a girl down there. True!'

'Gimme those glasses. Give give give!'

Shad said, 'In line with that big pool. Flat slab of rock on the opposite bank.'

Joe sang faint tenor, 'She's in the buff.'

As they crossed sloping moorland Butty leapt aside, pelting after a rising skylark, Joe hissing at him, furiously kicking him, the pup throwing yelps into the silence. The other dogs milled away, cringing—and the sunbathing girl, she gathered up her clothes, ran ghostly between the willow fringe and the stark rocks, fleeing without a backward glance down alongside the foamy pools. Joe stroked a single blow on Butty's ribs, the pup howling, Joe gone stony, swishing his walking stick.

Downstream a hundred yards, the tawny nude leisurely dressed herself. They saw her disappearing inside a yellow frock, become immobile for some minutes, watching them in turn. Joe raised his arm, beckoning. The girl sauntered away.

'She's a what's-a-name, a naiad,' said Shad, 'from my Carmarthen grancha's rubaiyat. Aye, lovely thing.'

'Stay still, you rowdy sod,' Joe said to the lurcher pup. Butty curried favour, tail between his legs, total submission in his eyes. 'I'll learn you,' warned Joe impassively, scratching the pup's ears.

'Lovely thing she was,' repeated Shad. 'Great sprinter. Beautiful action. Imagine her coming directly at you, Joe, top speed, like a wreath.'

'Ah?'

'Hymn then, like a hymn.'

'For Chrissake,' said Joe.

'Coming at you like Eve on the loose from Eden.'

'Nuh,' Joe sniggering, wobbling his knees, 'More like a butcher shop on fire. C'mon, let's move, Shad-boy.'

They worked Garreg-fawr, Joe taking the left flank with his three dogs, Shad and Duke some distance away, climbing parallel. The Jack Russell whined once, flushing a dozy buzzard from one of the hawthorns, Queenie turning slow motion, watching the raptor plane low over the boulders, tilt upwards from the pooled gutter, stall and descend, gracefully fold to standstill on a brightly mossed ant hill.

'Get on, Nails. Get on, Queenie,' ordered Joe, reluctant to use his voice while the dogs hunted among the echoing rocks.

They climbed carefully, watching, listening, Shad gradually angling across until they came to the first fox bury—merely a cleft holing down into dry peat. Nails spent a few seconds inside, came out and growled a warning at the lurcher pup. Now Joe and Shad moved on together, Duke swinging wider, Joe muttering at Shad to control the dog, timelessness suddenly upon them because the shaggy oatmeal-coloured bitch suddenly launched herself after the brindle. Her savage concentration streaked into Shad, stiffening his stomach.

'Goo-ood bitch,' whispered Joe, his strange yell gagging behind his soundbox, finding itself: 'Meat off him! Meat off him!'

All the dogs were away, the fox a ruddy blur skittering between black rocks.

'Head him off, head him off,' Joe was saying, running, goat-

196

leaping after the dogs. Clumsy Butty lost the scurrying little Jack Russell. Shad saw the young lurcher come to a whining halt on a big boulder, saw him teetering, fall as if thrown. 'Watch out for Butty!' cried Joe. 'On Nails, gerron dog!' Butty twitched on his pads, his slingy puppyhood bruised to a hobble. Shad picked him up, massaged his trembling belly, and he saw the fox again, travelling up an inclined gully, running flat-backed over broken shale. He thought, they've missed him, sure to miss the bugger, but on the instant he saw the fox making great low-curved bounds up the gully, the big brindle coming at full volley, Queenie behind Duke, labouring from the burden of her unborn litter. The fox vanished. Shad thought, if he clears Garreg-fawr he's ours. My Duke will outrun him.

Butty whined, nuzzling for comfort. 'All right, young un,' Shad said.

He hadn't moved from the huge boulder when Joe shouted, 'Coming down, Shad! Over on your left! Sha-ad! Nails coming down!'

The terrier squealed frenzy, hidden among rocks. Shad dropped the lurcher pup and ran, ran confounded, glancing up at his brindle and Queenie climbing the gully, and then sighting the Jack Russell down below, the *second* fox chopping back at him.

'Get him, Nails,' yelled Shad.

The terrier snorted, hanging on to the fox's brush, another lightning back-snap cleaving through his nose and upper lip.

'Hold him,' pleaded Shad.

He saw them on the smooth rock shelf where the girl had sunbathed, fox and terrier bundling over and over, the fox twisting airborne contortions, Nails hanging fast to his underbelly. Next they were coiled together in the pool.

Shad ran down, thinking, Nails must have fastened onto this one before he bolted.

There were chocolate wrappers and crimsoned cigarette butts on the flat rock.

He shouted, 'Hold him, Nails, hold him, dog!'

They churned under-water. Shad only saw matted fox-brown. 'Nails,' he said. 'Nails,' the fox's head surfacing, eyes slitted, grinning like a stuffed mask. 'Get him, Nails,' urged Shad. The fox slashed downwards. Again his head came aslant

197

the surface, grinning, and he slashed again, tumbling with it, sprung inwards upon himself.

'Let go, Nails,' cried Shad, pushing the excited pup away from his knees.

The terrier's hind quarters came floating up, the fox tightly curled around Nails' head and shoulders, violently unwinding himself, the sleek wet mask lolling, then snaking another chop at the terrier.

Shad turned, saw Joe Phelps toiling through tall summer fens above Garreg-fawr. He saw Queenie loping along a bare cut of skyline. Where's my big hound? he wondered, as he waded into the pool. Icy water prickled his sweaty legs. When the fox rolled up, he reached for the red-brown nape but the white teeth struck, too fast, slicing the flesh below his thumb. 'Right,' Shad said, lunging again. He missed, collapsing on one knee, chest deep, and the fox submerged, went down, down deeper with the terrier.

He ploughed in, cursing, chipped his ankle on a sharp bedded stone, thrashed to keep his balance, and he saw the refracted, elongated fox shape sneaking away, up and out, amphibiously, like an otter at the tail of the pool. The fox crawled from the water, disregarded Butty's yapping, steadily crawled up the peat crumbly bank, paused as if defeated, blood dripping from his holed paunch, then he dealt Butty a vulpine slash attack, ripping his ear. Butty yammered, shaking his head. The fox paraded wetly, firm on his feet, plumb straight across the open moorland.

Waist deep in the pool, Shad baulked, crying, 'Nails!' knowing it was useless, so he plunged for the Jack Russell, floundered headlong, dived twice, searching the grey-pebbled bottom, failing each time, the undertow trundling Nails down to the shallows.

'Nails,' he pleaded, 'come on, Nails, come to dog,' pumping the terrier's belly and rib box, forcing out greenish trickles, blood-stained, the trickles sundering to cold, lifeless froth. Nails had lost his left eye, the socket filled-in red, no longer bleeding, the surrounding bone rippling under Shad's fingertips.

Dazed, he knelt over the drowned terrier, elbowed off the young lurcher, time after time he pushed him away until Butty sprawled on the flat rock and whimpered misery. The hot sun dried Nails on one side. Shad patiently turned him over, exposing the red, puckered eye socket. He covered the terrier's head with his wet jacket. Joe, he thought, when he sees Nails he'll go crazy. This'll drive him mad. He'll rave. Ah, Jesus Christ. Then he thought, I could do with a smoke. My fags are ruined. Ah, Jesus Christ . . . jinx, that bloody girl, that bloody stripper out here . . . stuffing herself with Rowntrees. Hurry up, Joe. How much longer, Joe?

Joe came with Queenie and Duke, still Tarr-rrarr-rrarring his non-tune, a killed vixen slung along his walking stick.

'Nails is dead, Joe, he's a goner. They were scrapping in the pool. I didn't realise, thought sure Nails would put paid to the fox. He's killed a few, bad conditions an' all, up here in Garreg-fawr. Nails held on, wouldn't let go. I tried . . . look!' Shad held out his hand. I tried to break them apart! Christ, I tried, I tried!'

They wept briefly, shamefaced, kneeling beside the little terrier. Then Joe picked him up, held Nails under his left arm and he carried him back over Pen Arglwydd mountain, tramping through the blazing August afternoon, Shad Elias leading with the slung fox, the three lurchers padding single file behind Joe Phelps.

Reardon Jones, MM

Soldier Jones lived in a rotting half-timbered bungalow, with a garden of brambles, dock, nettles, skeletal prams, old tyres and rusted scraps of corrugated sheeting. Of his father and mother, he said, 'I lost two of the best.' As for his other relatives, 'They wouldn't give a man the skin off a grape.'

Soldier had the jocund refusal to despair of pre-war British swaddies, those Crown mercenaries wherever red showed on the map. Neighbours shunned him and Bunco, his Airedale dog. After a couple of pints Soldier used *language*, the familiar profanity of men isolated from women, so he was banned *sine die* from Tosteg Non-Political Club, the Earl Haig Club, and refused point-blank in six pubs. The Bridge Arms tolerated him, being the only pub in Tosteg catering for the sick, the lame and the lazy, social distinctions harking back to Parish Relief and the Means Test. Soldier had his Army pension plus a supplementary Giro cheque every Friday. He listened for the squeal and clack of the letter box, then called from the front door, 'Good on you, *brawd*!' and always from the veteran postman, 'Up the Borderers!'

Leaving the post office after cashing his Giro, Soldier would take the morning air, once around the bowling green for a friendly weather forecast palaver with the groundsman, down the river bank to the urinal, cross over to the supermarket (Bunco left couchant like a sphinx on the pavement), where Soldier filled a plastic hold-all with flagons of cider, because he was a long-time alcoholic. Nobody could or even wanted to help him any more. A rowdy man, blasphemous, heedless, totally non-violent, failing to distinguish between the sexes his only crime, consequently respectable folk despised him. Pub landladies regarded him as expendable.

Soldier's ideas on food were basic: bread, marg, cheese, bacon and eggs, tea, sugar and tinned milk. When he had no money, Soldier strolled the lower mountain slopes, Bunco ranging a few yards to either side, ineffectually sniffing, the humdrum activity of a townee dog. Soldier's treasures were remembrances, the warm bondage of men on active service, famous Welsh rugby players, old Hollywood stars (Carole Lombard, W. C. Fields, William Powell, Myrna Loy, Warner

Baxter, John Barrymore), and the blindly-committed forgiveness of his parents. Drink brought everything together, himself as the pulse of camaraderie, exclusive male loyalties removed from hearth and home and the responsibility of wage-earning. Life had meaning when he was drinking. Sober, coping with being sober, then life was something of a play-game, not to be taken seriously. Soldier felt himself immunized against grief and disaster, the fact of loneliness forgotten, surrendered to in 1937, when he signed on for seven with the South Wales Borderers. Following Dunkirk and a transient stomach ulcer, he soldiered in Tobruk and Italy, where he won his Military Medal, together with a piece of shrapnel which left a grey, puckered indent in his buttock. 'I never tried flogging my good looks, and it's too late now,' he said, trousers and pants down around his ankles in the Bridge Arms. 'For shame, *cwtch* you'self up, Reardon Jones!' screeched an elfin old woman, her white head bobbing through the hatch between the public bar and the snug.

He gave the medal to a barman on the train between Paddington and Cardiff, for a bottle of whisky. A memorable outing, Wales versus England at Twickenham.

Soldier was fifty-eight, wiry, upright in his bearing, dirt grained, his moustache and thick friz of hair turned stone grey. The flesh had fallen away from his ribs and collarbones, his remaining teeth were raggedly black, and sometimes morning stiffness affected his lower half. He endured bouts of malaria once a year, sitting in front of the fire with bottles of plonk. As he fed himself, he fed Bunco likewise, the Airedale dog his peer, neither superior nor subordinate. He referred to Bunco as 'my mate'.

Demands for rates on his father's bungalow were dismissed: 'Not worth a wank.' Ashes from the fire grate rose taller than a man against the backyard wall. Broken windows were tacked up with cardboard. The detritus of seven years (from the afternoon of his mother's funeral) cluttered the bungalow, smashed crockery, spilt food, newspapers, bottles, worn-out shoes and clothes, clotted dog fur, tea slops, Woodbine butts, dust, filth, proliferating mould. Blurred daylight hung outside the window panes. Cooking fat glazed hard around the gas ring. The wallpaper bulged, unfurled like ancient placards.

Towering above all this, Soldier Jones was gay, pleased as

punch to pass the time of day with man, woman or child. Teenage girls labelling prices in the supermarket, they enjoyed him. What a character, effing this and effing that. Not many real characters left in Tosteg. They flipped bits of broken biscuit to Bunco out on the pavement. The elderly staff supervisor detected a rancid smell on Soldier. He recognized it from his own povertied childhood. But a jovial customer without a care in the world, by all means keep him happy, remind him of items on offer, buckled tins of dog food and soggy pasties.

Then Soldier reached fifty-nine. A nasty Thursday morning, rain sheeting from the west and the pantry bare. Not a crust in the house. Curled on the couch, Bunco watched him.

'Tomorrow,' promised Soldier. 'Today we do without. No option, mate.' He opened the back door. 'Benghazi was never like this, not on your nelly, Fa-aquen roll on.'

Bunco yawned and tucked his nose.

At one o'clock Soldier pushed into the bar of the Bridge Arms. The landlord sanctioned two pints of scrumpy on the slate. Soldier sang 'The Bold Gendarmes' with mime, word perfect if strained for tone, encouraging a whip-around which paid for three more pints. Brimming goodwill, Soldier walked home. His clothes were saturated.

The Airedale curvetted inside the back door, whining.

'Call of nature, Bunco? Righto, butty, righto.'

Leaving the door open, Soldier slept on the couch until Friday morning. He heard the postman at eight o'clock, but he couldn't walk. The bones of his feet were locked in ache. Cool November sunshine flowed over the washed town. Soldier thought, up on your pins, man. This won't do at all-at all.

Shortly before eleven o'clock he hobbled to the post office. The postmistress eyed him from inside the louvred glass slats above the counter, a dumpy spinster, recipient and spreader of news, the best and worst of gossip in Tosteg.

'What's the matter with you, Mr Jones?'

'It's my feet, touch of the rheums.'

'No wonder. Saw you yesterday afternoon, sopping wet as a dishrag.'

'Aye, I got caught in it,' he said.

'You went out into it!'

Merriment snuffled through his moustache. 'That's how I got caught in it, lovely gel.'

202

She thumbed at the clock on the wall. 'Ten minutes before he closes the surgery. Leave the flagons this morning. See the doctor.'

'Ta very much,' he said, folding his Giro money.

He came out of the post office. 'Bunco! Hee-yaar, Bunco!' Soldier felt the gap in his mind. Well, I'm buggered, the dog's gone. Haven't set eyes on him since yesterday. That's right, not since I let him out for a piss. Yesterday. Oh by Christ . . .

The postmistress banged the flap in the counter. 'Soldier! Mr Jones, you go straight to the surgery! Do you hear me?'

'Aye, fair enough, I'm on my way,' he said.

There were a dozen people in the waiting-room, wan children, mothers comparing complaints and treatments, decrepit pensioners, a youth with half his head bandaged. Soldier hesitated, thinking, by the loving Jesus, there's nothing wrong with me that a few pints won't shift from my system. He saluted the patients and made his way to the supermarket. Unaware of his empty stomach, he lingered outside the chrome and glass doors with his purchases: two flagons of cider and a bottle of cheap red wine. Now he remembered. Grub. No effing, bastarding, spunk-drunk grub in the house. Soldier went back into the supermarket for bread, cheese and margarine. Once again out on the pavement, forgetful, he returned inside for a quarter of tea.

No sign of Bunco.

He found him at the bungalow, stretched on the doorstep, nose between his front paws. 'Night on the tiles,' he said. 'Bitch, ah, chasing after some bitch with her little minge on fire. Come and have some packing off the old Soldier.'

But the Airedale refused to eat. Soldier felt the dog's stomach, muttering, 'Tight as a bloody drum. You've had a good scoff somewhere, mate, no doubt about that.'

Soldier ate a cheese sandwich with cups of cider. He emptied one flagon, the untouched wine to hand on the table. He took a controlled mouthful, appreciating the acid tang drawn along his gullet. 'Decent drop of plonk, aye, not bad,' he said. 'Here goes, Bunco.'

Soldier drained the bottle.

It was dark when he awoke on the couch. The dog whimpered to be released. Soldier limped to the door. 'Get stuck in, mate,' he said. He closed the door. Bleary, pensive, he scratched the recurrent itch left by the piece of Italian shrapnel. He played with shadows of memory, tinged images of his mother, his father, his boyhood. He sniggered softly, wetly, waning to silence, emptiness, the vast vacuum of himself invaded, devastated. Dreadness struck him from the base of his spine to his feet. Soldier squirmed his arms and shoulders on the floor, cursing, grunting incomprehension. Fear came late, during Friday night, while he lay on the couch in torment, stubbornly finishing off the second flagon of cider. Not fear of death, but of helplessness beyond reach of his wit to carry on, survive as happy-go-lucky boozer.

Saturday, Sunday and Monday were spent indoors.

From an old allegiance to Soldier's mother, who attended his own mother's confinements during the Thirties, the coal merchant allowed him a hundredweight of coal on tick. So Monday was a good day for Soldier. He drank tea, made cheese on toast, stayed near the fire with wrappings of flannel blanket around his legs and up to his waist. Bunco came and went via the back door.

He said to the dog, 'Tomorrow I got to call in the post office. My pension, see! Must get there without fail. Ess-ent-shal!'

On Tuesday morning he collected his Army pension. The postmistress came out from behind the counter. She watched him tottering to the supermarket with his plastic bag. 'He won't last,' she said. 'The man won't last.' She repeated her message across the counter, imprinting Soldier Jones as a matter of and for public conscience, stressing to customers, 'Reardon Jones fought for us in our war against that lunatic Hitler and his gang, wickedest set on God's earth.'

Responses were mumbled, negative, cheated, governed by time and place, her time, Soldier's time, shared knowledge of both in Tosteg's time and place.

The doctor went to the bungalow after his surgery on Thursday evening. Soldier and Bunco were eating pasties and beans.

'Honest now, Doctor, I didn't send for you.'

'Others are concerned, if you aren't concerned about yourself.' The doctor was a curmudgeonly old man, more off-hand than clinical. 'Arthritis,' he said. 'I could place you in hospital, huh, this time next year, or put you on a course of tablets.'

'No hospital for this chick, thanks all the same. Twice they shoved me in dock when I was in the mob. As I say, thanks all the same.'

'Don't thank me. Obviously you prefer to live in this pig-sty.'

'Make 'em strong tablets, Doctor. I can't move in the mornings. I'm like a bloody stick.'

'Take this prescription to the chemist.'

'What are they?'

'Pain killers. I can't cure arthritis, nobody can.'

Soldier thought, fa-aquen roll on.

He put the prescription under a broken, face-down clock on the mantlepiece. Days went by. Visiting the chemist would have been a pleasing event for Soldier, his bones though, his feet, shins, knees, thighs and hips sent pain, pain begging for total stillness. Soldier had no defence. He fell into staring. Huddled on a bench by the bowling green, he stared across at the sky. In the Bridge Arms with a pint before him, he stared, slightly upwards, directed above the head of the landlord. The tablets relieved his suffering, but Soldier's zest withered. Passivity kept him apart. A kind of blankness denied communication.

The spinster postmistress again sent the doctor to see him. Soldier refused to go to hospital. He was detached, a fog of calm extending everywhere. Bunco came and departed as before, feeding from bins outside Tosteg's new custom-built comprehensive school, befriended by a serving lady who knew Reardon Jones from their classroom days, who remembered his return to civvy street in 1946, a drunken waster ever since, while her husband slogged his guts out in the coal-face until pit closures chucked him on the scrap heap.

Neither self-pity nor isolation affected Soldier. Dying, he obeyed dying, abandoning himself. He retained a meagre connection, a remnant of dignified whimsy, opening the back door for Bunco, saying, 'All the best. See you later.' Then, preparing the roving Airedale, 'So long, butty. Mind how you go.'

Unable to do his shopping, Soldier starved. Winter claimed him on the couch where his mother had nursed him on her lap. Bunco slept beside the cold hearth. He raised his curly head, blinked and growled deep in his throat for three minutes—Soldier's end.

Tosteg celebrated Christmas day. Families gathered to exchange gifts. In the Bridge Arms nobody queried Soldier's absence, the grizzled cider-drinker regarded as temporarily off the streets, safe, comfy by the fire with bottles of plonk. He bragged about his malaria as other men claimed esteem for factory production, or making London within two and a half hours on the M4, or the concocted exploits of Duke of Edinburgh Award winners. The postmistress knew what she had to do, arguing with the brandy-fugged doctor at the other end of the line; he advised her to contact the Deparment of Health and Social Security. She did, at 9 a.m. on 27th December. The officer apologized. Actually Mr Reardon Jones wasn't on their records as a person in need of care. After begging his pardon in her no-nonsense manner, she insisted someone should visit the bungalow. She telephoned for confirmation an hour later.

The Sick Visitor was a confident young woman, qualified SRN, daughter of a town councillor and determined to prove her worth as a civil servant. She heard Bunco barking inside the bungalow. 'Mr Jones!' she called through the letter box. 'Mr Jones, are you in there?'

She went around to the dirt lane behind the bungalow, where she met the coal merchant.

He said, 'It's not for want of trying on my part, believe you me. I can't make the bloody man listen. What it is, he's on the pop agen.'

'I must see him,' she said. 'I'm the Sick Visitor.'

He banged on the back door. 'Soldier, there's this young lady from the Welfare come to see you!'

Bunco stopped barking.

'Mr Jones,' she said, coaxing, 'please open the door. I'm here to help you.'

Bunco growled, winding up his courage.

'Bloody fool to hisself from the day he stepped out of khaki,' said the coal merchant.

They were standstill, listening, when the Airedale hurtled through the kitchen window. He staggered, then kept on running. The coal merchant took his cap off, bunched his fist inside it and cleared away spiky shards of glass until he could crane his head between the sash bars and look into the room.

206

'By God Almighty! Hey, Miss, if I was you I'd send for the amb'lance!'

'He's dead,' she said.

The coal merchant held his nose. 'Pong, I never smelt anythin' like it!'

'Open the window,' she said firmly. 'You can reach the latch.'

Reminded of his manners as she levered her thighs over the sill, the man hung his head. He waited, flicking tiny slivers of glass from his cap. She came out through the door in a flurry, gagging, stumbled among the winter weeds, stood straddled, retching.

'Whassamatter?' he said, simply resenting her as the daughter of a Tosteg councillor. 'Bloody hell, ent you seen a corpse before?'

She sniffed, backing away, distressed, wailing, 'The dog's been eating him!'

'The bloody dog?' shouted the coal merchant.

'His privates . . .'

The coal merchant and the SRN turned away from each other, his right arm flagging, thinning skeins of coal dust falling as he pummelled his cap against his knee.

Blood Money

Old Abe Rhys, he's 87, slurring Chaplin-footed to the post office on pension days, his inane banter ignored by customers. Mrs Dulcie Rhys ruled the roost until she died, and that was the end of her. Not even good riddance from Abe, because he neither grieves nor bears a grudge. He has no friends. Men shy away, they sense absence of weal, social give-and-take. Abe merely survived, mysteries of heart, giblets and the marrow of his bones committed to himself. He lived alone, his two daughters at each end of the same Pengelli street. Stubby-jawed Brenda, she's lean, scrawny as a nomad, her husband a long-time runaway. She flattered, cultivated the old man's favour, her wit tittering to his bogus chuckling.

Olive Rhys married Huco Melyn, a hangdog sloucher. She's top-heavy, with a numbing habit of changing faces, switching from pawky duchess to peasant malevolence. Olive ridiculed her father, she tyrannised him.

Trevor Rhys left home to join the army. More so than Brenda, Olive disregards their brother. Trevor La-di-dah, restaurant business of his own, nothing to do with them any more.

There aren't many of Abe's contemporaries left in Pengelli. As they pass away, he forgets them. Abe sleeps without dreaming, as if holy, pure, a fairy-tale saint. Only Brenda and Olive visit him. Olive does the shopping, she cooks his dinners. Brenda keeps the house clean, launders his clothes. Wary sisters, day-by-day nice to each other, guaranteed to share the old man's money. Umpteen thousands in Lloyds Bank, another twenty or twenty-five thou. from selling this house. Trevor? Pish-pish. He had loads. Posh place up there in London. Swanky. Waiters and serviettes. And that Cockney wife of his, her photo on Abe's sideboard. Proper slap-dash. Whoor for a cert. Enough said. Trevor married into money. Well-yes, father-in-law set him up, Trevor Rhys from Pengelli, cookhouse lackey, two stripes on his sleeve after five years. So there.

Nudging her sister, Brenda says, 'We'll have to let him know though.'

'I'll be down his throat sharpish if he comes yere interfering,' vows Olive. 'Who've been looking after Dad since Mam died?

Not Trev with his nancy-boy twang. He never came back to this house after our Mam's fun'ral. We didn't set eyes on him. It's we've tended Dad, me an' you.'

Brenda snickered behind a tissue, 'In case of emergency I've jotted down Trevor's number.'

'Pho-one, bleddy pho-one,' sneered Olive. 'He'll speak straight like the rest of us before I give him time of day.'

Brenda's amiable, 'Dad'll last for years yet, I mean he's always potching out in the garden or in his toolshed. Strong as a horse.'

Says Olive, 'Twice as *twp* too. I've warned him often enough. Menace to himself he is.'

'Gone sloppy,' agrees Brenda.

'Secant childhood!'

'No shame left in Dad. I can't get him to change his long-johns.'

Olive's eyes rage behind flick-up glasses. 'Him and his gammon rashers and onions boilt in milk!' She makes fierce scram-cat gestures, freezing as her husband edged around the kitchen door. 'Whattew after, 'Uco?'

'Nothin'.'

'Won't find it yere, man. Fetch Dad,' she says. 'Dinner's ready.'

'Huco dips obedience. 'Righto, Ol.'

Abe grows pansies for the delight of his isolate soul. Colours blaze two small plots outside the front porch. Lifting the letterbox flap, Olive sees him down on his knees, fingering the blossoms. Her screech sends him toppling forward on his elbows.

'Gerrup off of that damp ground!'

Abe pushed fear away from the shape of his mind. Not his fault, Olive's bad nerves. She's on tablets. Her and Brenda. Tablets, tablets. Bad nerves and bad stomach.

As Huco comes around from the kitchen, Abe surveys the gay welter of his pansies, and he's muttering, 'Strappers, out-and-out strappers.'

Huco grinned, 'Ne'mind about pigeon pie, Dad. Grub's on the table.' Pacing himself, Huco trailed Olive striding the pavement.

Brenda stays with Abe, beside him at the table, hooped over strong tea, dunking ginger-nut biscuits.

'Feeling al'right are you, Daddo?'

'Course I am! Feeling great!'

'Any news from Trevor at all? Don't suppose so.'

'Trevor, no, no news.'

'He'll be fifty-eight next month, Dad.'

'Sure to be! Fifty-eight!'

'Our Mam was thirty-eight when she had him.'

Abe hooted, '*Duw-Duw!*' on pretext of finding the memory. Munching serenely, he pares fat off a lamp chop. 'Done well for himself, my boy up there in the smoke.'

'Trevor used to be a lot like you, same stamp, same ways, bit stubborn.' Spooning mush from her cup, Brenda feels comfy. She can inveigle money for cigarettes, cadge milk, bread and veg. Now, gazing at the electric clock on the wall above the mantelpiece, 'Stopped again, Dad. For goodness' sake whyn't you buy yourself a new clock? I'll take that thing down, save you climbing on a chair.'

Suspicious grunts from Abe, 'Olive reckons it should be mended.'

Brenda strokes his arm, 'Listen, order a clock from my catalogue. Ever such a lovely selection. I'll tell her I chucked that thing in the ashbin.'

'How much they cost, gel?'

'Buy the best, you can't go wrong. About sixty quid, real quartz mantel clock, battery-operated.'

Abe squirted hisses through his teeth.

Coaxing, tousling his wispy grey hair, she rummages through his anxieties. Debasing herself, she uses him against Olive.

The mail-order quartz clock arrived in October.

A jack-of-all-trades repaired the electric clock. 'There, good as new for a drop of solder in the right place. For you, Brenda, just a packet of fags. That do?'

Devious Brenda, but of course Olive made the big decisions. Brenda swapped the clock for a carton of chicken portions filched from Pengelli Frozen Food Mart, threatening the teenage thief, 'Keep your mouth shut or worst it'll be for you.'

Days of north-west gales wiped out November. Abe Rhys stayed indoors. The glory of his pansies disintegrated, the plots a tangle of kinked stems and shredded petals battered to the soil.

Busy in his toolshed, Abe made a chronic job of nailing

rubber heels to his boots. Frustration parching his throat, he resented the shaky coordination of his hands and eyes, yet he persisted, striving to hammer home the bright tingles. The rubber heels were skewed. Daylight faded. Abe shuffled to the kitchen in a teeming squall of rain. Olive fumed, 'Silly old betsi you! Too minjy to send them boots to the cobblers! Find another cardi to put on your back and dry that daft head of yours!'

Abe day-dreamed in the lavatory, puhh-puhh-puhh squishing whiffs of smoke alongside his pipestem. I've been tapping my gardening boots for years, years . . . Dredged recall sieved away, emptying to limbo.

He levered upright, pins and needles trembling him. I'll have another go at those heels tomorrow.

That same evening he fell asleep before supper, blank television purring until 2.10 a.m. Abe climbed the stairs, hauling up the balusters like a worn-out ape.

Mid-morning when Olive came, the wheels of a shopping trolley squeaking behind her. 'Whassamatter, feeling rough?'

He's wheezing, 'This chest, my breath won't come. Best fetch the doctor.'

Olive sends Huco Melyn to Brenda's House. 'You gotto phone Doctor Gopal. Tell him urgent, rush quick as Dad's inna bad sweat.'

The sedate, delicately goateed Indian examined Abe. He turns from Brenda to Olive, 'Mrs Melyn, we must be very careful.' He writes a prescription, 'These will help his breathing.'

When they brought Abe's bed downstairs to the parlour, he protested, wailed, demanding attention. Before dawn he swarmed in delirium, a rambling mix of boyhood Welsh and demotic English.

Gopal made out another prescription. As bronchitis cleared, the old man's kidneys deteriorated. He soiled the bed.

Olive, she's frenzied, insisting, 'I say we should send him to hospital!'

Brenda's thin twined arms are clutched to her stomach. 'We've tried our best. I'm in agony. Everything I eat feels like poison inside of me.'

Gusting infantile shouts, tears crystallising on his stricken face, the old man doesn't want to go into hospital.

Brenda pleading on her knees, 'They'll take care of you, Daddo.'

'Typical,' from scowling Olive. 'All he ever does is think about hisself.'

Brenda's whispering, 'He's incontinent.'

'We'll be seeing bleddy Gopal,' says Olive.

Preceding Brenda, she seats herself in front of Doctor Gopal's desk. 'Being as our father's in-cont'nent, we'd like to put him in hospital, please, if you've no objection.'

'Well, there is difficulty, Mrs Melyn.' Gopal tries a winsome smile. 'The problem of finding a bed for Mr Rhys.' His chocolate-brown eyes promise naught in the Land of our Fathers. 'Long waiting list, Mrs Melyn, yes, long waiting list.'

Olive pitches suffering, 'My nerves are all in rags. How d'you 'spect me to sit up with him night after night?'

The doctor's shrugging has a kind of puppet veracity—he's been seven years in his custom-built surgery.

Brenda hugs herself, 'I can't either. I'm in pain with my gastric.'

Then bleak as gospel from Olive, 'Fact is, we're both of us under our own doctor.'

'God's honour,' says Brenda.

'Private bed for him?' inquires Gopal gently.

Olive sends her fingertips skidding from her knee across to Brenda's knee, 'We are in agreement. Private, certainly.'

Mission accomplished, the sisters returned to Abe's house by taxi.

'After all,' says Olive, 'Dad haven't spent a penny of his lump sum since he retired, and besides which, how much of his superann goes into Lloyds Bank I'd like to know.' She pinches a valium over her tongue before gulping the old man's Lucozade. 'As the Lord above's my judge, there's nobody can point a finger. Much more and we'll be ruined. We've done our best. Bad enough looking after our Mam, remember? He's worse, been a burden right throughout.' Pending soothe from the tablet she explodes rancour, 'No consideration for anybody 'cept hisself!'

Brenda complains, 'Hush, talking like that about our father.'

'Oh ye-es, verr-ry verr-ry nice. You're well-in with him, always been. I'm short-sighted but I'm not blind.'

212

'I'm not so nasty to him as you, Olive.'

'Of all the cheek! If it wasn't for me he'd 'ave some durrty slut takin' our Mam's place.'

Lull came, valium blunting Olive's hostility, 'Where's his bank book then, Brenda?'

'Don't know. *Cwtched* away somewhere.'

'It's he'll 'ave to pay for the private bed.'

Brenda squirms panic, saying, 'We can't. Never. Scrimping from one week to the next.'

'Been through all our Mam's things?'

'Only now and then, same as you'self, Olive.'

'The tight-fisted old bugger,' says Olive.

Brenda filled the kettle. 'Cup of coffee before we start searching.'

Olive bawled, ''Uco!'

He comes out from sitting with Abe in the parlour. 'Hey, after you went he cried like a *babi-lwsh*, kept on askin' for Trevor.'

Olive waved dismissal, 'No need to bother with Trevor.'

Brenda smirked weakness, 'Later on.'

'Whaffor later on? Leave Trevor be wherever he is up in London. He never offered before. Where's Trevor's feelings for Dad?'

Brenda's sniffling, 'He's our brother, Trevor's our brother.'

'I couldn't care less about bleddy Trevor.' Pacing dignified, sipping her coffee, puffing upwards from her lower lip to de-mist her glasses, Olive breaks into *do-ray* chanting, 'Bank book, bank book, bank book . . .'

'Must be in a secret place,' says Brenda.

'Oi, big-ears, get back to the front room,' ordered Olive.

Retreating, Huco thumbs over his shoulder, 'Try the toolshed. I'm not allowed. Door's kept locked.'

Which roused Brenda, 'Key's in his arse pocket! One of them Yales!'

They found Abe's bank book and never-used cheque book under a stack of newspapers, yellowing *Titbits* and a seed catalogue dated 1936—the year of Trevor's birth. Balance, £13,365.

Olive exulted, 'Kerrist Almighty!'

As they entered the parlour, guilt jerked Huco from dozing. 'Any luck, Olive?'

'None of your business. Dad! Dad, it's me, Olive. No lissen, Dad . . .'

Abe's mouth gapes, tongue lolling, furred with white glutinous nodules. His eyes open, close. Mottled sepia darkens from the root of his nose. Brenda folds back the bedclothes. The curve-necked bottle between Abe's shrunken thighs is empty but the sheets are stained with urine. Olive snarls at her husband, 'You waster.' Faint lament from Abe while they roll him to and fro, changing the sheets. Tucked to his chin, he's mouthing, 'Send for Trevor.'

Brenda leans closer. 'Of course, mustn't upset yourself. First though, Daddo, we want to make sure they look after you in hospital.'

Abe's husky yelp, 'Nuh!' and slowly slowly, 'Strappers, strappers.'

Said Olive, 'What's he on about?'

Huco's backing away, 'Somethin's on his mind.'

Olive hurls the cheque book, 'Tell him! Thousand like we settled, 'cause there's bound to be extra expenses. You,' she says to Huco, 'gerroff home.'

Abe's gasping, 'Send for my boy.'

Brenda's skinny hand wrestled to control Abe's, but she failed to make him scribe: *Olive Melyn. One thousand pounds only.* She's terrified, cowering from Olive's witchy threats, and succumbs, shuddering hysteria.

Olive's rat-squeal accompanies a wristy slap on Brenda's face. 'Shut it. Just you shut it.' Flagging the cheque book above Abe, 'Where's your bleddy gumption? For your own good this is! Unless you sign you'll be left to stink in this bed!'

Alone in the kitchen, droopy Brenda enjoyed a small fresh plaice, then she watched television, waiting for Huco Melyn.

'Try our Dad with some chicken soup, but don't force it down him. Olive's turn to sit up tonight.'

Huco swayed out of his duffle coat, 'Aye, you mean me, muggins.'

Two days later, Huco's message to Doctor Gopal. 'My Missis, Doctor, she said to cancel the bed for her old man, and awful sorry for any bother.'

As in living, likewise his dying, Abe Rhys alone, solitary, and flesh wasted away from his great, strong body. His hammer, last and boots were still on the toolshed bench when he died four weeks later. Between toolshed and the kitchen door, storm rain soaked through his cardigan, shirt and vest to his sweaty skin.

Trevor Rhys drove down on the morning of the funeral. He was a robust man, hardened in self-confidence. Familiar with cliches of mourning, the Welsh Methodist minister praised Olive and Brenda for their devotion to their father, respected senior citizen in Pengelli. Truly indeed, Abraham Rhys was safe in the hands of his Maker.

During the service Olive glared sidelong at Trevor, while Huco patted her shoulder. She had burned the bank and cheque books. Slow focussing Brenda's eyes shone ablaze, her lipsticked mouth flecked with alkaline rime. Olive's mute malice prompted Trevor. He introduced himself to the Lloyds Bank manager.

Traversing his forefinger across and across Abe's last will and testament, the Bank servant's solemn monotone summarised: Olive and Brenda Rhys, father(s) unknown, consequently the entire capital fell to the legitimate heir, Trevor Vaughan Rhys. 'Your father gave them a secure home,' commended the manager. 'He reared them as his own.'

Dissent narrowed Trevor's eyes, 'Over the years they must have treated him very shabbily, don't you think?'

Arms outflung, fingers dangling as in crucifixion, the manager bowed his head. Vagaries of human nature were not his province.

Trevor smiled his mouth, 'They are strange, especially Olive.' And still smiling, 'Pengelli is a small world. My solicitor will deal with the transfer to my account.'

'Regarding the property, Mr Rhys . . ?'

'I shall sell the house.' Eye to eye, Trevor continued, 'Can you arrange for Brenda and Olive to share the furniture? Good. Thank you. I'm grateful.'

They shook hands.

Whereon Trevor reflected, poor Brenda, poor Olive. My half sisters. Then, like his father, he forgot about them.

The Old Black Pasture

(1)

He dealt the pay clerk a wristy backhander across the mouth. Inside the office, the portly cashier strutted about-turn like a bantam cock.

'Lloyd! What on earth . . . Clear off! Go away from there!'

Pushing his head through the pay hatch, 'Gabe,' he said, 'the name's Gabe Lloyd. This isn't the first time I've been robbed by you clever bastards. My water allowance, fifty pence a shift. I want it now, straight away, or I'll be right in there with you.'

Anguished as a schoolgirl, the clerk licked flecks of blood off his lip. From righteous self-control, the cashier whiffed indignation, 'How dare you treat my staff like this! If it's trouble you want, rest assured you'll find it, oh yes, I'll warrant that!'

'Not before I bust you one,' says Gabe.

Sobersides colliers shouldered closer, 'Quieten down, Gabe, you'll cop the worst end of it.'

The cashier stressed, 'Be warned, you hooligan!'

The clerk scrunched his bloodstained handkerchief. He had overlooked the water allowance. Simple matter to put right but the adjustment would have to wait until next Friday— confirmed by the cashier with high-nosed dignity, having survived pay-day squabbles since before nationalisation. A sense of destiny ordered his soul and he stood aloof, authoritative, nimble fingers pianoing his waistcoat button.

Gabe lunged through the hatch, cursing. He missed hitting the clerk. Colliers hauled him away, sympathising, pacifying him at the same time. Gabe's cheekbones shone baby-pink, tight grey eyes menacing above the thickened splodge of his nose. He coughed abruptly, held it behind his tongue, alerting his wits, then he landed a dollop of black-streaked phlegm between his shoes, veeing his feet with instant accuracy. He returned to the hatch. They made a triangle: cashier, clerk and Gabe.

'My money, I want it today, *now*.'

The cashier plucked out a fountain-pen. He sloped his jowly head over the ledger. 'Petty cash,' he ordered the clerk, who

216

sorted £2.50 in coins and slid them across the hatch counter. Pen wagging, the cashier vowed a priestly edict, 'Lloyd, you will be sorry.'

'Very nice of you,' said Gabe. 'He isn't the first mammy's boy I've slapped across the chops. You sods fiddling in this office, you'd rise the bile in any man. You know sweet fuck all about what it's like down under. *You*, expert you are, on our consultative committee. What a laugh. The pair of you couldn't fill enough coal to cook a dinner.' Gabe turned to the pay queue, 'Harmony between workers and management? Load of ballocks. Don't take my word for it. Just remember my old man.' He shook both fists, 'Mansel Lloyd did more than his whack to improve conditions up here in Bothi Number 2. What did he get? Let me remind you. Bloody wreath from the NUM when we laid him in Moel cemetery.' Gabe rattled the stack of coins from hand to hand, 'These office blokes, they've never filled a dram, never cleared a top hole, they couldn't pack a waste or a cog, they've never cut up a rib face, they'd be smothered in diarrhoea working a low seam with the top pouncing like fucken Guy Fawkes' Night. How they going to *think* like us, ah?' Gabe let the coins fall, clinking, flashing, before dropping them into his pocket. 'Don't trust 'em,' he said. 'They don't know what day it is, they don't know crap from cream.'

'Stir it up, Gabe,' bantered a young miner.

'Stirrer,' they said, shuffling forward in the queue. 'Bank on Lloydie. Give him a big spoon.'

Gabe walked home, thinking, I'm different from my father. Different from my grandfather. They believed in the rank and file. I say, never mind about the rank and file. It's all mouth, always was, always will be. This life is for me, mine to do as I want with it. Some men are born slaves. Support the workers, nothing besides on my old man's mind. Bugger the rank and file. It'll take more than religion or politics to change human nature. Take more than yapping on television, management and workers arguing about wages and production. Poodles, grown men yapping like poodles. Jesus, they make me spew. I'm different. Definitely. They broke Mansel's spirit. They broke Grancha Tommy's leg in the '21 strike, aye, old Granch who worked on sinking Bothi in the first place. Lovely people, those wasters, bloody sons of workers marching up here,

217

bashing lumps off the strikers. Slaves in khaki, slaves with truncheons. Great people, the rank and file, cream of Socialism. Brainwash the dumbos, then just give them orders and they'll make a short-time Christ out of some chesty government leader. When his time comes, he's due for the boot too, on orders. That clerk I smacked across the teeth, by next Monday morning he'll have two shiners and all his teeth missing. More rumours floating round than bum paper. They all destest the mingy bastard. His name's rotten every Friday. Rumours and a bit of clap hands for Gabe Lloyd—him, fists up before you can say boo. Genuine enough bloke if you catch him in a good mood, but mostly you won't find Lloydie in any such mood. Chip on his shoulder. Daft as a luny once he gets started. Few years from now he'll settle down. Wife and kids, they'll tutor him. Sure to, same as everybody else. True as true.

Chinking the money in his pocket, Gabe muttered, 'It's me, first, second and last.'

July sunshine shone the saucer-cambered village from a naked mask of blue sky. Slanted windowpanes glittered, denied eyesight, and slate rooftops careened matt grey like the flanks of battleships below higgledy-piggledy sprouting TV aerials.

Gabe passed two punters, heads lowered as in prayer outside a betting shop, the street itself resonant with hard suavity, the voice of Peter O'Sullivan, his effortless commentary, and overall, everywhere, the same Ascot race, O'Sullivan plonking fearless precision, factual as a Gospel genealogist, the event crowding down to a final, laconic summary. But Gabe strode heedless, reflecting, I shan't see coal this weekend. Too warm for fires. That's another week wrapped up. Short week of short shifts. *Man's* job so the adverts reckon. You'd swear all the bureaucrats had filled their tonnage. Still though, man's job for definite, worth sticking at for the thirty-five hour week. Usual quota of tight-fisted scrapers in Bothi Number 2, mean grabbers here and there along the faces. In every industry the same shitty rodneys, same back-scratchers, back-stabbers, same fuck-you-jack-I'm-all-right.

He threw another gob of blackened phlegm. If you can't check your wages, too bad. You'll get robbed up, down and sideways. The NCB'll never pay us enough, but it's worth sticking for the short week. You won't dodge a wet singlet anywhere off the Five Deep, water cold as lollipops melting down your ribs. Some shifts you're wetter than others, some stents are worse than others. Useless making a song and dance. By grubtime you're sweated from eyebrows to ankles. Good old pit, Bothi, good by comparison.

Gabe drummed his fingernails on the kitchen-door window, warning Sue, his only sister.

She placed his dinner on the table.

He says, 'Ta, love.'

Sue Lloyd folded her arms. 'Why'd you lay your fist on that chap in the office? Her from next door came rushing to tell me.'

'By the Jesus, fast bit of news.'

'Everybody saw what you did. On colliery premises an' all. You couldn't have picked a better place to lose your temper. Time you used some gumption for a change.'

Slamming the oven door shut with her knee, Sue Lloyd brought a lamb chop and vegetables to the table. She was thirty-seven, her straight black hair bobbed for utility, the same principle affecting her clothes. Refusal to primp herself as feminine. Her ex-husband lived with another woman, their home a spick lodge behind the colliery manager's house. Now Sue existed on dour loyalty, her spirit annealed, proving herself by deeds towards Gabe or anyone who sought trust from her.

'Makes no odds,' he said. 'They can't do much, not for a little flip across the mouth. I was down on my wages.'

'There's the NUM. Let them sort it out, instead of you taking the law into your own hands.'

'Our committee's a right shower,' says Gabe.

'Point is you shouldn't use your fists. You're not a crot of a boy any more.'

He glanced at the de luxe travelling-clock tilted in its leather case on the middle shelf of a rosewood dresser. Below the clock, framed photographs of their parents, Mansel and Martha Lloyd, one each side, carefully quarter-turned towards a gilt-framed photograph of himself and Sue. Twice his size then, Sue had one arm around his shoulders. His hair stubbly above short back and sides, while hers rounded in a stiff aura of tightly-permed waves. Gabe wore a willing grin. Sue and Mrs Lloyd showed the same pent expression, humourless.

219

She said, 'Fetching that clock home didn't give you the right to take a poke at the least one who upsets you.'

'I must have been pretty good, Sue, couple of years ago.'

'Bull-headed,' she sneered bleakly. 'And you wanted to turn professional. God alive, by this time you wouldn't know if you were coming or going.'

'I can still do a bundle.'

'Don't talk rubbish.'

He watched gravy dripping off a forked potato. 'I beat every welterweight in the area for that clock.'

'Novices. Stop bragging. Eat your dinner.'

'I'm going for a swim later on,' he said.

From tiny streams fingering down through Ice Age bogland, Dyffryn Lake ballooned to smooth turnip shape. Birch, willow, alder and bramble thickets wound in and out with footpaths, covered the fat deep end bank. Gabe zig-zagged down steep, sheep-cropped turf. He followed the shoreline to level ground, where families were sun-bathing. The bulk of his meal pleasantly weighting his stomach, he stripped off his clothes, black rims of coaldust under his toenails, and whinberry-blue scars hung like tattooing behind his left shoulder, ending in a glazed pink indent above his left kidney. Gabe wiped his armpits, draped his towel on the grass, bow-tied the cord of his trunks and looked around for company. Some young colliers mauled in shallow water, pushing and tugging. Gabe raised slack fascist salutes, 'See you!'

He stared, elbows on his knees, Dyffryn Lake flat as glass, ripples catching the eye in fits and starts, dwindling to flatness again. Gabe conjured himself at the wheel of a red Triumph sports car, brand new, Lucy Passmore sitting beside him. Lucy the pit-head canteen manageress, his dolled-up woman, lush as a bath of warm milk. A gusted hiss blew the fantasy to absence.

From near the water's edge a frog sculled out before circling back to the undercut bank. Mildly fascinated, tongue dibbling out his lower lip, he groped for a pebble. Denied by grainy clay below the dry turf, he lay back on his towel. Inhale, exhale, palms over his belly, feet crossed at the ankles, Gabe felt supreme, luxuriating while the fullness of his dinner subsided.

Half an hour later he walked, slightly knock-kneed, into Dyffryn Lake. He swam half-gudgeon, half breaststroke,

220

joining the young colliers. They were all white skinned, from daily scrubbing under the pit-head showers. Tight muscled and white.

'Look at him, fastest clouter in Bothi Number 2. How's life then, Gabe?'

He humped into a clumsy dolphin dive. 'They paid up,' he said, spluttering. 'I had what was coming to me.'

'They might serve you a fortnight's notice as well.'

Gabe hacked water from his tubes, 'Aye, and I might clip the manager a goodbye present.'

'Cheeky bugger you. Only once you'll do that, butty.'

'Suit me,' says Gabe.

'They'll stick you behind bars for a few months. What you hit him with, Gabe, your bloody water jack?'

'Rumours,' he said.'

'Man, they'll get proof, doctor's paper etcetera, take you to court.'

Gabe snorted disgust, rolling over for a relaxed float across Dyffryn shallows. The sun was hot, the water mellow. Forget about Bothi. Just float. Why worry? Worry brought ruination. Biggest ruiner in the world, worry.

Rumour meshed with reality a fortnight later. A police sergeant came to the front door. He held out a summons folded in two places, 'Gabriel Lloyd, this is for you.'

Gabe grinned his teeth, saying, 'Seems like a gotto attend this farce.'

'Plead guilty,' advised the sergeant. 'The circumstance, fella, you assaulted a man while he was under the protection of his employer, namely the National Coal Board. In the eyes of the law, it's worse than you think, not that I want to blame you personally. Slogged in the pits myself years ago. Plead guilty, say you're sorry, won't happen again, and hope for the best.'

Gabe jibbed his shoulders, 'What about the times I been booked in the past?'

'They'll be set down against you.' The weary-eyed sergeant inquired, 'How many offences, fella?'

'Once for scrapping, once for foul language, once for obstruction as they call it, aye, the night your blokes locked me up.'

'Were you drunk?'

'More or less, yeh, suppose I was.'

The sergeant turned away. 'Good luck, fella.'

'Same to you,' says Gabe, mouthing like a silent film gangster, 'Drop dead.'

Due to appear in Dove Street Court at ten-thirty on a thundery August morning, Sue rowed him harshly while they were having breakfast. She polished his shoes, adjusted his tie, then sent him off with a slow stroke of her fingers on his forehead. Her blessing.

The case ended quickly after the colliery cashier gave evidence. Autocrat in his own milieu, the cashier took prompts from the magistrate as if bewildered. Gabe stared at the magistrate, tabbed him Monkey Lips, saw him whispering to his colleagues on the bench. They were nodding all together like marionettes.

'Lloyd, stand upright,' the flat tone of command, dead certain as God Almighty.

Gabe lowered his elbow off the rail.

The magistrate's trembling head glanced from the police superintendent to the clerk of the court. 'Gabriel Lloyd, we have ample information concerning your lack of discipline.' Pause to extrude, slide down his upper lip, hiding the lower lip, 'You have appeared in this court before, but obviously you aren't prepared to learn from experience. We must, therefore, conclude you have the disposition of a ruffian.' The magistrate interlocked his fingers, stable neurosis writhing his lips. 'The National Coal Board is determined to protect its employees from brutes such as yourself. We fine you fifty pounds, and furthermore, you shall remain on probation for a period of two years.'

Bloody old chimpanzee, thought Gabe Lloyd.

The clerk of the court sang out, 'Will you pay now?'

He held up his hand like a schoolboy, 'Give me a couple of weeks, sir?'—the *sir* granted as part of justice rigmarole.

'Seven days to pay,' announced the magistrate.

Chin tucked, Gabe smirked as he climbed down. Old stuff-pig, him telling me I lack discipline. He'd step over kiddies lying in the gutter. Better men than him on Assistance, better men six feet under with their toes turned up. Discipline. Slyness he should have said. Discipline's for puppydogs and born losers who can't think for themselves. Dirty old sod, he scraped and fiddled to where he is, the monkey-faced bastard. They're all scrapers. Justice, by Jesus, more justice in the weather.

The probation officer ushered him into a room below the court. A beefy man with sparse hair fighting off a centre parting, his Home Counties speech hurried through a gapped barrier of discoloured teeth. 'Smoke?' friendly as a visiting uncle.

'Ta,' said Gabe. 'I like a whiff now and again.'

'Did you enjoy hitting that wages clerk?'

'What d'you mean, enjoy?'

Flourishing a handkerchief to his nose, 'Tell me, were you infuriated or did you simply use the incident to inflict punishment?'

'I don't get you at all, mister,' argued Gabe. 'Look, we'd best leave it at that. They paid my water allowance, see, so I'm satisfied.'

The officer led him to a side-door exit. 'I say, Gabe, quite frankly, try to understand how I regard my job, the responsibility involved. On your part, stay out of trouble, behave yourself in public. In other words, the less we see of each other the better I shall be pleased.' They shook hands. 'Goodbye for now. I have your address, um, parents deceased, tch-tch, what a pity. Any change of circumstances, let me know immediately.'

Gabe walked Dove Street to a bus stop, fretting. Luck from now on, heaps of luck. I'll be watching my step for two years. They can nab me crossing a railway line, pissing in a *gwli*, fiddling a bus ticket. Any-bloody-thing at all. When I buy my Triumph, the Highway Code'll be stuck in my head like the Bible in Rosser Passmore's. Double rupture the law. Triple fuck the law and every chimp-faced magistrate since the one who played crafty with those early Jews. They're still accusing him, Sunday after Sunday. Aye, still chopsing, same old double-cross yarn for Wales and all the bloody world.

He sniggered, side-swerved to toecap an empty match box. Anyone with a black cap in his pocket or a black staff dangling against his leg, he's a menace to society. My kind of society. When I find it. And then from shallow turmoil, 'Lucy,' he breathed softly. Aye right, lovely Lucy.

2

She palmed the smooth bevelling of her tummy, her smile gracious, shared like unction. Lucy Passmore was thirty-eight, ten years older than she looked. Ageless glow sustained gestures of intimacy. Vestally buxom in the white, pit-head canteen uniform, Lucy veered from the counter, bending to a low cupboard, a soft-soft hostler clicks chucked off Gabe's tongue. She swung up and around, bible-stroking a hard cover Accounts ledger between her hands.

Helmet tipped back, he muttered over the rim of his NCB stamped mug, 'Same arrangement for tonight then?'

'Shh, boy, he's in the kitchen.'

'Just say the word.'

Pleasure seemed to moither her, 'I can't. Not tonight. Somehow I've lost a hundred Embassy. Hundred! I'm frantic, honestly.'

Gabe tasted coaldust off his lips, 'Nothing to panic about. Book the fags on my name. I'll make it good next Friday. Remind me.'

'Thanks, Gabie, thanks ever so . . . shh, he's coming.'

Rosser Passmore struggled out from the kitchen. He was anciently forty-four, gaunt, high-shouldered, subverted piety lurking in his suffering eyes. He chinned a pile of empty cartons and paper rubbish in his arms, 'This is the lot from in there.'

'Take your time, Ross,' she said.

Lifting the counter flap, '*Shwmae*, Ross,' said Gabe. 'Feeling better these days?'

'Chronic last night, couldn't find my breath. Sultry weather, no air about.'

'Want me to carry those?' asked Gabe.

'No-no, I'll manage.'

'That's the idea,' says Gabe.

Ross wavered between the tables, stalky legs ricking under his burden.

'Poor dab,' murmured Lucy formally.

Gabe grinned through pit grime, 'Eight o'clock behind the Great Western Arms.'

'You never give in, boy.'

'Never, you lovely thing.'

'Hush!'

'See you,' he said. 'Prompt on the dot.'

Maidenly, 'Okay,' escaped her lipsticked mouth and she continued palming her tummy.

At ten-past-eight Lucy's shiny blue Mini looped a fast U-turn outside the pub. Gabe sprawled low on the rear seat while she drove to the switchback summit of a mountain road. They were ten miles from home, a setting sun disappearing like an apricot slice on the horizon. For a while she held the ignition key in her left hand, occasionally jabbing the nape of his neck. Dark purple slowly came down, solid landscape merging with skyline.

'Let's gerrout from here,' he said.

She jerked away, complaining, 'Al'right, al'right, take your paws off me for God's sake.' Lucy dithered, feeling torn between familiar sacrifice and surrender. Blur-limned against a thin, gawping new moon, they were invisible even to themselves when Lucy's slender swan-necked legs wavered under the star-sieved sky. And shivering to stillness, she slept in his arms.

Past midnight when she dropped him off, a limping handyman from the Great Western Arms walking the pub alsatian, singing, 'I'm alone because I love you'.

Lucy caught Gabe's hand, 'That makes twenty-two times since last April.'

He expected this private arithmetic, Lucy's ritual testimony. 'Great and all,' he said, kissing her throat. 'We're a pair, we're the best.'

'It's because I love you, Gabie.'

'Hey, it's mutual, as you know. When I buy my car we'll have some weekend outings.'

'Respect though, do you respect me?'

'Hundred per cent. See you, my lovely.'

Subdued grumbling from Rosser Passmore when she entered the house. Lucy ate Bothi canteen sandwiches and biscuits for supper, disregarding him without malice, Rosser hooped in his fireside chair, watching her, morose, guilty, oppressed by cold ash of his ambiguous passion.

She said, 'Goodnight. I'm off duty until ten in the morning. My alarm is set for nine, so I'll have a nice lay-in.'

'Need any help in the canteen tomorrow?'

'Not at all, Ross,' smiled Lucy. 'You go for a walk, have some fresh air.'

3

'Next time use your loaf,' warned Sue Lloyd, watching Gabe burn the receipt for his fine in Dove Street magistrates' court.

'Too true,' says Gabe. 'I'm off now, darts in the Labour Club, bit of a challenge match.'

'Don't get drunk,' she said.

The following morning a Five Deep fireman came up the face—word-of-mouth had travelled the stents where colliers were shovelling coal on the conveyor belt.

Gabe saluted, '*Shwmae*, Jobie.'

Down on his kneepads, the fireman aimed tobacco juice fast as a chameleon's tongue. 'How old are you now, Gabe?'

He hunkered closer to the official, cap-lamps effectively killing the glare at half-way. 'Why, Jobie, any bother?'

'None, boy, no bother. They're inquiring in the office.'

'Twenty-two next month.'

Jobie Lewis grunted, poling to his feet on his safety stick. 'Manager wants to see you in the top-pit lodge at ha'-past two.' He speared at the coal, 'Lovely face slip that. Hole under her a few inches an' she'll spew out like a bag. Can't beat our Bothi coal. S'clean, mun, clean.' Jobie rolled his chew, 'Righto, Gabe, see you in the lodge.'

The fireman crab-legged up the face, Gabe thinking, there goes another fantastic Coal Board expert, elephant brainy between the ears. Roof streamers glinted ahead of Jobie's lamp; he ploughed on, stooped forward on his safety stick.

Gabe shovelled. They're up to something. Monte Leyshon and his clique, they'll be waiting for me in the lodge. Clever Monte, his missis no thicker than a rail. Funny old bitch, she always looks flummoxed. She's in a worse state than Sue. Monte though, what he doesn't know about coal production isn't worth mentioning. He'll warn me to keep my hands quiet. So cool head, Lloydie, you're on probation.

Hooter skirling from the roof of the winding house as Gabe stepped out of the cage, and dull echoes bansheed from gullied hills above Bothi Number 2. He crossed directly to the lodge. Jobie Lewis and two other firemen stood behind the manager. Gabe grinned amiably. They were like a photo from *Coal* magazine, as if the four were pigeon-fanciers or on the Institute committee or crack hands in their allotments or winners on the bowling green. Gabe folded his arms. Monte, I don't trust you, man.

Like an undertaker doffing his topper at a funeral, Monte Leyshon removed his pit helmet, placed it on the table, smiled cordially up at Gabe, the off-centre pupil of his left eye swollen fish-like behind his spectacles, 'Well now, no doubt you are wondering why I wanted to talk to you?'

Jobie scratched the nub of his chin, 'Don't you jump to conclusions, boy. Mr Leyshon doesn't intend victimising you or anybody else. Just take it easy.'

Gabe says, 'No messing about then.'

The manager tossed a confidential right eye wink, implying authority, his domain. He said, 'Gabe, I would like you to drive the cutter in the Five Deep. Of course Billy Holly drives the machine by night. I want you to help him until you get the hang of it.'

Innocently deflated, Gabe says, '*Behind* the cutter?'

'Until you can operate the machine. Let me explain. In practical terms you'll be your own boss, on top grade wages. That's important, certainly. It's a damned good opportunity, one of the most skilled jobs in our pit.'

'I'm satisfied pulling coal and chucking it on the belt,' he said.

'Yes, surely, but I need a reliable cutter operator . . .'

He interrupted the manager, 'Mr Leyshon, do me a favour, find somebody else.'

'Careful, lad, be careful. I won't have you dictating to me.'

'Bloody nights and then bloody afternoon shift.' He menaced the officials ganged behind the manager. Keep your bloody dagger-looks to yourselves.

'I'm afternoons regular,' complained one of the firemen, a jockey-sized man, prematurely wizened.

Gabe huffed animosity. This short-arsed clown with a scoot of kids, afternoon shift was good enough for him. 'Your fucken problem,' he said. 'Maybe afternoons suits your missis'— instantly realising he shouldn't have referred to the man's wife, but, if you speak out of turn you either back down or bash on regardless. He threw a reverse vee sign at the fireman, 'Up your jacksi.'

'I know what I'd do if I was Mr Leyshon! You'd be down the bloody road!'

227

The manager flagged his hands for peace and quiet. 'Look here, Gabe, until I find another man you'll have to go on night shift.'

'For how long?'

'Cantankerous bugger,' said Jobie.

Monte Leyshon tushed impatience, 'I shan't repeat myself. You'll work behind the cutter until I find a replacement.'

'I'm a collier!' shouted Gabe. 'I'll see our NUM about this!'

Jobie Lewis screwed his jaw, spent chew clamped between his inner dentures, 'Ignorant talk coming from you, boy. NUM can't do nothing, simple reason being Mr Leyshon isn't downgrading you. My own son, even, he spent a couple of years behind the cutter.'

'Aye, day shift,' says Gabe.

'More's the pity he smashed his fingers that time, put paid to him for definite. By now he'd be on cross shifts with Billy Holly, cutterman hisself.'

Gabe hardened his stomach. They had him over a barrel. Monte Leyshon knew the rule book. Trouble-makers never lasted on day shift. The principle was older than nationalisation. Trouble-makers were sacked. Dirty through and through, these NCB officials. Separate breed, and they had him where they wanted him. Gabe read the situation as true to family experience.

'Righto,' he said, grinning, 'Mr Leyshon, you can shove nights behind the cutter where the monkey shoves his nuts.' Family pride had removed the Triumph car from Gabe's ambition.

'So you prefer the alternative, a fortnight's notice.'

Old Jobie was shaking his head, 'It's a bad thing to sack a man, 'cause see, Gabe, they'll stop your dole money for six weeks. On top of that, boy, you're already fifty quid short. All I'm saying, boy, use some commonsense.'

'What's it to be?' asked Mr Leyshon.

Gog-eyed bastard, thought Gabe. He doesn't care either way. Me neither. And as the dream returned, 'I'm willing, Mr Leyshon, for two quid a week extra.'

The manager's smile flickered, 'One pound. Consider yourself lucky.'

'Two quid, Mr Leyshon'—there'll be a car outside our house next winter.'

'One.'

The under-sized afternoon shift fireman protested, 'I

wouldn't have him in my district. Lloyd thinks he can chuck his weight about since he boxed for the Coal Board.'

Monte Leyshon rose from his chair. 'We don't expect the cutter to run like a Swiss watch. There are bound to be snags occasionally, resulting in overtime. You'll make two pounds a week over and above the rate.'

Whereon Gabe conceded, 'Fair enough.'

'Start Monday night.' Distantly cheerful, the manager led his officials out of the top-pit lodge.

Soaping himself under the shower, Gabe realised an inkling of destiny. By the Christ, I went soft as butter in Monte's hands. It's what probation does to a man. At the end of two years I'll be down on my benders every night before creeping into bed. Blowing soapy dribbles from his mouth, he gurgled the absurdity! But the judgment mood was still on him as he went down the steps from the pithead baths. Here he met Jobie Lewis.

'Hey, Gabe, I'm nights reg'lar myself, starting next week. Done my share of traipsing up and down the faces. These legs of mine, see, knees gone stiff. Aye, I'll be overman by night, looking after repairers for a change.'

'Ought to be a medal pinned on your fucken chest with a horseshoe nail,' says Gabe. 'Give us a fag.'

Jobie shook kinked Woodbines from a packet. 'Genuine now, you and Billy Holly will make a go of it al'right. Like Monte Leyshon said, Billy's very nigh his own boss, y'know, give and take a bit either way.'

Gabe flared mockery, 'Come off it, you shitten old hypocrite. Why didn't you tell me when you came up the face this morning?'

Jobie unbuckled his kneepads, 'Mr Leyshon says where and when in this pit. He's paid for taking responsibility. Fair do's, Gabe, you took it better than I expected.'

Gabe lightly pressed his thumb on the old fireman's nose, 'You and me, we'll be in the last bon down next Monday night.'

(4)

Top pit bore the stamp of a modernised heavy industry. Mown sward bordered concrete walkways out to the car park. His first night shift and Gabe felt readier to put his feet up than change into pit clothes. He saw Billy Holly leaving the lamp-room, a pale, ginger-haired man in his forties, muscular as a work-dog, his feet misshapen from birth, which gave Billy a dire sense of dignity, the kind of rat-cornered righteousness for erupting as lunatic temper. Billy's blind outbursts were normally sanctioned in Bothi Number 2. Driving the Longwall coal-cutter, he could 'almost make it talk,' said the colliers, whereas Billy's chief concern was to make work easier for himself. Billy had the nous of perfectionism. Under dangerous roof conditions he served a skived undercut instead of the full extent of the jib. After a couple of feet, colliers were hand-cutting, temperately cursing the cutter-man, because a 4'6" undercut might have collapsed their stents in the face. Grafting with punchers and mandrels with a chance to reach the target, was better than bare day wage clearing heavy roof muck. Safer too.

Gabe said, 'Hullo, Cochyn. I'm your new butty.'

'None of your cheek if you don't mind. I heard Cochyn enough when I was a kid.'

'Doesn't mean a thing,' suggested Gabe.

Billy rocked on his deformed feet. 'Point is, Lloydie-boy, if you get really awful chopsy, well, aah, I can fuck you up good and proper, only we got to work together.'

'I'm with you all the way, no argument.' Gabe feinted friendly cuffs at his arm, then lifted a sack of sharpened cutter picks off Billy's shoulders, 'I'll lug these.'

Came a pleased cackle from Billy's neat, pursy mouth, 'Been hoping you'd offer, though I wasn't going to ask, not first shift.'

They stepped into the cage behind Jobie Lewis and a few elderly repairers. 'Last bon as usual,' intoned the banksman as if talking to himself.

'Mind your own bastardin' business,' said Billy politely, as if rebuking a mild pest. The banksman pretended boredom, having no warrant other than the safe, standby bickering of his job.

Suddenly a fireman came running from the officials' lodge. The banksman scowled, white teeth and eyeballs facing the cap-lamps in the cage. He swung the gate open again. Angry, wheezing breaths from the fireman as they dropped away. The official accused Billy Holly of negligence. The Longwall was buried under a fall in the fireman's district. Worse, he had no spare labourers. Who would clear the fall and timber the face?

'How much muck is there?' inquired Jobie.

'Seven, eight bloody drams! I shan't know 'til I see it for myself! Him, this man, he should have stuck up some posts around the cutter!'

Billy made forbearing gestures, his hands womanish, talon fingered, 'Wait now, listen,' he said. 'Before gallopin' on like you are, let's find out who shifted the cutter since last Saturday morning.'

'It's where you left the fucken thing! Up near the gate road!'

Billy hooked this thumbs in his waistcoat pockets, 'Well then, I think . . .'

'You're a dead loss!' snapped the fireman.

Garish cap-lamps bobbled to stillness in the pit cage. Gabe saw Billy's eyes retreat into creases. He seemed to contract his brow and cheekbones, and his steel-tipped boots went ominously tap tap-tap on the slab iron floor, like the march of metallic beetles. Proud Cochyn, he thought, he's entitled same as anyone else.

Every man automatically bent his knees, legs tightening as the dropping cage stalled to a ear-filling pause before gliding delicately to pit bottom.

They stepped out, the fireman rowing Jobie, demanding to know who was going to clear the fall. Jobie chewed, waiting his turn to speak. Meanwhile the pit-bottom hitcher pushed a tram of muck into the cage, hooked up the gate and pressed the button. Wrist-thick guide ropes squelched grease as the cage lifted into darkness.

Billy Holly snatched the sack of cutter picks off Gabe's shoulder. He held it at arm's length, the weight canting him as he hobbled around the repairers.

'Watch out,' said Jobie, stepping away from his colleague.

Small snorts from Billy's hooked nose as he advanced, wild in revenge to land a swinger with the sack of picks on the fireman's head. The fireman wobbled a run around the glistening guide ropes and beyond, to the brink of a walled sump.

Jobie poked Gabe with his stick, 'Stop him! Move, boy, quick!'

'Do your own dirty work,' says Gabe.

'Just stop him,' pleaded the overman.

231

Excited by drama in which he wasn't involved, Gabe yelled, *'Your* bloody orders, Jobie,' and charged past Billy, promising, 'I'll take care of him, butty.' He grabbed the fireman's lapel, 'Get out on pit bottom or you'll be in that sump.'

Bluster tinged with fear from the fireman, 'This all you're good for? I'm old enough to be your father?'

Gabe laughed. Decent guts for a Bothi official.

And, 'I'll see you back in Dove Street police court!' cried the fireman.

Billy Holly screamed falsetto, 'I'll show the bastard who's a dead loss!'

Gabe ducked, wrenching the fireman aside, under the loaded sack, but Billy missed anyway. The fireman wriggled free. He scurried around to the traffic side of pit bottom. Billy was teetering from the momentum of his attack, as the flying sack of cutter picks splashed into the sump. They watched it bubbling to the bottom. Sixty sharp picks in five feet of black water. They spent an hour hooking the sack out with a slender 6½ foot post, the end spiked with a grapple of six inch nails, guaranteeing the incident as legend.

Gabe and Billy established themselves as workmates. Jobie sent labourers from another district to help clear the buried coal-cutter. At three o'clock in the morning they began cutting coal. Gabe behind the machine, his round-nosed shovel scooping away hot, fine gumming as it churned out from the jib. He felt easy. We'll never get round to a proper bust-up, me and Cochyn Holly. One thing, this is easier than working a stent. Slightly cushier, forgetting about pneumo. Aye indeed, the dust. Supposing a paratrooper worried? He'd never manage to live rough and shoot to kill. Similar applies down here. You can have the House of Lords and the House of Commons, two loads of shit for sure, but you can't have coal and pure spit. Therefore, no reason why a man should respect any system at all. Bugger respect . . . Lucy Passmore, my woman, by the Christ, my woman.

Shovelling in dream, Gabe ignored the awkward fact. Lucy was almost twice his age.

Shuffling in front, Billy kept his right hand on the bull-nosed machine, near the control chipper. He watched the roof, overhanging coal slips, and he threw clear the electric cable as the cutter crept forward, steel tow-rope lapping on its drum housed nearside in the machine. Billy listened. Danger creaks from the roof, then he lifted the chipper handle. In seconds the jib cleared iself, grinding roar diminishing as the freed picks chained around, rattling bedlam above the heavy, droning electric motor. Following behind, watching, listening, Gabe learned to hold still, poised alert as a wild animal.

A few shifts and he was orientated to the Longwall racket. Night shift itself soured Gabe's outlook. Broken sleep by day, early morning and late afternoon, made him grouchy, 'Like a bear with a sore backside,' in Sue's words. Pitiless Sue, she tormented him. No yielding in her. No sympathy. Outside the house he made his own way, obeying the only law. Fight to have and keep what's yours.

He cultivated dozing while standing on his feet, drooped forward over his shovel, wafer of consciousness sensing the roof and crackling, sagging coal. Sometimes the machine thundered on, leaving him, duff spreading a dense level carpet, six inches deep, deepening, the Longwall ploughing slower, slower, groaning, burning the life out of the picks. Billy left him alone when conditions were hazardous. He'd chip hauling speed in spurts to zero until the jib cleared. Next morning wary colliers tapped, sounding the roof above untouched layers of gumming in their stents.

Gabe repaid his butty by taking on strongman graft. He dragged out the cable before they started cutting each face, he heaved on a crowbar after they flitted out from the coal, levering the Longwall onto a transporter trolley. At the end of each cut, Gabe hauled forward the steel tow-rope. He fixed the two-post. Learning how to operate the cutter came pat. But he often dozed on his feet, awakening instantly, guiltless, roused by lessening roar, protesting to himself, 'Bloody night shift, I'll never adjust. Goes against human nature.'

Most nights they catnapped at snack-time. Billy planned, nominating a dry section of face where they knocked off, chatted over sandwiches and a swig before settling down for their little sleep—breaking mining law, prosecution certain despite Billy's noble alibi. 'It takes a really sly waster to sneak up on a man when he's at his grub.'

Slumped in powdery, warmed duff, Gabe agreed. The bastard deserved a running kick.

And Billy explaining further, 'What I mean to say, once a man's on top of his job.'

Gabe confirmed, 'Right. Wake me, Coch.'

He relied on Billy. Always the prescribed ten or fifteen minutes. Disciple of Greenwich, Billy pulled himself to his senses, slammed the lid on his tommy box, loudly gargle from his water jack, or he told dirty jokes, encouragement for Gabe to come around. Cruel the harrow between duty and the flesh, Billy affirming *duty* with sanguine rectitude, while ever scheming to make it bearable.

One night they were in D conveyor face off the Five Deep. Broken roof had collapsed behind them as they were cutting down. This slavery shift meant everything went wrong. Three times the two-post pulled loose. The picks blunted from chewing through a freak layer of slag inside the coal. Moreover, Billy swore he was in the opening throes of tonsillitis. Sweat gleamed his bony face, coalescing with water drippings from the roof. Globules shining in his gingery eyebrows, ran off the tip of his beaky nose. Hard, grubbing shift aggravated by visits from Jobie Lewis, old Jobie preaching the theme of production. Fevered Billy taking risks, neglecting caution, his role as cutter-man. Mindless risks men take when threatened by failure.

Jobie squatted with them at snack-time, shooting tobacco juice, costing estimates per man-hour per stent if day-shift colliers had no machine-cut coal ready for them in the morning.

Stubborn behind the cutter, Gabe felt harassed, onus upon himself to keep the jib clear. He crouched from one Dowty post to the next, cold steel solid against his ribs easing his worried soul. Often he shovelled one-handed at the full reach of his arm. On ahead of the Longwall, two repairers were hurriedly sledging up extra timber props. Behind them the entire face creaked and groaned, pounded, slips of coal crashed down, roof fissures powdered, cracked, fell, splintered each side of flats above the props. Time after time Gabe scrabbled up in front of the cutter to dodge jagged chunks of roof.

Standard squeeze, localised, intensified by the Longwall cutter. For Gabe Lloyd and his butty, safety hinged on experience foretelling chance.

Worn out at the end of the shift, Billy tottered back to pit bottom like a rag-stuffed doll. The following night as usual,

'We'll change the picks first thing,' he said, squeaky from his inflamed glottis.

'Didn't expect to see you tonight,' says Gabe. 'Missis boot you out of the house?'

'Mine's a good un, don't you fret. Any road, I got four mouths to feed. Seen Jobie?'

'He went down earlier.'

'Bit of a cunt, Jobie is, on the quiet. He gets his pound of flesh out of the daft likes of you an' me. Hear his bullshit last night! Firemen laying down the law to me, I don't like it, boy, not at all.'

'We won't see much of Jobie this shift. They're re-laying the double parting to Gomer's heading.'

Billy rocked tap-tap-tap on his heels. 'Better not, else I'll be fast into him.'

'Bloody nog for punishment you are,' says Gabe.

They found Jobie waiting for them in the face, sprays of tobacco juice on the flat, steel-clad machine.

'News for you, Gabe. Mr Leyshon says you're ready to cross Billy on afternoons. I told him you could handle the cutter a treat.'

Gabe dropped the sack of sharp picks. 'The lying bastard, he promised I'd be doing this job till he found another man.'

Sliding his backside off the cutter, Jobie came out to the roadway. He frowned up at Gabe, 'You're in the same position as previous, s'far as I understand from Monte Leyshon. Either drive the cutter by afternoon, or take fourteen days notice. See, boy, there's so many on the dole, they can play dip-dap-doh.'

'On your way then, don't rub it in,' says Gabe, thinking, this is it, *discipline*. Old Monkey Lips in Dove Street, he put the jinx on me. He should have been with us last night, cutting down D face. He'd weep for mercy, bastard-born chimp as he is.

Billy shouted after Jobie's retreating cap-lamp, 'Switch the power on, Jobie!' Whereon he confided, 'Yes, boy, I told you he was sly as a whoor's minj. Him and Monte make a right pair.'

'We'll go slow motion changing the picks,' says Gabe.

'Course, man, and there's a pretty dry run in front of us tonight, thank Christ.'

5

10.45 Friday night, their last shift together, Gabe waiting for Billy in the canteen. Lucy came out from the tiled kitchen behind the counter, Nita trailing her. Dumpily built Nita, waddle-footed and tireless, who worked off-shifts serving in Bothi Number 2 canteen.

'Clear the tables, Nita, please,' Lucy said.

Gabe paid for his mug of tea, saying, 'Know what, Lucy, for next week I'll be on afternoons.'

She fluted sympathy, 'Sha-ame, bed to work. Of course afternoons doesn't affect the older blokes so much.'

'I'll save money,' says Gabe.

Her hands were demurely cupped, presenting bliss against forces of malice and dissolution, 'We're only young once in our lives, Gabie.'

'Perhaps I'll sling it in when I get my car on the road. Find another job.'

'Marvellous!' her smile measuring him for glory.

He boasted, 'I can feel the itch coming on. If I hadn't changed into these working clothes I'd sacrifice a shift's pay. Hey, girl, your bedroom window, leave it open tomorrow night. I'll shin up off the outhouse roof.'

'Don't you dare,' Lucy hugging herself inside her summer cardigan, silent laughter shaping her red mouth.

'Here's my suggestion then. We'll have a few drinks somewhere out in the country, bed and breakfast place, okay?'

'Oh, dear God . . .' as Billy came in and she remarked politely, 'Hullo, Billy.'

They sat at a table near the door, Billy beckoning for a mouthful of Gabe's tea. He took it swiftly in short sips, like a bird drinking. 'Ta,' he said, adding, 'Cow of a woman she is. Old Rosser Passmore's worn the same suit on his back for years, and there she's togged up like a bookie's tart. Beats me how she runs that car. You can't run a bloody car, not on the wages she's getting.'

'She's manageress,' said Gabe.

'Man-age-urr-ess!'

'Stop back-biting, Coch, you'll turn pure green.'

'Bright fucker to talk,' from Billy.

'What's her maiden name, Lucy's I mean?'

'Rollins,' said Billy, 'and if she was my missis she'd be rollin' 'round the floor of our bloody scullery.'

Gabe mimed a left hook, 'That's what I like about you, Coch, you're such a nice gentleman. How's the sore throat?'

'Better now, boy, y'know, not so raw.'

'This'll be our last shift.'

'Aye, worse luck,' says Billy.

They rode down in the last bon, Billy Holly for the last time.

And Gabe, he missed his Saturday night date with Lucy Passmore.

At one o'clock in the morning a miracle saved Gabe from losing his foot. He unlocked the cutter jib prior to changing the picks. Heeding his signal, Billy switched on and hauled forward a couple of yards until the jib straightened out from under the seam, then Billy hooked the tow-rope to the jib, ready to chip it back under the coal at 45 degrees to the machine. Billy trilled a pigeon fancier's whistle for Gabe to start changing the picks.

Reaching for the sack, Gabe smeared his hand on Jobie's tobacco juice. Seconds later Billy did the same thing. They cursed the overman and his family, reviled him in the idiom of miners, soldiers, sailors, prisoners, all victims of civilisation. Imagery inane to the eye, alien to domesticity and nemesis of any dialectic.

Gabe changed the picks. Short stubby picks locked in the chain by single, nut-headed grubscrews. It was simple. Tug on the spanner. Remove the blunt pick from its socket. Tighten in the sharp pick. Blunt picks were left in the blacksmith shop every morning. Billy kneeled at the controls, chipping the chain around the jib. Between times he oiled the machine, finally sloshing a pint of oil over Jobie's trade marks before scraping it all off with a shovel.

Contented in the silent face, Billy sang his doleful version of 'O, more and more I adore you, Gianina Mia'. Snugged over the jib, Gabe glanced at him now and then. Comrade Cochyn fancies himself as the great lover. Him hopping around on his buckled feet, crooning from that bitsy mouth under that small Shylock nose, hair the colour of Sue's nightie over his lugholes, the nightie she boiled to shreds. Good old Billy Coch, he's like a half-scragged parrot. God alive, you'll only find Billy's kind in Wales, these scruffy valleys where the *gummel* of every man's ancestors has taken a homing from proving himself stronger in the balls than in gumption. I reckon old Coch's a sticker on the nest, grunt-grunt like an Easter frog. Still, he's *real*. Billy's settled himself with a woman and kids, which is more than I can say. After I buy my car we'll make some arrangement, Gabe Lloyd and Lucy. Aye, carry on, Gabriel, she's all yours. Unless you've had a dabble you don't know where you are. Buy a Triumph first. Jesus, afternoons from now on. By the loving Christ, best shift ever for saving a few quid every Friday.

He moved away from the jib. 'Okay, man,' he said.

Billy tipped the control chipper, inching the chain around.

Gabe waggled the spanner, 'That'll do.' The chain stopped and he shuffled in close again on his left knee, dragging the sack of picks with his left hand, his right leg outstretched.

Then it happened. Perhaps a lump of coal fell on the controls, or a flake of scaling from the roof. Later, Billy pledged on the lives of his children. He hadn't touched the chipper. The chain cogged around, the tow-rope began hauling the jib into the coal seam, and one of the picks jabbed through Gabe's right boot, thinly slicing the skin where the arch curves under. His boot rammed against the coal, the cutter *stalled*, stopped dead, power to mince granite whining, raging from the motor. But the chain stopped dead—as the ravelled tow-rope unhooked itself, whanged from the jib. Miracle, luck, anything nameless beyond reason.

Billy cut the motor. He's frantic, unscrewing the pick and untying Gabe's bootlace. Gabe withdrew his foot. It pulsed fire.

'My jack, Cochyn, douse some water over the fucken thing.'

Billy fingered the west underside of Gabe's sock. He's stuttering, 'Buh-bleeding, boy. Buh-best take a look at it first.' He removed the sock, 'Ah, Christ, I don't like seeing blood.'

Gabe angled the foot up across his left thigh. 'Looks worse than it feels. Bruised and that bit of a gash. Fetch my jack.'

'Bones all right, Gabe?'

Flexing toes and ankle, 'Aye, definitely.'

'Keep it clean,' Billy said. 'You wait here while I fetch Jobie.'

'All I need is some bandage. Gimme my jack before you go.'

Now, reaching for the water jack, Billy vowed he hadn't touched the controls. How could he with his back to the cutter, tucking the empty oil can in the gob wall? 'On my life,' he said, 'on my kids' life, jonnack, boy, I didn't touch the chipper. Honest to God, honest.'

Said Gabe, 'I'm not blaming you, for Christ's sake.'

'What's the pain like? Can you walk out?'

'I'm staying. Those mean bastards in the office, they'll crop me half a shift.'

'Sure now, Gabe?'

Who laughed, 'Bugger off, get me a bandage.'

It was late in the shift when Jobie Lewis asked them if they would help one of the heading miners.

'What's it worth?' Billy said.

Jobie unclipped his lamp, hit the glass bullseye with a tiny squirt of tobacco juice, wiped it clean with his thumb, offering, 'I'll book you in for a quarter.'

Billy insisted, 'Remember, you're taking us off our job.'

'So book it down now,' says Gabe. 'Next time you plant your filthy gobs on this cutter I hope your tongue blows out as well.'

They walked the two hundred yards to the development heading. N.C.B. planners were re-opening an old supply road to exploit a new district. Jobie left them at a junction off the main, 'I'm only asking you blokes to give Stan Evans a hand with a pair of rings, that's all. It's pinching a bit in there, but do your best. See you on top pit.'

Gabe and Billy entered the mouth of the old heading. 'Stan's making four quid a yard,' said Billy. 'Us two, boy, we'll be booked in as dead-work. Stan'll gain the benefit.' He paused, teetering on his heels, singing, 'Tell me the old, old story,' then 'Bullshit baffles brains. Members of the working class, we been fed bullshit since day one.'

'You remind me of my old man, except you're fucken vulgar,' says Gabe.

Far ahead, flickering like a glow-worm, they saw the heading man's lamp.

Gabe held Billy's wrist, 'Hush a minute. Listen. Hear that? Wouldn't mind betting it's a proper crib in there.' He flung his arms around Billy, 'Butty, you bolt up the fishplates. Got your skyhooks handy?'

Billy tilted his head back, gazing at twelve foot rings arching the heading. Some were twisted, fishplates gaping, held by

239

skewed nuts and bolts. Thin puffs of dust jerked down through mildewed timber lagging lapping from ring to ring. They heard their own breathing and the persistent whispering of moving earth. 'It's pinchin' al'right,' Billy said.

'Pinching! It's all on the bloody move. Steady, hold on, Coch, plenty of time.'

Small rivulets of grained rubble drifted down behind the dry-stone walled sides of the heading. They dribbled, stopped abruptly like scatterings from the claws of watchful rats. High up inside the roof, booming rolled, nagging on and on, echoing distant as fading thunder. Billy sniggered, stepped backwards, impelled by the tension of his neck, his raised chin exposing the jig of his Adam's apple. A fist-sized piece of rock thumped muffled on the overhead canvas air-bag which ventilated the re-opened heading. Dust shone innocently, swirled away to nothing. Another stone fell on the air bag. Billy darted, tucking himself close to the roadside, one boot resting on a 2" compressed air pipe column clipped low down on the rings. 'Long way off yet,' said Billy.

Says Gabe, 'Aye, hope it stays a long way off.'

They walked in fifty yards, halted, hearing harsh tearing of timber, like crossed branches strained by winds. Common enough, the way it creaked slow and steady.

Billy said, 'Old ground, she'll settle by and by.'

Gabe spat superficial anger, 'Let's put this bloody ring up and clear off out.'

The heading man grumbled, 'Where the hell you been? I asked Jobie for help hour an' a half ago.' Bulky Stan Evans, middle-aged, wearing a half-sleeved woollen vest, badgerly hair like lathe shavings bushed on his chest. A cud of tobacco seldom left his nibbling front teeth. Brown stain crystallised on the rims of his pink lips.

Gabe said casually, 'Go easy on the mouth, Stan. We came straight off the cutter.'

'Where's your reg'lar butty?' inquired Billy genially.

Lifting off his helmet, Stan wiped his bald skull with a hairy forearm. 'Christ knows. Youngsters these days, they chuck money away like it was dirt.'

'No worse than miserable old buggers like yourself,' said Gabe. 'C'mon, let's shove this ring up.'

'Keep you eyes open,' warned the heading man.

240

6

4½′ posts stacked near Stan's last pair of rings, new timber for lagging, and a level-bedded tram of muck, sprags locking the front wheels. Both halves of the new roofing ring sloped against the sides of the tram. Small, meaningless puddles and shattered rock from previous shot firing, concealed the end of the tram track. A narrow seam of rider coal glistened damply some ten feet above the rubble.

Stan indicated the rider, 'When she runs out we'll be into four feet of clean coal. She's causing all the trouble, that dirty little rashing of *mum-glo.* Wouldn't be so bad if there was something solid up above.'

Back in the roadway, stones cascaded, echoed on the overhead lagging.

Billy screwed up his small mouth, 'Coming closer.'

Stan tossed a pair of fishplates and four nuts and bolts on the tram of muck. 'Who's fixing?'

Billy clambered up off the hitching plate. 'Let's have the bloody spanner.'

'I'll fetch it once you've got the bolts through,' said Stan. 'It's on my toolbar.' He and Gabe lifted one half of the new twelve-foot ring, resting the butt on a thick wooden sill. They raised the other half. Billy drew the crowns flush together. Gabe and Stan held perfectly still. Skinny, dextrous on the tram of muck, Billy slotted the fishplates in position and sent the bolts through. He gave the nuts a few turns by hand.

Stan's toolbar was ten yards back in the road. He lumbered hestitantly as timber squealed, rending across the grain, followed by sibilous roaring soft shale pouring out from a break in walling between the rings. 'Damn and blast, couple of drams of muck back there,' complained Stan, plodding out for his spanner.

Billy looked down at Gabe, still humped against his half of the ring, 'Slacken off, butty, she won't topple now.'

'Where's he off to, for Jesus' sake?' says Gabe.

The heading man was near the fallen shale, his cap-lamp dancing as he examined dry-rotted overhead lagging. They heard his furious shout before the roar of the next fall drifted mazy curtains of dust. Stan's light disappeared. From his perch on top of the tram, Billy saw it again, moving away, and Stan's bellow rang up to tenor screaming, 'Come on out!'

'Get moving,' urged Gabe, offering his shoulder for Billy to jump down. Billy landed like a thrown bundle, rose to all-fours, unhurt. He set off, trotting out. Gabe's jacket hung over a corner of the tram. He snatched for it, saw Billy stop suddenly, heard heavy stuff rumbling farther out in the roadway, lags snapping, and Stan's light disappeared again. Billy came backing away, soft stepping like a wary primitive.

'Keep going!' yelled Gabe, glimpsing the heading man's lamp shining far out, a small white glitter in blackness.

'Can't,' Billy said.

'We gotto make it,' Gabe nudging him forward. 'C'mon, Cochyn!'

They were a few yards beyond Stan's toolbar. Another fall spewed out from the left side of the road. They waited, cursing, praying for it to stop. Fishplates squealed like bats, releasing shrapnel-pinging stones. Gabe reasoned from his gut. There's a bloody huge *cwmp* on the way. He said, 'Let's get out from here.'

Baulked by frailty, his boots scuffling dust, 'Back to the dram,' said Billy.

'We'll soon be out on the main,' argued Gabe, bundling him over the rubble. But there were more falls. Every few yards the walls burst open. Softly roaring slides of crushed shale spilled out. Overhead rock cramming down on the rings, broke the lagging, jagged stones smashing through, pelting like volcanic hail in the roadway. And not a flicker of Stan's cap-lamp.

They were isolated, the earth roiling original chaos.

A small stone struck Billy's shoulder, up near the neck. As he pitched sideways another bigger stone skidded off his left buttock, ripping his trousers. The torn cloth flapped down. Gabe saw Billy's underpants spread loose over his lean shape. Billy yelped to growling, rolling himself into a hedgehog ball. Gabe grabbed him beneath the armpits, hauled him towards the base of the rings until his grip was broken by chuting stones deflecting off his forearms. Gabe crouched low, tight to the rings. Floods of rubble continued, burying Billy's head and shoulders. Grazed hands shielded between his thighs, without realising Gabe heard the sickening knock of stone against bone. The bones of his butty's skull.

Frenzy quelled Gabe Lloyd's fear, gave him the blind power of heroes and agonised cowards. He caught Billy's boots,

242

dragging him clear, the cap-lamp trailing on its flex from the battery clipped to Billy's belt. Unbuckling the belt, Gabe hitched it over his own. He thrust Billy's lamp into his jacket pocket. With Billy dead in his arms, he lurched back to the tram. Seconds into minutes later came the biggest fall in memories of Bothi Number 2. Forty yards of heading blanket crashed, leaving eight new rings, strained but upright behind Stan Evans's tram of debris.

Head bent against slow-surging clouds of dust, Gabe sat on the hitching plate with Billy across his lap. He's muttering, 'You were right, Coch. Man, you were right.'

Pain registered. He dangled his right arm. There were lacerations along the back of his hand, blood clotting, glints blackening. Fist clenched, he tightened the forearm muscles, a sense of wonder beguiling him. It was okay, the arm, proved by digging his fingernails into his palm. Gabe waggled his bandaged foot, feeling it tolerably sore. The soreness comforted his existence.

'Cochyn, hey, Billy . . .' Widening the spread of his thighs, bending over to lever up Billy's head and shoulders, he saw a blood bubble film out of the small mouth, burst soundless, the lips set still.

He's crying, 'Billy, Billy, Billy,' and staring at the pulped flesh behind Billy's ear, bone punched inwards, all of it wet black, minute highlights shrinking, fading to over-all matt black. 'Ah, Christ, Billy,' he grieved, wrung bankrupt, desolated, and lowered him over his thighs again, letting the slack head loll down.

Gabe didn't know what to do. He sat on the hitching plate, listening to the roof sounding off. High up air pockets imploded in rock molten and sealed for three hundred million years. Tension drained away. Reveries surfaced, disconnected, the mixture unstoppable: Sue's wedding day, her new husband bragging in the kitchen, already half-pissed, confetti peppering his curly hair. Flabbergasted Sue. She dapped him in his place before the first week was over. Very likely banned cock on him. No doubt, aye. Sue, she's a Lloyd. Married a runaway husband. His father fixing stair carpet with blue tintacks. Mansel's big welcome for Martha when she came home from hospital. Martha created ructions. Carpet clashed with the wallpaper and they hadn't bought stair rods. Last round of his match against Nobby Graham. Two straight lefts smack on the point, then Nobby fetched a right-hander from nowhere, and they wobbled back to wrong corners like in a comedy. Shoni Joseph's gang of boys racing up the old big tip incline, Shoni in front with a new wristwatch. Shoni's record for running up the incline. He could gallop along like a *milgi*. Crumped-up Grancha Lloyd showing newspaper cuttings, reports about pit owners who refused to allow food sent down the shaft when colliers were on stay-in strike. Police on guard around the pit-head, batons keeping away wives and lodge committee-men. Grancha Tommy's walking stick bouncing off the mantelpiece, him reciting olden times, his voice quavery inside his chest, 'Durrty swines, they'd leave men rot so as to make their profits!' The winter weekend of twenty-foot snowdrifts, top-pit horses sledging groceries from the shops. Everything altered. Hedges vanished. Bank manager's bungalow just a white tump. Sheep down off the hills, they'd crash into your pantry. Lucy last night . . . up there in the canteen, blonde hair like Goldilocks. Lovely Lucy.

His breath groaned for himself stranded alone. Muttering, 'One-two-three,' he staggered lop-sidedly to his feet, hoiked Billy over the rim of the tram. Thus Gabe laid out his butty on the rubble. Didn't matter any more. Cuts on Gabe's hands were burning, his fingers stiff as he unclipped his cap-lamp. He tried the pilot bulb. The faint glow swung his head, stare pop-eyed at the full glare of Billy's lamp. Gabe switched it off, waited, adjusting his eyes to the dim light: 'Give a bloody rabbit nystagmus.' And he switched it on again.

He drained his water jack, the last half cupful chilling inside his chest, then he settled down on his heels, tired but sure of his strength, and compelled to dismiss Billy Holly, dead. Concentrate on himself, trapped in this heading. Air for instance. Aye. Christ, aye! The big canvas ventilation bag from the main was under the fall, smashed to smithereens.

Gabe went searching for the 2″ compressed air pipeline which powered Stan Evans's boring machine. It was buried.

7

Hunkered in the roadway, Gabe felt confident, untested yet confident, conscientious, talking to himself as if discussing pit-work over beer, 'Pipe column finishes this side of Stan's toolbar, blast hose connected to the column and the valve's turned off. Must be turned off because Stan's drills and boring machine are stacked behind his toolbar. There's roughly four yards of fall between me and that bloody valve. Eight, ten drams of muck if I can timber up as I drive through. Big IF. Umpteen drams if the heavy stuff starts shifting again. It won't move though, not if I go careful on the timbering.' Gabe climbed to his feet. 'Hey, any case it's shit or bust.'

Stan's shovel, pick and hatchet were propped against the side of the tram. Testing the blade with his thumb, he remembered the other hatchet buried under the fall. He carried the new 4½' posts to the edge of the fall. Three journeys and he was sweating. He sniffed for air. There wasn't much circulating. None at all, maybe. The canvas ventilation bag was in ribbons, some twenty yards out from the tram.

Filling his water jack from a thin streamer glinting below the high, narrow seam of mothering-coal, he kept his eyes averted from Billy Holly. Pointless examining a corpse. First things first. Drive through to the stop-valve. Knock on the pipe column. Remind anyone at the other side that he was alive and kicking. Time enough to worry about Billy when they could bring in a stretcher for him.

Gabe worked hard, careless of his durability, following the left-side tramrail, intent upon digging a low burrow between the rail and slewed butts of the collapsed rings. Every shovelful had to be thrown well back. The muck would have to be handled twice. At least twice. For a couple of hours he cleared sliding rubble. No alternative. He had to reach the solid, stone packed fall. Again Gabe counted his posts. Thirteen. One extra, Welshman's luck. Flats, he thought, I'm without flats. Strong flats, else I'll have muck tamping off my bloody helmet. Can't expect to hold big stuff up with these thin four'n halves. He cooped on his heels, expectant, waiting for ideas, thinking, I shan't travel far trimming these lagging timbers. Flats? Bloody flats . . . Sleepers! Yes, by Christ, sleepers. Rip the lot up.

He prised out rail cramps from the end sleeper. Slackening the wheel sprags, he pushed the tram forward over the loose rails. Then he removed four more sleepers. Pleased with himself, he said, 'Now for the real fucken graft.'

Massive slant-locked stones were his enemies. Gabe tackled them cautiously, loosening rubble with his pick, his head always protected by a half-length of sleeper flatted across short props. He chopped 18" off the posts, using off-cuts for wedges. His small burrow meant less digging. Less muck to clear. Twice the service from his sleepers.

Seven hours after Billy Holly's death, Gabe sounded a steeply-raked slab of rock with his pick-head, and he put the pick aside. Groping upwards, he finger-tipped delicate fern shapes, rippled tracings etched in the edge of the stone. They signified naught. He crawled out. Rest, *think*—instead he wondered about the rescue team working into the fall from the other side. Jammy sods, plenty of timber and steel flats. 'Few six'n-half posts would do me al'right,' he said. Two six-and-a-halves, that's all I need. There're thousands mouldering on collieries all over Wales. Fuck Wales. Fuck the mines. How would Mansel and Tommy perform, stuck in a crib like this? No-answer bloody question.

Then, straightening out his legs, instinct crowed from him, his bootstuds scraping on the nearside rail. 'Just the job,' his touch of joy. Gabe knew he'd found a way to work under the big stone. Plant a couple of 2 yard rails up against it. Rails and heavy wedges.

Prolonged toil wearied him. He struggled, hooking out shovelfuls of packed shale inside the line of rings, working back to a firm base upon which to slope the tramrails against the slab of rock. God knows how many feet of broken ground above the slab.

Muttering, 'So far so good,' he came kneeling out for a drink of water. And tired, weary, the gristle of his bones fiery. Sleep, he decided, save light, save my battery. Precious cap-lamp held to his stomach, he slept in the dark. Dull pain from his bruised foot and grazed hand failed to message his senses.

Gabe awoke fearfully, conscious of time spent. How much time? He inhaled, testing the air. It smelt familiar, the stale atmosphere of abandoned districts. Stale, like a dead-end airway road before knocking through to a ventilated coal face.

Not *too* bad. I can stick a lot of this. Besides, doesn't seem to be any gas here inside the fall. No killer gas, thank God.

Head turned from glancing at Billy Holly on the tram of muck, Gabe returned to his burrow.

He plodded now. Fatigue centred his body. He fiddled with the mandrel instead of hacking debris loose enough to shovel away. And his shovelfuls fell short. Crawling out, he remained stooped until he fell sideways, his limbs creeping to slumped rest. Rest, peace.

Often he simply listened. Surely to Christ they were working on the fall from the other side, day-shift colliers fresh from the kitchen table. Rescue teams from all over this bloody Number Three Eastern Area. Working side by side in pairs, under new rings, turn and turn about every few minutes. Slash into it, you dim-witted buggers. Bang on the pipe column, you bastards, let a man know you're getting stuck into it.

Gabe crawled out.

Clear sterile water dripped, spun candlewick streamers from the high, narrow layer of impure coal. Small puddles spread around the grey heap of rubble. Water seeped back under the tram, dampness invading dust in the shallow indent left by the far side rail, swelling half an inch wide to surface-coiling current where it leaked beneath the fall. Resting outside his burrow, Gabe thought, Thank Christ it's over there, otherwise I'd be soaked to my knees in this bloody dug-out. I've shifted tons of muck. Few more hours should put me by the stop-valve, near as damn it, I hope. By then I'll be knackered. Just about knackered as it is. There's old Cochyn my butty, he's out of it. He's finished. His missis'll go off her rocker when she sees him. As Mansel would say, here's the price of the old black diamonds. He was never stuck in a crack like this. Stan Evans's heading, right place for trying out our N.C.B. office staff, our collar-and-tie brigade.

Gabe's mind feathered as drift around himself and Lucy Passmore, finally vanishing, become phantasmal. He drank from his jack before crawling into the hole.

Raging, 'Anyone back there?' careless insanity promised to protect him. He slaved briefly, desperately. Exhaustion and stale air drained his spirit. He threw muck twice, clearing the burrow. He dragged in his last two props. When they were fixed in position, Gabe crawled out and slept. Cap-lamp in his hand, consciousness settled greyly peaceful. *Stop-valve*, get on to the pipe column or you'll wind up a deader like Billy Cochyn, which sparked defiance. *Never.* But torpor held his unfeeling body.

He hacked slowly at the rubble, levering away larger stones, rolling them behind him. The rail was his base for shovelling, screwing aside, turning every shovelful over his left thigh.

As in dream, impacting like divine insight, a streak of black low down in the debris, Gabe scrabbled with his fingers, freeing a loop of rubber hose. The blast hose connected to the 2″ pipeline. Confidence swam warmth, magic hurrahs singing his blood. Uncoiling the tough rubber hose, scratching forward through rubble, he found the smooth iron pipe. Gabe turned the stop-valve wheel, clung to it with a searing wrench of strength as compressed air whined, howled from a leak at the hose connection, purging the burrow with pricking dust and grit. Sobbing breaths, he eased back the knurled wheel until gentle air purred out, consistent, like a soft chimney draught drawing a fire. Gabe lashed his muffler around the leak. He crawled back to the tram. He felt convinced. All he had to do now was rest, wait for rescue teams to work through the fall.

Sprawled in the roadway, cap-lamp and helmet held to his stomach, he listened to cool, flowing air. Memory fragments bobbled like spawn. His fight-training days in the basement below the Institute. Sweat and snobs. Hard. Nothing like this.

Few minutes rest, relax all over, then start banging on the pipe column. Battery's just about flattened. He switched on as he stood upright. Glimmer focussed on Billy's studded bootsoles projecting above the rim of the tram. And Gabe's throat lamented, 'Poor old Cochyn.'

Whispery, human sounding air flowed out from the threaded nozzle of the blast hose. Gabe pulled on his jacket, feeling his bones worn, feeble. He dragged Stan Evans's hammer-headed hatchet into the burrow, poised it over the 2″ pipe and knocked six hard bangs. He waited, eyes shut, his mouth open. Six far-off signals resounded faintly. He hammered aggressively until he realised the danger of dislodging stones above his head.

As before, answers came softly pecking along the pipeline.

He's mumbling, 'Christ . . . Christ-man, it'll take 'em ages to cut through.'

248

Gabe huddled at the end of his burrow. The banging clacked on and on, all the time far, far away. He couldn't calculate how far. Head wrapped in his arms, he lapsed into misery worse than any physical beating, worse than the deaths of his father and mother. He was reduced, flawed in power, Gabe's secret faith where he lived heroically.

Frightened, he skulked around the tram to peer at Billy Holly's shrunken face, 'Billy Coch,' he said, mawkishly superior, 'we're trapped inside a bloody big dose of it, heading's blocked right out to the main, way they're knocking through on the blast pipe. Trapped, see?' He reached over and buttoned Billy's jacket, tidily, the way Sue straightened his tie before he went to Dove Street court. 'But you're safe, Cochyn, lucky man you.'

He circled around the tram. Cracked saucepan tappings were still coming from the burrow, endless, and he thought, they've put a youngster on the job, just bashing the pipe column. Monte Leyshon's back there, Monte the gog-eyed wonder, in charge of operations. He'd better be. I hope he is for Christ's sake. I'm relying on more than brains to get me out from here.

When the knocking ceased, he stilled himself in listening. Abruptly then, with blind certainty, Gabe leaned over the tram and rifled Billy's waistcoat pockets. Jacket pockets never carried anything except water jack and tommy box. A harmless WHUMP froze him in the act. He gazed up at the new untightened ring. Shot firing on big stuff back there.

The distant explosion shook down diminutive whiffs of dust.

He crouched into the burrow. Billy had small change and a return bus ticket in a Zube tin, a piece of hacksaw blade attached to a wrist loop of baling string, pair of pliers, box spanner to fit nuts on the Longwall cable pommel, and two sticky boiled sweets wrapped in paper. Gabe switched off his cap-lamp, lowered his mouth to the sweets, sucked, a king of clockwork suck-suck-suck, then crunched, savouring fragments to his upper palate, draining juice out of them, twitchy like a rodent. Hours later he replaced the articles in Billy's waistcoat pockets.

He licked buttery crumbs off greaseproof paper which had wrapped Billy's sandwiches—Sue Lloyd always packed his sandwiches in a plastic bag. Sleep, he thought, for the time

249

being, sleep. She's heard the news by now, odds are Sue's on top pit, blinding holy Jesus out of officials. Sue and Cochyn's wife, that queer little sprat of a woman. Strange little piece, Mrs Holly, busy-busy like women with kids are supposed to be.

Gabe examined ground around the tram for a dry, shaly place to sleep. Knock first, he thought. Ease off the blast or I'll freeze.

He clanged the pipe six times with the hatchet, returned to the driest side of the tram and curled up with his head tucked inside his jacket. Nine hours later, when he roused feeling broken, nerves sapped beyond cure, a fourth rescue team were beginning their work on the fall.

Gabe drank too much water, felt it grip his insides like colic. The worthless mystery of his heart said, 'I'm starving.' I'm starving. Jesus Christ, I could eat now, put away the eggs and heaps of rashers. Forearms pressed to his stomach, he see-sawed from the waist, defending himself against gnawing chill. Bound to wear off, he thought. Gripe. I'll have to go steady on the water. It's easing already. Must keep warm. At a pinch I'll borrow some of Billy's clothes. Dead cert there won't be any grub. Set my mind on that. God help me if I can't go without grub for a couple of shifts.

Insectile vibrations plagued along the metal. He's squawking, 'Slash into it!' the same dumb answer along the compressed air pipeline.

Idle bastards, he thought, they're not putting their backs into the job. Every man in Bothi Number 2 should be out there, all the rings, timber and flats they want coming up right behind their legs. Everything to hand for the asking, while me, I'm . . .

He rubbed his eyes, quenching tears. The knockings were punishing his mind. But tears flowed as he crawled from the hole, clogging runnels in his blackened face. Gabe sobbed, warning himself, 'Hang on, gotto hang on to my nerve. Once my nerve goes I'll be useless. I won't lose my nerve. I *won't*. No matter what, I'll stick it out. Must hang on,' thinking, If it takes them a few shifts to clear the fall, I'll be al'right. Just hang on, stick it until the first lamp comes up the heading.

By way of inane authority, he shouted, 'Cochyn, I'll stay company with you.' Then mumbling defeat, 'Ah, poor old Cochyn.'

On in front of the tram, waxily black against grey rock, the rider seam of inferior coal wheezed airily, handfuls spraying down over the rubble. Gabe hunkered motionless, chin on his chest. He was failing to estimate how long he'd been cut off in this bloody death-trap of a heading.

(8)

Like a drugged man he scuffed his shape in the shaly rubble. Gabe laid flat on his back, Billy Holly's jacket wrapped around his legs. Staring at darkness, cap-lamp clipped to the front of his belt, he invented tactics: The longer I'll sleep, less I'll panic. There's enough strength left in me. I'm a long way from beaten, hell of a long way yet, as I'd show if Lucy Passmore was here. I could use a good woman, put some life in my guts. She'll be waiting. Lush blonde. I had the green light off her again last night. Last . . ? How long since the fall? We'd finished cutting when Jobie came. Say around six o'clock in the morning. *Saturday*. I worked at least a full shift digging through to the stop valve. Then slept. Slept three, four times. Making it Sunday evening. Sunday night at the latest.

He drowsed, hungering, cuddling his privates for warmth, the only wistful reach of life in his humanity. Subsequently through his drowse, emerged a large amorphous female, soft concubine of dream to give succour, dissolving benevolence throughout his bones and flesh. Instantly losing her. Afterwards deep sleep, peaceful, and all lost forever in the spastic rigor of his awakening.

The pilot bulb glowed like a cigarette, outlining its single filament. Gabe stared, his other hand reaching for the lamp on the tram of debris. Now he curled himself with Billy's lamp ready between his knees. He gazed at the slender curve of reddened wire, waiting for the glow to die but the glow remained, ceasing when he was already blind, tranced from staring at it. He thought, I should be working from this end. No timber, nothing, nothing. Nothing left. Despair chuckled, 'I'm not a fucken mole.' It's me, Gabe Lloyd . . . N.C.B. champion two years ago.

He switched on Billy's lamp and briefly wept, pleading, 'I can't last much longer. My butty, he's dead in here.'

251

Water trickled under the far side of the tram, spreading outwards to Gabe's shaly bed. Unclipping his own lamp and spent battery, he placed them beside Billy Holly's feet, 'Mine for yours, Coch-boy. You don't need light any more.'

The fragile corpse stank, stained teeth bared inside tightened, spread-away lips. Like a foolish, sentimental child, Gabe caught up the nozzle end of the tough rubber hose and he fanned softly purring compressed air over Billy's face, saying, 'Can't bury you, Coch. Pointless even if I could, same it would be, the stink. I'm taking a real bloody hammering, honest now, Billy. Awful. Real hammering. I'm weak as a kitten. Aye, weak.'

He dropped to his knees, complaining as he crept into the burrow, 'God knows how long I've been in here.'

One knock on the pipe brought immediate ringing reply, nearer, urgent, distinct, as if the rescue teams were a couple of rooms away. Gabe clanged the pipe with the blade of his shovel. Someone answered furiously, loud kettle-drum syntax, reverberations thrumming the narrow burrow. Stupefied, Gabe crawled out. Unable to lever upright, he kept moving, hands and feet each side of the rail. Face down on the shale, light switched off, Gabe breathed shallowly across the back of his hand. Asleep, he lowered into disintegration. Eighteen hours later, chewing and swallowing pellets of greaseproof paper, ugly jeering taunted as threat: *Jibber, you're jibbing, Gabe.*

'Nuh,' he said, sinking away.

He lay there to the eighth day, curled in darkness, small pieces of leather bootlace inside his mouth. Total blackness no longer disturbed him. There weren't any terrors. Billy's broken hacksaw blade hung from his wrist. Short lengths of bootlace clustered meaninglessly in his stomach. Like an infant he licked the dried, coal-grained cuts on his hand, puckered skin cold against scant warmth of his tongue. He moaned to sighing, very, very slowly creeping his thighs to his belly, sighing, sighed into the coma which sustained him on ebb until Monday evening, when the first rescue miner found him.

Crouching out from Gabe's burrow, he came bowling forward on hands and feet like a grounded ape. Pausing short of the team, hand clamped over his nostrils, the beam of his lamp shone on Gabe. He shouted into the hole, 'Come on! Safe! We're too late by the looks of it!'

Rescue miners were grouped around the tram. Saying,

'Right now,' they lowered and covered Billy Holly's body on a Stokes stretcher. Heads shook, twisting aside, 'Ach,' they said against the foul smell. The ambulance man trickled diluted brandy down Gabe's throat. He convulsed, jack-knifing trembles from his groins. They wrapped him in blankets.

'Carry Billy out to the main,' ordered the team leader. He spoke quietly to the ambulance man, 'What about him, will he make it?'

'Should, unless there's something busted inside. No signs. These, they're superficial.' He tucked Gabe's hand back under the blankets. 'We'll try him with some warm soup.'

Monte Leyshon elbowed through the group. 'Let the doctor examine him. He's waiting on top pit.'

'Aye, but he isn't down here, Mr Leyshon,' said the ambulance man. 'Open the flask.'

The ambulance man spooned patiently, 'Good on you, son, you're all right, you're safe. Slow now, slowly does it.'

Gabe strained for consciousness. Neural tics plucked his face. His tongue felt huge, wooden.

The ambulance man laughed up at the team leader, 'He's ours! Aye, great!'

Monte Leyshon finger-wiped his nose, inquiring, 'Where's Jobie Lewis?'

'Top pit cabin,' they said. 'Old Jobie's knackered, been working too many doublers.'

The manager kneeled into the burrow. 'Bring Gabe out to pit bottom when you're ready. I must speak to Jobie. He'll have to let Mrs Holly know about her man.'

A miner said, 'Don't forget Sue Lloyd, for Christ's sake.'

Another miner said, 'Sooner Jobie than me.'

Gabe's speech broke through whining, 'I was licked. Billy Coch, see, it kill't Billy.'

The ambulance man wiped his mouth with cotton wool. 'We're taking you out, Gabe.' He cautioned the miners each end of the stretcher, 'Gentle, lads, lift altogether.'

Gabe moaned as they dragged him through the hole, 'Ah, Christ, I was all in, I was beat.'

'Talking bloody daft,' said a man at his feet. 'I saw you fighting Nobby Graham. Guts, boy, you won on guts.'

Out on the main, Stan Evans leaned over him, 'Gabe, I didn't expect it to come in like that, indeed to God I didn't.

Whole place fell in. I couldn't do anything, couldn't warn you in time.'

The team leader pushed at Stan's chest, 'Be quiet. No call for you to take it on yourself. Nobody's bloody fault.'

They lifted Gabe on his stretcher into a tram, men squatting each side, easing jolts as they journeyed back to pit bottom. A chatty young G.P. examined him in the ambulance centre. Gabe swallowed more soup. Sue was holding his hand. Beffudled, Gabe grinned at her and the world before sleep collapsed his senses. He fell away, emptied into warmth.

(9)

Mid October and after-dark chill scuttling customers into the public bar. Gabe stepped to the curb as Lucy Passmore's little car circled outside the prototype Edwardian Great Western Arms.

'I didn't expect to see you so soon, Gabe.'

'Me neither,' he said. 'How's trade in the canteen?'

'Pard'n?'

He gripped her knee, squeezing hard. 'Knocking somebody else off these days, girl?'

'You're hurting me!'

He rolled his shoulder against hers, saying, 'Dyffryn Lake, let's find out if it's same as it used to be.'

'My knee! You're cruel, Gabe, cruel.'

He said, 'Aye, I know that too.'

'Everyone kept saying you were dead. Morning, noon and night in the canteen, Gabe Lloyd is gone, he's bound to be dead. Even Mr Leyshon, he believed you were dead.'

He jammed his fists into his pockets. 'Okay, I don't want to hear any more.'

Lucy turned into a lane at the lower end of Dyffryn Lake to the gate of a derelict sheepfold.

He loosened his shirt collar, 'We'll stay inside tonight.'

Her lips found his mouth, 'I'm trying to be nice to you, Gabie-love.'

'You were in my mind, Lucy. *That* was cruel.'

'I missed you, darling.' Carefully moving away from their kiss, she opened her handbag, 'Cigarette?' Her lighter spurted

254

flame. She puffed contentment, glow-'puhh' glow-'puhh' glow-'puhh', her plump, perfumed body sagged behind the wheel. Awkwardly in the cramped space, the seats creaking, pulling closer to her, his hand reached down between her thighs. Lucy sat motionless. Cigarette smoke whoofed softly at his ear, preceding benign fatalism, 'Poor Gabie, you've picked the wrong night.' Crossing her legs, she embraced him affectionately, 'There, that's better. Now we can have a lovely *cwtch*.'

'Jesus Christ,' he said.

'You're ever so greedy. For one thing you're not fit yet. They kept you in hospital for ages. I mean to say, I had no intention of meeting you tonight, only you insisted. You did, Gabe, after all you've been through.'

He said, 'You should have told me straight off.'

'Dear God, what a way to talk, as if I'm some kind of um, well, y'know Gabie, you're only concerned about sex.'

'Lay it on, girl,' he said.

'I'm telling the truth.' Strange to his ears, Lucy giggled, 'Matter of fact the under-manager, he asked me, offered to make a date.' She pressed her knuckles over his mouth, 'Ssh, wait till you've heard the bleddy story. It was for Rosser's sake. The under-manager promised he'd try to find Rosser a job in Bothi stores. My husband can't do heavy work, his chest being the way it is. By damn, I've kept our home going for years and years!'

Gabe said, 'Been out with him?'

'Once. We saw a show in Cardiff.' She gushed nasally, 'Bleddy Kairdiff. Lousy it was, I couldn't follow it myself. As for him, he was really chuffed.'

'What about after the show?'

'We had a meal. Oh, shurrup, Gabe. No reason for you to criticise. Stop quibbling. Honest to God, you're narrow-minded like all the rest. 'Tisn't as if there's any future. Where's our future? Least we can do is be friends. Don't make bad blood between us.'

It was a serene Autumn morning when Sue went upstairs to Gabe's room. She stood beside his bed.

'C'mon, move, it's eleven o'clock.'

'Be right down.'

255

'When you starting work?'

'Monday, day shift an' all, my own stent.'

'Wake up, you loafer.'

'Al'right, al'right.'

After breakfast he walked alongside a feeder stream to Dyffryn Lake. Drought-weather fog capped the low hills. Dark-mossed stones were drying out above water level and still green clods of sedge tufted vagrant pointillism. His first long ramble since rescue teams stretchered him from Bothi Number 2, Gabe making the most of it, scorning his sloth, the flabbiness of his belly muscles. He broke into jog-trotting, leapt to-and-fro across the brook, made short sprints, and turned, setting himself a brisk homeward pace.

Near the village football field, Gabe met Rosser Passmore.

Riven-faced, tormented by sickness and conscience, Rosser stamped his walking stick, 'Glad to see you out and about, my boy. Must have been terr-rrible for you down there in the bowels of the earth. Remember the proverb, The finest blades are tempered in the fiercest fires. Oh yes, our time of trial will come. Tell me true, you prayed to the Lord when you were trapped down there.'

Gabe stroked his nose, 'Can't say I did.'

Rosser made high, shaky baton strokes with his stick. 'There isn't a man alive who can afford to neglect the Almighty in his hour of need. Every day of the week Christian lives are saved by prayer.' Climbing to the pentecostal fervour, Rosser hovered his stick above Gabe's shoulder, 'Without prayer our sins mount up higher and higher! There can be no salvation . . .'

Gabe snatched the end of the stick, Rosser blinking skywards, gulps of irritation stringing his throat. 'Excuse me,' said Gabe. 'If you don't mind, Ross, You're spouting to the wrong fella.'

'Then you are blind and proud!' accused Rosser.

'Doesn't matter about that for now,' suggested Gabe, ready to appease. This man was a wreck, old Bible-puncher not far short of his coffin. He says, 'Cheerio, Ross. My dinner's waiting for me.'

'Hear the word of the Lord!'

The walking stick whiffled above his shoulder again, victimising him.

'Don't fucken-well do that,' snarled Gabe, attack glinting his grey eyes. He flung down the stick. 'Belt up, you drippy old bastard. Buy a pair of working boots and get your missis to fill your tommy box.' He returned the walking stick to Rosser, 'I'm on my way home. Just leave me alone. You go your way, I'll go mine.'

Rosser was gasping, 'God-bless, God-bless, God-bless,' his arms jerking fore and aft, seeking to propel his legs.

Gabe nodded, 'No offence, it's only, aah for Chrissake listen a minute.' And it blurted out, 'Do something about your wife, will you! She's chasing 'round like a bitch on heat.'

Rosser Passmore's head planed forward, vulture hanging.

Short-cutting across the field, Gabe cursed himself for a bloody fool. Typical. No better and no worse than Sue. Two beauts under the same roof. What in the name of Christ am I any good for? What? Five bloody stents a week. So he talked to the grass under his shoes, 'Act your age, Lloydie, for Christ's sake grow up, man.'

Boy and Girl

Her perfection, theirs, wilted in kisses. Then on and on, the nowhere end of kissing. Like a sickness, blight at the mouth for two: Herself/Himself. Incurable.

'I wish I was a boy,' she fretted, wincing her pale blue eyes. 'Tch, you boys, free to come and go anywhere just as you please.'

Fear sent him leaping across the brook, expertly hopping boulders like a lurcher dog.

'Emyr, wait for me!'

He said, 'Shall we climb up to the big waterfall?'

'Is it safe?'

'Easy,' he said.

'Wait then, wait for me!'

Bell in every tooth, he thought. Rowdy, Gwyneth, she's very rowdy for a girl. Proper screamer. Sixteen, sixteen years old. We started school the same day, up through every class, finished school on the same day last July. Everybody knows we are supposed to be courting.

A pair of grey wagtails looped ahead of them, delicate birds seeping anxious call-notes, tails flickering, all nerves, nervy— like Gwyneth.

She rushed at him from behind, toppling, her arms wide, her breasts buffeting his shoulders. Emyr smiled seriously, flaw waxing between them as they kissed. Kissed.

'They must be nesting nearby, feeding younkers,' he said.

'Pard'n?'

'Wagtails, pair of 'em.'

He roved up and down ivied ledges, searching the wagtails zipping downstream, silent, their territory safe. Deceived, he realised the nest was lower down, somewhere near the double-trunked sycamore, one swollen heart enclosing EMYR and GWYNETH carved on a high branch flooded by summer leaves. He fingered the knife in his jacket pocket, stainless steel handle, three inch blade, disgorger, corkscrew, scissors, can-opener. His father said, 'Best on the market, this knife. Look after it, son. Last you another fourteen years.'

Her father, he thought, different kind of man altogether, strange beyond, wrapped up in private misery, stranger in his own house, even to his wife and daughter. Daughter Gwyneth, oval face, brown hair, gorgeous figure, haunting, small hands, small feet, same-shaped lips, uncanny eyes, pale, lost—her father's eyes.

He cleared the brook, hop, step and jump, climbed a narrow gully, foamy water gushing alongside his head, lunged to the top and froze. The dipper swam oar-winged, a dark blur over mottled gravel, skidded into fresh air, glistening, bobbing, squirted its turd and whistled upstream. Marvel, he thought, sheer marvel.

Gwyneth shrivelled his rapture, crying, 'Wait for me!'

Emyr helped her climb the gully. She whooped panicky screams, groped up to him from tip-toes, clinging, perfumed, her body rigid. She transferred herself upon him. Mouth to mouth he exchanged himself for Gwyneth, pairing fate.

'C'mon,' he said, but she dawdled, knelt beside a pool, cleaning a mucky sandal with handfuls of wet grass.

Less than half a mile away the waterfall hung roaring, arched outwards from the rock face, white as a slot of cloud. A kestrel stood in blue sky above the falls, lowered itself plumb as a spider, paused, dipped below the horizon, a rufus smudge swooping across the dark rock. Emyr heard a new cooing sound lulling through the harsh roar, so he moved faster, skirting overhangs, criss-crossing the stream, sprinting over crumbling shale, carefully prising his weight up steep banks of whinberry bushes, Gwyneth still calling, 'Wait for me!'

Attached as ever, witless, he refused, turned, waved to her, scented Gwyneth in her summer blouse, calling, 'Emyr! Emyr!'

'C'mon, girl,' he urged quietly.

While she buckled her sandal he swiftly levered his rump up and over a slanted alder tree, hauled clear and rounded mossy scree back to the stream. Top Pool, boiled by torrent tumbling the height of a house. Stunted brownies flicked away from the tail of the Pool. Here, Top Pool, marked the terminus of a scanty sewin run from the Bristol Channel. Barren water above, curving into distant peat bogs. Emyr scooped up a raft of scudding froth. A bronzy tinted nymph wriggled free. He placed his hand under the water, watched the busy wriggler, reversed his hand; the nymph vanished.

Climbing the left bank, he caught sight of Gwyneth balancing her route through a patch of quag. Sheep-path, she can't *see* the path. It's under her nose. He wondered why she resented being a girl. Mystery of mysteries. And again the alien cooing floated down to him. Out swung the kestrel, wheeling clock-wise circles, riding thermals above the damp ravine. Then Emyr saw the doves fluttering behind stalky heather niched to the rock face. Not homers, he thought, wood pigeons neither, can't be, not at this altitude, these rocks and bare hills. *Kee kee kee* from the kestrel, flying back over the mountain-top. A lunatic jenny wren trilled among jumbled boulders, prompting *chackchackchack* from two ring ouzels fleeing to higher scree. Emyr laughed, stuttering his Latin limit: 'Troglodytes troglodytes,' making connection with his coalminer father, the old man's rollicking amusement at their mutual discovery: The Observer's Book of Birds cross-referenced to a tattered Chamber's dictionary.

He reached the waterfall, skimming away low, close to the hillside. Definitely not wood pigeons. He clambered around behind the towering falls, spume dampening his trousers, streaming moss wetting the shoulders of his jacket. Around into glaring sunshine again, Gwyneth down below, brightly coloured, calling, her mouth opening, closing, her hand beckoning, demanding, the familiar gesture, token of her imperious dream. Unafraid, he murmured, 'Iesu mawr,' ending with a tongue click like a Zulu, more an awareness of himself than a dismissal of her, of what he was doing, had done, his solo climb up to the waterfall, finally declaring, vowing, 'I can't fathom her at all, 'specially the ideas in her mind.'

He squatted for a while, facing the endless pour of the falls. Gwyneth seated herself on a flat stone, legs tucked like a houri. His tranced stare brought on slight vertigo, wobbly sensation broken by lowering his head, arms hanging over his knees, all relaxed, dropped, slack mouthed, eyes blinking in slow motion, time itself dissolving, vanquished until he saw, registered the off-set twins of his testicles bulging his taut trousers. Emyr touched them stood up, shook loose the trousers from his crotch, glanced down-valley at the motionless girl, and began climbing slant-wise out of the deafening cul-de-sac, outwards and upwards to tussocky pasture above the waterfall. Stretched flat on his stomach, he watched her slow escape from the ravine. Gwyneth quit the stream to wade through summer ferns on the right-hand bank. Humourlessly reflective, he thought, she'll be plastered with cuckoo spit.

Lying there, the round of his head nubbed to the rim of the mountain, he found the unremarkable truth of their relationship. Two whole years together, Gaiety cinema once a week, youth club dance every Saturday night, cafe discussions, hundreds of arguments—from thousands of kids doing the same thing everywhere. Kissing and slapping. She always slapped his hands. Blind frenzy, stern, calm, more frenzy, total confusion, Gwyneth slapping his hands away from her secret body. Merely the formal embrace, lips meeting, their bodies separate. 'Like separate species,' he said, plain awe quelling his sullen temper, his hunger for her, for girls, any girl.

'Emm-mheer!' she screamed, thigh-deep in ferns.

'Ah, be quiet,' he said; the epithet spurting from his throat: 'Prick-teaser.'

Skylarks diverted him. He counted five. Three were lofting, shivery dots ringing in the blue; two came down, volplaning as they neared the ground, songs cut off for hidden landings. A lone raven flew directly upstream. He heard the whuff-whuffing of its ragged primaries. Dead sheep, he thought, mutton feast somewhere up there in the bog.

Where to now? Cross over to the next valley, or walk along the mountain-top. Let her see me, follow if she wants to, or otherwise. She can please herself.

Gwyneth kept track of him, ploughing through ferns on the lower slopes. Clouds piled from the west, wearing out the afternoon. Larks, wheatears, magpies, scavenging crows retreated before him. Hands in pockets, he hiked contentedly over the coarse millennia grass. Emyr revelled in naked space. She no longer screamed his name, simply remained abreast with him until he descended, heeling short zig-zags down the hill above their home town.

He said, 'Sorry you couldn't make it up to the waterfall.'

'That was insulting,' she accused, 'Nothing but a deliberate insult to me personally.'

Emyr shrugged. 'Matter of opinion, girl. We'd better catch a bus before the rain comes.'

Gwyneth linked arms with him. 'Mmm, it is changing. End of the heat wave.'

'I like it when the sun's belting down,' he said. 'Although my old man, he's praying for rain for his garden.'

* * *

She twitched a sprinkling of salt over her left shoulder. 'I don't want bad luck on my birthday. We get enough of it throughout the year.'

Emyr folded his newspaper. 'Luck? More like tit-for-tat.' He pushed back from the breakfast table. 'That clock on the mantelpiece is my worst enemy. Cheerio, see you ha'-past five.'

All day without stress he delivered sides of beef, sheep and pig carcasses, kidneys, livers, hearts, pies and sausages. Lunch-time he called in the Railway Bar.

'You've come,' she said. 'I'm ever so glad.'

'About tonight, it's her birthday, um, consequently I'm lumbered. Gwyneth expects me to take her out. Habit, see, Ruth, from ages ago, the old days. Something I can't dodge.'

'Get divorced. I went through it, with a couple of kids clinging to my apron strings.'

'Too late now. I'm forty-eight.'

'Half that in bed,' she said.

Emyr grinned, 'Aye, we're a genuine pair al'right. Listen, Sunday morning I'll show you the mountains where I used to spend my time when I was a lad. Pick you up at nine o'clock.'

'*You* listen! I'*m* manageress of this pub.'

Right,' he said. 'I'll pay your brother to look after the bar.'

Ruth argued, 'Expensive bit of romance! If she refuses a divorce, I don't mind living tally. As it is I'm on the pill, and you've no kids to worry about.'

'She'll create hell.'

'Afraid, Em?'

'Maybe. We've been married a long, long time.'

'I'm thirty-six,' Ruth said. 'Make up your mind.'

She went down the counter to serve customers. A good looking woman, brunette, vital, unselfish, buxom . . . loving, he reminded himself, Ruthie understands loving, the give and take, the *sharing*. I've shared hard-earned wages and meals with Gwyneth. Twenty-nine wasted years, more, ever since our schooldays. One long bloody sacrifice, buying the house,

262

furniture, her notion of home comforts. Millstones. Deprivation and a status missis. His jowly image scowled in a mirror behind the counter. Fattening romeo, not far short of middle age. Zombie between the ears. Without Ruthie I'm just a bag of bones and giblets.

'Sorry, my love,' she said.

'Me too, Ruth.'

'I'll bring sandwiches for our outing next Sunday. We'll have all day and each other.'

'Yeh.' He looked at her. 'Know what I'm afraid of? Hysterics, screams, me rushing for help, suicide. She refers to suicide as if it's a dose of 'flu.'

Ruth said, 'You worry. Worry makes a bad conscience.'

'Yeh,' he repeated. 'I'm brain-washed, but, oh but Christ Almighty, it's coming to the end!'

She responded to his pent fury. 'I'll stick by you Em,' promising, 'on my childrens' life.'

'This is my responsibility. I'm going to settle it,' he said. 'Once and for always, believing he could face Gwyneth, logically break away from her; he even fixed the day, the hour for confrontation. Emyr's delusion. Late on Saturday afternoon, with six pints of beer swarming his senses, and still wearing his long white, bloodstained coat, he slammed into the deserted house, and fell asleep in front of the television. Gwyneth had the car, her once-a-month excursion to Cardiff, his money spent on clothes, posh dinner in solitary style, followed by a theatre or cinema show.

She arrived home after midnight. Emyr was in bed.

The alarm clock woke him at seven o'clock, his work-day time. Sunshine yellowed the curtains. Great, he thought. We're in for a scorcher. Dressed in his underpants and slippers, he shaved before entering her bedroom. She slept as if unwakeable, lying on her back. The immaculate counterpane mounded in classical effigy: feet, buttocks and breasts. Equally perfect, crafted to waved stillness, the chestnut hair around her oval face.

'Gwyneth!'

The lustre-less topaz eyes resented his presence in her room, the estranging hulk of his hairy body, thick-set, ugly, heavy arms waving like a gorilla.

'Gwyn, I'm away for the day, taking the car.'

'You might have left a note downstairs.'

He turned at the door. 'Some men do that when they've had enough of married life. Would it bother you, I mean if I went with another woman?'

She sat up, fragile fingertips palping her mouth, the same-shaped, same-size lips quivering, failing to expose the enigma of her pale eyes. 'Must you torment me like this?'

He said, 'It wasn't intended.'

'My capsules, they're on the dressing table.'

Emyr gave her the plastic bottle.

'Water,' she said, 'and for God's sake put some clothes on.'

Again he turned back from the door. 'It wouldn't bother you much, not really, not so long as you could do the things you want to do, titivate here in the house, buy nice clothes, trip into town whenever you feel inclined. A show-piece wife, right?'

He brought a tumbler of water from the bathroom.

'I've suspected,' she said. 'Who wouldn't, knowing your private nature. I don't want to hear about it. Carry on with your whoring. In future take your filthy underclothes to the laundry.'

She reached for the tumbler.

'Gwyneth, he said, pouring the water over her head, 'Gwyneth, I can't stay under this roof any longer.'

Her screaming tingled his nape hairs, but his rationale survived, came through. 'I'll pack my clothes. You won't see me again.'

'Pig!' she wailed, keening her high pitched moan.

'I've always known you were a vulgar pig. Go away, leave me alone. You won't see me again either. Why should I! I don't want to live any more!' Clutching her bottle of capsules, she ran into the bathroom.

His purpose held. Lucid in his mind, he waited on the stair landing.

'Emyr!'

'I'm here.'

'Fetch the doctor! I've taken all my capsules!'

'You sound normal.'

She unlocked the door. 'I said fetch the doctor! Look!' The bottle was empty.

'You'll survive,' he said, pitying her, ineffectual pity the only real feeling grown from his marriage.

'Ugh, get out of my sight!' she screamed, screamed, howled

264

down to bereft moans while he crammed his clothes into a suitcase. Then he returned to her bedroom.

'I'll ring the doctor from the phone box out on the corner. How many of those capsules did you take?'

'Sadist,' she whimpered. 'You shouldn't have thrown that water over me.'

'How many capsules?'

'Leave me alone, I want to die.'

'Were they for your nerves?'

'My nerves, of course my nerves!'

He crossed the landing to the bathroom. There were tiny smears, grains dissolving around the plughole of the wash basin. Almost, he thought, she almost beat me. Besides everything else, she's a liar. Unaware, suddenly sighting himself in the bathroom mirror, Emyr flashed a toothy grin. 'Young enough, boyo,' he said, pummelling his bare stomach and chest. 'Healthy body, gut in fair condition considering the regular weekend boozing,' the therapy continuing inside his head: start all over again with Ruthie. She's my woman. Mine while I live and breathe.

'Emyr!'

He stood at the foot of her bed for the last time.

'I want the doctor!'

'Sure, okay. Go to sleep. I'll ring him from the phone box. So-long, Gwyneth.'

He stopped the car on the greening side of an old colliery, bulldozed flat, top-soiled and seeded while miners were picketing power stations throughout the country, proving the durable barbarism of twentieth-century man, his raw economic gospel of Us and Them. Mid-summer heat shimmered, charming abadoned allotments, bedstead and patch-work fences over-run by brambles and saplings. The hillside where Gwyneth once waded through sappy ferns was now under Forestry Commission conifers.

'This is it,' he said. 'See up there, the big waterfall. We'll climb the gully, easy does it all the way. Let me carry the haversack.'

Ruth said, 'My kids would love to roam these mountains.'

'Next time,' he confirmed. 'And the next time, and the next time.'

'Speak straight.'

'Aye, it's finished. I've broken free at last. My suitcase is in the boot of the car.'

'She's agreed on a divorce?'

'We'll settle that later.'

'Time is on our side, Em-love. We can't lose.'

They climbed together, happy in the hot morning, birdsong reduced to odd bursts and everywhere the lonely belling of ring ouzels. Ruth stripped off at the Top Pool, thrashed strokes out and back to the bank, scuttled about huffing and puffing, goose-pimpled, frantic, joyous.

'Where's your gumption,' he said. 'The water's like ice.'

'Your turn, mister!' dripping over him, white thighs, white belly, the gay, plump venus of his adolescent longing, alive, tearing off his shirt buttons, insisting until he too, stripped to the buff, dived in and out of Top Pool, panting, 'Crazy, we must be stone crazy.'

They were crouched, passing behind the big waterfall, Emyr leading, gripping her hand, when Ruth tugged, held him back.

'What?'

Incisive above the pounding roar, her ultimatum stiffened his diaphragm. 'Em, I shan't take the pill any more!'

'No more!' he yelled. 'Righto, girl, if that's how you feel.'

And later, after lurching and dozing beside her on the mountain-top, he remembered that moment in the glaucous light behind the waterfall of his boyhood. He tried and failed to remember his previous dip in Top Pool. Boyhood again. Brave Ruthie, fearless, the bravest of all, and he turned to her, his revelation in the warm grass. I'm forty-eight, he thought; goodbye daftness, goodbye ignorance.

Winding sheep-paths returned them to the parked car. A long trek. He showed her snipe clipping away from the shore-line of a peaty pool. They watched two far-apart buzzards winding upwards, soaring to vanishing specks. But they were tired, dulled by heat, energy on ebb. He said, 'Had a good day?'

'The best.'

'I'm whacked.'

'I need a bath.' They sat in the trapped warmth of the car. 'Em, I'm not stealing you away from her, am I?'

'I'm sorry for Gwyneth,' he said. 'Just sorry.'

'Does she expect so much a week from your wage packet?'

'She can find herself a job.'

Ruth drove the car, saying, 'These are matters we must discuss. Another thing, my two kids . . .'

'*Ours*,' he said. 'I'm committed now. You've shown me the way.'

'Shown each other, I mean deep down, as sweethearts. The world can look after its own damn business. Open the windows, my love! Let's sing!'

'Thank the Christ,' he said.

Who Belonged Just Long Enough Ago

Rapid consumption buried Jack Argest at twenty-two, this innocent man of honour ringing Graig-ddu main with 'Show me the way to go home' or 'I'm alone because I love you'. Genuine Jack Argest, butty to Frank Minty for six years. Heading man Frank, who fathered eleven sons and daughters, all thriving like grass. Giantess Mrs Minty was Border stock. She looked Scandinavian, covertly related to Jack's distaff side, to wit elsewhere than between the sheets. Jack had black curly hair and ten stone twelve pounds of healthy innards, bone and muscle. Good as gold bloke, generous as Eden without the temptation—those bible-makers buggered themselves and mistook snakes. But we're all born quite ignorant. Or call it grace.

Frank Minty grafted to sixty-five and died below his runner beans at sixty-nine. Years too soon because fifty per cent dust clogged his sponges. Not to be lightly stressed, working coalfaces shorten living breath, yet GPs continued scribbling cause and effect death certificates. Maybe doctoring does them damage, hearts and heads conditioned to stoic sync. Perhaps stoics are small-souled.

Jack Argest wasn't pledged on oath or brain-washed from pulpits. Nobody imagined Jack as the proofed replica of Frank Minty, the hard, hard man, true as any weather. No singing in Frank's heading. Occasional serenely random dah-deh-dah-dah humming back in the road while sliding tools off or locking them safe on Frank's toolbar. Respecting work, every smidgen behove experience. Forget short cuts. Left and right hand road posts were dead on point. Drill and fire top holes Mondays and Thursdays. Five-foot holes, six pills of powder in each. Rip down and clear the muck, gob walls tidy, packed to the roof. Timber the face. Fill out the turn and never keep the haulier waiting. Frank's law. Jack's apprenticeship. Their inheritance.

Twenty-four trams a week. Every tram raced to 1 ton 2 or 3 cwts. Lump coal only.

Bravely inoffensive, Jack began social drinking at seventeen. Saturday nights he foxtrotted girls like a sensible dervish in

Croes Parc Club dance hall. He usually sat out on the tango. Three flashpoint loves sufficed his adolescence: Myrtle, Lucy and Eva. Then Cranwen. At twenty he had to marry Cran under the aegis of her widowed mother (Mrs Herbert), glazed convert to Spiritualism when a tranced medium referred to a family legend, i.e. of great Grancha Joshua Herbert born in a Hansom cab en route back to Morgannwg, blue blood son of the second Earl of Powis's third son, one Gabriel Herbert, soldier who perished in the Zulu War.

Monday morning, first shift in his own stall, Jack Argest in sanguine chorus, singing from the mouth of Graig-ddu to the double-parting servicing Frank Minty's heading.

Said Harry Harry the district fireman, 'New stall like the manager promised. Now you're on your own. Few minutes and I'll send in your butty'.

Harry put sixteen-year-old skinamalink Lennie Taylor with Jack. Coincidentally, Cranwen was second cousin to Lennie's mother, sad Rian Taylor with a shrunken arm and no husband. Nat Taylor disappeared, took his clothes and the alarm clock while Rian and schoolboy Lennie were watching Warner Baxter in the Plaza. Cruel, such human nature. Merciless since way back when you think of it.

Says Lennie, 'Tellew to your face, I'd sooner go butty with Frank Minty.'

'He'd get shot of you in a week, Lennie.'

'I can chuck it in the dram, don't you fret,' bragged Lennie.

Jack said, 'What's up then, apart from feeling our feet?'

'I been fucked about,' complained Lennie. 'What I'm after's a reg'lar butty who pays good trumps. Hey, how's Cran by the way? See, my old lady's bound to ask. In the puddin' club 'ccordin' to talk.'

Ignoring Lenny, laughing Jack spun a little jig.

Lennie pleaded, 'I can keep my mouth shut.'

They filled four trams.

Weary Jack, he trudged through pans of slurry on the way out. After scrubbing in a tub by the fire, he slumped and jerked from dozing over his dinner. Cranwen, she smiling at him, knitting a baby's cardigan and listening to pasteurised Cockney comedy on the wireless.

Sweeping rain bleared Tuesday morning. Frank squinted at Jack hooded under a feedsack. 'How's it going, fella?'

Jack replied, 'Great, man. By Saturday I'll clear a couple of top holes in my stall'. So he did, but he lost three trams.

Quite gently he hoiked up Lennie's jacket collar, 'You'll have to pull your weight, sonny-boy, else we'll be on the Min.'

'Won't be the first time since I raised my lamp,' peeved Lennie.

As always, men and collier-boys walking the main, they enjoyed Jack's stentorian, tingling baritone serenading 'Marta, rambling rose of the wildwood'.

Says Lennie to his mother, 'Ask me, she's busted his guts.'

'Damn you, be quiet. None of our business.' Rian Taylor felt wounded by nasty gossip about husbands and wives.

Lennie protested, 'Mam, I know when I'm well off. I've 'ad my share of wasters in Graig-ddu.'

'They come from respectable families, Jack and Cain Argest,' said Rian.

They were too, durable Croesgwyn natives with ancestors who mined coal before steam engines, ancient of days villagers who compared to machinists, furniture assemblers and paint sprayers on three-miles-away Oaktree Trading Estate.

However, or nevertheless, morning sickness helped promote Cran's dawdling. Inconsequential day-time dawdling. She luxuriated in Jack's manhood, their nightly ravishment natural as intended, normal as Wales itself since people built roads and chapels.

The midwife's verdict over their still-born son, 'Act of God. Start another one, best thing you can do,' adding rule of thumb comfort, 'There's no option.'

One to the other, Jack and Cran mourned. And of course among neighbours a deeper empathy than humane sympathy. Depression ruled Britannia's sceptred isle. Gruelling ups and downs verged on inevitable. Reality warranted fatalism devoid of prophecy. Acceptance sustained pitiless hope.

Jack Argest joined Croesgwyn Male Voice. He took on tonic sol-fa. Worth the struggle eventually, their conductor rapping and quivering his baton.

'Hold it a minute. Now them, um, Jack, I want you to try taking the chorus solo. Just quietly for a start-off. We'll polish once you're confident.' Mel Jenkins marched forward. 'All you boys come in as before for the verse. For the *final* chorus, understand, everybody joins in. And remember, get the timing right. Also, total silence for Jack. I'm thinking about more variety, say one of you top tenors, someone to blend with Jack Argest. Don't let me down.' Mel returned to his stance. 'Any questions?'

Jack balled his only hankie in his fist:

'*Home, home, sweet, sweet home, be it ever so humble there's no place like home.*'

Politely curt as a sergeant to Miss Houghton the Pianist, 'Legato next time, Angharad,' ordered Mel the conductor.

Miss Houghton a less-than-fey, middle-aged spinster, being sister to Graig-ddu's under-manager, somehow acquired a grace-and-favour Company bungalow behind the mechanic's house in private woodland across the G.W.R. tracks in Croesgwyn.

Jack respected Miss Houghton. He brimmed endeavour in his soloist role. By the end of choir practice tension rawed his throat-hole. Later, Cran snugged around him in bed, the whole of "Home sweet home" swung remorseless inside his head, vanquishing sleep, and Cran covetous as a harem lady, until she levered aside and wiped themselves with the hem of her nightie.

When she murmured, 'Jack-love, time to get up,' six dongs were echoing from the Clarke's catalogue wall clock down below the stairwell.

'I'm a bit off colour this morning,' says Jack. 'But don't bother, Cran, I'll manage.'

'Sure?'

'Aye, course I'm sure. S'long girl.'

He filled his tommy box with corned beef sandwiches. Two cups of tea and a Woodbine later, he tramped alongside same-paced colliers to Graig-ddu. Arctic February morning, all-night fires glowing in oil drums on the screens and near the weighbridge, where the collar-and-tie checkweigher logged every collier's tonnage below his official number. The checkweigher (Central Welsh Board education certificate) never smiled. Flighty Mrs Sylvia Gethin had a string of affairs, chosen paramours, transient, who confirmed by word of mouth, boasting in pubs and clubs.

'*Shwmae,* Morlais,' called Jack on his way home, passing the checkweigher's dust-mazed window at ten past three.

Morlais Gethin triggered his forefinger. He's grave as a

deacon against the doorjamb, 'No offence, Jack, you're filling out dirty coal. Manager asked me to let you know. In future he'll be seeing you in his office. Sorry, Jack.'

'How much, Morlais?'

'Hundredweight plus in a particular dram last week. All slag, no roof muck.'

'Thanks for telling me,' says Jack. 'My butty thinks he's clever.'

'Shall I have a word with your fireman?' offered the checkweigher.

Jack said, 'Take a better man than me or Harry Harry to tutor him.'

'Well?'

'Lennie Taylor's sly as his father.'

'Ah yes, Nathan Taylor, shifty customer. 'Bye, Jack.'

'See you, Morlais.'

Jack couldn't handle guilt; Lennie chalks my number on every dram we fill. *My* name goes to the office for dirty coal.

Conscience nagging his awareness of Lennie's treachery, he told Cranwen. Unbeknown to Jack she visited Rian, who simply wept. Lennie was seventeen, committed to his awkward streak, blaming his mother for runaway Nat Taylor.

Until sideways Fate arrived.

Quinsy induced delirium as infection spread into Lennie's system. Fevered in bed for three weeks, he spent a month watching the kitchen fire. Spring sunshine sent him mooching about, scruffy, hands in his pockets, wandering back lanes alone or rummaging on the Council ashtip. So Lennie *changed*. Stolid apathy held him hangdog. When his Sickness Benefit ceased, sad Rian eked out on Parish Relief.

Streets, terraces, rows in Croesgwyn and old Oaktree had loners, enigmatic failures, expendables in the market of human souls. Some were endlessly beloved, kept alive. More were tolerated. Others perished ungrieved by one and all.

By now Jack Argest felt absolved, with a new butty, Ieuan Rodgers, ex-junior technical school pupil with thick brown hair and the alien, feral features of Johnny Weismuller. In fact eighteen-year old Ieuan performed, he crooned with Joey Bianchi's dance band in Croes Parc Club.

'It's practice-practice-practice,' insisted Ieuan. 'I wouldn't know what to do in the Male Voice.'

'Point there,' agreed Jack. 'Honest, myself I'd be lost without our conductor.'

Ieuan prupped his lips, 'Mel Jenkins, he's a crafty old arsehole scraper. Him and his daughter want shooting.'

'What's the aggravation then?'

'Not a bad stall this,' says Ieuan. 'Top's solid rock. Easy face slips. All that clod peels off a treat. See much of Frank Minty these days?'

Jack hooted instant joy. 'Fair enough, I'll keep my nose out. Nigh on every shift I bump into Frank on the double-parting.'

'He's the goods,' guaranteed Ieuan. 'My old man was mates with Frank during the twenty-one stride. They went on tramp.' Ieuan grimaced to merriment, 'Happy days, ah!'

Whereon, '*Happy day, happy day,*' bellowed Jack, '*when Jesus washed my sins away.*'

They dueted, '*He taught me how to watch and pray, and sing rejoicing every day, happy day, happy day, when Jesus washed my sins away.*'

'Hey, Jack, there's some power in you, like John Boles in *Desert Song*. Sheer bloody power.'

'Since I was a kid,' he said. 'What I haven't got, your special style. The way you put it over. I can't match your timing.'

'Only practice, nothing but. Don't know why the fuck I'm working on the coal. I'll pick up two and a half quid every Saturday night.'

'Man-o-man, have a go at it,' says Jack.

Ieuan's hugging himself. 'Trouble is, I couldn't stomach leaving home. Last winter I did five weeks in the Army. They chucked me out 'cause I was under age. Never again, *never.*'

'Ah well,' sympathised Jack—mystery beyond reach, this new butty. The way he crooned, all feelings direct from the heart. 'I'll work my left hand side,' he said. 'C'mon, you pull on top of the road.'

They filled two trams and bored a top hole by eleven o'clock.

'Grub-up,' says Jack. 'Hefty bloke you are, Ieuan. Me, I'm a pretty good stayer.'

Ieuan jutted his basin chin, 'Frank Minty's the best collier in Graig-ddu.'

'Without doubt, and I should know.'

'How come? Look, try one of these.'

273

They exchanged pieces of cake.

'I worked with Frank from leaving school. Why'd you pack in the Tech., Ieuan?'

'Couple of years ago now, my old man caught me mitching. Straight'way he took me out. Like he told my mother, "Best let the world teach our son". Too true an' all, but I'm not worried. I could work a stall like this.'

'Might be you'll think different once you've sampled a bit of the real rough shit.'

'Know what you mean, yeh, right enough,' Ieuan grinned, 'My old man's copped a few bumps.'

'Right again,' says Jack. 'Your old man worked the big Nine Foot seam above Tŷ-glas sidings.'

'Broke his arm twice, once he was trapped, airway fell in behind him, another time he brought half his thumb home in his tommy box.'

'Bumps,' says Jack, knuckling his forehead, 'touch wood I've only had a few cuts and bruises.'

Ieuan lofted his water jack, 'More luck than judgment in it!'

Two hours later, pushing forward and spragging their last empty for the shift, Ieuan said, 'When I'm on stage I make sure I don't get slewed.'

'Oh?' queried Jack.

'That's my agreement with Joey Bianci. Joey won't have a boozer in his outfit.'

Says Jack, 'Now there's a man with the gift.'

Ieuan's hacking private giggling, 'Joey's way out on his own.'

'You'd know best, boy,' conceded Jack, thinking, this Ieuan's on his tod and all. Besides being gutsy. He must have tangled with Mel Jenkins over Gwen the daughter . . . *Miss Gwendoline Jenkins* dressed in white and black behind the counter in Lloyds Bank. *Crachach* girl. Aye-aye. And Sylvia Gethin, she's cream in her own eyes. Funny sometimes, what goes on. Funny ideas. Morlais Gethin though, he's straight as a die.

Striding out with Frank Minty, they briefly remarked about their wives, Mrs Minty having a wisdom tooth extracted; Cranwen's ingrowing toenail.

'How's young Rodgers?' says Frank.

'Ieuan's a decent butty, brainy too, uses his loaf. Tell me,

Frank, how'd you cope with old Ivor Rodgers during the long strike?'

'Cheeky bugger, Ivor. Shitten times they were. No money about. Beg, borrow or steal was Ivor's motto. Any man worth his salt, he wouldn't care either way when there's mouths to be fed. Truth to tell, I never thought of coming home to Croesgwyn. Bloody cruel, myself only three years out of the mob and singing hymns and "Swanee River" in the gutter with Ivor Rodgers. No coin in Gloucester either. We did best in Bristol. Better grub. But sleeping rough isn't a picnic.' Frank spat aside, 'Favour, Jack, leave it there. You're fetching old stuff back into my mind!'

'Take it easy,' says Jack. 'Know what, man, you left a mark on Ivor and he shoved it onto Ieuan. So there.'

Frank Minty huffed against remembrance, 'Lots of fuckin' half-starved heroes on the road in them days.'

Jack Argest belted out, *'Look down, look down that lonesome road, before you travel on.'*

Frank cuffed his shoulder, 'Good on you, fella.'

* * *

Into summer, diphtheria plaguing Croesgwyn and full wards in the Isolation Hospital, a 20 mile roundabout trip by bus and Shanks' pony.

Cranwen Argest was seven months pregnant, feeding herself with slabs of cottage pie, chips and gravy dinners, while Jack ached through the worst bout of 'flu in his life, sweat reeking his pants, vests and bedclothes.

'Don't be pig-headed,' warned Doctor Humphries. 'If you start work next week I shan't be responsible.'

In October Jack endured pleurisy.

Cranwen delivered their baby girl in the adjoining bedroom.

'Girl!' shouted the same blunt midwife.

He's squeaking guttural. 'Girl! Betty Argest! Lovely, Cran, Lovely!' his head rolling rockabye on the pillow, his chest swathed in pink lint soaked in wintergreen oil.

From the midwife at his bedside, 'Your wife's better off than you are by the looks of it. Everything's all right, Jack. Perfect baby. I'll be calling in the morning.'

Cran's backslider Spiritualist mother and two aunties were

275

coming and going. They laundered and cleaned and cooked, supplying him with basins of *cawl*, mutton-fat rings coiling, bacon, egg and fried mast, cups of tea and the *Daily Herald*. Proud and whitely gaunt, he watched Cran cradling the baby before the black ambulance van ferried him to and from the X-Ray Clinic.

Doctor Humphries clumped upstairs. Jack saluted, 'Hullo there, Doctor.'

After a while, bellicose by familiar route, the Doctor let his stethoscope flop into his leather bag. 'You must stay where you are. Set your mind on it, mister, you'll be in this bed a long time.' From workaday logic Humphries vaguely faulted universal helplessness, contra his steadfast Methodist faith— young Argest, another TB case. Nineteen bacillus sufferers in Croesgwyn, eight in Oaktree village. No beds in the Sanatorium.

Jack Argest lost dignity. Lost innocence in malign drowse and morphia. He went in flaming June, whispering to Cranwen, 'Didn't expect this.' She cooped him in her arms, her lips reading the falter and finish of his pulse. *Gone*. Gone forever. She waited, tics gawping her eyes and mouth. Came stillness. As in dream she laid him out, raised and draped the sheet over his head.

The unholy bastardy of nemesis and celebration wreaked excelsior at Jack's funeral, "In the sweet by and by" pouring from tenors, baritones, profound basso and sopranos and contraltos.

The romantic preach, the evil unction of "Those whom the gods love die young".

Evil.

Evil.

Short Stories

End of Season, *New Welsh Review* (no. 22, 1993), pp. 38-40.

Summer's End: Snaketown, *New Welsh Review* (no. 6, 1989), pp. 47-53.

Market Forces, *New Welsh Review* (no. 38, 1997), pp. 23-25.

My Uncle Dan, *Anglo-Welsh Review* (no. 88, 1988), pp. 66-68.

Before Forever After, *Penguin Book of Welsh Short Stories*, ed. Alun Richards (Middlesex: Penguin, 1976), pp. 264-279.

July Saturday in 1940, *Planet* (no. 55, 1986), pp. 34-41.

A Hero of 1938, *Anglo-Welsh Review* (no. 84, 1986), pp. 54-68.

Comrade in Arms, *Planet* (May, 1995), pp. 46-51.

Reaping the Sown, *Planet* (no. 72, 1988), pp. 81-92.

Natives, *Pieces of Eight* ed. Robert Nisbet (Llandysul: Gomer, 1982), pp. 39-48.

Left Behind, *Pieces of Eight* ed. Robert Nisbet (Llandysul: Gomer, 1982), pp. 33-38.

Time Spent, *Pieces of Eight* ed. Robert Nisbet (Llandysul, Gomer, 1982), pp. 21-32.

Ben, the T.V. Playwright and his wife, Lottie, *Planet* (Autumn, 1993), pp. 77-86.

November Kill, *New Welsh Review* (no. 1, 1988), pp. 37-41.

Spoils of Circumstance, *The Strand* (Spring, 1995), pp. 65-71.

Max Thomas, *Planet* (no. 36, 1977), pp. 46-49.

Nice Clean Place, *New Welsh Review* (no. 32, 1996), pp. 29-30.

Clarion Boys, *New Welsh Review* (no. 35, 1997), pp. 16-17.

Lew's Old Man, *New Welsh Review* (no. 25, 1994), pp. 39-42.

King of Fo'c'sle, *Cambrensis* (June 1995), pp. 12-16.

Rosebud Prosser, *The Green Bridge* ed. John Davies (Bridgend: Seren, 1988), pp. 177-185.

Protocol Spin-Off, *The Works* (Cardiff, Union of Welsh Writers, 1991), pp. 155-163.

Homecomforts, Besides the Convenience All Round, *The Valleys* eds. John Davies and Mike Jenkins (Bridgend: Poetry Wales Press, 1984), pp. 113-122.

The Foxhunters, *New Stories* (London: British Arts Council, 1977), pp. 30-38.

Reardon Jones M. M., *New Stories 2* (London: British Arts Council, 1978), pp. 22-30.

Bloody Money (BBC Radio Wales: Spring 1994).

The Old Black Pasture, *Panurge* (April 1996), pp. 10-29.

Boy and Girl, unpublished m/s.

Who Belonged Just Long Enough Ago, *New Welsh Review* (no. 40, 1998), pp. 22-25.

Other Works by Ron Berry

NOVELS
Hunter and Hunted (London: Hutchison, 1960).
Travelling Loaded (London: W. H. Allen, 1963).
The Full-Time Amateur (London: W. H. Allen, 1966).
Flame and Slag (London: W. H. Allen, 1968).
So Long, Hector Bebb (London: MacMillan, 1970).
This Bygone (Llandysul: Gomer, 1996).

AUTOBIOGRAPHY
History is what you live (Llandysul: Gomer, 1998).

GENERAL INTEREST
Peregrine Watching (Llandysul: Gomer, 1987).

RADIO AND TELEVISION PLAYS
Everybody Loves Saturday Night (radio, 1963).
But now they are fled (television, 1968).
Death of a Dog (television, 1969).
Uncle Rollo (television, 1971).
Where darts the Gar, where floats the Wrack (television, 1976).

TELEVISION AND VIDEO RECORDINGS
Ron Berry (Writers of Fiction Collection no. 5: Centre for the Study of Welsh Writing in English, 1992).
'Read All About Us': Ron Berry (BBC2, 14 October, 1996).

SELECTED ARTICLES ON RON BERRY
'Ron Berry', *Profiles* eds. Glyn Jones and John Rowlands (Llandysul: Gomer, 1980), pp. 323-325.
'No Through Road', *Arcade* (no. 12, April 17, 1981), pp. 18-19. Interview.
'Ron Berry', *Oxford Companion to the Literature of Wales* ed. Meic Stephens (Cardiff: University of Wales Press, 1985), p. 36.
'Word-of-mouth cultures end in cemeteries', *New Welsh Review* (no. 34, 1996), pp. 9-15. Feature article by John Pikoulis.
Tributes to Berry by Alun Richards, Robert Minhinnick and Robert Thomas, *New Welsh Review* (no. 38, 1997), pp. 13-25.

Glossary of words and phrases used in the text which are derived from the Welsh language

babi-lwsh	cry-baby
brawd	brother
cariad	love
cawl	broth
crachach	élite, snobs
cwmp	a fall
Cymru am byth	Wales forever
diolch	thanks
Duw	God
gwli	back lane
hiraeth	longing
hwyl	excitement, raised spirit
Iesu Grist	Jesus Christ
milgi	greyhound
mochyn	pig
mum-glo	mothering-coal
Saeson	Englishmen
shwmae	how's it going?
twp	stupid
ych	expression of distaste